Arthur K

THE GLADIATORS

TRANSLATED BY
Edith Simon

WITH A POSTSCRIPT BY
Arthur Koestler

V
VINTAGE

Published by Vintage 1999

2 4 6 8 10 9 7 5 3 1

First published in Great Britain by
Hutchinson & Co Ltd in 1939
This edition published in 1965

Vintage
Random House, 20 Vauxhall Bridge Road,
London SW1V 2SA

Random House Australia (Pty) Limited
20 Alfred Street, Milsons Point, Sydney
New South Wales 2061, Australia

Random House New Zealand Limited
18 Poland Road, Glenfield,
Auckland 10, New Zealand

Random House South Africa (Pty) Limited
Endulini, 5A Jubilee Road, Parktown 2193,
South Africa

The Random House Group Limited Reg. No. 954009
www.randomhouse.co.uk

A CIP catalogue record for this book
is available from the British Library

ISBN 0 09 945981 7

Papers used by Random House are natural, recyclable
products made from wood grown in sustainable forests.
The manufacturing processes conform to the environ-
mental regulations of the country of origin

Printed and bound in Great Britain by
Cox & Wyman Limited, Reading, Berkshire

Contents

CONTENTS

The events historically known as the Slave War,
or Gladiators' War, took place during the years
73–71 before Christ

'When we had passed the gate, I pulled my hat down over my eyes and wept a little; and no one saw it.'

Silvio Pellico

Prologue

THE DOLPHINS

It is night still.
Still no cock has crowed.

But Quintus Apronius, First Scribe of the Market Court, is used to the fact that clerks have to be earlier risers than cocks. He groans as his toes fish for the sandals on the grimy wooden floor. Once again the sandals stand the wrong way, toes facing the bed: the young day's first offence; how many more are to come?

He shuffles along to the window, looks down into the courtyard, a deep shaft surrounded by five storeys. A bony old woman comes climbing up the fire escape: Pomponia, his housekeeper and only slave, brings breakfast and the pail of hot water. She is punctual, he will say that for her. Punctual, old and bony.

The water is lukewarm, breakfast awful: second vexation. But then the Dolphins swim across his mind, the anticipation of his day's splendid climax chases a smile across his face. Pomponia prattles and nags as she bustles about the room, brushing his clothes, helping to adjust the complicated pleats of his clerk's habit. In worried dignity he descends the fire escape, cautiously snatching up his gown, that its hem may not sweep the rungs; he knows that, broom in hand, Pomponia is watching him from the window.

It dawns. Still holding on to his robe, he edges along the houses, for a continuous train of ox- and horse-carts migrates through the narrow alley, with much rumbling and gee-ups: the Driving of Vehicles Through the Streets of Capua During the Day is Strictly Prohibited.

9

A group of workmen is coming towards him along the street that divides the perfume- and ointment-stalls from the fish market. They are municipal slaves, ruffians staring woodenly with unshaven faces. Harassed, he flattens himself still closer to the housefront, gathers his cloak, mutters with scorn. The slaves march past, two of them jostle against him, unmindful and unrepentant. The Scribe quivers with rage, yet he dare not say anything: the men are unshackled—cursed newfangled slackness—and the overseers dally far behind the gang.

At last they have all passed, Apronius may go on his way; but his day is spoilt. Times are growing more and more menacing, it is five years since Great Dictator Sulla's death, and once more the world is off its hinges. Sulla, that was a man for you, he knew how to keep order, how to crush the rabble with an iron heel. A whole century's revolutionary unrest had preceded him: the Gracchi with their mad plans of reform, the horrible slave risings in Sicily, the terror of a mob let loose when Marius and Cinna armed the slaves of Rome and sent them out against the Aristocrats' Party. World civilisation rocked in its foundations: slaves, blunted, stinking crowds, threatened to take power, posed as the lords of Tomorrow. But lo! came Sulla, the saviour, and took the reins in his hand. And he shut the People's Tribunes' mouths for them, cut off the most rebellious heads, drove the leaders of the People's Party into exile, to Spain. He abolished the gratuitous distribution of grain, prize for idlers and loafers; he gave to the people a new, severe constitution—to last for thousands of years to come, for the duration of time; after that unfortunately the lice got hold of Great Sulla and ate him up. Which they call Phthiriasis.

Only five years—yet how distant were those goodly times! Again the world is threatened and troubled, again there is free corn for lazybones and loiterers; People's Tribunes and demagogues may once more hold forth with their blood-curdling speeches. Bereft of its leader, the nobility compromises, vacillates; and once more the rabble rears its head.

Quintus Apronius, First Scribe of the Market Court, feels that his day is definitely spoilt; thinking of the Dolphins even, splendid climax of his day, fails to cheer him. A wooden hoarding attracts his gaze; scriptors are busy adorning it with a new announcement. It is a very grand announcement, nearly finished: on top is painted a crimson sun with many rays bristling in all directions. Underneath, Director Lentulus Batuatus, owner of the city's greatest school of gladiators, is proud to invite the gracious Capuan public to a super-performance. The festival will take place the day after tomorrow in any weather, for the director Batuatus, heedless of enormous expense, will have awnings spread over the arena, designed to keep possible rain, not to mention sun, off the honoured public. Moreover, perfume will be sprayed throughout the auditorium during the intervals.

'Quake and hurry thither, ye lovers of festive games, esteemed citizens of Capua; ye who witnessed the feats of a Pacidejanus, winner in a hundred and six combats, ye who once admired invincible Carpophore, do not miss this singular opportunity of seeing the famous fighters from Lentulus Batuatus's school fight and die. . . .'

Follows the lengthy list of the performing teams, the main feature being a fight between the Gallic gladiator Crixus and the Thracian ring-bearer Spartacus. The notice further announces that one hundred and fifty novices will duel AD GLADIUM, that is, man against man; one hundred and fifty more AD BESTIARIUM, man against beast. During the noon-interval, and while the arena is disinfected, dwarfs, cripples, women and clowns are to fight mock-duels. Tickets from three Asses to fifty Sestertii may be booked in advance at Titus's bakery, in the open-air baths of Hermios, as well as from the authorised agents who may be found at the entrance to the Minerva Temple.

Quintus Apronius mutters with scorn; in Rome they have long ago changed over to the system of free games, offered by ambitious politicians as electioneering stunts. But in this backward provincial city of Capua everyone has actually got to pay for his bit of fun. Apronius decides to ask Director Lentulus Batuatus, whom he knows by sight, for a free ticket. The games-director, one of Capua's most distinguished citizens, is also an habitué of the Dolphins; time and again Apronius had intended to make his acquaintance.

Slightly cheered by this resolution, Apronius continues on his way; a few moments later he has reached his destination, Minerva Temple Hall, where the Municipal Market Court is in session.

The sun rises, the colleagues appear; sleepy minor clerks first, grumpily on their dignity. Two parties in a law-suit are already there, fishmongers quarrelling about a stand in the market; they are told to wait outside until the beadle calls them in. The officials move drowsily around the hall, push benches about, arrange the documents on the president's desk. Quintus Apronius enjoys a certain amount of respect among his colleagues, due partly to his seventeen years of service, partly to his position of an Honorary Secretary to a Sociability-Society-and-Funeral-Club.

Even now he is busy trying to recruit a younger colleague to his club, the 'Worshippers of Diana and Antinous'; he explains the club-rules with benevolent condescension. New members have to pay an entrance fee of one hundred Sestertii, the annual subscription is fifteen Sestertii, payable in monthly instalments of five Asses. The club fund, on the other hand, pays three hundred Sestertii towards the cremation of each deceased member; suicides are excepted. Fifty Sestertii are deducted for the funeral train and divided among them on arrival at the pyre.

Whosoever starts a quarrel at one of the socials is fined four Sestertii, whosoever starts to fight pays twelve Sestertii, whosoever insults the chairman twenty. The banquets are seen to by four annually replaced members who have to provide rugs or bolsters for the dining sofas, hot water and crockery, as well as four amphorae of decent wine, and one loaf at two Asses and four sardines for each member. Quintus Apronius has talked himself quite pink, but his colleague, instead of feeling honoured, merely says he will think it over. Disappointed and irritated, Apronius turns his back on the irreverent youth.

Other officials are filing in, ever higher and mightier ones, up to the Municipal Councillor who acts as judge. Graciously he takes leave of his suite, patronisingly he nods at Apronius who is busy fussing about chair and documents for him. Adversaries and public stream inside, the session has begun, and with it Apronius's business, profession and hobby: Writing. His pinched face lights up; with tender pleasure he traces word after word on that nice virgin parchment—no one writes such an ornate hand, no one takes minutes as efficiently as Apronius, who has gained his superiors' implicit confidence in seventeen years of service. Opponents get personal, attorneys talk, witnesses are examined, experts interrogated, documents pile up, laws and lawlets are read out—all of this is but a pretext to let Apronius prove the Fine Art of minute-writing; he is the true hero of this stage, the others are mere crowd. As the sun beams its noon and the beadle announces the court's adjournment, Apronius has long forgotten what the suit was all about. But the unusually successful flourish which both closed and embellished his record of the defendant's speech, still undulates behind his eyelids.

He neatly stacks records and documents, salutes the Councillor respectfully, the colleagues affably; pressing his pleats to his hips he leaves the scene of his official activities. He strides towards the Tavern of the Twin-Wolves in the Oscian quarter, where a table is reserved for the Worshippers of Diana and Antinous. For the last seven years, ever since the day of his promotion to First Scribe of the Market Court, he has eaten his midday meal here, a meal specially and personally prepared by the proprietor according to a prescribed diet, for Apronius has stomach trouble; but there is no extra charge.

The meal is over. Apronius superintends the washing of his private drinking bowl, snips the crumbs off his dress, departs from the Tavern of the Twin-Wolves and betakes himself to the New Steambaths.

Here too the attendant welcomes the regular guest with deference, hands him the key to Apronius's reserved locker, receives with a forgiving smile the tip of two Asses. The spacious marble hall swarms with life as usual, groups lounge in gossip, news and compliments are exchanged; public speakers, ambitious poets and other opportunists lecture in the arch-roofed shelter, interrupted by their public with heckling, applause and laughter. Apronius enjoys having his intellect titillated in advance of the manifold physical delights of the baths. He joins one group, then another, one ear half-catches a few phrases of an attack on abortion and the falling birthrate; he turns an indignant back as soon as the next speaker has quite finished a dirty story; gown snatched up, he saunters forth, towards a third group. In its centre is a fat real estate agent and broker. He carries on an obscure little bank somewhere in the Oscian quarter, and is trying to hook himself customers by extolling the shares of a new resin refinery in Bruttium. Out of the purest philanthropy he urges the listener to buy at once, resin is a good proposition, resin has a future. Apronius pulls a wry face, mutters with scorn, walks on.

Of course, the largest audience, quite an assembly, has collected round that hole-in-the-corner lawyer and author Fulvius again, that dangerous agitator. Apronius has heard many tales told of this small, insignificant-looking man with the bumpy bald pate; they say he used to be Somebody in the Democratic Party at one time till they suspended him on account of his notoriously radical sentiments. Since then he has been living here in Capua, in some miserable attic or other, inciting the people against the order of things left to them by Sulla. The little lawyer speaks dryly and complacently as though quoting a cookery book; and yet those imbeciles seem to lap it up. Full of resentment, pleated robe held high, Apronius squeezes into the listening crowd; not from curiosity, but because he knows well that anger before bath is good for his digestion.

—Doomed is the Roman Republic, declares the lawyer in his scholarly manner of stating dry fact. Once upon a time Rome was an agricultural state, now the peasantry has been bled empty, the State with it. The world had expanded meanwhile, cheap corn was imported from all lands, farmers had to sell their fields and live on alms. The world had expanded, cheap slave labour was imported from all lands: artisans starved and workmen went abegging. Rome was flooded with corn, it rotted in the granaries; and for the poor there was no bread. Rome was full of working hands, they opened begging or closed to fists; no hands were wanted. The scheme of distribution was at fault, Rome's economic system had not adapted itself to a wider world, it was gradually petrifying; the necessity for a fundamental change had been obvious to all thinking men for nearly a century. But wherever such wisdom aired itself it was killed, together with its progenitor.

'We live,' remarks Fulvius, and gravely strokes his indented pate, 'in a century of abortive revolutions. . . .'

The Scribe Apronius has heard quite enough now. This is going too far. Truly, that kind of talk undermines the very base of civilisation. Trembling with wrath and concealing his secret satisfaction—for he can feel anger doing its intended work— Quintus Apronius finally walks inside, to his first station of delight: the Hall of the Dolphins.

This is a well-lit room, at once pleasant and severe. All along its marble walls are high marble chairs of utilitarian construction the elbow-pieces of which represent dolphins, carved by a master hand. These are the seats of homely wisdom exchanged by neighbours in circumspect discourse, where thoughts fly high as bowels ease. For, to combine both activities harmoniously is the purpose of the Hall of Dolphins.

The Scribe Quintus Apronius's annoyance yields to a gala-mood; and his joy multiplies at the sight of a well-known, well-fed figure enthroned between two dolphins: Lentulus Batuatus, owner of the gladiator-school, whom Apronius is going to ask for a free ticket. The marble seat next to him has just been vacated; Apronius lifts his folds ceremoniously, sits down with a grunt of happiness, and tenderly strokes a dolphin's head with each hand.

That revolutionist has really provoked a most effective wrath. In pious emotion Apronius pays the dolphins their toll, and watches his neighbour out of the corner of his eye. The director's brow, however, appears clouded, and all does not seem to be going well with his physical endeavours. Apronius braces himself and sighs sympathetically that the chief thing in life is after all a good digestion; and that for a long time he has been evolving a theory: the majority of all rebellious discontent and revolutionary fanaticism are actually caused by an irregular digestion, or, to be more exact, by chronic constipation. As a matter of fact, he goes on, he has been considering whether to make this the subject of a philosophical pamphlet which he hopes to write as soon as his time permits it.

The impresario brushes him with a casual look, nods, answers sullenly that this is quite possible.

—Not only possible, it's an established fact, says Apronius heatedly. And he would pledge himself to explain many an historical incident simply by means of this theory—incidents whose importance has been exaggerated beyond proportion by seditious philosophers.

But all his fervour does not succeed in rousing his neighbour. As far as he is concerned, the director grumbles, he has always fed his people decently, and he has been employing the best of doctors to watch over their physical condition and their diet. And yet, in spite of all that, the wretches have repaid his expensive trouble with the basest ingratitude.

—Apronius inquires compassionately whether Lentulus has business worries; his hopes for a free ticket dwindle sadly.

—Indeed he has, moans the impresario, there is no point in keeping it a secret any longer; seventy of his best gladiators have run away during the night, and the police have found no trace of them in spite of all their efforts.

And once started off, the corpulent man with the untarnished business reputation gives way to his chagrin and lets himself go in a lengthy lament on how times are bad and business worse.

The Scribe Apronius listens reverently, his torso bent forward in an attitude of extreme attention, his garments gathered up with affected fingertips. He knows that, apart from the public respect he enjoys on account of his prosperous ventures, Lentulus has also had a remarkable political career in Rome. He came to Capua only two years ago, and founded his gladiator-school which already enjoys an excellent reputation. His business connections spread, net-like, all over Italy and the provinces; his agents buy the human raw material at the Deli slave market and sell it, transformed into model-gladiators, to Spain, Sicily and the Asiatic courts, after one year's thorough training. Lentulus owes his success mainly to his business integrity; his establishment employs only renowned trainers, medical specialists superintend the pupils' diet and exercise. But above all, he has succeeded in impressing on his men as an iron rule that, once beaten, they should never ask to be spared, should cut a good figure whilst being finished off and not disgust the audience with any sort of fuss.

'Anyone can live—but dying is an art and takes some learning,' he kept on admonishing his gladiators. It was due to that very attribute, their delicate dying discipline, that Lentulus's gladiators fetched an average of fifty per cent more rent than those from any other school.

And yet, even Lentulus is affected by these unpleasant times; flattered and compassionate, the Scribe listens to the great man's plaint:

'You see, my good man,' explains Lentulus, 'most games contractors are going through a crisis at present, which is entirely the public's fault. The public no longer appreciates qualified, carefully trained fighters and the trouble, the expense, involved in manufacturing them. Quantity is indeed supplanting quality, the public demands that each performance close with one of those disgusting mass-executions of men by beasts, and all that sort of thing. Have you any idea what that means for the business? Quite simply this: in the classic duel form AD GLADIUM, that is man against man, the losses are obviously one out of two, which means, in other words, that the consumption amounts to fifty per cent. Add a safety margin of ten per cent for fatally wounded cases—and we arrive at a material-consumption of sixty per cent per show. Right you are—here we have the classic calculation on which we base our balance sheet.

'But now the public comes along and demands animal stunts. They will insist on the picturesque, and of course it never occurs to them that exposing my gladiators AD BESTIARIUM raises consumption to eighty-five or ninety per cent. Only a few days ago my son's tutor, an extremely able mathematician, worked out that even the best gladiator's chance to survive three years' active service is about one in twenty-five. Logically this means that the contractor must make up for the amount spent on each man's training in one and a half or two performances, to name an average.

'You, the outsider, the Public, of course think the arena is a gold mine,' says Lentulus with a bitter smile; 'you'll be surprised when I tell you that this kind of enterprise, responsibly conducted, brings a profit of at most ten per cent per annum. Sometimes I do honestly wonder why I don't invest my money in land or why I don't take up actual farming professionally. After all, even an inferior field brings in its yearly six per cent. . . .'

Apronius sees his hopes for a free ticket lie dead and buried, and on top of that he is apparently expected to supply comfort. 'Well, surely you will be able to get over that loss of a mere fifty men,' he says encouragingly.

—'Seventy,' the director corrects him, exasperated. 'And seventy of the best. One of them is Crixus, my Gallic gladiator-trainer, you've probably seen him at work: a gloomy-looking, heavy man with a seal's-head and slow, dangerous movements. A dead loss. And Castus, the little fellow, agile, malignant, sharp as a jackal. And quite a number of other eminent fighters: Ursus, a giant of a man; Spartacus, a quiet, appealing character who always wore a pretty fur-skin round his shoulders; Oenomaus, a promising debutant; and many more. First-class material, I assure you, and very pleasant-spoken people.'

The impresario's voice takes on a positively pathetic tone as he recites his list of lost ones. 'Now I'll have to reduce admission by fifty per cent; and already I've had several hundred tickets distributed among paid enthusiasts and free-ticket-scroungers.'

Apronius swallows and hastens to raise the conversation to a more generally philosophical level. It must be a rather queer feeling for those gladiators, he reflects, to go on living from performance to performance, always in the shadow of death. He, Quintus Apronius, finds it difficult to imagine himself in the state of mind of one of those creatures.

Lentulus smiles, he is used to laymen asking him such questions. 'One gets used to it, you know,' he says. 'You as an official have no idea how quickly men get used to the most extraordinary conditions. It's like war; and anyway, fate may overtake every one of us any day. Besides, these people, who have the assurance of a firm roof over their heads and of good, healthy food, really have a far better time of it than me with the entire responsibility resting on my shoulders, what with those daily worries, business trouble, and so on. Believe me, sometimes I almost envy my pupils.'

Apronius confirms with nods that a pupil's life seems indeed to have its points.

'But, you see, man is never satisfied; it seems to be human nature,' the contractor continues talking pessimism. Particularly just before a performance, he adds, there is always a certain amount of unrest among the men, and a lot of silly talk. This time it had got round somehow that, by public request, the director was forced to expose the surviving AD GLADIUM-victors to renewed fighting AD BESTIARIUM. Naturally the men rather disliked the idea of it; there were some positively embarrassing scenes and finally, last night, in a manner so far inexplicable, the said incident took place.

Despite the fact that he, Lentulus Batuatus himself, is the person most deeply concerned, he cannot but agree to some extent with the men's indignation. For the public's behaviour aggravates even him, Lentulus, far more than the business aspect; there is, for example, the latest superstitious belief that fresh gladiators' blood cures certain female complaints. He will spare himself and his esteemed listener a description of the incredible scenes that have been enacted since in the arena. As for his own health, it has been so shattered by all these happenings that he cannot without nausea hear the word 'blood' pronounced, and his physician has seriously counselled him to visit a hydropathic institution at Baiae or Pompeii in the near future.

The director sighs and closes his tale with a resigned gesture which might equally point to the vanity of his physical endeavours or the general state of the world.

Apronius realises that there is no hope of getting anything out of this man today; disappointed, he rises from his marble seat, rearranges the pleats of his gown, makes his adieux. During his dinner at the Tavern of the Twin-Wolves he remains grumpy and preoccupied, and actually forgets to superintend the washing of his drinking-bowl.

Dusk veils the narrow criss-cross streets of the Oscian quarter as he sets out for home. Not for one single moment does the thought that he failed to get a free ticket leave his saddened mind. He is gorged with bitterness as he clambers up the fire escape to his apartment; what good are seventeen years of service?—an outcast from the feast of life, not even the crumbs stray your way.

Mechanically he lets the clothes down his gaunt body, repleats them carefully and lays them on the wobbly tripod; then extinguishes the light. Rhythmically thudding footsteps echo from the street: the municipal building-slaves are returning from work. He can see their ill-boding, numbed faces as when they pushed him aside and went on without apologising.

Quintus Apronius, First Scribe of the Market Court, stares sadly into his bedroom's night. Is this what one labours for, a whole toilsome life long full of grievance and privation? Can there be gods in such a world?

Since his childhood Apronius has never been so near to tears. In vain he waits for sleep to come, scared of the dreams it will bring. For he knows they will be bad and nasty dreams.

BOOK ONE

RISE

I

THE INN BY
THE APPIAN WAY

THE Appian Way tapered southward, an endless procession of
milestones, trees and benches. It was paved with large, square
stone blocks; recurring sections of cactus hedge ran along its
sloping sides; stone and plant alike were covered by a layer of
floury dust. It was quiet, and very hot.

At the second milestone south of Capua stood the inn of
Fannius. It was the busiest time in the year, but the inn was
empty. Times were bad and uncertain; only he who had to,
travelled; gangs of roughnecked rabble loitered around the
countryside, making traffic and trade unsafe. The road had
brought no prospective customers since midday, excepting two
aristocratic travelling parties on their way to Baiae, and in their
eyes Fannius's tavern did not even exist.

Fannius stood behind the counter listening to his book-keeper
reading out the accounts. The room was filled with stinging
smoke, it smelled of thyme and onions. Two painted waitresses
threw dice on a table to decide who should serve the next guest.
The male servants, strong-boned, bull-necked men equal to any
situation, were busy in the stables, or held their afternoon naps
under clouds of flies in the shady yard.

A tumult of voices approached from the gateway. When
Fannius rose to see what was up, the door had already been
pushed open, and a noisy crowd thronged inside. The place was
full with them at once; there were between fifty and sixty of
them. They carried odd instruments such as one might see used by
men at the circus. Most of them were rather bashful and raised

superfluous shouts and laughter. One of them wore the skin of a beast thrown over his shoulder instead of decent clothes. They stood around uncomfortably and leered at the serving maids. One demanded that a table should be laid for them in the courtyard.

Fannius looked this bunch of people over and, without undue hurry, bade his servants carry benches and stools outside. In the yard large tables formed a horseshoe. The waitresses moistened their eyebrows, made faces at each other and began to lay the table. The guests sat down; an expectant silence reigned. Several women were among them. At the head of the table sat a fat man with drooping moustaches and the eyes of a fish; he wore a silver necklace and looked like a sad seal. The waitresses came and went, they put jugs and cups down. The fat man brushed them on the floor with his elbow.

'Take them away,' he said. 'We want a barrel.'

The earthen tankards shattered on the cobbles; all the others laughed. One of the women, a slim, dark one, banged the table with her childish little fists.

Fannius slouched over to the fat man, his bull-necked servants forming a wall behind him. He touched the fat one's arm, and everyone grew quiet. Fannius had only one eye left, he was stocky and broad-shouldered. Musingly he looked up, down and past his customers.

'What arena has given you leave of absence?' he asked them. The fat man took Fannius's hand off his arm and said:

'He who asks much gets an earful. Now we want our barrel.'

Fannius stood for a while, looking at the guests. The guests looked at Fannius and said nothing. The silence lasted for a time; finally Fannius winked his eye, and his men shoved a barrel to the table. The plug was pulled out, and Fannius went away. The maids returned to fill the cups, but the guests were crowding round the barrel and helped themselves. Then they demanded food. The waitresses brought dishes in and the guests ate and drank. They got very cheerful. The bull-necked inn-servants leaned side by side against the wall and looked on.

When it began to grow dark, the fat man called for the proprietor. Fannius came. Several guests were sleeping over the table and some held waitresses on their laps; the waitresses were now very cheerful too.

The fat man, still as doleful as before, asked Fannius to prepare lodgings for the whole party. Some of the guests protested, yelling it was necessary to go on. The fat one said this place was as good as any other for a night's rest. Fannius was silent. The slender, dark-haired girl called out that the fat man was right, and that one might put guards in all the doorways. The fat man said there had been enough talk for now, and the innkeeper should get beds and bedding ready. Fannius answered that he had neither beds nor bedding, and would his guests pay and go.

The guests were quiet. After they had been quiet for some time, the man with the fur-skin told Fannius not to be afraid, for they had enough money to pay the bill. He had a wide, good-natured face with many freckles all over it; his angular limbs, and the way he sat, ponderous elbows propped on his knees, made him look rather like a woodcutter of the mountains. Fannius looked at him and the man with the fur-skin looked at Fannius and Fannius averted his eye. One of the guests, a lean little fellow, laughed unpleasantly and threw Fannius a purse. Fannius picked it up and said the guests should go now. The guests were silent. Fannius waited a little, then he winked his eye and his bull-necked men came closer. The fat guest got up and Fannius backed slightly. They stood belly on belly. Fannius eyed the fat man and said he had finished off many a bigger and better bandit in his time. His sudden grasp was swift and clever, but the fat one pushed his knee up into the other's belly and the inn-keeper was hurled against the wall, where he curled up whimpering.

One of the bull-necks raised his arm and all of them charged upon the fat customer. The sleepers awoke and the waitresses screeched, the tripods splintered, and the thud of the jars drowned the cracking of breaking bones against which they were smashed. But the guests' strange weapons were superior to the clubs of the servants, and the whole thing did not take long.

The yard was one riotous mess. The servants were driven back and huddled by the barn. The waitresses bandaged them, but two of the men were past their aid and were dragged off. The guests hung about irresolutely, joked and abused the bull-necks. The bull-necks were quiet. A few looked at Fannius, who crouched against the wall.

The lean little fellow walked mincingly over to Fannius and

bent over him. Fannius turned his head to the other side and spat. The little fellow solicitously kicked Fannius's groin with the tip of his toe. Fannius retched.

'First someone spills your eye for you, now something else has gone,' said the little fellow, 'that's what happens to people who go looking for trouble. And with Crixus too, of all people.' He laughed and patted the fat one's paunch. But the fat man Crixus did not laugh. He only looked like a sad seal with dangling whiskers and dull eyes.

The bull-necked servants stood still clustered in silence before the barn and several of the guests, armed, stood guard over them. The man with the skins on his shoulder walked across the yard and stopped in front of the servants. Everybody was looking.

'And now what shall we do with you?' said the man with the fur-skin to the servants. The servants looked at him. His eyes were quiet and attentive. They liked that.

'What sort of people are you, anyway?' one of them asked.

'Guess,' bawled the little fellow. 'Senators, probably.'

One of the bull-necks said: 'We don't care if you do sleep here, if you hop it in the morning.'

'Thank you very kindly,' said the man with the skins and smiled. Everybody laughed, even some of the bull-necks joined in.

'We'll lock you up with the cows for the night,' said the man in the skins.

'For rights we ought to kill you,' said Crixus. 'If one of you tries to get out he'll be finished off at once.'

The men were locked in the cowshed and the iron bolts made fast. Two of the guests remained to guard it. Two other sentries were placed in the outer entrance.

The maids went to get beds ready and prepared themselves for an exhausting night.

A hundred Campanian mercenaries marched along the highway. They had been sent out in the afternoon to recover the fugitives, and four hours had seen them trudging aimlessly through hamlets and by-paths. They sent out patrols, and after a time the patrols came back reporting that peasants and field-hands here and there had seen the escaped horde. But none of these tracks had led them anywhere; everybody had seen the runaways and none could say whither they had turned, or maybe they did not want to.

The platoon was accompanied by a few of Lentulus's slaves who were to aid identification. They were the most excited, for they felt responsible to their master for the success of the expedition. The mercenaries considered the whole affair a fairly disagreeable one. They were supposed to capture the fugitives, alive if possible—the bland fancy of the Town Councillors in their steam-baths. There was no possible reward in decorations or bloody glory, and a wrestling match with gladiators was no pleasant prospect. Everyone knew those men were little more than animals, trained beasts; they had nothing to lose, either. Apart from that they had those extraordinary weapons: nets, lassos, tridents, javelins, which rather upset all battle rules.

Dusk fell, and the platoon stopped at a tavern by the sixth milestone just after where the road forked off near the county of Calatia. It seemed as though the expedition would result in nothing, and the soldiers did not mind. Most of them were elderly people: impoverished artisans and pedlars, workless workmen and ruined farmers. They had enlisted with the auxiliaries for the sake of daily rations, regular pay and the old-age pension. In outlook they were more like rural militia than Roman Legionaries.

They ate and drank.

Two hours after sunset they started on their way back. The moon was young, it was very dark. Half-way one of their mounted scouts hurried towards them, he had with him a breathless, limping man. The man was badly tattered and said that his name was Fannius and that the runaways had broken into his inn where they killed the servants and made a filthy mess generally. Now they were sleeping with his maids, and by surrounding the house one might catch them with great ease like trapped rats in a hole. After that he inquired whether there was any reward.

The soldiers would have loved to kill him. They were damned tired, heavy with wine. But their captain had his ambitions, and the march was resumed. About a mile from the fork in the road was a farm. Its servants were roused and provided the regiment with torches. Twenty minutes later they arrived at Fannius's inn.

The building appeared dead and deserted; the torches smoked. After having the house surrounded, the captain knocked at the

outer door with the hilt of his sword. It was a very solid door of
hard wood. No answer came. 'Maybe they've already gone,' said
a soldier. They had to make up their minds to break the door in.

Ten men were sent back to the farm to get axes. Again time
passed. The house showed only two small windows, one at the
front and one in the wall overlooking the fields, both were on the
top floor. All other windows opened into the inner courts. There
was nothing else for it, they had to wait for the axes.

The mercenaries sat down on the road, some fell asleep. They
waited. From time to time a man went to the door, knocked,
bawled a bantering word; but the inside remained dead. Perhaps
they had really gone. The whole thing looked completely senseless to everybody.

After about an hour's time the axes arrived and the men got
ready to smash the door in. It was in truth a solid door. When
it finally gave way, there was still no sound from within. Fannius
was ordered to lead the way, but he yielded precedence to the
captain. The rest flocked in after them. They came to a square
yard which looked strange in the torchlight. At every window on
the top floor the gladiators stood and looked down.

The captain—his name was Mammius and he was a youth of
quality—forced his voice to an unnecessary shout. 'Now then,
stop making trouble,' he bellowed, turning his head in every
direction, at a loss which window to address, 'come on down,
resistance is useless.'—When he had done the yard was as still as
before.

'Show us the stairs,' said the captain to Fannius. Fannius
pointed to the kitchen quarters. The captain walked towards the
stairs.

'Better go home,' drawled a voice from above. The captain
stood still.

'Will you or won't you come voluntarily?' he said to the voice.
From above there was laughter.

'. . . And there's old Nicos, too,' someone shouted from one of
the windows, 'are you bringing us the master's love and kisses?'

Nicos, an old slave of Lentulus, looked up. 'Don't be so silly,'
he said, 'come on home. The master is very annoyed.'

There was some more laughter.

The mercenaries stood around and stared up at the windows.
'Where is Spartacus?' Nicos asked, searching among the windows.

The man with the skins leaned out of a window on the other side of the court and sent him a friendly grin: 'Ave, Nicos!'

'Can't you make them see reason?' Nicos asked him. 'You used to be more sensible than that.' The one in the skins smiled and did not answer.

The torches spread smoke instead of light. 'Now then,' said the captain, 'are you coming or aren't you?' Again he took a few steps towards the stairs.

'Stay where you are, shorn onion,' barked a window over the stairs. The captain took a few more steps. Then something shapeless came floating down and the captain lay on the floor, cursing; his hands and feet struggled in the net which drew together around him. The men in the windows roared.

'Pull him up!' cried one whose voice rose above the rest. The captain swore so violently that his voice broke and squeaked. Several reluctant mercenaries approached the corner by the stairs, intending to free their captain; one of them fell instantly, screaming, the others stopped short, and now hell was let loose; knives, stones, javelins, whole pieces of furniture shot from the windows.

The soldiers ran about holding their shields over their heads, and dropped the torches; but the shields were no use at all, the terrible missiles came from everywhere. Some tried to throw their spears and pikes up into the windows, but they always fell back. The torches smoked and died, the complete darkness made everything still worse, and worst of all were the roars from above. The soldiers pressed towards the outer doorway, but they found the door bolted, and those who ventured near it were stabbed or clubbed; the gladiators stormed down the stairs into the yard, and the soldiers were swept into a corner. Over their heads new torches were lit and held from the windows so that they formed an illuminated target, unable to protect themselves. The voice that had yelled 'Pull him up!' before, rang out now:

'Drop your arms!' After that it grew more quiet.

Several soldiers flung their swords off and sat down on the ground, the others remained standing. One of them cried not to throw anything away. Crixus went to the centre of the court and asked the man to step out. The other did not move. Crixus repeated that he should step out; one against one, he said, would be more sensible than everybody battering everybody else's heads in. The soldiers thought this a good idea and they shifted to make a gap for the man who had said they should hold on to their weapons. He did not budge. So then they all put their arms away and sat down in their corner of the courtyard.

The gladiators collected all the arms and carried them upstairs; they joked and were in a very genial mood. The dead and wounded were carried to the shed; Fannius was dead and so was the captain, he had been trampled to death in his net. Castus, the little fellow of the swaying hips, said the shed was their spolarium; that was the name of the place to which the corpses of the arena were dragged. Everyone laughed. They fetched the servants from the cowshed and pushed them into the soldiers' corner. The servants blinked stupidly, they had heard all the din in their stable, and they had preferred to stay where they were.

The waitresses reappeared, but no one took any notice of them. The gladiators stood around; some of them went upstairs to resume their sleep. Among the soldiers, in their corner, Nicos sat against the wall, an old man. The man in the fur-skin walked over to him across the courtyard. 'You'll come to a bad end,' said Nicos.

'Listen to me, Nicos,' said the man with the skins slowly, 'do you think the arena is a beautiful end?' Everybody in the courtyard was listening.

'It's all against the law and the order of things,' said Nicos. 'What can it lead to?'

'To hell with law and order,' said Castus, the little fellow with the swaying hips. But no one laughed.

'What will the master say when we come back without you?' said Nicos.

'It's very uncertain that you will get back at all,' said Castus. They were all quiet at this.

'You could come with us, Nicos, you know,' said the man with the fur-skin.

'I haven't been an honest servant for forty years,' said Nicos, 'to end as a thug and cut-throat.' Gradually a circle of gladiators had assembled around him.

'And what are you going to do with those over there?' Nicos asked, jerking his chin at the soldiers, some of whom had now stretched out on the ground. They were mostly elderly people. The gladiators were quiet.

.   .   .   .   .

They stood about in threes and fours and stared at the disarmed soldiers in their corner. Some of the soldiers snored, others were sitting on the cobbles and talked.

'. . . When we get back,' said an elderly soldier, 'they'll dismiss us all, or even worse. Maybe they'll hang us all on the cross.'

'And serve you right,' said a gladiator.

'Why?' said the soldier.

Some of the gladiators gathered around the group. 'The question is whether you will get back at all,' said Castus.

'Are you going to kill every one of us?' asked another soldier.

'You first of all,' said the little fellow, 'you lousy son of a bitch.'

'Be quiet,' said the man with the fur-skin.

Castus was quiet. Like the other Gauls he wore a little silver necklace.

The gladiators had formed a cluster in front of the soldiers' corner, shifting their feet in silence.

'The most sensible thing to do would be for all of you to come back with us,' said Nicos.

'Try and think, Nicos,' said the man with the fur-skin thoughtfully, 'think and talk after.'

Nicos said nothing.

'Put yourself in our position, Nicos,' said Oenomaus, a younger gladiator of rather slim and shy appearance, 'try and imagine that someone gives you a spear, and gives me one too, and then he says you and me are to skewer each other for other people's amusement.'

'I have never regarded the profession from that point of view,' said Nicos.

'But that is what it is like,' said the one with the fur-skin, 'think it over.'

Nicos thought it over and did not answer.

'Stop jabbering,' said Crixus, leaning gloomily against the wall.

'What are you going to do next?' Nicos asked.

The gladiators were quiet. 'We'll let them elect us to the Senate,' said Castus. Nobody laughed.

'There is Lucania—full of hills and woods,' said Oenomaus and looked shyly up at the man with the skins.

'The world is wide,' said the man with the skins, 'come with us, Nicos.'

'Lucania, eh?' said one of the soldiers, a former shepherd with wide cheekbones and the yellow teeth of a horse.

'If you lose your way there they can go look for you all right . . .', '. . . and herds of wild horses,' said another soldier, 'and the herdsmen are all robbers in Lucania. Their masters don't pay them any wages, so they have to live on what they can get.'

'There's game too, and fish—as many as you like, the brooks are full of them,' said the shepherd, 'I wouldn't mind going to Lucania with you . . .'

'Neither would I,' said the other. 'Your pay just about buys polenta and lettuce.'

'They'll hang you all, that's what they'll do,' said Nicos. 'You haven't even got any leaders.'

'Stop jabbering,' said Crixus and left his wall. 'We'll elect a leader, and then we're off.'

'Crixus will be Tribune,' said a gladiator, and everybody laughed.

'Will you take me with you?' asked the shepherd.

'They'll all be hanged,' said an old soldier.

Dawn came, the sky over the courtyard grew grey. The torches were put out. The yard looked more spacious and strangely different.

'I'd go too, you know,' said one of the bull-necked servants.

'And then what'll happen to the tavern?' asked another one.

'Maybe they'll hang us all because of Fannius,' said the first. 'Or else they might send us to the mines. . . .'

The bull-necks put their heads together and conferred. Then they all got up and came towards the gladiators. 'Back, you!' yelled Castus, the little fellow.

'We'd all come with you,' said the spokesman of the servants, 'if you'd take us.'

The gladiators looked at them doubtfully. 'We won't arm you, though,' said Castus. The servants conferred.

'They say that there will be arms in time,' said the spokesman. 'And that one there should be the leader.' He pointed at Spartacus. Spartacus looked at him with quietly attentive eyes, then he turned and grinned at Crixus:

'You're the fattest round here,' he said. Crixus eyed him mournfully. The gladiators cheered up. The Gauls wanted Crixus, all the others were for Spartacus. Finally they agreed to have both.

Again all grew quiet. The gladiators hung about, embarrassed: so now they had chosen commanders. The servants went to the barn, fetched some clubs and axes, and shared them out between them. Then they arranged themselves in a single file along the wall. The gladiators looked on in silence. The one with the fur-skin went over to the corner of the soldiers. 'What shall we do about you?' he asked them.

'Take us with you too,' said the shepherd with the teeth. 'I know the woods of Lucania.'

'We haven't any arms for them,' said Crixus. 'And anyway, they're too old.'

'How do you know we want to come?' said another soldier. 'You'll be caught and you'll hang, all of you.'

The soldiers hesitated and consulted together. The shepherd and a few others stepped forward.

'We'll take you along,' said Spartacus to the shepherd. The shepherd leapt high up in the air and rushed over to the gladi-ators. The gladiators next to him shifted a bit.

'And what's the matter with you?' said Crixus.

The shepherd cocked his head and went to join the servants. One of them handed him a bludgeon. The shepherd bared his horsy teeth and tried the bludgeon on the air.

The one in the skins asked the other soldiers who had come forward their age and previous professions. Each was voted on by the gladiators, about some the votes differed and they wrangled for a while. The whole thing was very funny; only a few of the younger ones were accepted, they joined the bull-necks by the wall and received clubs or swords or tridents. Those who were rejected went back and sat down on the cobbles again.

Dawn broke in earnest now and dyed the skies red. The mica in the window frames began to sparkle. Crixus and the man in the skins stood side by side and listened to the confusion of excited talk. After a while Crixus turned to the other:

'If the two of us went off now,' he said, snorting audibly, 'they'd never catch us. We might go to Alexandria. There are heaps of women in Alexandria.' The man with the fur-skin looked at him attentively:

'The two of us alone—that would be easier,' he said.

'There are all kinds of people in Puteoli,' said Crixus.

'If you have money, no skipper will bother about passports.'

'No,' said Spartacus. Crixus looked at him in silence.

'It can't be done,' said the one with the skins. Crixus said nothing. 'Later on, maybe,' said the one with the skins.

'Yes, later on,' said Crixus, 'when they've hanged us.'

The man with the skins thought for a while and looked at the gladiators scurrying back and forth and getting their things together.

'It can't be done—not now,' he said. 'Do you want to go off on your own?' he asked after a pause, and looked at Crixus.

Crixus said nothing. He left Spartacus and stood by the wall. The gladiators were noisily trying to determine what to do. All of them were very cheerful now.

Suddenly the one in the fur-skin climbed up on the table. He raised his arms high, as though to cut trees:

'We're off,' he roared with all his might. 'We're off for Lucania.' He grinned a great, freckly grin.

The gladiators shouted all at once and got themselves ready. The servants and those of the soldiers allowed to go too were still standing against the wall. 'Well, are you coming?' Spartacus called out to them.

'We said we would,' their spokesman answered gravely.

The other soldiers sat on the cobbles and peered, some of them were still asleep. The gladiators took their money away, and everything they had left in the way of daggers and knives. One of the soldiers resisted and died; the others looked on. They were elderly men and knew they would either be dismissed or sent to work in the mines.

The women came walking across the court; they had been watching everything from the windows. The dark, slender one stopped before Spartacus, who jumped off his table with a crash. The bull-necked servants looked at him in mute surprise, they were puzzled by his sudden change from thoughtfulness to activity. But they liked this abrupt vehemence too.

'And now what?' asked the girl and lifted her head to the man.

'We're going to Lucania,' he said.

'We'll have a merry time in the woods,' said the woman.

'Very merry,' said the man with the skins and smiled at her, 'we'll all be hanged.'

He went over to Nicos. 'Are you coming with us, Nicos?' he asked.

'No,' said Nicos. He sat against the wall, and he looked very old.

'Farewell, Father,' said he with the skins.

'Farewell,' said Nicos.

Disorderly, the gladiators pushed and pressed through the gateway on to the road. The servants and soldiers marched behind them, the three women followed last.

They numbered over a hundred now.

It was almost daylight.

2

THE BANDITS

They had intended to march to Lucania, but when they gained the rougher, mountainous regions where fields grew scarcer and spoils were scanty, they turned back. For the land Campania, praised, blessed land, let go of no man—not even a robber. Capricious country, this; its loose black soil bore fruit thrice a year, and was decked in roses even before sowing time. The intoxicating breeze from its gardens drugged the blood; and on Mount Vesuvius herbs grew whose extracts transformed virgins into Bacchantes. In spring the mares, on heat, would canter up high cliffs, turn their back to the sea, and become pregnant by the hot wind.

Hell had erected its prettiest ante-room in this land Campania. The big devils wore snowy white, magnificently pleated; the little devils served them in submissive piety and dreamed of killing them dead. As old as the very hills was the conflict as to who should control Campania, granary of the Legions, most valued of national assets. Ever since Tiberius Gracchus's time, patriots had attempted to free the country from the big landlords' grasp, to divide it among the landless people; they were drowned, battered, stoned to death; the usurers and speculators returned. Farmers and petty tenants were drained of blood by the aristocracy, they were ousted, their property bought up; there was no escape. The peasantry was supplanted by the great landowners, and free-born workers elbowed out by slave-labour which was constantly replenished through every war; there was no escape. Bands of destitute Campanian farmers swarmed about the roads, turned to robbery, hid in the mountains. There was no escape.

Rumours trailed across the land Campania.

A robber band of unheard-of audacity fell upon inns and taverns, robbed travellers, pillaged wagon loads of goods, burned down the noble country houses; stole the ox from his manger, the stallion from his stud. The brigands were everywhere and no-where at once. This night they might be camping in the swamps by the river Clanius, the next in the forests of Verginia's moun-tains. Soldiers were sent out against them, hurriedly composed regiments from smaller towns; but the soldiers deserted or joined the bandits. Their number increased day by day; they inspired alarm and admiration; for they did not respect life and they scoffed at death.

Rumours trailed across the land Campania. Slaves and farm-hands sat together and talked of the bandits when the sun stood high and the midday demon stalked the fields and inflicted bad dreams on the sleeping overseers. The brigands had two leaders: a fat Gaul, sad and cruel, and a Thracian of luminous eyes who wore a gay fur-skin. There was also a girl, dark, slender and of childlike airs, a Thracian priestess who could read the stars and the future. She was the woman of the one with the fur-skin, but she slept with others too and afflicted all men with like desire.

They were no ordinary bandits, they were gladiators. Never before had there been such bandits in Campania, for gladiators are hardly human and destined to die in the arena. But, on the other hand, they were humans after all, and quite right if they did not want to die. They butchered the shepherds' sheep and devoured the grapes of the vineyards, and took for the men the best racers of the stud-farms, and for the luggage the hardiest mules. Wherever they had been no grass grew henceforth and no maiden was what she had been and no barrel was left in the cellars. Whosoever resisted them was slain and whosoever ran away was caught; but him who threw himself on their mercy they might take along with them, and there were some people who actually asked to be taken. That's what those gladiators were like.

Rumours and legends trailed across the land of Campania. The women recounted them as they milked the cows, and the old

men when they could not fall asleep at nights in their musty
vaults, when they crept close together and thought out loud
many thoughts of cattle, weather and death.

What was that story of Naso the stableman?

On the Lord Statius's estate near Suessula all three oxen had
fallen sick. They had blown-up bellies, snotty noses, constrained
nerves, dull eyes; they would not feed, nor ruminate, nor as much
as lick. One might have thought them bewitched, but in truth
the Lord's steward had supplied them with inferior and in-
sufficient fodder, for the Lord Statius's estate had not enough
pasture ground of its own, so that fodder had to be bought, and
the Lord's steward put the money aside for himself and let the
oxen starve. Naso the stableman had always foretold that the
oxen would get sick on such bad food, and asked the Lord's
steward for better, but all he got for his good advice was thrash-
ings. And when the oxen fell sick in all seriousness and their
innards went all wrong and they would not work, Naso tried to
cure them with unfailing remedies: he gave them pounded fig-
seed in cypress leaves, forced pigeons' eggs down their throats,
poured garlic crushed in wine into their nostrils, gave them
clysters of salted honey with myrrh and snail's-blood, and bled
them below the tail, after which he bandaged the incision with
papyrus-fibre, which is the correct way of doing it.

But when none of this helped any, that thief of a steward got the
wind up. In order to make someone else take the blame, he
accused Naso of having let a pig and a chicken into the stable,
whose excrement was supposed to have mixed with the fodder
and so caused the oxen's illness. In vain Naso the stableman
protested his innocence: he was put in chains, branded with the
red-hot iron and condemned to work in the mill.

Now, as everyone knows, work in the mill is one of the most
terrible punishments, second only to those of death, work in the
mines, and work in the quarries; the unfortunate delinquent must
trudge round and round the millstone in unending circles, his
feet weighed down in irons. Gradually his eyes grow sightless with
all that dust and steam; and an iron wheel is forged around his
neck so that he cannot put his hand to his mouth and taste of the
flour.

In this manner Naso would soon have pegged out, although
not he but the steward was the real culprit. But one fine night

the bandits raided the Lord Statius's estate and ransacked everything as was their wont. So they came upon the mill too and dragged off the sacks of meal; and so they came to hear of Naso the stableman's fate.

And so the man with the fur-skin had the Lord's steward brought before him, and they tied him to the mill-beam. And they released Naso and had him whip the steward with a whip to make him walk his circles quicker—all that had been done to Naso himself. And when they left, they told the steward that they would come back and whip him to death if they heard that he had stopped pulling the beam around. But the Lord's steward went crazy and circled the millstone for two days and nights without stopping, until he fell down dead the third morning.

Rumours trailed across the land Campania, gruesome and touching tales. The bandits were here today and gone tomorrow, they might appear from anywhere, at any time. Travellers ventured to cross the country only under armed escort, and at times even that did not avail them. A lady journeying to Salernum had left Capua by the Albanian Gate with fifty Numidian horsemen and five baggage wagons; but she arrived in Suessula all alone on a mule cart and had not a shred of clothing left on her body.

And then there had been that strange affair which happened at an estate near Acerrae. Its field slaves were badly treated; they were kept chained together in groups of ten. But when the bandits came to this estate, the slaves stood as though rooted in the earth, determined to resist. The bandits were about to pounce on them and slaughter every one, when the solemn Thracian stood up before them and in a ringing voice ordered them to wait; and delivered a sudden speech, which surprised everybody very much.

'Truly,' he said to the slaves, 'your chains must be dear to your hearts and of great bliss to your bodies. I for one cannot see anything else on this estate that you can call your own and could wish to defend with your lives. Or did they tell me lies, or do those fowls lay eggs for *your* breakfast, do those cows yearn for the bull to increase *your* herds, do those bees store nectar in the hives to sweeten *your* cakes? . . .'

When the slaves did not say a word to this, the man with the skins told one of the brigands who was a locksmith to unshackle them. A few resisted, saying they would not owe their freedom to anyone but their master. They were killed; but the rest went along with the bandits.

Many such tales were borne across the land Campania, and they were as the hot sirocco breathing from the seas to blow feverish unrest into the heads of men and beasts.

Suspense racked most the lords and their bailiffs, overseers, accountants and foremen; they were stricter than ever and reinforced the guards. But the common slaves, the ploughmen, weeders, diggers, mowers in the fields; the stablemen, shepherds, and cattle-drivers, grew still more lazy and rebellious, damaged their tools and their own bodies, shammed illness, avoided work, and seemed to be waiting for something. Every morning some were missing, in spite of heavy bolts guarding the vault-doors, in spite of high-up windows that could not be reached by the tallest man's lifted hand—they went to join the bandits, and some even took their women and children with them.

A fever gripped the land of Campania. The towns with their impotent little garrisons watched it spread. They sent messages to Rome, and put more guards on their walls at night. The gentry hurriedly left their Campanian mansions for the summer, drove back to Rome and complained to the Senate about this scandalous state of affairs.

But the Senate had greater worries. Their Gallic worry was: Sertorious and the revolutionary emigrants' army. If they won, it meant revolution in Rome; if Rome's own general Pompeius won, it meant a new dictatorship. Their Asiatic worry was: King Mithridates. If he won, the province was lost; if Rome won, the price of corn would fall. Further worries were: the pirates, unimpaired sovereigns of the seas; the people and its demagogues, keener than ever; the economic crisis; the necessity of minting bad coin.

The Campanian trouble was far too unimportant to be included in the worries-list.

3

THE ISLAND

THEY were a horde now of more than three hundred men and
about thirty women.

They had horses for their vanguard and mules for their
baggage, they had tents to sleep in, and proper arms for every
second man. Their numbers increased day by day.

There had been frequent squabbles on account of the people
who came to join them. The gladiators were distrustful. They
wished to keep themselves to themselves, and wondered what all
this would lead to. The people who came to join them brought
presents: a sack of flour, a lamb, two horses. If chased away,
they would settle next to the camp, eat their provisions, wait.
Some were killed, robbed of their possessions. But one could not
simply kill all of them.

Often they tramped the countryside for several days and nights
before they found the camp. They were crafty, asking whomso-
ever they met whether the road was safe: where had the bandits
last been seen? Slaves were often caught and returned to their
masters, it meant death for them, or worse; yet they could not
be deterred.

Field-hands came, shepherds and day-labourers, slaves and
freemen, without distinction. Cattle-drivers came, from Hirpinia,
beggars and bandits from Samnium, slaves of Greek, Asiatic,
Thracian, Gallic origin; prisoners of war came, and those born
in servitude. From land and town they came, artisans, loungers,
ragged doctrinaires.

Sextus Libanius came, citizen of Capua. He was of old artisan

41

stock; his grandfather Quintus Libanius had made statues. The
craft had become more and more specialised; his father already
fashioned exclusively heads, the son now merely inserted eyes,
blue, green, red, yellow eyes of coloured stone. He was a sturdy,
respectable man of advanced years and very good standing
among his neighbours, opposed to any disturbance of existing
conditions. But then crisis descended, and civil war; no one
bought statues. His workshop was closed down, and Sextus
Libanius went to join the robbers.

Proctor came, field-hand from a medium-sized southern estate.
His erstwhile employer, a pig-headed man, acted the Roman
burgess of ancient times, when speech smelled of onion and garlic,
but hearts were hale. He treated his servants according to Old
Cato's maxim: slaves must either work or sleep. He kept meticulously within the law which ruled that the plough rest on holidays;
so he let the plough rest, and had the slaves mend barn-roofs and
empty manure-pits—occupations not expressly mentioned by the
law. In the end Proctor slashed off three of his fingers on purpose
with the scythe, was dismissed as useless, and joined the
bandits.

Zozimos came, a grammar scholar and rhetorician. Starting
out as a beadle to the Oplontis Council, he had talked his chief
into making him his children's tutor; having made connections,
he then set up a school of his own, which soon taught about
twenty children of greater or lesser rank whose parents liked the
odd man well. Zozimos made good money, but success went to
his head: he began to fancy himself as a public orator, disbanded
his school, wrote poetry, failed through contemporary lack of
appreciation, went hungry, and joined the bandits. Arrived at his
destination, he at once delivered a political diatribe; the bandits
laughed like anything and gave him a good hiding. But they took
him along; he had a smattering of many matters strange and
curious, and they liked listening to him.

Women came, too.

Laetitia came, a maidservant with a face of leather and breasts
like emptied wine-bags. Ten years ago her master had promised
that she need work no more if she bore three sons. In ten years
Laetitia had brought forth ten children, eight of them were
female and only two were male. Now her womb was no longer
fruitful; so the servant Laetitia went to join the bandits.

Cynthia came, aged sorceress from a mountain village. For fifty years she had been engaged in apparently contradictory activities, which were, however, all definitely connected and had each their fixed price. She assisted at births, two Asses; lamented the dead, four Asses; lay down to men in the graveyard, five Asses. She read the future out of offal, the flight of birds or the pattern of lightning: five Sestertii. She cured illness, sold pills and love-potions, all at fixed rates, from the cheapest which facilitated conception, up to the dearest which caused abortion. But one day a Greek medico appeared in her village, a follower of Erisistratos who claimed that the blood in its vessels streams up and downward, and more such drivel. That quack bagged her clientele, Cynthia lost her livelihood; she joined the robbers.

Young women came also, harlots and abandoned brides, lecherous and spent ones; the majority were hideous, a few attractive. At first they caused strife and death, later people got used to their presence, and every woman lived with one man or with two.

The influx of runaways never ceased. Everyone had got used to it, accepted it; at night people wondered how many new ones had come that day, laid wagers as to whether the next would bring a physician of whose owner's patients too many had died, or a prostitute who had quarrelled with her landlady. On the march, the horde looked more like the guilds' procession on Minerva's Day than a band of gladiators. Previously they had managed easily thirty miles a day, now all they could do was twelve.

They were forced to look round for a permanent camp. A suitable site was found west of Acerrae, an island in the swamps by the Clanius.

It was a quiet enough island, sheltered by rushes on three sides. The moon rose late, her face scratched by the reed. The frogs' dirges were the night's sole sound; an occasional marsh bird would plunge from the rushes, ascend spirally and glide down on the thick, yellow water of the river. The tents were stuffy with the swamp's close breath, so that at early dawn many people tottered out into the open, wrapped in their blankets, to sleep outside. Their limbs were stiff in the morning; but the sun came out and sucked prickly sweat from their skins.

Many fell sick of fever. Cynthia the witch sold herbs and bitter

pills of a morning. No one liked her, but all took her powders.
Some people died and were burnt on reed and brushwood fires.

But at night there always were great goings on in the camp.

By then it had grown cooler. Red-tinged mist hung over the
rushes.

Eating and drinking over, some sat by the river, legs dangling
from the bank, and watched the water eddy round their toes.

Some were fishing.

The bull-necked servants of Fannius faced each other in two
rows and competed in throwing stones. They never laughed and
strictly observed succession.

Several younger men and women squatted in the rushes,
listening to a player. Her head lolling backwards, her dyed eyelids closed, she repeated the same stanza over and over in a
throaty tremolo.

Scattered couples ducked into the rushes; after only a few
paces they perceived the hubbub of the camp as muted, distant
echoes. Now and then forceful neighs could be heard: a stallion
shepherded into the enclosure together with his herd.

The largest group flocked round the day's new-comers. This
time they were an old man with a stiff leg and a young one,
thick-necked and pop-eyed. The old man was taciturn and
reserved, the lad too intimidated to talk. The ice could not be
broken, so they called for Castus. The little fellow and a number
of his cronies strolled towards the group. They were a dreaded
clique and had been dubbed 'The Hyaenas'.

'They come from a vineyard-estate near the Sebethos,' a man
informed Castus, 'they've run away because their corn-ration was
too meagre, and on top of that they had to pay extra to have it
ground.'

'They're probably lying,' said Castus. 'They think here we'll
give them corn for nothing. They're just the kind of people we're
dying to have.'

The old man said nothing. The lad cast frightened eyes at
Castus; his lips were full and moist, and he wore little ear-rings.
The spectators grinned.

'What have you come here for?' Castus said to the old one. 'I
daresay you think we steal sheep and rape girls, and other
naughty things like that. What's your name, anyway?'

'Vibius,' said the old man, 'and that's my son.'

'And what's yours?' Castus asked the lad.

'Vibius,' said the lad, and plucked uncomfortably at his ear-ring.

The onlookers laughed. Castus laughed as well; he had a pretty, girlish mouth, his nose was peeling. When he bent forward, a white strip of skin showed underneath his necklace.

'Vibius,' repeated the little fellow, 'plain and simple, just like his father. My name, for instance, is Castus Retiarius Tirone.'

He checked himself to watch the effect. The lad looked at him admiringly.

'There's nothing to it,' said Castus, 'every nobleman has three names.'

'Are you a nobleman, sir?' asked the lad. The onlookers laughed.

'All former gladiators are aristocrats round here,' said Castus, 'and new-comers like you are vulgar rabble.'

'Are you a gladiator, sir?' asked the lad respectfully.

'Certainly,' said Castus.

Vibius the Younger thought hard, pursed his lips: 'That man with the fur-skin—is he an aristocrat too?'

'Certainly, Vibius,' said Castus, 'all gladiators are noblemen and scions of important princes. Spartacus, that's the man with the skins, is a scion of important Thracian princes.'

The onlookers chuckled with glee.

Zozimos, tutor and rhetorician, sauntered past the group. Castus appealed to him:

'Am I speaking the truth, Zozimos?'

'All that may be clothed in speech is truth,' said the tutor, always careful not to cross Castus and his friends. 'For, all that can be expressed in terms of words is possible, and that which is possible may well come true one day.'

'And can a cow have piglets then?' questioned one of the onlookers.

'Even that is possible,' said Zozimos. 'If a god can turn himself into a swan and so beget a child by a woman—surely a cow may one day produce piglets.'

The onlookers laughed. 'Sit down, Zozimos, and tell us something,' said Hermios, the Lucanian shepherd with the horsy teeth.

'I had rather stand,' said Zozimos, 'for upright is the noble word.'

'Tell us a story,' coaxed the shepherd.

'Selah,' said Zozimos. 'Hearken then: a hundred years ago the Greeks had a republic. Before their Consuls entered upon office, they had to swear the following oath: "I shall be an enemy of the people, and I shall concoct every sort of plan to damage the people." '

'And what did everybody else say?' asked Castus.

'Everybody else?' said Zozimos. 'You mean the People. The People said exactly what they say today—for you may have noticed that we have the same state of affairs this day and age, only that our Senators no longer swear that oath in public.'

The onlookers were quiet and disappointed.

'Ah well, that's how things are,' said Hermios the shepherd without conviction, 'and what they always were like . . .' he bared his teeth and sighed.

'Zozimos,' said the little fellow, 'you're boring us. If you can't think of anything better than that you can hop it.'

'I depart,' said Zozimos. 'My master sent me packing on account of my revolutionary ideals; I had hoped, however, to find you more understanding. But I will not conceal aught from you, Castus mine: I am disappointed.'

Bonfires burned in a number of circular hollows which had been dug in a triangular clearing. They suffused stinging smoke good for keeping the gnats away. Each group had its particular fire, lit always in the self-same place. And each group had its particular story.

There was the women's fire, the fire of Fannius's servants, the Celtic fire, the Thracian fire. The Celts and Thracians were numerically strongest and detested each other. Crixus was the leader of the Celts, among them the little fellow and his Hyaenas. Leader of the Thracians was Spartacus.

The Celts were moody, irascible creatures; mostly born in Roman bondage, they knew of their native land only by hearsay. The fathers of most of them had been menials, their mothers prostitutes; they swore beautifully intricate oaths and fought one another at the slightest provocation; afterwards the survivors sobbed in each other's arms.

The Thracians on the other hand had entered Italy only a few years ago as captives of Appius Claudius's campaign. They were of sombre demeanour and coarse build, and had tiny blue spots tattooed on brow and shoulder. They were strangely meditative; they drank much without ever getting boisterous. God knew where they had found the huge drinking horn which they passed round the fire tranquilly; if someone spoke up loud, they looked at him, amazed and inattentive. There were twenty of them and they never disagreed, in which last trait they resembled Fannius's servants, with whom they shared unuttered fellow-feeling. They had their one drinking horn going the rounds, and they had their three women, likewise going the rounds; they were used to that: women are scarce in the mountains.

They had kept awake misty, dreamlike memories of their mountains, of the lowing yellow flocks, the black goat-skin tents —where drought brought death to man and beast, and poverty unending strife with the tribes of the neighbouring valleys: Basternae, Triballi and Peukines. Life was hard in the mountains. Down in the vale lay big cities: Usedoma and Tomoi, Kollatis and Odessos, fraught with splendour and wild opulence; the mountains held poverty, herds, and ancient customs. When a child was born unto them there was much sorrow and wailing, for life stores suffering for the newborn; but at deathbeds there was glad hilarity, for the dead one passes into the colourful realm of timelessness. They had feast-days too: once a year Bromius the Clamourer and Bacchos the Caller broke out of the forest, in their wake men and women united. And Ares the Wrathful had to be placated, although it was burdensome to dance for him in nude contortions, face and body flecked with paint. Life was hard in the mountains; the large herds were hungry, and ate on and on without bothering about dearth or enemies. But the mountains were also good and right; everything was fenced in meaning and custom—until the Roman forced his way into the forests, with much hooting of tubae and shouting, to hunt human quarry. Wherever the mountain-folk came across him they murdered that naked-skull and moved higher up among the rocks; but the Roman never left off the pursuit. For many years this went on, until finally they were caught: shepherds and flocks, many thousands of men and sheep.

It was only then they heard that they had infringed the law

and were therefore to be duly sold and condemned, for the Apuleian Law accurately specified their crimes: Offence against Safety and Grandeur of the Roman Republic.

This then was the Thracian contingent, and they were quiet, rather sombre folk, these twenty. The man with the fur-skin was one of them and yet not one of them: he had lived in Italy longer, knew more of tongue and usage; and no one knew quite what he had been up to.

The twelfth day after the establishment of the camp by the Clanius, the twentieth after the flight from Capua, a mounted messenger was intercepted on the Highway between Suessula and Nola. He was a municipal slave of Capua, destined to give a message to the Nola Council.

Castus and his cronies, bent upon a private excursion, had held him up out of pure mischief; besides, they liked the look of his horse. In his fear the man talked such gibberish that they grew suspicious and began to examine him. Castus and his friends had their own methods of extracting information: after a quarter of an hour they knew the message. Its gist said that the Praetor Clodius Glaber and three thousand selected mercenaries would leave Rome for Campania in the next few days in order to exterminate the robber-plague. The Nola Council is requested to provide quarter, and to obtain reliable information as regards number and shelter of the bandits.

Castus and his friends strung the messenger's remains up on a tree by the highway, and tacked a welcoming letter to the Praetor Clodius Glaber on his chest. In silence they galloped back to the camp.

The camp was just as usual. The Hyaenas were surrounded at once and asked what they had brought back. They said the expedition had been fruitless. Castus had ordered them to keep silence, and they kept silence.

Castus himself went into Crixus's tent. Crixus sat on a rug doing something to his shoes which had suffered from the damp. He did not look up when Castus entered, and hammered on.

'It's all up,' said Castus. 'Three thousand are on their way from Rome. We held up their courier.'

They fetched the one with the fur-skin and a few of the leading gladiators. It was stifling hot inside Crixus's tent. They talked back and forth for some time. Castus suggested that they disperse, each trying his luck apart. The others were not pleased with this; they argued, sweating. Attracted by the uproar, people in the camp collected in front of the tent, not bold enough to enter. Crixus stared glumly in front of him, wiped the sweat off his forehead, and said nothing. The man with the fur-skin said nothing either, his musing glance resting on each successive speaker as though seeing him for the first time. By and by, every one directed his words to him.

When finally they tired of talking, the man with the fur-skin began to tell them of a mountain on the coast, not far away, which was called Vesuvius. Several people who had come to the camp from that particular district had reported that this mountain had a hole burnt into its middle by internal fire; before there were men on earth, all mountains had glowed with such intense heat as to make them transparent, and blind the animals who looked on and saw it happen. But those fires had died many ages ago, and instead of a peak the mountain now had a funnel-shaped hole inside, half a mile deep and as big as two amphitheatres together. . . .

The gladiators could not see what he was getting at. They listened open-mouthed; he sat with hunched shoulders, his bony cheek propped on his hand, as though he were telling wood-cutters' tales over the nightly camp fires in the mountains.

The foot of that montain, he went on, was clothed in woods and vineyards, and the cities of Pompeii, Herculaneum and Oplontis spread close by. But farther up it grew bald and steep, and was beset by precipitous rocks. It was said, he told them, that some years ago two thieves had camped at the bottom of the hole, and they had never been caught because there was only one single path across the rock leading up to the crater-rim, which was easy to defend.

By and by, understanding dawned in the gladiators' minds; the idea of living inside a hollow mountain seemed to them exceedingly alluring and droll; they worked up more and more enthusiasm, raised a tumult of shouts and laughter and praised the man with the fur-skin who always had such mad ideas and who sat among them, smiling, elbows propped on his knees, and let his musing eyes rest on every one in turn. The anxious folk outside also regained their confidence; soon the news spread that they would leave this fever-island to live on a mountain which bore a fortress in its bowels.

That night saw song and dance on the island, the wine-bags were drunk empty, and groups from the separate fires mingled in great merriment.

In the morning the tents were taken down, and the robbers with their mounted vanguard, their sumpters, ox-carts, and train of women and children, started plodding towards the mountain Vesuvius.

They were a horde now of more than five hundred men and nearly a hundred women.

4

THE CRATER

PRAETOR CLODIUS GLABER turned grumpily in his saddle and signalled his forces to sing. The forces sang. Their voices emerged hoarsely from the cloud of dust which had enveloped them for miles and hours; it did not sound too pleasant. The men sang a satirical ditty on the Praetor's shiny pate which illuminated his faithful soldiers' way day and night. It was not very brilliant; but every true general and every true army must have their satirical song. And was not he a true general, were not his true troops? Undoubtedly they were. True, the foe was neither King Mithridates nor Boiorix, the Cimbri chieftain. He could have wished for a more showy enemy—especially as he had waited fifteen years for the moment that would find him riding in command.

How he had waited! Distressing times, these, for honest souls like Clodius Glaber: the road to power was no longer paved with intrepid deeds, but with petticoats, bribes and intrigue. One after the other, his contemporaries had sneaked to position while he laboured like an honest fool from station to station—the Service, Quaestorship, Praetorship; not even the Aedilate had he been spared. And all that in spite of his father's having been Consul, in spite of all the prophecies of a glorious career for Clodius Glaber himself.

To hell with his soldiers, why were they not singing? They were in full view of Capua's necropolis now, the Campanian people awaited him, their saviour—what kind of an advent was this without song? He turned round, the soldiers raised their voices anew in the Hymn of the Pate.

51

Take Marcus Crassus, for example. He had never distinguished himself with warlike feats, but had brought dozens of Sulla's opponents to the Dictator's gallows, after which he pocketed their estates, thus laying the foundations of his fabulous wealth. Now half the Senate is in his debt, the highest State officials dance to his tune; he has grown hard of hearing, hog-eyed and fat— and of course ignores Clodius Glaber, companion of his youth. The other day he had been indicted for unchastity, committed with a Vestal, but procedures had brought to light that his nocturnal visits to the Virgin had been nothing but negotiations concerning the sale of her country villa; all Rome had laughed at the story.

The Praetor's spirits rise. In a moment he will enter Capua, Campania's saviour on ambling horse. Why are those confounded soldiers not singing? He turns a smiling face, signals to them. For the third time the Hymn of the Pate resounds; the Praetor rejoices and pats his horse.

Furthermore, there is that stodgy Pompeius: many consider him the next dictator. His late and lamented father had been cross-eyed and was killed by lightning—what a death for a nobleman! Young Pompeius himself had been summoned to court at the very outset of his career for purloining bird-snares and books, part of the booty from Asculum. Bird-snares and books! But while the law-suit was still pending, he got betrothed to the president's ugly daughter, and was acquitted. When judgment was pronounced, the public cried 'Nuptial Congratulations' instead of 'Long Live Innocence!' Soon after, he got divorced, and married Dictator Sulla's stepdaughter, with child by someone else. Returned from Africa, he weeps and pleads until his father-in-law grants him a triumphal entry; so Pompeius has four elephants harnessed to his chariot, but the arch is too narrow, the elephants must be unharnessed, and Pompeius has hysterical fits of weeping. And the people adore him just the same.

The people! If the people knew its heroes the way he, Clodius Glaber, knows them, there would not be many heroes left. Had he not been brought up with them, admittedly the most decent of the whole clique—and where has it got him to? All and sundry have overtaken him; Lucullus is about to conquer Mithridates, and to drench his glory in booze and guzzling; Pompeius is a general in Spain and calls himself 'Pompeius the Great'; Marcus

Crassus sits at home without ever touching a sword, and has everyone else trapped in his pocket; even little Caesar who fulfilled his ambassadorial mission in the bed of the King of Bythinia, to the mirth of all Rome—even he is rising in the world and airs his gift of the gab in the Democratic Party. But the reward for his, Clodius Glaber's, forty years of virtue is the conducting of a ridiculous campaign against bandits and circus-folk, at the head of a rotten army of hastily gathered recruits and veterans who will not even sing.

'Sing up!' roars the Praetor, red with rage, at his fatigued, hoarse men. They are now a mere two hundred feet from the city gate, where the Municipal Council of Capua queues in welcome.

The Hymn of the Pate rises to the skies, the Praetor's horse trots a fancy canter, Clodius Glaber himself, furious tears in his eyes, receives the slightly surprised and measured welcoming speech of the oldest Councillor.

It was the tenth day of the siege.

Praetor Clodius Glaber walked about as in a weird dream. As far as he knew, in the history of the Roman wars there had never before been such a peculiar siege. For they were not besetting a town, but a mountain, and not even a mountain but a hole in the mountain, with one single accessible path leading up to it. The besiegers could not get up. The besieged could not get down. The path was slim as a gutter-pipe, and so steep that a mule could not climb up unless pulled in front and pushed from behind; but this was, of course, unthinkable.

Praetor Clodius Glaber had several sheep-skin bags of wine fetched up every day, and got drunk together with his officers; they were all veterans with rheumatism in their legs and vociferously warlike speech in their mouths. That at least was something.

The Praetor's camp had been pitched, more serviceably than artistically, in the crescent-shaped highland valley named 'Hell's Ante-room' by the natives. It had to be sheltered from javelins and bits of rock hurtling from above. Even though distance lessened serious danger, it seemed wiser to adapt tent-pitching to the existing natural cover afforded by the cleft, furrowed ground. The classic regulations for camp-building had to be disregarded, much to Clodius Glaber's regret, as he had a great taste for decoration.

The valley embraced the blunt head of Vesuvius in an inland semi-circle, thus separating it from Mount Somma. The summit's other, seaward, side dashed steeply and impassably down to the wooded lower regions. There was no possible way out for the bandits; the sole path ran to earth in the valley which was Clodius Glaber's camp—had been for ten days.

On the first and second days the soldiers had repeatedly tried to attack the crater rim. It was, of course, quite hopeless. Up top one man was enough to defend the path single-handed, and who wanted to duel with gladiators? To give the regiment its due, twenty men had tried it; fifteen died in the attempt, five were caught alive and arrived dead at the foot of the rocks some time after. This did not greatly encourage the rest, and the Praetor felt he could hardly blame them.

During those first attempts a number of soldiers had tried to climb up the bare rocks. Some fell down, unversed in the art of climbing, others were easy mark for the gladiators' missiles, the rest had to leave off.

The only way left to them was to starve the enemy out of his hole. The besieged were estimated at five or six hundred; even if they did have mules and horses—for when the nights were quiet down below they could hear ghostly whinneys from the mountain's bowels—and could kill and eat them before the animals themselves died from starvation, even then their water supply was bound to last only for a few days longer. So they would either have to give up or perish with thirst, since one could not count on rain at this time of year.

In consequence, the Praetor decided to forgo further un-necessary sacrifices; he and his soldiers bided their time.

The third day passed peacefully. The view was lovely. The valley was framed in shady forests of chestnut and pine, sidling down gentle hillocks. The soldiers rambled all over the valley and its woods; they were very contented and sang the Hymn of the Praetor's kindly Pate. The bandits were not to be seen; they were crouching in that crater-lair of theirs; every once in a while, though, their sentries and scouts, minute toys, were seen to scamper about the extreme rim.

The fourth day passed likewise. Glaber calculated that to-morrow at the latest would see the end of the bandits' drinking water. In his head he planned his first message of victory to Rome, which was to be of a clipped simplicity reminiscent of Sulla's: 'Three hundred bandits executed, two hundred captured alive. One Roman dead.' The other fifty who had been killed could safely remain unnamed—had not Sulla in his battle report spirited away about one hundred thousand of the dead?

The first day was particularly hot. The Praetor's men swallowed incredible amounts of water and wine; the thought of the thirsting robbers acted on them as a stimulant. When the pigmy sentries and scouts appeared on the rim of the crater, the soldiers poured whole bagsful of wine out on the ground, although it was uncertain whether they would notice it way up there.

But they must have noticed it after all, for the following night the first deserters, two women and one man, came rolling down the mountain. All three were still alive; their tongues were swollen and their adam's-apples bobbed continually up and down. The soldiers let them have a drink and spread-eagled them on crudely constructed crosses put up in such a way as to be clearly visible from above. The deserters did not complain and only asked towards morning to be given more water. The soldiers passed moistened sponges up to them and let them hang.

On the sixth day silence reigned above. The sentries and scouts had disappeared. Tired of waiting, the Praetor asked for volunteers and had them clamber up the path in order to negotiate surrender. They waved the ensign of truce, but all five were killed. The Praetor thought he might as well wait a little longer, five more corpses discreetly concealed would make no difference to his report.

That night fifty desperate men and two women came down the slope, half-climbing and half rolling. They gripped knives in their teeth which they had not let go even in falling, so that some arrived with lacerated faces. They were all killed, but several of the Praetor's men received knife-wounds, and two died of them.

The seventh day brought disaster.

It budded as a dark spot on the sky in the direction of the sea, travelled rapidly and was a giant cloud. So far it was uncertain whether it would really drift towards them. Out of the crater of Vesuvius rose a rumbling growl: the robbers were imploring the gods to make the cloud pour out its rain over their mountain.

And then the sun was suddenly gone, and the rim of the crater
became alive with distant skipping dwarfs whose arms sprawled
over their heads in the desire to show the cloud the way. Clodius
Glaber looked up, and he too felt a furtive hope that rain might
fall—which hope, if realized, might mean the end of his political
career; the soldiers were betting meanwhile, and put the odds at
three to one against rain. But the cloud floated nearer, its dusky,
fumy, pregnant body trailing wisps as of torn veil. The veil
hovered over the mountain-head, swallowed it up, and rapid
torrents of water fell with gushing patter.

The soldiers laughed, pulled their hoods over their heads,
caught the water in their gaping mouths, raised, in hitherto un-
dreamed of harmony, the Hymn of their darling Praetor's Pate.
One of the three crucified deserters, a man, was still alive though
unconscious; he stirred, tried to lift his head, to catch with
swollen tongue the raindrops running down his cheek. The
soldiers, rapt with gaiety, embraced, and danced with the rain;
they took the deserter down and poured wine into his mouth
until they noticed he was dead. Gradually the rain waned,
stopped, and almost immediately the sun set.

The Praetor knew that the enemy was now supplied with water
for at least three days, and that again he could do nothing but
wait. Wait—until their tongues swelled up once more, until they
hurled themselves down the slope to have one drink and be
crucified. A nightmare.

The elderly little Praetor got drunk and entreated the forgotten gods of his childhood not to let any more rain lengthen
indefinitely this most ludicrous of campaigns for which he had
waited fifteen years.

In such manner passed the eighth day, the ninth and the
tenth.

On the tenth day Old Vibius sat perched on the crater rim next
to Hermios the shepherd. The old man's lame leg stood out from
the rock like a flagpole.

'Over there is the Via Popilia,' said the shepherd. 'If you look
close you can see the aqueduct behind Capua, and watch it come
down from Mount Tifata.' He spoke slowly and felt at his gums
which had been swelling in the last few days and were beginning
to bleed.

'Can't see a thing,' said Old Vibius, 'it's much too far.'

They were silent. The curving bowl of horizon behind their backs was brimful with the sea's rigid shine. The shepherd craned his neck to look down at the tents of the Praetor Clodius Glaber, tucked into the crescent-shaped valley.

'Everything is quiet down there,' he said. He was silent, bared his teeth; eventually he said:

'They're probably having dinner now.'

'They're not,' said the old man. 'Much too early for it.'

Hermios grinned sheepishly, annoyed at having said it. You did not want to talk of it and then you did talk all the same, as though anything were improved by talking. Wasn't there enough talk down there at the bottom of the crater? They had a bad enough time as it was, and on top of that they had to go and quarrel. Where will it all end?

'Where will it all end?' said Hermios, surprised that he had given word to it without intending to.

'Better this way than the other,' said the old man.

He should talk, thought the shepherd, that one, withered and weatherbeaten as he was, like an old tree; if you cut his arm it was sure to sprinkle the ground with wood-worms.

The old man was silent. He shut his eyes, for he liked the red sun to filter without glare through the skin of his lids.

'Do you think anything will come of that rope-idea?' Hermios asked.

'Maybe,' said the old man.

'I don't think so,' said the shepherd.

They were silent.

'There's Oenomaus,' said Hermios. 'And what a sight he is!'

The young Thracian sat down beside them.

'How's it going?' the old man asked him.

Oenomaus shrugged and looked at the scenery.

Beyond the highland valley spread the plain of Campania. In the river beds flowed the crystal sweat of the black earth, the highways threaded the abundant pastures like arteries, the orchards seemed inflated with their own sweet juices. The air flickered over the plain, pregnant with unashamed fertility.

The shepherd was off again:

'I just can't bear to look at the horses,' he said. 'They look like skeletons sewn into skins.' He showed his teeth.

'You look like a horse yourself,' said the old man without malice.

Hermios grinned: 'Shepherds and animals understand each other,' he said. 'Last night there's suddenly something warm in my ear, like the sirocco blowing in, you might say. I wake up, and what do you think it is? A mule, just standing there and snorting and licking my head. He meant to ask me why he can't go grazing.'

'How did you explain it to him?' asked Oenomaus.

Hermios grinned: 'I went—kss, kss—and then I went on sleeping.'

'We can't go grazing either,' he said after a pause and felt his gums. 'And no one can tell us why.'

Vibius the Older was silent and blinked into the sun.

'I can tell you all right,' he said, suddenly. 'I saw a juggler at a fair once, he was vile and dirty, but awfully agile. He could put his head between his thighs, and pissed in his own face. That's what human law and order is like.'

The shepherd bared his teeth in perplexity. 'Why?' he asked.

The old man did not answer.

Zozimos the orator was coming towards them. His large, keen nose had grown even keener, but the pleats of his toga were cleverly arranged as ever. Like a huge, skinny bird he came staggering over the rocks.

'They are quarrelling again,' he said.

Hermios shook his head disapprovingly, the other two were silent. Zozimos sat down beside them.

'It is about the water,' he told them. 'There is a Thracian water-vessel now, a Celtic water-vessel, and one for everybody else. But the Celtic one is nearly empty because they have no self-control, so now they are demanding redivision.'

'They're always like that,' said the shepherd who had no love for Castus, Crixus and the other Gauls.

'Spartacus would have let them have their way, but his own people came and protested.'

'Quite right too,' said the shepherd.

'You can't let them die with thirst, can you?' said Oenomaus.

'That is just it,' said Zozimos; 'law must bow to necessity, though it seldom does.'

'What have they agreed on now?' asked the shepherd.

'A common basin for everybody,' said Zozimos, 'and very strict control. One cup per day per head. Fannius's servants are supervisors.'

The other three were silent. They were all thinking of the same thing, and each knew the others thought the same. They thought: All this is really stupid. You simply walk down the mountain, quite peacefully, the Praetor is probably quite different from what we think he is like—an educated man, and he has even got a bald head. 'Give us something to drink, please,' you say in a friendly, simple way. 'Let's all go back to what used to be, each in his proper place. It wasn't as bad as all that.' The soldiers fetch cool wine, bread, bacon and polenta, and everybody is happy that misunderstandings and torments are over.

'Ah yes,' said the shepherd and swallowed. He tried to think of what they had last spoken.

'That was silly—those three basins. In the old days when things were going well, nobody bothered whether you were Gallic or Thracian.'

'The mentalities of the peoples differ,' said the rhetorician. 'The Celts are brave but vain, temperamental and undisciplined. The Thracians are generous-minded, blue-eyed, red-haired, and live in polygamy.'

'That's what your textbooks say,' said Old Vibius. 'A hungry Thracian is just like a thirsty Celt.'

They were silent, and looked down.

White, self-satisfied smoke rose from the Praetor's camp. They were cooking dinner down there. All over the Campanian plain, from Volturnus to the Sorrentum mountains, farmers, shepherds, and field-labourers were cooking their midday meal: polenta, lettuce, bacon and boiling turnips.

'Spartacus might have been a great general,' said the rhetorician. 'If he had been Hannibal, he would have conquered Rome.'

'Hannibal,' said the shepherd. 'I hear he tied burning straw to the horns of some cows and chased them at the Roman camp. But the Romans put the fires out and ate the cows.' He grinned with an effort.

'The nonsense you do talk,' said Zozimos.

'You know history by heart, I know it by stomach, so to speak,' said the shepherd. He was strangely exhilarated, and kept on baring his yellow teeth; his eyes oddly agleam, a flush on their lids.

'Was he really a prince?' he asked hastily and absent-mindedly.

'Who?' asked Zozimos. 'Hannibal?'

'No, Spartacus.'

'Oh,' said Zozimos. 'Nobody knows for certain.' He turned to Oenomaus: 'You ought to know.'

Oenomaus winced, he had been lost in thought. Oenomaus had a high, delicate forehead with a bluish vein showing beneath the skin.

'I don't know,' said Oenomaus.

'If he used to be a prince,' cried Hermios, 'then he used to eat fieldfare with bacon. All princes eat fieldfare with bacon.' He repeated it several times over and his eyes filled with tears.

'Be quiet, won't you,' said the old man without annoyance.

The shepherd was quiet.

'What a glutton,' said Zozimos, shamefacedly. Zozimos always found ways and means to get something to eat from somewhere, besides his ration.

'I like him just the same,' said the shepherd who had quietened down a little. 'I like him because none of us knows what we're doing all this for, and he does know.'

'What does he know?' asked Zozimos.

The shepherd did not reply; but after a while he began anew: 'He's always so full of ideas,' he said, 'just think of this new idea—the ropes.'

'That is a crazy idea,' said Zozimos. 'I feel sure it will come to nothing.'

'So do I,' said the shepherd, 'but that he *gets* such ideas. . . .'

After that all four of them were silent and looked down at the plain. Now and then small clouds of dust crawled slowly along a highway; it meant that a carriage or a horseman were on the road and could go wherever they wished; for them there were no barriers, and the land was wide.

From the inside of the crater came the noise of flurried climbing and falling fragments of rock. Zozimos turned to look.

'There is your son,' he said to the old man, 'he is sweating and spitting and apparently bursting with great news.'

Vibius the Younger emerged from the crater-hole, gasping; his full lips were dry and cracked, his eyes popped more than ever.

'You're all to come down,' he said, 'everybody must help with the ropes. The fun starts tonight.'

'What fun?' inquired the shepherd and perked up.

'You must all come down right away,' said Young Vibius, 'everybody's tearing their clothes into strips for ropes. All has been decided. You're to come right away.'

The shepherd rose and hit the air with his stick. 'You see,' he said to Zozimos and began to climb down the rocky slope with alacrity.

'It is a maniacal idea,' said the rhetorician, getting up quickly all the same. 'Whoever heard of climbing down a mountain by means of ropes!'

The crunching of their steps was stunned by the pebbles. The old man rose, cast a look at the camp of Praetor Clodius Glaber, spat down on it:

'Hope you have a nice meal,' he said.

'Do you hate them as much as that?' asked Oenomaus as they climbed down the side of the crater.

'Sometimes I do,' said the old man. 'But they hate *us* always. And that's our disadvantage.'

The massacre of Praetor Clodius Glaber's army took place during the night after the tenth day of the siege.

The side of the mountain that faced the Roman camp was steep, but not wholly impassable. Deserters had attempted descending there repeatedly; they had rolled down the harsh slope, yet they arrived still alive and were killed only then by the soldiers down below. The careful Praetor remembered this and had put sentries along the entire semi-circular valley called 'Hell's Ante-room'.

The other half of the summit which faced the sea consisted of almost vertical rocks that formed an obviously impassable, steep wall between the upper rubble-field and the forests below. On this side Nature herself had undertaken to stand guard over the robbers, to ease Clodius Glaber's task. And over this very side the gladiators let themselves down on ropes, one at a time, in the second hour after sunset, walked around the mountain and fell upon the unsuspecting Praetor from behind.

The descent took roughly three hours and proceeded nearly soundlessly. Two ropes and one rope-ladder, made from plaited strips of linen, were let down over three vertical crevices in the rock. The rope-ladder with its rungs of tough wild vines—the only vegetation inside the cavity—served partly the transport of arms and partly the descent of the more clumsy. Evenly distributed moonshine aided their exploit.

The gladiators went down first, after them came Fannius's servants, the mercenaries of captain Mammius's regiment, and every man fit to bear arms. Those who had reached level ground lay down in the grass and waited. Some had whispered conversations.

About midnight one of the ropes snapped, two men fell and broke their bones. They suppressed their groans in order not to endanger the others. As no one could help them, they were killed; they died without a murmur.

In the fifth hour after sunset, two hundred men with regular weapons and a hundred armed with clubs, axes and gladiators' equipment, were assembled at the foot of the rock. A few women who did not want to miss anything had come down too, the rest had stayed behind inside the crater, together with the old people and the cattle.

The horde began its march. They had to walk a southward circle round the mountain-head along the edge of the forest-zone. This soundless approach took over an hour; Campanian shepherds, familiar with the mountain tracks, acted as guides.

The gladiators reached the southern end of the crescent-shaped valley named 'Hell's Ante-room' and killed the first Roman sentry before he had time to cry out. The alarm raised by the next sentries was already lost in the gladiators' war-cries which shattered the sleep of the camp and filled the tents with husky echoes, distorted by the rocks' proximity. The massacre began before the massacred woke up to their plight; so that only a few veterans resisted. But the irregular, unmilitary lay-out of the camp and the fearful confusion convinced even the most hardened soldier that resistance was useless and flight his only chance.

The gladiators, prepared for battle, found themselves in the role of mere butchers. The lack of resistance lashed them to blind frenzy and at the same time left them unsatisfied. And the victims, who cried for mercy and found none, lying with their consciousness fading into death, felt that these opponents whom they had never seen until they fell upon them at night with strident yells, were not human, but demons let loose.

Thus ended the tenth day, and feasting followed the massacre. But fulfilment came only with sleep on the soft Roman quilts; the dreamless sleep of duty done and necessity satisfied.

On foot—for his horse had been left with the robbers—the bald-headed Praetor Clodius Glaber climbed down into the plain. He had been separated from his fleeing soldiers, and walked through the night, alone. He strayed from the trodden path, stumbled over the crooked, stony edge of a vineyard, looked around. The vineyard, studded with pointed stakes, looked like a graveyard by the stars' light. It was very quiet; bandits and Vesuvius dimmed to unreality, Rome and Senate were blotted out; yet one more deed asked to be done. He opened his cloak, felt the place with his fingers, gently pressed the sword-point to it.

The deed asked to be done, but it was only now he understood its full meaning. Little by little the point must be driven home; little by little it must tear through tissue, cut tendons and muscles, splinter the ribs. Not till then the lung is reached, tender, mucous, thinly veined: it must be ripped asunder. Now a slimy shell, and now the heart itself, a bulbous bag of blood—its touch beyond imagination. Had ever a man accomplished this? Well he might, with a sudden thrust, perhaps. But once you knew of the process and every one of its stages, you would never be able to do it.

'Death', up to now a word like any other, seemed removed into unattainable distance. All the relatives of Death, such as Honour, Shame and Duty, exist for him only who has no ken of reality. For reality, mucous, unspeakably delicate, with its mesh of thin veins, is not made to be torn to bits by some pointed object. And now Praetor Clodius Glaber knows that dying is unutterably stupid—more stupid still than life itself.

He realizes that his shoes are full of pebbles. He sits down on a stone and empties the shoes; he observes that the pebbly discomfort had been a responsible element of his despair. As compared to the ignominious defeat of his army, the sharp little pebbles—seven in all—admittedly shrink into ridiculous insignificance. But how can you sift the important from the unimportant if both speak to your senses with equal vehemence? His tongue and palate are still covered with the stale taste of interrupted sleep; a few forgotten grapes lurk between the vines. He plucks a few, looks around: only the stars are witnessing the curious sequence of his actions, and their sight is no rebuke to him.

He feels ashamed and yet he must admit that his actions are in no way senseless: no amount of philosophy can alter the fact that grapes were made to be eaten. Besides, he has never before enjoyed grapes as much. He sips their juice together with the tears of an unexplained emotion. He smacks his lips with defiance and shame.

And night with the lights of its indifferent stars gave as a further knowledge unto Praetor Clodius Glaber: all pleasure, not only defined versions of it, and Life itself, are based on age-old, secret shamelessness.

5

THE MAN WITH
THE BULLET-HEAD

His heavy head propped up by his left hand, Crixus rested sideways on the rug; his bared biceps was threaded with red and blue veins. Spartacus lay on his back, arms crossed behind his neck; a gap in the tent-roof unveiled a strip of the crater with a few stars above it. Their mats lay parallel, the table stood in between—there was no room for more in the tent of Praetor Clodius Glaber.

Crixus was still eating. From time to time his right hand reached across the table-top which towered above his head, groped for a chunk of meat, placed it in his mouth, and sent great draughts of wine from the jug after it. Greasy rivulets dropped from the table.

The horde outside had grown quieter, then quiet. In short intervals, shorter than necessary, sentries called out the passwords. The horde played at soldiers.

Crixus grew attentive, listened, became conscious of the silence. He smacked his lips, wiped his greasy fingers slowly on the rug. Spartacus turned his head to him and looked fixedly at the fat man's face. Crixus screwed up his eyes and dug bits of food out of his teeth with his tongue. The other's glance discomfited him; he averted his.

'The corpses should be burned,' said Spartacus. 'There are still plenty lying about, six or eight hundred. They stink.'

'Have them burnt then,' said the Gaul.

They were silent and Crixus took a gulp of wine.

Spartacus lay back again, crossed his arms behind his neck; the mountain's outline drew a black line across the gap in the tent. 'I know what you're thinking of,' he said. 'It's the women of Alexandria.'

'Glaber will run right back to Rome,' said Crixus. 'He will stir up the Senate, and they'll chase the Legions after us.'

The torn roof gaped, black, over Spartacus's head. He was very weary, his eyes had lost their usual attentive steadiness. 'And then what?' he asked.

'We'll eat them up,' said Crixus.

'And then?'

'More Legions.'

'And then?' asked Spartacus, staring through the gap.

'Then they'll eat us up.'

'And then?'

Crixus yawned, made a fist with the thumb pointing to the ground; the slow fist passed downward in front of Spartacus's eyes.

'Then *that*. Do you want to wait till then?'

So there it was again, the Sign on which the gladiator's fate depended. There was no escape from it. Jewelled, loosely wrinkled, that thumb pointed down, dishonoured life and de-graded death to a spectacle, pierced even one's dreams.

Crixus lay back again.

Moonlight dripped through the gap in the roof, the crater displayed sharp-edged shadows. The passwords were coming more scantily.

'Who said I was staying?' said Spartacus. He sounded as though talking in his sleep; he was so tired.

'Who says I'll stay with you? Chase a man and he will run when he has run far enough he will stop to catch his breath, and, go about his business. Only a fool will run and run for ever. . . .'

Crixus was silent.

'Only a fool will run on and on until foam flows from his mouth and until an evil spirit makes him cut down all he meets. We had a man like that, out there . . .'

'Where?' asked Crixus.

'Out there in the woods. He was bowlegged like an infant, his ears gaped from his head and he had pigs'-eyes. We used to call him "the Hog", and we made him crawl on all fours, and made him grunt like a pig. One day he jumped up and ran. Everything in his way he destroyed, and he kept on running. They never caught him.'

'What happened to him?'

'That's what nobody knows. Maybe he is still running.'

'He died out in the forests, that's what happened to him,' said Crixus, 'or else they did catch him and hung him on a cross.'

'Nobody knows, I tell you,' said Spartacus. 'But maybe he did get somewhere in the end. You never know. Somewhere—anywhere.'

After a pause Crixus said: 'Somewhere—on to a cross.'

'Maybe on to a cross,' said Spartacus. 'Why don't you rather go to Alexandria? I have never been in Alexandria. It must be a very beautiful place. Once I lay with a girl, and she sang. That is what Alexandria must be like. Go on, Crixus, go and let your phallus rove. Who told you that I would stay?'

'How did she sing?' asked Crixus. 'Madly or softly?'

'Softly.'

Crixus was silent. Then he said:

'Tomorrow maybe it'll be too late.'

'Tomorrow, tomorrow,' said Spartacus. 'Maybe we'll go off tomorrow.' He yawned. 'Maybe we will go to Alexandria.'

They became silent. Crixus dozed. He breathed more evenly, he snored. Again his head rested on the naked left arm with its veined biceps.

Spartacus peered through the gap, closed his eyes, opened them. He got himself a hunk of meat, chewed, drank wine from the tankard. Fumes of strong Falernian were gradually rising inside him, and clouded his sight. The sentries had finally grown quiet. He had some more wine, rose, and stepped out of the tent.

The coast down below was screened by white mists. The queer outline of the crater stood out jagged and black against the starry sky. Emaciated olive trees strained their crippled limbs in the valley.

He walked past the sleeping guards, away from the camp. He reached a stony slope and went up, the scrape of his sandals on the rubble sounded noisily exaggerated. The slope flattened into a horizontal, narrow mead, and up there, among bushels of dried-out grass, roots and underwood, lay a man wrapped in his blanket. Only his head was visible, it was clean-shaven, globular,

and looked very peaceful. His eyebrows were drawn up high as
though the man were amazed at his own dream. His lips were
thin and ascetic, but the nose was fleshy and crinkled with sleep
like that of a merry faun.

Spartacus regarded him for a while, then he kicked his hip.
The man's eyes opened, not in the least startled. His eyes were
dark, deceptive moonlight had filled the sockets with shadows.

'Who are you?'

'One of your camp,' said the man and sat up slowly.

'Do you know who I am?'

'Zpardokos, Prince of Thrace, liberator of slaves, leader of the
disinherited. Peace and blessings, Zpardokos. Come and sit on
my blanket.'

'Fool,' said Spartacus. He stood undecided, touched the sitting
man with his foot:

'Go on sleeping. Tomorrow the Romans will come back and
hang you on a cross, and the rest of us with you. Can you read the
stars?'

'Not the stars,' said the man with the bullet-head. 'But I can
read in eyes and books.'

'If you can read you are a runaway tutor,' said Spartacus. 'So
you will be the eleventh. We now have eleven tutors, seven
accountants, six doctors, three poets with us. If the Senate lets
us live we might found a university on Vesuvius.'

'But I'm not a tutor, I'm a masseur.'

'A masseur?' Spartacus was surprised. 'A man who can read is
not used for massage but for teaching.'

'Until three days ago I was employed in the fourth public bath
at Stabiae. When they first sold me I did not tell them I could
read.'

'What did you do that for?'

'So that they should not be able to force me to teach lies,' said
the bullet-headed man.

'You don't say,' said Spartacus, ill at ease. 'We have some more
lunatics like you. There is a man called Zozimos, for instance,
also a one-time tutor, who always makes political speeches. I
never used to know there was so much madness in the world.'

'Nor so much sadness,' said the man with the bullet-head. 'You
didn't know of that either, did you?'

Spartacus was silent, his discomfort growing. You just did not talk of such things. 'The sadness of the world.' He had heard such talk often of late, the chatter of poets and world-reformers. He wanted to go away now, but he was in no mood to be alone.

Shivering, the other pulled the blanket around him, for with the approach of day the moon-mists were sending up cold white fumes. Spartacus stood beside him, undecided, big and awkward in his fur-skin. He felt more and more embarrassed, with the learned masseur looking up at him out of those darkly shaded eye-sockets. That's what they were all like, these learned men and chatterers; they offered their feelings for sale to any passer-by, their very core crawled out of its shell like a slimy snail.

'I did not see you yesterday,' said Spartacus. 'Where were you during the fighting?'

'I was kneading your heroes,' said the bullet-head and wrinkled his nose.

Spartacus grinned: 'A coward—that is what you are.'

The other thought it over: 'I do not think I am a coward. But when someone goes for me with a spear I get a shock.'

Amused, Spartacus sat down beside him and propped his elbows on his knees. The other pushed a corner of his blanket over.

'Fool,' said Spartacus. 'Why did you address me so foolishly just now: "liberator of slaves, leader of the disinherited"?'

The question was to sound casual, but his eyes had regained their customary attentiveness.

'Why did I?' said the bullet-head. 'It is written thus: "The power of the Four Beasts has ended, and I beheld One like the Son of man come in clouds of heaven, and come to the Ancient of days, and there was given him might and glory and a kingdom, an everlasting dominion" . . .'

'This is pure rot.' Spartacus was disappointed.

'The Four Beasts are the Senate, the big land-owners, the Legions, and the bailiffs,' said the bullet-headed man and counted the four on his fingers.

'Beasts,' said Spartacus, 'are in arenas.'

'It is a figure of speech,' said the other one.

'The only thing that fits is the clouds of heaven,' said Spartacus, for the mists around the mountain continued to thicken. 'And what about that Ancient, power-giving one?'

'That is meant to be poetry,' said the bullet-headed one. 'Or it might be God.'

'There are many gods,' said Spartacus, bored.

'It is also written: "He shews his strength against the proud, he overthrows the mighty from their seats and exalts the lowly and humble; he fills the hungry with good things and the rich he sends away empty." And it is written further: "The spirit of the Lord is upon me because he has anointed me to bring the glad tidings to the poor, he has sent me to mend the broken hearts, to comfort the captives, to open the eyes of the blind, to free the oppressed." '

'That sounds better,' said Spartacus. 'Do you believe in prophecies?'

'Not really,' said the bullet-headed and creased his nose. But no clowning or grimace changed the narrow hardness of his lips.

'I don't either,' said Spartacus. 'All prophets and augurs are swindlers.'

'It takes all sorts to make a world. There is one sort who speaks words pleasing to the ear of the mighty, and there are those who cry out into the night with their wrath and their sorrow.'

'But their talk is always sticky and obscure.'

'That is a trick of the trade. A good tailor makes garments that will fit many men.'

Spartacus meditated; he meant to put a question, but it was an awkward one and he was ashamed of it. In the end he asked after all:

'If you do not believe in prophecies, why did you call me the One whose coming is predicted—the Son of man?'

'Me?' said the man with the bullet-head. 'I didn't call you that. I said it is written One will come . . .' He shivered, wrapped the blanket closer:

'It is the same with prophecies as with clothes. There they hang in the tailor's shop, many men pass them, many a man they would fit. One comes and takes the robe. And so it is made for him—for he has taken it unto him. . . . What really matters is, that it suits fashion and period. It must fit in with the taste of the time—the wishes of many—the need and longing desire of many. . . .'

He screwed up his nose and turned away. Spartacus was silent; he gazed at the moon, the stars, the crater, his fingernails; then said in sudden, unguessed hostility:

'Before, you said yourself you didn't believe in prophecies.'

'I do not believe in the spoken word at all,' said the man with the bullet-head. 'I only believe in its effect. Words are so much air, but air will be wind and make ships sail.'

Spartacus was silent. He sat on the rug with his legs astraddle and his head propped on his fists, the moon shone straihgt at his face, he closed his eyes. The light was so strong that he could feel its glittering silver through his lids.

He knew not how long he had sat thus, perhaps he had been asleep. He stretched his limbs, yawned, felt cold.

'Are you still here?' said Spartacus. 'Give me your blanket.'

The bullet-headed one got up, shook out the blanket, handed it to Spartacus. As they stood side to side, the other was a whole head smaller than he, and looked thin and frail.

'You should have been a tutor instead of a masseur after all,' said Spartacus as he pulled the still warm blanket about him, yawned, and lay back. 'You might stay here and talk to me.'

Shivering, the other man sat down on a stone two paces from Spartacus's head.

'Better get some sleep,' he said.

'That's just it, I cannot sleep,' said Spartacus. 'Lots of flies seem to hum inside my head.'

'You're just tired out,' said the bullet-head. 'Shall I massage you?'

'Tell me a story,' said Spartacus. 'You talk from your palate, so you must be either Syrian or Jewish.'

'I'm an Essene.'

'What is that?'

'It's a long story,' said the other one.

'Tell me.'

'Right,' said the Essene. 'It is written: "There are four kinds among men. The first say: What is mine is mine, and what is thine is thine: that is the tribe of the middle classes or, as some say, Sodom. The second sort say: What is mine is thine, and what is thine is mine: that is the people of the ordinary and humble. A third kind say: What is mine is thine, and what is thine is also thine: those are the pious. Others again say: What is mine is mine, and what is thine is also mine: they are the wicked." Thus it is written. The scholars say to this: the first among men to act in the mine-is-mine, thine-is-thine manner, was Cain who murdered Abel his brother, and founded the first city. Therefore this outlook is rejected, though it is very common in our days, and it is called the way of Sodom. The third opinion, that of the pious, is also rejected. Because they possess not the goods of the earth, they shed even the little that they have in order to prove that their need is virtue. That is a very special hypocrisy which one might call the haughtiness of the weak and which is, above all, stupid. The fourth way is that of the great landowners and usurers. It is abominable and is rejected. Remains the second kind—"thine-is-mine-and-mine-is-thine"—and that is ours.'

'You have common property, then?'

'We have.'

'And are your slaves too the common property of all?'

'We have no slaves.'

Spartacus deliberated: 'I see, so you are a tribe of hunters and herdsmen?'

'We are not, we are farmers and craftsmen. We all work, and we all share in the profits.'

'Funny,' said Spartacus. 'If you are freemen and work all the same, you are your own slaves. Never have I heard anything like that.'

'That may well be,' said the Essene, wagging his head. 'You may be right there.'

'You see?' said Spartacus. 'There you talk and talk and you stick fast in your own pulpy words. One's own slave—that is as though a man were his own wife. Hunters and herdsmen need no slaves for they do no work. But where you sow and reap, make things and trade, there you must have slaves, that is how it must be. Man commands, woman bears, and the slave works, for such is the order of things. And anything else is sticky chit-chat, against reason and order.'

'Think so?' said the Essene and wagged his head. 'You haven't spread disorder in Campania, have you now?'

'Be quiet,' said Spartacus. 'He who is hunted cannot abide by law and order. But that has nothing to do with your babbling.'

'Think so?' said the Essene. He took up a pebble, weighed it in his hand, sent it rolling down the hill. The stone tumbled on and soon disappeared from sight, for the mists swallowed it in their depths, but the sound of its striking ground could still be heard.

When the noise had stopped, the Essene said: 'Had you asked this stone whither it rolls it would have answered that it had been pushed. The stone believes that the only thing that matters is the particular push it got. Yet it obeys unwittingly the common law that everything is pulled downward.'

Spartacus did not answer. He lay on his back; to his right rose the dark mountain wall, to his left fell the steep slope. He was too tired to follow the Essene's words, but he felt his mind absorb them like a sponge.

The bullet-headed one, however, paid no attention to him. He seemed to have forgotten all about Spartacus. Like an alert, timorous animal he sat crumpled on his stone; his head swung slowly back and forth, he seemed to be talking to himself and was probably wrinkling his nose once more, for in his voice was a soft chuckle:

'. . . Neither their silver nor their gold shall save them in the day of the wrath of Yahve, but the whole land shall be devoured by the fire of his jealousy. Weep, ye that live by the mills, for the merchants are gone, and all who hoarded money are eradicated. Woe be to the shepherds that feed themselves but feed not their flocks. Woe unto them that join house to house and field to field till there is no room, till they possess alone the lands of the earth. Woe unto them that decree false laws and take the right from the poor of the people so that these poor may be their prey. Woe, for your heads judge for reward, your priests teach for hire, and your seers prophesy for money. Woe, for they chant to the sound of harps, and invent to themselves music, they drink wine in bowls and anoint themselves, but they are not grieved for the affliction of the people.

'But the justice of Yahve will be upon them and every one that is proud and lofty and he shall be brought low, and upon all the cedars of Lebanon, upon all the oaks of Bashan, and upon the merchantmen of the seas, upon the lords of the Senate and upon the masters of the bloody games, and upon all luxury; for the Lord will bare the daughters of Rome and strip them of their jewels. And there will be great cries before the East Gate and alarm before the other gates, and loud laments from the seven hills. For He is come, sent by Yahve with his sword and net and his trident, He who is anointed by the Lord to mend the broken hearts, to bring light to the eyes of the blind, to free the oppressed.'

'But that you have heard before,' concluded the man with the bullet-head with a sudden change of voice, and his head stopped wagging—by which one could see that he had not been talking to himself alone after all.

'Go on,' said Spartacus.

'I'm cold,' said the Essene. 'Give me back my blanket.'

'I will,' said Spartacus and did not stir. He lay open-eyed.

The Essene seemed to have forgotten the blanket again. Quietly he sat on his rock and stared at the sheet of mist which crept up sluggishly.

'I have never heard of a God who curses like that Yahve of yours,' said Spartacus. 'He is so wild at the rich, one might think he was a God of slaves.'

'Yahve is dead,' said the bullet-headed man. 'And he was no slave God, he was a desert God. He was good at things of the desert: he knew how to open up springs in the rocks and how to make bread rain from the heavens. But he knew nothing of industry and agriculture. He could not make the vineyard bear fruit, nor the olive tree and the wheat, he was no luxuriant God, he was hard and just like the desert itself. Therefore he scolds at modern life and gets lost in it.'

'You see?' said Spartacus disappointedly. 'If he is dead his prophecies are no longer worth anything.'

'Prophecies are never worth anything,' said the Essene. 'I explained that before, but in the meantime you've been asleep. Prophecies do not count, he who receives them counts.'

Spartacus lay in thought, his eyes open.

'He who receives them will see evil days,' he said after a while.

'Aye,' said the Essene. 'He'll have a pretty rotten time.'

'He who receives them,' said Spartacus, 'will have to run and run, on and on, until he foams at the mouth and until he has destroyed every thing in his way with his great wrath. He'll run and run, and the Sign won't let go of him, and the demon of wrath will tear through his entrails.'

Freezing, the Essene squinted at the blanket. Spartacus was silent, then he said:

'As for where he'll land—even you cannot say.'

'Who?' asked the man with the bullet-head.

Spartacus said nothing.

'I can even tell you that,' said the Essene after a while. 'For there have been many who recognised the Sign and received the word.'

'And do you know what befell them?'

'I do, for there were many, and none was the first. There was, for instance, a certain Agis, he was King in Laconia. This man Agis had heard from his tutor that once there had been an age of justice and common property which is called the Golden Age, and this he meant to reawaken. His aristocrats and the wealthy naturally objected to this, but the King gave away his riches to the people and brought back the ancient laws.'

'And what happened to him?' asked Spartacus.

'He was hanged. Then there was a man by the name of Jambulos who went on a long sea-voyage with a friend. In the middle of the ocean they found an island on which the Golden Age is alive to this day. The natives of this island were called Panchees and, because of their just mode of living, they are of truly wonderful body. They share property, food and shelter, and share their women too, so that no man may know his children. In this manner they not only avoid the pride of property, but the haughtiness of blood as well. So, in order to do away with a good example, the wealthy in Jambulos's country killed him, peace and blessings to his memory—and now no one knows where the Panchee island is.'

Spartacus was silent, he lay open-eyed and watched the darkness decrease. The Essene crouched near his head. He resumed:

'It is always the same. Again and again one man arises, recognises the sign and receives the word, and goes on his way with the great wrath in his bowels; and he knows of the people's homesickness for the buried times of old that were ruled by justice and kindness. How just was Israel and how fine its tents when it lived in the desert, branched out in tidy tribes, on a friendly footing with Yahve . . .'

'Leave your Yahve alone and tell on.'

'It is always the same. Not long ago, for example, the man Eunus, a slave, lived in Sicily. He had a friend called Kleon, also a slave, he came from Macedon. These two ran away from their master, a great landowner and slave-sweater. They collected a few other slaves and camped in woods and on hills. They fought and beat the mercenaries, without much purpose at first, no doubt.'

The man with the bullet-head paused and wagged his head. But Spartacus was sitting upright, impatiently urging him to go on.

'Ah well,' said the Essene. 'As I say, they collected more and more people without a definite purpose. But purpose or no, that's nothing to do with the facts. Quicker than they could fathom it their numbers increased, soon there were a hundred, a thousand, ten thousands, seventy thousand of them. Seventy thousand—and all of them slaves, an army of slaves; every slave in Sicily joined them.'

'And then?' said Spartacus.

'The Senate sent out Legion after Legion, and the slaves finished off one Legion after the other. For three years they ruled over nearly the whole of Sicily. As soon as Rome left them alone they intended to found a Sun State, a state of justice and good-will.'

'And then?' said Spartacus.

'And then they were beaten,' said the Essene. 'Twenty thous-and were crucified, Sicily grew more crosses than trees; and upon every one a slave hung and died and cursed Eunus the Syrian and Kleon the Macedonian his friend, for they were guilty of their deaths.'

'Guilty?' said Spartacus. 'How were they guilty?'

'By letting themselves be beaten,' said the bullet-head and wagged.

'Go on,' said Spartacus hoarsely.

'There is no "go on" so far,' said the bullet-headed one. 'For these last events occurred only a few decades ago. But you can see how right I was in saying that the common peoples' longing for lost justice is an everlasting one, and that again and again one man stands up and receives the Word, and rushes on his way with the great wrath in his bowels.

'Let the powers of Sodom conquer and crucify him: after a time another man will rise, after him again another, and they pass on the Great Wrath from decade to decade, and it is like a gigantic relay race that began the day when the wanton god of towns and agriculture murdered the god of deserts and herds-men.'

Gradually the rhythmic motion of his head had got hold of the Essene's body; he swayed back and forth on his rock and, as the first glow of dawn pierced the mists at last, Spartacus saw that the learned masseur was an old man. The black shadows in his eye-sockets had, as it were, evaporated, his startled eyebrows arched over heavy pouches, and the faun-like nose projected sadly over the severe, narrow lips. His body swayed and swayed as though he had no hip-bones.

Spartacus rose, adjusted the skins on his back, stretched his arms until the joints cracked. Thus he stood for some time, legs apart, arms raised, huge and splendid-looking in the loose fur-skin. He bent down to give the old man his blanket; the Essene instantly arrested his monotonous sway and began to wrap the rug around him.

Spartacus approached the slope, looked again at the glowing East and at the mountain whose everyday shape gradually broke the spell of its nightly distortion. He did not hear or return the old man's salutation, and bore down upon the camp with mighty steps that were echoed by the stony rubble.

From the tents sounded distant, noisy confusion, for some of the horde had awoken. In the pallid twilight overhead circled clumsy black birds; he remembered to have the corpses burned at once—those six hundred or eight hundred that were left of the beaten army of Praetor Clodius Glaber.

BOOK TWO

THE LAW OF DETOURS

Interlude

THE DOLPHINS

THE scribe Quintus Apronius has been feeling low and grumpy lately. His digestion does not function properly, he is tortured by spasms in stomach and abdomen; he has overslept, a thing that has but rarely happened in his eighteen years of service. With flurried gait, holding up his gown and wedging it against his hip, he hurries through the streets, fallow with morn.

Where the perfume- and ointment-stalls meet the fish market, a new announcement was painted some days ago, with letters one inch thick, alternately red and blue: the impresario Marcus Cornelius Rufus is proud to recommend his most excellent of troupes to the gracious Capuan public. The first performance will take place tomorrow; the play will be called *Bucco the Peasant*; it is advisable to secure seats in advance.

Apronius knows it by heart; he has been stopping in front of the announcement every day, studying it anew and shaking his head. There has been a lot of talk about this play. A theatre scandal is mentioned in connection with it, supposed to have occurred when the company played in Pompeii; an incident with a political background and two casualties; but of course, the price of admission is quite, quite exorbitant. Games-Director Lentulus, though, did promise to introduce him to the impresario at the Dolphins' today, so that he might obtain a free ticket—it remains to be seen whether he will keep his word.

During the dragging hours in the Market Court, while Apronius traces his endless minutes, the pangs in abdomen and stomach come on again. He can hardly wait for the Market Judge

81

to adjourn proceedings, and instantly after he hurries to the
Steambaths without even looking in at the Tavern of the Twin-
Wolves.

The covered walk is full of its customary genial life, but
Apronius wastes no time with either recitations or smutty stories.
As he forces his way through the gossiping groups, he can see that
even more people than usual are assembled around Fulvius the
author; the insignificant little man with the bumpy pate is
evidently making one of his usual seditious, incendiary speeches.
What did he say last time—'We live in a century of abortive
revolutions.' Today he is probably preaching of the robbers up
on Mount Vesuvius, who menace the peaceable citizens of
Campania; probably he is longing for them to come.

At last Apronius enters the marble Hall of the Dolphins, takes
his habitual seat and heaves a sigh; but soon his mien darkens
once more; every endeavour seems to be futile today. He is just
about to rise resignedly and depart, when Lentulus comes in,
zealously conversing with a rotund gentleman in a very smart
bathrobe: the impresario Marcus Cornelius Rufus.

The two gentlemen sit down on two Dolphins' thrones at
Apronius's right. In a slightly derogatory manner the clerk is
introduced to the distinguished stranger who bows a little from
his chair and resumes his conversation with Lentulus. They are
talking of old times; it is apparent they they have not met for
years. Apronius gathers from their remarks that their acquaintance dates back to the time of Lentulus's political activities in
Rome, and that the well-dressed impresario was then a man of
important position; respectfully he hears the names of great
politicians: Sulla, Chrysogomus, Crassus, Pompeius, Cethegus,
as they keep cropping up in connection with smiling allusions
clear only to the initiated.

The well-dressed impresario is obviously of Greek origin,
possibly with a sprinkling of the Levant. Apronius has heard it
said that he was one of those ten thousand men whom dictator
Sulla freed from slavery and endowed with the civic rights in
order to strengthen his party. Owing to his nimble astuteness,
combined with exquisite manners, he had rapidly risen in the
world, and after Sulla's death he was generally believed to be a
future leader of the Democratic Party—until about two years ago
he disappeared overnight from the scene of politics: a sordid

liaison with a Vestal had proved his stumbling block. Since then, Rufus had turned to the spheres of wheat-import and other business activities, and of late he had taken up tripping through the provinces with an actor's company.

Rufus is a man of interesting small-talk; gracefully bent forward, he sits enthroned between his Dolphins, and his mundane loquacity represses the worthy games-director into the part of a provincial bumpkin. He tells an amusing tale of the shock his troupe had caused the reactionary Pompeian public, until Lentulus interrupts him with the query whether the robber-gang on Mount Vesuvius, the talk of all the town, is also mentioned in the play—for Lentulus is secretly proud of the fact that these famous robbers were, so to speak, bred in his school.

No, answers Rufus; the stage police, who interfere enough as it is, would most certainly ban a play with any direct reference to those Spartacus-people. But indirectly, as a matter of fact, they form the motif of the entire play; which actually ends with the hero, Bucco the Peasant, deciding after all sorts of adventures to join the bandits on Vesuvius, as both gentlemen will be able to see for themselves. And, turning directly to Apronius for the first time, the impresario expresses his expectant hope of seeing him in the auditorium.

Quintus Apronius, First Scribe of the Market Court, knows that the decisive moment is now upon him. But Rufus's political past and, even more, his smart bathrobe, have thoroughly intimidated him; lean and drab, he has been squatting on his throne next these two imposing men, listening respectfully, and racking his brains all the while to find an opening for the topic of the desired free ticket. Now, as the never-to-be-repeated opportunity is here, he pales; without forethought and indeed almost without his agency, his lips stammer regret because of previous engagement. And at the same time he realises that he has irrevocably lost out.

Polite and slightly surprised, the impresario in turn expresses his regret, rises from his seat, links his arm in Lentulus's, and betakes himself to the inner baths. Apronius follows three paces behind. With loathing he observes them enjoy the detailed ceremonies of the baths: lukewarm water, hot water, steam, cold water—watches them being kneaded and slapped, sweating and groaning, sighing with pleasure. Their spirits rise to such heights

that they decide to have a game of ball; with much merry shriek-
ing and bickering, naked, oily and chubby, the two respectable
men of affairs prance about like ingenuous children, playing with
heart and soul, and are sincerely glad that their carefree, happy
dispositions have withstood all of life's storms.

But as they repose side by side afterwards, pleasantly tired,
tucked in soft blankets, the clerk Quintus Apronius's mood is
induced to change. He remembers that never in all his eighteen
years of service has he come in such close contact with men of
such important political past. He is suddenly overcome by
emotion; the great sorrow of his life, a secret never as yet divulged
to any human soul, not even to Pomponia, comes to his mind.
Prone, eyes ceilingward, he feels the urge to confess grow irre-
sistible.

Haltingly he tells the impresario how he had once cherished
lofty ambitions, intended to retire, travel to foreign lands, and
achieve honoured recognition by writing his philosophical
treatise on constipation as the germ of all revolutions. In order to
reach this goal he had invested his entire savings, the fruits of ten
laborious years, in the shares of an Asiatic tax contractor's
company. Three months later Sulla had the company dissolved,
the shares became so much worthless parchment overnight, and
he, Quintus Apronius, had been ruined for life.

The impresario, whose belly the muscular female attendant is
just plastering with hot towels, turns his head and inspects the
clerk more extensively. His glance travels down Apronius's lean
figure, from the sloping shoulders to the peaked knees, the un-
cared for nails of his hairy toes. Apronius feels that this man Rufus
knows all about him: knows of his monthly budget, the attic and
the fire escape, even of bony old Pomponia with the broom in her
hand. Rufus turns aside, he smiles half in amusement, half in
pity.

'Look here, my friend,' he says, 'you were not the only one
affected. The story of the Asiatic Tax Company is a little complicated, but instructive. Would you like to hear it?'

Apronius swallows and nods without a word.

'Listen then,' Rufus begins, still smiling, as though talking to
a child. 'The company in question who had rented the tax
collection of the Asiatic province from the State, and to whom
you entrusted your money, was actually a very sound business

proposition. But its directors were all members of the knighthood, that is, the young financial aristocracy; and Sulla had an incurable preference for ancient pedigree. He hated the financial aristocracy; whoever wished to sit in office had to prove his descent from wolf-suckled ancestors. Therefore he declared that the company was robbing the tax-payers; all of a sudden he dissolved it and decreed that the taxes would henceforth be collected by the State itself, by the governor of the Asiatic province. The natural consequences were devastating for all concerned. In the first place, the small shareholders lost their money. And secondly, Asia's tax-payers were worse off now than before, because the governor—you will remember it was young Lucullus—had no inkling of how to manage elastically the complicated business of tax-collecting, though I will say he had a lovely family tree.

'By the way, it might comfort you to know that the most prominent people in Rome suffered just like you. Would you like me to go on? Young Cicero was at that time on the upgrade of his career. He was twenty-seven years old and his mistress was Dame Cerelia who had strong financial interests in the Asiatic Company. Like you, she lost half her fortune; Cicero was so moved by this that he very nearly turned against Sulla. "Protect the Secondary Nobles", he cried in an open tirade right there on the Forum. "Protect the knights who found us treasures!" He nearly talked his head off, in more senses than one.'

Rufus smiles, lost in reminiscences. The clerk Apronius wags a bewildered head. He expected comfort, understanding, words of sympathy; instead, the great man talks of foggy business deals beyond his comprehension, which seem to him sinister conspiracies with the sole aim of robbing him, Quintus Apronius, of his savings.

'. . . But the tale goes on,' Rufus continues his smiling verbosity, 'would you like to hear more about it? Lucullus's successor was a certain Gneius Cornelius Dolabella. He was a more easygoing sort, and on the quiet he began to hire out the tax-collection once more to various knights and their companies. The banker Marcus Crassus and a certain Chrysogomus who was known to be a favourite of Sulla's, acted as intermediaries. Asia's tax-payers, sad to say, were again no better off; on the contrary, their tribute was raised from twenty thousand to forty thousand Talents in order to reimburse the company's losses. The unhappy natives had to mortgage their temple treasuries, pawn their theatre revenue, sell their children on the Deli slave market, or fly and join the pirates. Dolabella was therefore charged with extortion as soon as his term of office had expired. But Crassus and his friends managed to secure him an effective acquittal. The accusation was brought forward by a young aristocrat whose affaires and adventures at the court of the King of Bythynia had amused all Rome, and whose name was Gaius Iulius Caesar.'

Quintus Apronius, First Scribe of the Market Court, returns alone. The pangs in stomach and abdomen have set in again; he is quite dizzy with all he has been hearing. In all his eighteen years of service he has never heard half as much about the hidden reasons behind Roman politics as on this one eventful afternoon; he shakes a bewildered head, mutters with scorn. What a jungle of political decay, what a chasm has opened before his very eyes! Scum like these men, upstarts and business sharks, invisibly pull the strings of the Republic, plot and rob the honest citizen; are the cause of all misfortunes. And he, Quintus Apronius, First Scribe of the Market Court, had behaved like a timid schoolboy in their presence, looked up to them in awe!

But things are going to be different from now on. Next time he meets one of them he'll give him a piece of his mind! And at the annual reunion of the 'Worshippers of Diana and Antinous', he will deliver a speech virulent with disclosures: High time it is, he will say, that these corrupted scoundrels are shoved down the drainpipe by a strong man who clears the muddy stable of the State relentlessly! A good job if those robbers really did come to the town Capua and made a shambles of everything, Court Hall, Steambaths, Dolphins, and put an end to all anxiety and toil.

Darkness lies over the Oscian quarter when the scribe Apronius leaves the Tavern of the Twin-Wolves to go home. Contrary to his habits, he has had wine with his dinner, potent Falernian, to drown melancholy and belly-ache. As he strides through the empty streets, trailing his clerk's gown carelessly through the dust, he sings a reckless, provocative song, a bandits' song.

As he clambers up the fire escape to his apartment, he slips and nearly falls. But he sings on, sits down on the rungs between the second and third storeys; not in the least giddy, he sings into the night with his bandits' song and beats time with his scraggy, hairy legs.

Let him come, that Barbarian chieftain, that Spartacus, let him bring turmoil and destruction to everything—houses, Dolphins, Market Court; ye gods, who'll be sorry for this kind of a world?

I

THE MEETING

THE horde lived in the crescent-shaped highland-valley, in the tents which had been Clodius Glaber's, eating his provisions and drinking his wine. But in the bowels of the mountain, inside the crater, great fires were lit every night which diffused light far into the country.

It looked as though Vesuvius were spitting flames again as in legendary times; and the nightly red smoke which the crater emitted was to the people of the valleys as the ensign of that victory over the Legions of Rome fought by an army of robbers bold and just.

For rumour, crossing the country quicker than the Senate's fastest courier, said this and nothing else. The farther removed from the scene of origin, the more winged and joyous these tales did become; and as the wave ashore has forgotten the shape of the stone which splashed it, the legend had forgotten about the bald Praetor's hastily gathered army, just good enough to fight a gang of tattered brigands and mangy gladiators; all rumour knew was: Rome had been conquered and the conquerors were slaves. And it knew of even more, knew of that adversary born to Rome, that hero of tall stature clothed in only a fur-skin, who received the poor and oppressed into his avenging horde.

In ever-widening circles the towering head of the mountain radiated this message to the country. It penetrated into the barren highland valleys of Lucania, promised land of herdsmen and bandits; it stormed across that garden of debris by the

88

grace of Sulla which had once been the proud county of Samnium. But in Campania herself the masses were now on the move.

Before, they had come in isolated ones and twos—now they came in their hundreds. Before, they had slunk over concealed paths to the island in the swamps—now they jostled up the mountain in upright troops and sang songs of great temerity.

Two hundred serfs from the estate of a Senator near Cumae, a stern procession, marched into the camp; they were half-naked, barefoot, in rags. The foremost three carried a high mast like the standard of the Legions, with the iron ankle-fetters and a cat-o'-nine-tails dangling from it.

A long train of sappers came, who had been employed at the building of Lucullus's fish pond; a giant muraena-eel was borne in front of them, with a human head in its jaws.

The guild of free builders from Nuceria came, who had become workless when the Town Council purchased a ship-load of Syrian slaves and let them out in cheap batches to all building contractors. They were neatly dressed, respectable people; they brought with them the funds of their savings society whose interest paid for their annual birthday celebration.

The first Lucanian shepherds came. They had huge, vicious dogs and knotty, club-like sticks. They wore boars'-hides or wolf-skins over their backs like Barbarian warriors, grew long beards, and had shaggy hair all over their bodies.

The two hundred servants of a Pompeian man-about-town came; they carried a wooden phallus with this inscription: 'Behold Gaius our master, no other part of him is worthy of note.'

But the majority of those who came carried as their emblem the simple patibulum, the wooden slave-cross.

Each group built its own camp in the crescent-shaped valley named 'Hell's Ante-room'. They cooked their own meals, sang their own songs. They spoke Celtic, Thracian, Oscian, Syrian, Latin, Cimbric, German. They did not care for one another, and clashes were rather frequent. They swapped bacon for clubs, wine for shoes, women for weapons, weapons for money.

The members of the original horde walked about the camp

with a bad grace, and looked at the throng, silent and annoyed. The gladiators had put on airs; they wore the best clothes, uniforms of Roman officers; one could recognise them at first glance and pointed them out to new-comers. There were still fifty gladiators left from Lentulus's school in Capua; their horde, known as the gladiators' horde, soon embraced five thousand.

The camp boasted a number of celebrities; people turned and stared after them. Zozimos the rhetorician wandered from group to group, joked and squandered learned phrases, was applauded and gibed at; he was the only one in the whole camp who wore a toga. Hermios the shepherd played the great man towards his compatriots, the uncivilised Lucanians, flashed his teeth and bragged about his service with the Campanian army, he who had seen the world. Castus, the little fellow, minced affectedly past the crowds, stopped by a group here and there, played with his silver necklace, spoke of the Old Horde's exploits in the swamps of the Clanius; was admired and very little loved. The women ran after Oenomaus, enamoured of his girlish face: it was said he had never lain with a woman yet, and that he made poetry though he was a gladiator. Crixus inspired abashed deference; when he walked through the camp—fat, inert, dull-and-slow-eyed—conversation became unnatural, and the young people avoided his glance. Scurrilous tales circulated about him; it was said he slept with Jack today and Jill tomorrow: in itself there was nothing wrong with that, but you ought to look different if you did it.

And then there was Spartacus.

Many of the new-comers wondered after the first few days what thing about him was so special; it was a popular topic for evening chatter, and they chattered much for they had time.

Some said the special thing was his eyes; others, his cleverness. Women said it was his voice or his freckles. But there were others among them who had the same kind of eyes and were maybe just as clever, and there was no dearth in pleasant voices or freckles.

Philosophers and learned people said that it was not one trait or the other, but the Whole that did it: that certain something called 'personality'. Well, yes, it did sound learned, and pulpy as everything learned—but in the end everybody had a 'personality', one in this way, the next in another; that did not explain a thing.

Zozimos put a finger to his nose, said: 'Man's will it is, that force which giveth power', and more such comely, rhythmic sentences. But when you thought it over and were not taken in by the rhythm: where was the man who did not *will*, and if all that mattered was the strength of your will, every landowner in Italy would have died of pestilence long ago, and every maiden in Italy would have her belly great.

Well, said Zozimos, he had not meant quite *that*, not the will of desire mattered, but the will of action. Action? There had been the brothers Eunus of Beneventum, the three of them had killed their master and harangued their colleagues to the effect that they should all become free bandits instead of remaining servants. And what happened? They were hanged, were these Eunus brothers, hanged, all three of them, together with their will, their action and personality.

In short, if you looked close, one man was like the next; one was a little plumper, the next a little cleverer, the third could talk like an angel, a fourth had a crooked nose—all this did not in the least explain what was so special about Spartacus. And if you thought it over and thrashed it out you might find that in the end there wasn't anything special about him at all. Spartacus was Spartacus: he went about the camp, tall, slightly hunched like a wood-cutter in his fur-skin; let his eyes wander, said little—but what he did say was exactly that which scorched your own tongue, and if he said the opposite, it seemed at once as though the opposite had been scorching your tongue. He smiled seldom and when he did smile he certainly had good reason, and it positively warmed your heart. He had little time, and when he came to sit with one group—say, the servants of Fannius or the herdsmen of Lucania—you did not make a fuss, but you were glad, and it seemed as though at last you knew why you were busy killing time on this mad mountain, instead of continuing your life according to reason, order, and your station in life.

When Castus ordered you to do something you obeyed because it was ill-advised to disagree with the Hyaenas. When Crixus issued a command, you obeyed because you shrank from the heavy, dismal man. But when Spartacus said anything you never dreamt of a contradiction—simply because none occurred to you. Where was the sense in wanting something different from Spartacus; did he not want exactly the same as everybody wanted?

It must, of course, not be forgotten that every one did want
something different. One man wanted to stay here for ever and
gorge his fill to the end of his days. Another wanted them all to
march to Puteoli to burn his master's house with the master in it.
A third wanted them all to conquer and take a ship on which to
go to Alexandria where women were plentiful. A fourth wanted
them to go to Capua, raze the city to the ground and erect a new
one. A fifth wanted to make war on Rome. The sixth wanted to
go home, to his flocks—what in hell had they come for? The
seventh wanted to go to Sicily where the slaves had stood up to
Rome once before. The eighth wanted to join the pirates of
Cilicia, the ninth wanted communal wives, a tenth man wanted
to enforce the prohibition of eating fish. Everybody wanted something different, and talked, quarrelled or kept silence about it.
But each one felt and knew that the man with the fur-skin who
had nothing special about him, wanted exactly the same as he
himself—that he was the common denominator of all their
opposed hopes and desires—and nothing else.

But maybe that was the special thing about him.

The rains were approaching.

Half a month had passed since they vanquished Clodius
Glaber; counted from the flight of the Seventy from Capua, nearly
three had gone by.

Provisions were dwindling on Mount Vesuvius. Expeditions
into the valleys yielded less and less; the entire district, including
Herculaneum, Nola and Pompeii, had been laid waste. In a
circuit of ten miles the plain of Campania, the paradise, lay bald
and bare as though eaten by locusts. The cities were closed, their
garrisons reinforced, and their walls repaired.

And still humanity came flocking up the mountain, bearded,
ragged, with branding scars on their shoulders and sore feet.
They plundered the estates on their way and avoided the towns.
They brought scythes, shovels, hatchets, sticks. They were the
dregs of the blessed country, the refuse that fertilised her fields;
they stank and there was no health left in their bodies. They
carried disease and bad habits into the camp, brought a dower of
hunger and nebulous hopes.

They were not kindly received. Those who had lived in the
camp for ten days looked down on the three-day-olds, those who

had come three days ago regarded themselves as old inmates and treated new-comers accordingly. People in the camp began to get bored; there they were, waiting, and did not know for what. They began to grumble, some went home. No one prevented them. Five thousand people lived on the mountain, spoke various languages, ate, argued, talked, quarrelled about booty or women, formed friendships, sang, killed one another. They were waiting, and knew not for what.

Even the gladiators were at variance over what should be done. They held meetings to which none but the Fifty were admitted, conferences preceded by mysterious preparations, held inside the crater. Fannius's servants had to fetch up many bags of wine before it commenced, and the gladiators wore important-looking faces like Senators, as they went to a conference. But nothing much was ever decided; for, each time they drew near to the question of what was to be done, it was evaded, unimportant subjects were discussed, quarrel or laughter raised, and the necessity of coming to a decision forgotten.

Spartacus never took sides to the projects that sprouted up every day. In silence he listened to the others, and only towards the end, when everything threatened to be lost in confused back-chat, did he speak briefly on subordinate questions which could not be postponed: provisions, the sharing out of arms, camping sites for new-comers. He was never once contradicted, for his suggestions were sensible and simple; but all were disappointed as they expected him to supply the deciding cue, which he did not seem to notice.

Instead, he achieved the gradual re-formation of the divers groups into cohorts and centuries, with one gladiator at the head of each column. Then he told them of the ways in which the hunters of the Thracian mountains made their arms: round shields of wickerwork covered with fresh hide, and wooden lances whose points were hardened in fire. Finally he divided them up into categories: vanguard, reserves, and regular infantry; heavy cavalry with the armour and spears of the fallen Romans; light cavalry armed with swords and slings.

All of this took time; day followed day, hardly one without discord and killings; food supply diminished, and the rains approached ever closer.

But when two months had passed after the defeat of Clodius

Glaber, he had accomplished it; from the shapeless clay on Mount Vesuvius he had moulded an army.

One fine day two months after the defeat of Clodius Glaber, the servants of Fannius went from one group to another with the same message: 'Elect aldermen, and representatives of every ten among you,' they said, 'and send them to the crater. A general meeting is going to be held.'

Commotion went through the camp. The groups mingled, they voted, argued, conjectured, lapped up rumours. The camp had woken and shook off the waiting like a deep sleep.

An endless procession ascended the path leading to the rim of the cavity. Only aldermen and delegates of every ten were supposed to attend, but the entire camp crowded the path; the boldest climbed over naked rock. When they arrived at the summit, they beheld for the first time the inside crater with its charred rock and queer-shaped, corroded blocks of stone. They scurried down through loose pebbles and rubble, streamed together at the bottom, fidgeted excitedly and showed new-comers the memorials of the siege: the Thracian basin, the Celtic basin, the skeletons of the slaughtered mules. The sun sent harsh rays into the crater and on the growing multitude at the bottom, whom he melted into a piebald, sweating massive lump. Even the crater walls were studded with people; they sat on blackened rocks, clutching the tough mesh of wild vines which grew all over the rubble. Some littered the rim and looked down. Like a giant sea-shell, the crater sent a hollow buzzing up into the broiling air.

When Spartacus started to speak, his voice was drowned in the hum. Clothed in his fur-skin, he stood on a large, projecting tooth of rock half-way up the wall; with him were Crixus, and some of the gladiators and of Fannius's servants. The odour of the many became one odour, their expectation mobbed him as one expectation. Clumsily he raised his arm—immediately the gladiators and bull-necks behind him raised theirs, and silence descended. For the second time Spartacus began; the walls of the crater caught and amplified his voice.

'The rains are on their way,' said Spartacus, 'and food is getting scarce; we must have winter quarters.'

'He's right,' thought Hermios the shepherd, who huddled in

the rubble on the other side. 'That's just what worried me too,' he thought, bared his teeth approvingly and looked at Spartacus on his rock, tall and very splendid in his fur-skin. His voice was not much louder than usual, and calm, as though he were speaking to the shepherd alone.

'Maybe the Romans will send another army,' said Spartacus. 'We must have a town for the winter, a town with walls around it, a town of our own.'

That was not what he had meant to say. It was impossible to take a walled city without appropriate siege machines. Crixus who had stood, fat and heavy, by his side, turned his head and looked at him cloudily. He knew that you could not take a city without siege machinery, and those Five Thousand in the crater knew it as well.

But the Five Thousand were quiet, heard the wheezing breath of the Many, their own breath, smelled the smell of the Many, their own smell, and they knew that this man Spartacus up on his rock was right, and that everything became possible as soon as they willed it.

'A town,' said Spartacus, 'a town of houses and firm walls, a town of our own. Then, when the Romans come, they will break their heads against the walls of the town which belongs to us—a gladiators' town, a slaves' town.'

Only now he felt the silence. He heard his own voice rebounding from every side of the crater. He heard the breath of the Many as one breath, as he felt the one expectation of the multitude.

'And the name of this Town shall be the Town of Slaves,' said Spartacus and perceived his own alien voice resounding through the crater. 'Remember that we'll get what we want and that no one will serve in our town. But maybe we will not have one town only, but many, a brotherhood of Slave Towns. Don't think I am just talking, for such a thing existed once before, a long, long time ago. It was called The Sun State. . . .'

All the time he was thinking of the siege machines they did not have. They were what he meant to talk of, but he talked of the Sun State. As through a dancing hot veil he saw the Essene sitting on a stone opposite and wagging his head with the stern lips in listening. He saw Hermios the shepherd bare his teeth and stare. And the smell of the crowd was in his nostrils.

'Why should the strong serve the weak?' he roared at them, his arms suddenly flung high as though invisibly pulled up. 'Why should the hard serve the soft, the Many serve the Few? We guard their cattle and drag the bloody calf out of its mother, but not into our herds. We build them ponds and may not bathe in them. We are the Many and are to serve the Few—why, tell me, why?'

Now he was no longer thinking of siege machinery, he listened to the words that spurted out of him from an unknown source; they became a stream which swirled around those in the crater, swallowing them in its whirlpool. The words frothed in their ears, and their eyes drank in the sight of the man in the fur-skin sharply outlined against the bare wall of rock.

'We are the Many,' said Spartacus, 'and we have served them because we were blind and did not ask for reasons. But once we start asking they have no more power over us. And I tell you, when we start asking it is the end of them, and they rot away like the body of a man whose arms and legs have been sawed off. And we will go our own way and laugh at them. If we will it, all Italy will laugh, from Gaul to Tarentum and Africa. And behold, what laughter that will be, and what cries will go up before the Eastern Gate and what alarm at the other gates, what loud laments from the seven hills! For then they will be as nothing before us, and the walls of their cities will crumble without siege machinery.'

He paused to listen in astonishment to the echo of his own words. Again the horde grew indistinct; all he saw was the bullet-headed Essene over on the other side, sitting on his stone, his head asway. Then the siege machines came back into his thoughts:

'Again I tell you: we must have a walled town, a town of our own. A town that is ours, whose walls protect us. But we have no siege machines. . . .'

A wave of restlessness passed over the multitude. Those who were herded at the bottom shuffled and stirred, as though waking from a great enchanted silence, and testing their limbs.

'. . . We have no siege machines, and it is not true that the walls of cities tumble on their own accord. But we will camp in front of their gates and through every gate and gap we will send our message to the serfs of the town, and will repeat and repeat it until the message fills their ears: "The gladiators of Lentulus Batuatus of Capua want to ask you why the strong should serve the weak and the Many serve the Few." This question will rain on them like stony hail from mighty catapults, and the serfs in the city will hear it, and they will raise their voices and unite their strength with ours. And then there will be no walls.'

Now he could distinguish several women. From their eyes which never left him he saw that their breath went haltingly and that he touched them with his voice. And there the men stood, and if he wished it they would kill Crixus; and if he wished it they would start off.

He spoke of the distant beginnings of the horde, and how the Fifty became Five Thousand. He spoke of the anger of the fettered and oppressed which weighted down heavily over Italy, told them how this wrath had dug roads to roam like the brooks that spring forth from the pressure and sweat of the mountains. And how they, Lentulus's fifty gladiators, dug one broad bed for all the small angry brooks, so that they united in one mighty stream which drowned Glaber and his army. And how necessary it was to dam the flow and guide it, so its force might not be wasted. And that therefore they must conquer the first fortified town before the rains set in, how the brotherhood of Slave Towns would grow up in Italia; the great state of justice and goodwill, which will be called—and here he said it for the second time— which will be called the *Sun State*.

But among the crowd were two elderly clerks from the city of Nola, sent out by the Senior Councillor, Aulus Egnatus, with the secret commission of ascertaining the robbers' intentions. They stood pressed in the crowd, heard like them the words of the man in the fur-skin; and they understood—for they were old and experienced men—that from this moment on not only the fate of their town was in the balance, but the fate of the land Italy, the Roman Empire—and hence the fate of the whole inhabited world.

T.G.—D

2

DESTRUCTION
OF THE TOWN NOLA

THE impresario Marcus Cornelius Rufus saw with satisfaction
that he had succeeded in making the first performance of his
company in Nola a social event. He had his own ideas on up-to-
date methods of publicity and he had seen to it that the rumour
of his play's insolent politics traversed the city in good time.

For five days the city of Nola had been cut off from the rest of
the world; before its gates lay the scourge of Campania, the slave
army. The general feeling among the serfs grew more and more
threatening, arson and looting were every-night crimes; if relief
as promised by Rome did not come soon, things might become
unpleasant.

In spite—or perhaps because—of all this, Rufus had succeeded
in making his première the season's event. The open-air theatre
was overcrowded, on the privileged benches sat the Councillors
with their ladies, white-pleated and dignified. The entire nobility
of the town was there, with the exception of the Senior Councillor,
aged Aulus Egnatus, who was too old-fashioned to visit a theatre.
The county representatives, stocky and bashful, sat among the
native knights in an attempt to hobnob with them; a few rows
farther on sat Nola's famed Jeunesse Dorée, sons of good families
with painted cheeks and oil-waved hair. Behind the benches, on
the stairs-like stands, jumbled the People, noisy, sweating and
chewing chick-peas.

Auditorium and stage were sheltered from the sun by a
coloured canvas roof. A couple of flowerpots-full of wheat played
at being a cornfield in front of a plain back-cloth. The piece was
called *Bucco the Peasant*.

First to appear was Bucco, with a scarlet, puff-cheeked mask and bright yellow hair. Babbling incessantly, he stumbled jerkily on to the stage as though moved by invisible wires.

'I am Bucco the Peasant,' he said. 'I've just come from the war in Asia where I killed seventeen men and two elephants and was greatly commended by my captain. "Bucco," said my captain to me, "now you've killed off enough enemies and committed enough heroism, now you go home nicely, and till your soil, steeped in glory and honours as you are." But where are my wife and child, not to mention my field-hand, who are to receive me exultantly? Hey, come here, wife and child and field-hand, Bucco has returned victorious!'

He clapped his hands and revolved a few times on his heel, but nothing stirred. As he peeped and pried and clapped, Maccus the Glutton mounted the stage in funereal tardiness. He was the soul of laziness and ugliness, a phallus made of rags dangled lewdly down to his knee. He nibbled an enormous turnip and tore out the corn-stalks that hemmed his way.

'Hey, you Cappadocian scarecrow,' cried Bucco the Peasant, 'you shorn onion whose sight brings tears to my eyes, you lascivious frog, what are you doing on my field?'

'I am reaping the harvest,' said Maccus, bit a piece off the turnip and went on plucking.

'Praised be the gods!' cried Bucco the Peasant. 'So they made a brand-new field-hand grow unto me during my absence! And even if he is not handsome, he doubtless is a man, as anyone can see.'

'I daresay you got sunstroke in Asia,' said Maccus measuredly. 'I daresay your brains evaporated through your ears, if you think that this field is your field. Know it then: this field belongs to the exalted Lord Dossena.'

On hearing this Bucco the Peasant broke into loud lamentations. But that was not all. Bucco learned that the exalted Lord Dossena had not only taken his field, but had led away his wife and child; every shred of land all around now belonged to the exalted Lord Dossena; Maccus the Glutton was also one of the slaves of the Lord Dossena. Weeping and sobbing, Bucco the Peasant paced the field that was no longer his. He hurled atrocious curses at the mighty Lords for whom he had fought the war and killed seventeen men besides two elephants; this, then, was the fatherland's gratitude!

But what good were curses; Bucco had to try and find a livelihood; so he decided to go into service on the land that had
formerly been his own. Whereupon the Lord Dossena, hunch-
backed and beak-nosed, made his entry, and Bucco the Peasant
delivered his request.

But the Lord Dossena, who spoke an affectedly literary Latin
in contrast to Bucco's deep-vowelled Oscian brogue, declined: he
employed only slaves, he said, and would not have anything to
do with free labourers, for they are pretentious, demand high pay,
and decent treatment even. No, no, said the Lord Dossena, he
would have none of that, and off he went.

So there stood Bucco the Peasant, helpless and lonely, and
walked the stage, he could not even curse any more. Fortunately
Pappus came, the Good-natured Sage, and knew of a way out:
Bucco must go to Rome, for in Rome everybody whom bad times
have deprived of his living, is supported by the State by means of
monthly distributions of free corn. 'Go to the capital, my son,'
said Pappus, 'and live on the wheat you can reap without sowing.'

Bucco became quite enthusiastic on hearing this; humming a
jaunty tune he departed for Rome.

The wheatpots were swiftly removed and a new back-cloth let
down, which represented a street; and there was Bucco already
marvelling at the size, traffic and stink of the capital. But then he
got hungry and asked the next passer-by where it was they distributed corn to unemployed citizens.

The passer-by, a fat man with documents under his arm, nearly
threw a fit with surprise at this question. Where, he asked, did
Bucco come from—was it the moon or the German province? Did he
not know that glorious and dauntless dictator Sulla—whose name,
he begs to point out, he only mentioned with all due reverence—has
abolished the corn-benefit because the State needs all its money
for the wars? And anyway, Bucco had better disappear at once,
unless he would like to be suspected of extreme oppositionism and
high treason, and see his name advertised in the proscription-list.

Thus all of Bucco's beautiful hopes were gone, and he was wan
and hungry again. Fortunately a turbulent crowd came by; its
leader asked Bucco whether he would vote for Gaius or for
Gneius at the elections. Bucco the Peasant replied that worried
him as little as a fart of slumber. So the leader said he should vote
for Gneius and slipped a coin into his hand. Delighted, Bucco

skipped to the bakershop to buy bread; but the baker said it was one of the recent coins with which the State cheated the people, for, though silvered outside, it was only copper inside, and he would not take it. So then Bucco sat down on a cobble in front of the bakery and wept.

But now another man passed by and asked Bucco why he was weeping. Bucco told him that he had been to the wars where he had slain twenty-seven men as well as two elephants, and now he could not even buy a loaf of bread. So then the man said Bucco was a hero, and did he not know that dictator Sulla—whose name, be it noted, he only mentioned with all due reverence— had promised fields to the faithful veterans of his army. No, said Bucco, still bathed in tears, he did *not* know, for they had not given him land but taken it away. A crying shame, this, said the man, and he would see to it that Bucco got a new and better field in compensation for his lost one.

After that the back-cloth with its streets was pulled away and the flowerpots with wheat returned: Bucco was a farmer again.

But things got really bad only now. The new field assigned to Bucco was full of stones, and he had to sell the sparse corn it bore at a loss, because the wheat from overseas lowered the price. Apart from that, Bucco again owed money to the hunch-backed Lord Dossena, as he had been forced to borrow from him in order to buy the necessary tools. Lo, came Dossena with a smug bailiff who read out some unintelligible document; whereupon the field was taken from him again.

So there was Bucco the Peasant, alone on the stage, chubby-faced, bright-haired, and speaking a monologue: 'It's fiendish,' said he, 'every day is worse. The justice of our State develops backwards like a cow's tail. Cross my heart and hope to die if I believe that all this is Divine ruling. What will you do with yourself now, poor old Bucco? All you can do is leap about and wonder and worry, like a mouse in a chamber-pot. . . .'

But when Dossena and the smug bailiff came back to order him off the field, Bucco the Peasant took a big stick and began to thrash them soundly; he yelled he would go to the bandits now, to Mount Vesuvius, in order to smash this bloody country to bits; and thus the play ended happily in the obligatory row, under the raging applause of the spectators.

.   .   .   .   .

Old Aulus Egnatus, Senior Councillor of Nola and greatest art-collector in the town, was expecting two guests for dinner after the performance: the popular leader of the Progressive Party, Herius Mutilus, and the impresario Marcus Cornelius Rufus.

The old gentleman paced his dining-room; irritated, he examined the arrangement of plates and altered the position of a many-armed candelabrum whose light fell at an unfavourable angle on the new vase which he wished to show his guests.

He was looking forward to his guests, that old cynic Rufus and the youthful, popular and clever People's Tribune, although the latter was an adherent of the Democrat's Party, abhorred by old Egnatus. At the same time it saddened him that the menu was not all it should be; Nola had been cut off from the rest of humanity for five days, no fresh vegetables were to be had, and the old gentleman had even had to forgo his accustomed morning ride outside the city gates—a pleasure he had not renounced in years, neither for the storms of the Council, nor the confinement of his young wife who had presented him with an heir when he was over sixty.

Mutilus arrived first. The Tribune of the opposition was his guest for the first time, the Senator went to meet him in the garden, and greeted him with a cordiality not altogether devoid of ceremony. As he chatted at him, a trifle too lively in order to get over the first awkward minutes, he felt vexed with his wife who, presumably indulging her toilet, was keeping them waiting. At the same time he noted with amusement that the candlelight subtracted much of the glamour with which the fêted democrat was imbued on the rostrum; he looked squat and a bit provincial; probably he wore his linen artificially starched. Also, his progressive principles did not seem to be aiding him past that embarrassment which took hold of every one who entered Egnatus's house in Nola for the first time; for even passing Roman noblemen who visited old Egnatus, found to their surprise that they could not utter any of their wonted smutty stories which were just then all the vogue in society.

The Senator showed his guest the new black vase, and when he noticed that the other did not understand, he felt a gentle regret that nowadays you could become a famous man without knowing anything of vases. He attempted to explain the difference between antique Etruscan or Cretan vases, and the modern mass-products from Samos and Arezzo; volubly he pointed out the scrupulous laws of form and ornament, reviled the muck-manufacturers' criminal handling of material. His blue-veined hand curved the air with the outline of the black vase which, in spite of its solidity, seemed to revoke its own weight; he compelled the Tribune to scrutinise the vase's sole ornament, a Pompeian dancing girl whose fragile figure, nude and as though suspended between the spreading wings of her veils, stood out in joyous red varnish from the black ground. The more evident his guest's disinterest, the more Egnatus worked himself up; and he broke off only when the two doors which faced each other on opposite sides of the dining-room opened almost simultaneously, one of them letting forth the impresario, the other Egnatus's young wife. The hostess stood framed in the doorway for an instant, then she saluted her husband and guests in her manner of vaguely theatrical charm.

'I see,' said Rufus, 'that our friend is again in love with a morsel of clay and will rave about it all night while his guests starve. You, dear friend, are the veritable eighth wonder of the world, slim and youthful like a man of twenty, while parvenus like myself get out of shape at forty, unless they undergo four weeks' hot mud-bath treatment every year. What good is democracy when there are two kinds of men: one who get fat with age, and the other who grow slender and willowy?'

Without interrupting his verbose amiability, he walked towards the hostess, complimented her on her pretty dress, mixing Greek words unobtrusively with his speech; despite his apparent lack of formality, he never lost a subdued trace of respect, almost of aloof dignity. Smiling, old Aulus admired this accomplishment of taking more than ten steps across empty mosaic floor, incessantly talking, and never, in spite of a paunch, diminishing in poise. But when he proceeded to introduce Tribune Herius Mutilus to his wife, he observed that she was almost a whole head taller than the square-built man.

Standing, they chatted on, an aged servant offered snacks and coloured herb-liqueurs. The hostess smilingly refused responsibility for the food: half their servants had left them in the lurch, run to join the besiegers, there had been absolutely no holding them.

'Why aren't you drinking?' she cut herself short, when she saw the Tribune refuse the third species of liqueur, offered to him again and again in mute obstinacy by the offended old servant.

'I take nothing but pure wine,' said the Tribune. 'Last night approximately two hundred people climbed over the walls. One hears those Spartacus-people receive them with open arms. Please consider that the deserters were by no means all serfs, but nearly as many of them were artisans, workmen and small gardeners. Also, looting occurred again in the suburbs near Regio Romana.'

'What simply divine times for your play,' said the hostess to Rufus. 'I hear you have a scandal every day. I really must go to see it, but one simply can't drag Aulus near a theatre.'

They sat down at the dining table.

'Have you seen it?' Rufus turned to the Tribune and snugly began to eat some fish. 'It is quite a primitive extempore affair, in the style of the ancient plays of Atella—but strangely enough, people get frightfully excited over it.'

'I've seen it,' said the Tribune. 'The very fact that it is so primitive makes it all the more seditious. If I had any say with the stage police—' he glanced quickly at the Senator, 'I should have it banned.'

The bit of fish stuck in Rufus's throat, the host looked at him and smiled. 'What about democratic principles, my friend?' he asked Mutilus.

The Tribune did not return his smile. 'You ought to go and see it, Egnatus. It proves to the people, shall we say arithmetically, that the most sensible thing to do is to join the bandits.'

'In your last speech,' said Rufus, piqued, 'you said something rather similar, only much more seditious. True, you did it so prettily as to impress a certain part on my memory.' Grinning sarcastically, he quoted: ' "The wild beasts in Italy have their caves, but the men who fight and die for her have no abode; homeless, they have to straggle about the land with their wives and their children. The politicians lie when they encourage the poor to defend their homes against the enemies, for they have neither homes nor any other sort of property worth defending. They are called the lords of the world and yet they do not own a single crumb of earth." Can you say this is not seditious?'

'It appears,' laughed the hostess, 'that both our guests are in complete agreement with the bandits.'

'I was merely referring to the land reform,' said the Tribune, whose face had gone red. 'Besides, it was only a quotation from a speech by the Elder Gracchus.'

'If I permitted my actors to quote the classics,' said Rufus, 'such as Plato and Phaleas of Chalchedonia with their inciting speeches on equality and communal property, I would long have been in prison.'

'If my husband has you locked up,' said the hostess, 'I'll send you some ham to prison every day.'

'You are too kind,' said Rufus. 'I only fear, if Rome goes on precipitating reinforcements as much as up to now, none of us will be in a position to lock the other up, or even to be nice to him. . . .'

'Do you really think this Spartacus so dangerous?' asked the hostess.

Rufus shrugged.

'Last night's lootings,' said the Tribune, 'were undoubtedly of an organised nature. And those masses of deserters rather make you think. The Spartacus-people must have smuggled through quite a number of emissaries.'

'The best emissary, my friend,' said Rufus, 'is the affinity of all hungry stomachs. When one stomach rumbles in Capua, it is as though someone had touched a tuning-fork, and all the hungry stomachs of Italy sing up.'

At this moment Rufus felt that everyone at table had the same thought: that of Rufus himself having been a serf only ten years ago, and probably therefore knowing so much about the acoustics of hungry stomachs. He put the bite of food back on his plate, dried his fingers, looked old Egnatus straight in the eye:

'After all, I'm the one to know,' he said without particular stress, and his interest seemed once more wrapped up in the roast meat.

The Councillor's young wife swiftly drained her glass—her fourth or fifth—and held it over her shoulder to be refilled. The aged servant behind her filled it only half and avoided looking at the Councillor.

'I'd love to find out,' said the hostess, 'what there is so special about this Spartacus-fellow. Three months ago nobody knew that he as much as existed, today he is a walking legend. I cannot conceive how such a man can gain such power over the masses.'

'No more can I,' said old Egnatus. 'But our Rufus will probably explain it by saying that his stomach rumbles loudest throughout Italy.'

'I shouldn't think this explanation quite sufficient,' said Rufus.

The Tribune cleared his throat, he was visibly jealous of the absent man's reputation. 'He's supposed to be a remarkably good speaker, and I consider that sufficient explanation.'

'I don't, though,' said the hostess and thrust her glass again at the servant. 'He must have an additional certain something. Do you know,' she said to Rufus and touched his shoulder, 'what I imagine him to look like? Hairy all over, with a naked chest and a look in his eyes that goes right through you. Last year I was present at the execution of a man who assaulted little children in the mountains—he had such a look in his eyes.' She laughed excitedly, and Rufus thought it was not so good after all for a man of over sixty to marry a young girl. Possibly Egnatus read the thought in his eyes, for he broke in with deliberate briskness:

'You know what *I* think he's like? Bald, fat and perspiring, like the luggage porters of the Suburra. When he speaks, he changes from pathos to obscenity; besides, he is probably sentimental and keeps little boy friends.'

'So now we are all at one,' said Rufus jovially. 'By the way, I know him personally.'

'Ah!' made the hostess. 'And you didn't tell us before?'

Rufus was pleased with the effect he had produced. 'I saw him at the gladiator-school of my friend Lentulus in Capua. He showed me over his school when the gladiators took their morning exercise.'

'What did he look like? Weren't you struck with him at once?' asked the hostess.

'I can't say I was. I only remember that he wore a fur-skin round his shoulders, but there's nothing special in that among Barbarians.'

'What sort of face did he have?' asked the hostess.

'I'm afraid I must disappoint you: I can't remember accurately. You can see he made no particular impression on me—an average sort of face, I should say, wide, good-natured, on a well set-up, slightly bony body. The only thing about him I can remember is that he had a sort of thoughtful way of moving about, rather reminiscent of a wood-cutter.'

'But didn't you feel something—something mysterious, some magic force?'

'Not as far as I know,' said Rufus. He was glad to let the young woman down, from a feeling of solidarity with old Egnatus. 'There is a difference, you know, between seeing King Oedipus on the stage, and brushing his teeth.'

'But he must have *something* to get on to the stage in the first place,' said the hostess, irritated.

'I agree,' said Rufus. 'Although I personally believe that conditions produce the hero, not the other way round, but conditions rather tend to pick the right man anyhow. Take it from me, history has an instinct for discovering such people.'

Conversation dulled, they ate and drank. The servants came and went. One of them bent to his master's ear.

'Lootings again?' asked Rufus, whom nothing ever escaped.

'Nothing of consequence—in the suburbs,' said old Aulus and looked covertly at his wife. She seemed in no way agitated but drank a lot and became ever more animated; Rufus felt her thigh snuggling against his knee.

'We're used to worse than that in Nola,' said the old gentleman. 'When I think back to the civil war . . .' he gave the Tribune a confused look and said no more.

'Were you at all related to Gaius Papius?' Rufus asked the Tribune. At the same time he withdrew his knee, with a paternal glance at the hostess.

'He was an uncle of mine,' said the Tribune, curtly and scowlingly.

Tribune Herius Mutilus had been aged twenty when the South Italian nations, the Samnites, Marsians and Lucanians, rebelled against Rome. One of the leaders of insurrection had been his uncle, Gaius Papius Mutilus. Nola, whose populace was wholly Samnite, had been the first city to join the rebels, despite the resistance of its pro-Roman aristocracy. For six years the Romans besieged Nola, and Nola held its ground. Then Rome itself erupted with the democratic revolution under Marius and Cinna. At once the people of Nola opened their gates wide and fraternised with the Roman arch-enemy under the banner of revolution—despite the resistance from the aristocracy who suddenly forgot their pro-Roman sentiments and avowed themselves separatists. Three years later restoration under Sulla took hold of Rome, and again there was a change round in Nola: the aristocrats declared they had always said the city's salvation lay exclusively in an alliance with Rome—but the People's Party closed the gates and staunchly withstood two more years of siege. In the end the insurgents had to flee, not omitting to set the aristocrats' houses on fire; the last leader of the South Italian rebellion, Gaius Papius Mutilus, was killed while escaping.

'. . . I used to know your uncle well,' said the hostess. 'I was very young at the time, and he used to dandle me on his knee. He had the loveliest beard—like this . . .' She indicated what kind of beard the national hero of Samnium had had.

'He was a great patriot,' said Egnatus solemnly, as he feared his wife might have hurt the Tribune's feelings. 'But a ruthless chauvinist and Roman-eater,' he added.

'Don't talk nonsense, Aulus,' said the Tribune. 'Why do *you* not exhibit any of that renowned chauvinism, you, a member of one of the oldest families here? Because you and your party's interests are insolubly bound up with the interests of the Roman aristocracy who are continually preventing the land reform and protecting the big landowners. The South Italian rebellion was nothing but a rebellion of peasants, herdsmen and artisans against the usurers and big landowners. Its programme was neither Samnite, nor Lucanian, nor Marsian, but a programme of land reforms and civic rights. In fact, you can summarise the last hundred years of Roman domestic policy in one phrase: the desperate fight between the rural middle classes and the big landowners. All the rest is but the lullaby of officious chroniclers.'

'. . . Have some more fish?' asked the hostess.

'No, thank you,' said the Tribune, enraged that she should have happened on the one argument which put him in the wrong; he was incapable of handling fish gracefully.

'These modern theories,' said old Egnatus, 'are very specious, but I don't believe in them. In my opinion the root of all misfortunes must be sought in the moral degeneracy of the Roman aristocracy, their luxury and their corruption. Now, Old Cato . . .'

'For peace's sake leave Old Cato out of it,' said Rufus. 'These sententious sighs of the Forefathers' virtues no longer impress anyone. Old Cato—and you know it as well as I do—was charged with blackmail exactly forty-four times.'

'Admitted—both of you are so very versed in history,' said old Aulus whose expression had grown tired during the last part of the discussion. He rose, walked slowly through the room, stopped absently before the black vase, touched it tenderly with one finger: 'What do you think of this piece, Rufus?'

'A lovely piece,' said Rufus. 'I've been looking at it all night.'

'I have no arguments against you,' said the Senior Councillor, 'and you will think it ridiculously sentimental when I tell you now: this vase is *my* argument, and a more forceful one than any of you can put forward.'

'You mean . . .' began Rufus.

'I mean nothing,' said the old man, irritated. 'One need not argue about everything.'

Rufus said calmly: 'I merely wanted to point out that even this vase is not of Italian but of Cretan origin. Correct me if I'm wrong.'

'But I bought it!' snapped the old man. 'And wherever in the world such things are modelled, or painted, or written, or invented—they come to us. Without us, the much-reviled Roman aristocracy, none of it would ever be produced.'

'Perhaps so,' said Rufus. He bowed slightly, and for his part regarded the argument as terminated. A faintly disagreeable pause ensued. The Tribune smiled sneeringly, not even he himself knew whether at the old aristocrat or the upstart.

'Why don't we all go into the garden?' said the hostess. She looked past Rufus. 'Anyhow it is far too hot for politics.' She clapped her hands, and the aged manservant appeared.

'Have torches brought,' said the Councillor. 'We're going into the garden.'

'I'll fetch torches at once, Aulus Egnatus,' said the servant.

'Not *you*—I said you were to have them brought,' said the Councillor, who could not rid himself of his irritation. All of them were standing by the open door which led into the garden. Outside it was cool and very dark, but in the direction of the inner city a broad, reddish band crossed the skies.

The old servant stood still, embarrassed.

'Can't you understand,' said the hostess to her husband with a nervous laugh. 'The servants have all gone. Now the fun will start. . . .'

During that night the slave army, let into the town by the looting mob, sacked the city of Nola. The army commanders, Spartacus, Crixus and young Oenomaus, were unable to prevent the pogrom against the inhabitants, victims of which were half the free citizens of the town. Among those killed were the Senior Councillor Aulus Egnatus with his wife, and the democratic Tribune Herius Mutilus.

A lucky coincidence had enabled the impresario Marcus Cornelius Rufus to escape. He lost his actors, as well as all his baggage and money; all he saved apart from his life was a vase of clay which he rescued from the burning house of Egnatus—a vase with a Pompeian dancing girl, whose fragile figure, nude, and as though suspended between the spread-out wings of her veil, stood out in joyous red varnish against the black ground.

3

STRAIGHT ROAD

Ten thousand of them, on foot and on horseback, they moved
north along the highway.

Behind them, the rain puts out the last burning houses of Nola.
The rain is dyed black by the charred beams; it flows in grubby,
gushing rivulets over the cobbles between the demolished houses.

Many corpses are still lying about the skulking alleys of the
inner city; the rain has washed and soaken them, they are as the
bodies of drowned men. They lie strewn between the ruins of the
ransacked houses, between furniture and household implements,
mirrors and cupboards, beds and saucepans, chairs and clothes.
Women squat on the debris, up to their elbows in mud, they dig
for their buried belongings; men sit beside them and weep in
silence. A temple has spilled golden vessels and candelabra of
solid silver into the sooty mud; no one touches any of them. Nola
is silent.

Nola is silent; the preceding night had thundered through her
with a cloud of madness, the chorus of the murdered and burning, the crash of falling houses, the bellow of cattle, and the
pinched squall of the children. But now Nola is silent; only the
sound of the rainy brooks gargles through the streets.

Now they have gone. Have they really gone? Will they not
come back? The army of the destitute tramps into the upper
town, built of stone and brick. On wheelbarrows and mule-carts
they bring broken tables with dainty legs, distaffs with rain-
soaked bobbins, guitars, frying pans, gaping children's coffins, a
dead calf, wooden idols of unseeing eyes. They are met by the

first voluntary helpers, young men of quality in military formation; the slums are being evacuated.

Have they gone? Have they really gone? The debris is cleared away and searched; corpses and parts of corpses are piled in the amphitheatre. The upper city, strangely enough, suffered remarkably little; although numerous wealthy mansions have been plundered and demolished, the main force of the bandits concentrated on the inner city; intimidated by the quiet avenues with their dark, well-kept gardens, they felt more at home among the taverns, cook-shops and brothels of the slums; also, here whole streets flared up easily like torches, for the inner city was built of wood.

Have they gone? Have they really gone? The rain drizzles down unceasingly. The homeless are provisionally quartered in the market-halls and public buildings; towards noon the surviving Councillors assemble in the town hall. The session starts in a mood of depression among the heaped-up lumber, the deputy Senior Councillor delivers the mourning speech. A terrible fate, he says, has carried off a third of their colleagues, among them their venerated Aulus Egnatus, in whose place he inadequately stands today before this assembly. But, continues the speaker, whose venomous jealousy of old Egnatus was common knowledge, things might have been worse; fortunately the fury of the depraved had mainly ravaged the slums, raged among their equals, and relatively spared the better-class residential quarters; the time has come to take the necessary measures and, above all, to claim indemnity. The pathos of despair is gradually replaced by more material considerations. Measures must be taken, a loan negotiated, the city must bring forward her first option on unclaimed sites. A terrible slump in the price of land must be expected, steps against speculation taken. Noticeable gaps appear among the rows of benches; in the lobbies the Councillors secretly conclude the first land-deals.

Have they gone? Have they really gone?

Night falls, the rain has not ceased, the Voluntary Aid Brigade, young men of quality, leave the inner city in military formation. They meet a crowd of looters in chains who had lain drunk in the cellars of a villa, and so had missed the general departure; the criminals are torn from the militia and battered down then and there. A few suspicious characters seem to be hanging about the town hall—they are old servants and sedan-chair bearers waiting for their masters inside to come out—they are surrounded and killed; and the chase begins, the chase for those serfs who stayed in the city. They had stood by their masters, would have nothing to do with disorder and rebellion: now they pay for it. The slave-massacre lasts the whole night through, the rain does not stop either: in the morning the Aid, young men of quality, have slain more slaves than there were victims of the uprising.

Not many serfs in Nola survived the night. But those who did survive thought the dead deserved their fate, and cursed the man Spartacus who was responsible for their plight.

Fifteen thousand of them, on foot and on horseback, they moved north along the highway.

Behind them lie the ruins of the town Suessula, half her houses burnt, three thousand people killed; one night's work. At noon, when they marched to the North Gate through the stunned town, they beheld it again in the sun's harsh light. The black skeletons of houses were still smouldering, the smell of burnt flesh still flavoured the air; the streets which they had to pass were walled with corpses, piled there on both sides by unknown hands. The man with the fur-skin saw them lie as he rode slowly past them at the head of his horde; some clutched the air with their fingers, others showed their teeth, some were charred and black, dead women lay on their backs with shamelessly straddling thighs, children on their bellies, with dislocated limbs. This was the Sun State.

He did not know how it had happened, nor how it could have been prevented; all he knew was: it was Crixus's fault. Heavy in his saddle, the fat man rode his horse as though it were a mule, drowsing inscrutably. Ever since the battle on Vesuvius things had been like that. He, Spartacus, had divided up the horde into cohorts and regiments, had taught them the fashioning of weapons, had shaped an army out of a lump of clay. And Crixus had stood by, gloomy and dull-eyed, had neither interfered nor helped, had lain with women and men, and drowsed, murky and fathomless. Then came the night which saw the gates of Nola open to them, and Crixus woke up; his hour had come. The town of Nola was to have been their secure winter quarter; but the first night they spent within her walls had become the night of

Crixus, the night of the little fellow Castus and of his Hyaenas. The horde had been overcome as by poison or drunkenness, words had meant nothing to them. The prattle of the wag-headed Essene, all that talk of justice and goodwill, had gone with the wind like chaff, gone with the hot wind that bore the odour of the burning towns. And under their ruins lay buried the Sun State.

What had he done wrong, what had he omitted, to allow the horde to wriggle from his hold, so that his words meant nothing to them? He had walked the straight road, evil past behind and goal in front, had turned neither left nor right. Or was this the very error, to walk the straight and direct road—was it necessary to make detours, to walk the crooked roads?

He tore the reins round and rode back, along the silent column of the horde. Crixus turned his head, glanced lazily after him, trotted on, his immobile buttocks heavy on the horse which he rode as though it were a mule. He was probably dreaming of Alexandria.

But the horde, marching along the highway with equanimity, saw Spartacus ride past, stiff and upright on his horse, his face very lean now, his eyes sunken and listless. His lips had grown stern and thin, his eyes narrow; there was no more good-nature in his face. The men turned as he rode past them through the dust, they signalled each other; they sighed, partly with compunction and partly with grief that Spartacus should be so sternly unreasonable. What did he want of them? Had they offended him by settling accounts with the masters and slave-drivers? If we do not kill them, they will kill us. Had they not spared all serfs who took their part, had they not even taken them along?

What did the man Spartacus want, why was he cross with them? By all the frowning gods, what were they, after all? Were they bandits—or were they pious pilgrims, a travelling sect of fools?

Twenty thousand of them, on foot and on horseback, they moved north along the highway.

The third town, now a heap of smoking ruins, which lay behind them, had been called Calatia. She had offered no resistance whatever. As under an evil spell her gates had opened, and she gave herself up, trembling and moaning, as life gives itself up to death. Those who lived within her walls had hoped for deliverance by Roman troops; but the troops did not come. Some had prayed for mercy; but there was no mercy for them. For death knows neither mercy nor forbearance nor justice; he is Death. And only those escaped him who became murderers themselves and thus fraternised with Death.

Rain flogged the land of Campania and dribbled turbid streams over the Appian Way. It fell from the clouds to water crops, scrub roofs and windows clean—and died, sizzling in blackened debris and sticky blood. It was the end of the land Campania, she was overwhelmed by a horde of demons, many thousands of them, who crushed her marrow and stamped from town to town, a baneful curse.

Rain flogged the Appian Way. Over its large, shining stone blocks, between its sloping sides, the horde marched to the north, a train many miles long. The vanguard first, with its broad shields, javelins and swords, each cohort led by a captain: the gladiators. They were flanked by cavalry: the Syrians and the Lucanian shepherds. After them the guards in heavy armour, arms and legs clad in mail: the servants of Fannius. Behind them the endless, wild, crawling mass of people without proper arms brandishing clubs, axes, scythes, cudgels—bare-footed, limping, swearing, singing, ragged. Behind them the camp-following: mules and ox-carts, booty and baggage, women, children, cripples, beggars and whores.

The vicious shaggy dogs of the Lucanian shepherds, half wolves, grown plump on the flesh of the dead, ran yelping along the slave train.

They had come down from Mount Vesuvius to found the Sun State, had sown fire and reaped ashes.

Now they were marching towards the town Capua.

4

THE TIDES OF CAPUA

Capua resisted.

Nola, Suessula, Calatia had surrendered, Spartacus's message had penetrated their entrenchments, the serfs had opened the gates, and the walls had crumbled without a struggle and without siege machines. But Capua resisted.

Strange things had happened in the city of Capua.

The first to bring the news of Nola's downfall to Capua was the impresario Rufus. Rufus arrived alone on a sweat-drenched horse without servants or luggage; he looked so harassed and woebegone that the city guards would at first not let him pass. He went straight to his friend Lentulus's house, had a bath, and conferred with him for some time. He had gained several hours' start over the official couriers of the Senate and the messengers of the big Trading Companies. The report of Nola's fall was graver news than a dozen bulletins from the Asiatic front. It was the signal for civil war. Verily, the fate of the Roman Republic was in the balance; the breath of history blew through Lentulus's spacious bathroom. The two men in their bathrobes felt it fan their brows and decided to buy corn, without delay and at any price.

Together they took the necessary steps—a matter of several hours; after which they went to see the First Urban Councillor in order to inform him of what had happened.

Meanwhile the first rumours of the burning and destruction of Nola had found their way into the town; the populace crammed the fish market and balsam market, in the covered walks, public

116

halls and baths they stood and talked of the event. They formed groups, argued and gesticulated; some of them openly professed their delight, others shook their heads without succeeding to hide a certain amount of secret satisfaction. This feeling of general content soon burst out into exclamations of open triumph and, although its cause varied with everybody, it was blended into one common emotion as more and more people thronged the streets. Crowds caused obstruction in Capua when the Slave Army was still miles away.

The pettifogger and orator Fulvius, notorious for the rebellious speeches he gave daily in the lobby of the steambaths, was later to write a treatise which summarised the reasons for this turbulent unrest. It was never published and its title read:

ON THE CAUSES OF THE SERFS' AND COMMON PEOPLE'S EXULTATION AT THE NEWS OF THE GLADIATOR AND BRIGAND-CHIEF SPARTACUS HAVING CONQUERED THE CITY OF NOLA.

Those favoured with insight into the people's mentality, said this treatise, were able to distinguish the following motives in the riots of Capua: Firstly, malignant joy, for the cities of Capua and Nola had never got on too well. Secondly, local pride, for the said man Spartacus had, in a manner of speaking, begun his career in the town Capua. Thirdly, fourthly and fifthly, the serfs and common people had lived in such acute misery in the blessed town Capua, in consequence of the soaring prices, bad unemployment and worse arrogance of the nobility, as to receive with glad excitement any event which promised a change of conditions, no matter in what direction; for they could lose nothing but their chains. Why then—thus closed the unpublished treatise whose author was eventually to join the bandits, discourse with an Essene skilled in divinity, and die next to him on a cross before the argument's conclusion—why then should the common people of Capua not audibly express its joyous excitement, or violent triumph, for that matter?

When Rufus and the games-director came to speak to him, the First Councillor had already heard the news. In frigid courtesy he listened to the impresario who had insisted on entering his house without appointment at such an unusual hour, and whom he heartily disliked on account of his memories of a certain play called *Bucco the Peasant*.

But when Rufus overreached himself by alleging that danger actually threatened the town of Capua itself, the Councillor could not but smile a benign patrician smile at this upstart's exaggerations, and dampen his meddlesome zeal with the hint that the Magistrate would know when to take requisite steps. Thus the audience ended, and the Councillor was about to discharge the shrugging impresario with a few reserved words of thanks— Lentulus had only tacitly attended, as he still felt gauche and shy in the presence of aristocrats—when confused noise from the streets poured into the room.

First there were isolated cries as from afar, then came the approaching footfall of a tumultuous crowd; and immediately after, the street was flooded with people whose simmering mumble broke through the window.

The Councillor paled, he interrupted his farewells to Rufus, and the three men went to the window. Below in the street, a fat and sweating individual with the bearing of a navvy from the Oscian quarter had mounted one of those wooden wine barrels invariably rallying to join any riot. The man on the barrel addressed a speech to the Urban Councillor, punctuated by applause. The speaker showed himself brief and to the point: he said the politics and misery of Capua were raising such malevolent odours that the stink of the Slave Legion could be no worse; in other words, the Urban Councillor should open the gates to Spartacus.

The crowd roared approbation, the Councillor withdrew from the window. At that very time looting occurred already in the western suburbs.

One week later the Slave Army reached Capua, found the gates barred and the town's inhabitants, free citizens and serfs, united against them in flaming enthusiasm.

Strange things had come to pass in the town Capua. How had it come about, that total change in the people's mood, a few days only after it had demanded that the gates be thrown open, and had longed for Spartacus its deliverer?

How had it come about, their barring the gates and marching to man the walls in flaming enthusiasm—the serfs to defend their bondage, the wretched to guard their misery, the hungry to risk life and limb for the growling of their guts?

A certain pettifogger and rhetorician whom they had nearly killed for his remaining outside the great patriotic upheaval—his name was Fulvius and his fate the cross—went home that day and took in his hand a quill pen, intending to write down what things had come to pass in the city of Capua, and why they had happened. He was a lawyer as well as an author, knew of the wiles and intricacies of the human soul, knew its greed and its serene want of reason. He wrote his treatise in his hovel of an attic on the fifth floor of a tenement-house by the fish market. Above his shaky desk stretched the wooden cross-beam which supported the roof, so that he was forced to write in a permanently stooping position. Whenever, struck by a happy idea, he started up, his head would bang against the massive beam; the author Fulvius had to pay with a bump on his skull for every lucid thought. The atmosphere in the attic was compact with the stench of rotting fish, and the window let in the buzz of the martial crowd on the ramparts and in the streets.

The first part of the treatise, dealing with the original enthusiasm for Spartacus and its causes, was finished, he was now about to embark on the second part: the sudden hostility with which the slaves of Capua now reacted against the Slave Army; and this was far more difficult. He wrote down the title of this second part:

ON THE CAUSES WHICH INDUCE MAN TO ACT CONTRARY TO HIS OWN INTERESTS.

But as soon as he had written this, he realised that it was incorrect; he remembered the numerous suits he had conducted in his capacity of lawyer, recalled the tenacity and artfulness of his clients guarding their interests, ever ready to hound their neighbours to dungeon or scaffold for the sake of one stolen goat.

From below came the hubbub of a marching brigade. They were not soldiers, but slaves armed by their masters, now off to the ramparts to fight Spartacus—to fight in serene enthusiasm, for their tormentors and against their equals. He crossed out his heading and wrote underneath:

ON THE CAUSES WHICH INDUCE MAN TO ACT CONTRARY TO THE INTERESTS OF OTHERS WHEN ISOLATED, AND TO ACT CONTRARY TO HIS OWN INTERESTS WHEN ASSOCIATED IN GROUPS OR CROWDS.

A long while he brooded over this first phrase, but nothing more occurred to him. He had often thought about what made man act contrary to his interests where great issues were concerned, whereas he guarded his advantage with so much cunning and obstinacy when small matters were at stake. But the many warlike noises from the streets saddened him, and the enthusiasm of these poor fools who were ready to receive their deliverers with javelins and boiling tar, this intense ardour choked his thoughts. He left his work—many eventful months were to go by before he took it up again, although it was never completely finished—and went down into the streets.

Speakers stood everywhere; those who were not speaking listened and applauded. There was much fellow-feeling and elation; Fulvius made a mental note that in times like these man was driven by an urge constantly to speak and hear the same speeches over and over: he evidently does not trust his own feelings, does not believe they will thrive and last, without being watered with permanent reiteration.

Speakers stood on every corner, friends of the people, all of them progressively minded men. They reported atrocities as committed under Spartacus, related how a certain Castus and his infamous Hyaenas murdered and ravished—and what they said was true. They praised peace and praised order—and most of them were honest in doing so. They spoke of approaching Land Reform, and almost believed their own talk. They spoke of the burnt-down houses of Nola, Suessula and Calatia, and were honestly shocked. They spoke of the resistance which united all Capua, poor and rich, masters and slaves, in one common fold, and felt uplifted. They were neither members of the nobility nor of the Sulla-Party, they were democrats, oppositionals, friends of the people; they did not lie. Every word they uttered was plain, sensible and well-intentioned. They poured forth their arguments, their little, rounded, agreeable truths, like so much petty coin. The people believed them; and did not notice that they concealed the one great dreadful truth: that of mankind being still divided into masters and slaves. Only the author Fulvius knew it; many bumps grew on his head, the sun stung at him, the unreasonableness of mankind pained him, he possessed the great truth and carried it about with him, but no one wanted to partake of it.

.   .   .   .   .

The tide had turned in Capua. The friends of the people spoke at once in every street, on every market place, in every public hall; no Senate had appointed and no party paid them, yet there they were, doing their duty. They were patriotic. They warned the serfs and common people of those foolish, misguided affairs, rebellion and civil war. They restored the people's faith in the Republic and in the great community of Roman citizens. They won the hearts of the serfs with the tidings that the City Council would arm them as a sign of confidence. Thus the slave would have the chance of defending his master and demonstrating that he deserved to be a member of Rome's great family. For, whether sheltered by palace or hut, whether clad in white toga or the worthy chains of honest work, they were all children to the Roman she-wolf and they all drank from her teats the milk of human law, order and civic reason.

Feeling ran high among the lower classes and the slaves. All of yesterday's vile emotions, all the baser instincts of hunger and bitterness, were forgotten. They waved flags and rattled spears. The serfs of the town especially were intoxicated with joy after the Council had really distributed arms among them and thus— though only for the time being and revocably—raised them to the rank of free and martial citizens of Rome.

The little lawyer with the indented skull who edged round the streets, alone with his misery and his truth, later observed in his diary: 'They disarm the slaves by pressing swords into their fists —so terribly blind are those for ever forced to gaze at light only from out of darkness.'

But the present demanded no such aphorisms, nor was there a demand for rumours which professed to know that the Democratic Party's whole patriotic passion had been engineered by their mortal foes, the aristocrats and members of the City Council, by the agency of a certain Lentulus Batuatus, a gladiator-dealer and former electioneering-hog of Rome. People who spread such rumours were wretched agitators and kill-joys; several were un-masked as agents of Spartacus. They were torn from their pulpits and beaten to death.

5

DETOUR

Nola, Suessula, Calatia had surrendered to Spartacus. Capua resisted.

The tents of the bandits formed a sweeping circle around the entrenched city. Like a calamitous swarm of locusts they stood in the wet southern cornfields, within the blessed Campanian wheat. The grey soaked tents grew up the sloping vineyards of Mount Tifata; irregular huddles, overtaking each other like flights of steps, lay scattered between desolate manors and denuded marble terraces. From both sides they pushed towards the banks of the Volturnus which had transgressed the dams and flushed squalid mire into the sea. Grey and haughty behind the veils of rain were the walls of the town Capua.

On the summit of Mount Tifata stood the Temple of Diana, surrounded by fastidious arcades and arbours; the dwelling of the fifty virginal priestesses. They had trodden their grapes without outside help, had watched over the wine's fermenting in the dusky vaults, and were often drunken and had loved each other sinfully; no man had been allowed to approach their sacred grounds. Now the gladiators Spartacus and Crixus and the other commanders of the Slave Legion sat in the Convent of Diana, had conferences and quarrels and never reached an agreement.

They had no siege machines. As before, they had sent secret emissaries into the town, to summon the slaves into the great brotherhood of a Sun State. But the Sun State lay buried under the black ruins of Nola and Calatia, and the mouthpieces were murdered behind the walls without ceremony or repercussions.

And the slaves of Capua stood on the ramparts, they had received arms from those inside and aimed them at those outside; they rattled their spears and would have nothing of a Sun State.

In the dainty Temple of Diana, still flavoured with the fragrance of the priestesses' ointments and perfumes, the gladiators sat and quarrelled; only Spartacus and Crixus were silent. Gradually the camp had split into two sections, one who sided with Crixus and the little fellow, and the majority who stuck to Spartacus. A reaction of sobriety had gradually developed among them, they said the Hyaenas' insane raging against the conquered towns was the reason for the slaves of Capua not wanting anything to do with them. Great depression haunted the horde; here they had rain, dripping tents, annoyance and disappointment; over there was the town, dry and warm, filled with the smells of cook-shops and the spices of the markets, Italy's most luscious city after Rome. And the odious little fellow with his Hyaenas had spoilt all that for them.

On the twelfth day of the siege of Capua, when the rain waned, a delegate from the town came to the slave camp. Escorted by two of Fannius's servants he walked his tent-edged way, turned not left nor right, leaned heavily on his stick, an old man, and trudged up the slope of Mount Tifata. He caused sensation, amazement and laughter: here was a delegate from the city of Capua who came to negotiate, it was all just like a regular war. Fannius's servants, silent and bull-necked, walked at his side; when the old man stopped to get his breath they also stood, gazing straight in front, and silently continued walking uphill, with the laughter and cat-calls from the camp behind them.

Spartacus sat on a couch in the sanctuary of the Diana Temple and waited for the delegate. The servants of Fannius ushered the delegate in and withdrew. Spartacus had risen; he recognised the old man at once and smiled—it was the first smile which had moved his features since the burning of Nola.

'Nicos,' he said, gently and kindly, 'how is the master, Nicos?'

The aged servant was quiet, cleared his throat, receded the slightest fraction.

'I stand here in the name of the City Council of Capua.'

'Aye,' said Spartacus, and the smile tinged his voice. 'You're quite an official personage, my father. You see, neither of us would have thought it, would we?'

He broke off because the other said nothing and remained frigidly in the doorway. But he himself was overrun by memories: the large, square yard of the gladiator-school, the dormitories with their tepid stable-atmosphere, even the fraternal proximity of death, had all taken on the intimate warmth of things past.

'Are you a civil serf now?' Spartacus asked. 'A municipal slave? Did the master sell you away?'

'I have been freed,' said Nicos dryly. 'I am an official of the Council of Capua with all civic rights, delegated to negotiate with the rebels and their leader Spartacus the raising of the siege.'

He babbles like a man in second childhood, thought Spartacus, he has learnt it all by heart. He is Nicos, a good man whom I used to call father, now here he stands and prattles, and no warmth goes out from him. You cannot look to anybody for anything. 'In the old days you used to talk differently to me,' he said and sat down on the couch again.

'In the old days,' said Nicos, 'you and me talked differently. Your face has changed, I would not have known you. The way of evil has made your features sharp and bitter, your eyes, too, are not what they used to be. I am here to negotiate your raising the siege.'

'Negotiate, then,' said Spartacus and smiled.

The old man was silent.

'The way of evil,' said Spartacus again, 'what do you know of it? For forty years you worked in service and waited to be freed, and now you're old. What do you know of Ways?'

'It is the way of evil you have taken,' said Nicos. 'The way of disruption. Look,' he said and sat down on the couch beside Spartacus, 'look, I am old and righteous and arid. Forty years I served for freedom, now I'm old, and it is an arid freedom. But when you say: "what do you know of it?" then I say I know more than you. Maybe we'll talk of it some day, but the hour is not yet come.'

'I didn't know you were that much of a philosopher, Nicos,' said Spartacus. 'Last time I saw you, at the tavern by the Appian Way, you just kept on saying all of us would be hanged. And very nearly you came with us.'

'I was misguided, but only for a moment,' said the old man. 'But I didn't come with you because I knew you would walk the way of evil and of disruption. Nola, Suessula, Calatia—what did your friends do to them! Our tidy country—you poured blood all over it. You sowed fire and reaped black cinders. Everybody says so.'

'The serfs were all for us,' said Spartacus. 'They opened the gates to us in Nola, Suessula, Calatia.'

'Nobody is for you in Capua,' said the old man. 'People opened their gates to you and you destroyed their towns, now no one will open any gates to you. Disorderly folk you are, and everybody knows it, and everybody has turned against you.'

Spartacus was silent.

'Nicos,' he said after a pause. 'The orders were good ones, but there are many men who won't obey. There are some like that among us. How can one separate them off? How can one sift the chaff from the wheat? That is what you should tell me.'

'That I don't know,' said the old man. And, with senile stubbornness: 'It is the evil way,' he repeated.

Spartacus rose, he smiled no longer. Cool and gloomy was the sacred chamber. 'Be quiet,' he said. 'I know more about the Way Nicos. I recognised it on Vesuvius, between the clouds I met. There I found an old man, wiser than you; I used to call you Father, but he called me the Son of man. And this old one—he knew the Way and told me its name.'

'What kind of a name?' asked Nicos.

'The Sun State,' said Spartacus after a pause. 'That is the name of the way.'

'I don't know about that,' said Nicos. 'All I know about is Nola, Suessula and Calatia.'

'That is true,' said Spartacus, 'but those are the little truths. And those who recognise only the little truths are very foolish, you have just taught me that.'

The old man could find no retort, he was tired and did not understand the talk of Spartacus, who had become a stranger to him. The servants of Fannius came and brought some torches. The chamber was suddenly high and light, the stone walls moved apart.

Old Nicos straightened his gouty limbs, brittle and stiff, he stood before the man who sat there, whom he had cherished as a son and who now was a brigand.

'The Council of the City of Capua,' said old Nicos, 'warns you to raise the siege. The City of Capua has enough grain in her

granaries and wine in her cellars to wait until the rain has
softened your bones and washed you to hell—thus speaks the
Council. The morale of our soldiers is excellent, and you have no
siege machines. The Council warns you that it does not mind
your camping before our good walls and trampling our cornfields—for again Rome is swamped with corn from overseas, and
we would not mind a boom in wheat. Still, the Council has reasons of its own to wish you would camp elsewhere—in Samnium,
maybe, or Lucania. The Council is of the opinion that this wish
should correspond with your own interests.'

'You babble and keep on babbling,' said Spartacus. 'Old you
are, and not ashamed. I wanted you to tell me how to sort chaff
from wheat, for that is advice we greatly need. We have two
kinds of people with us, and they should be separated: one kind
carry the great, just wrath in their hearts, the others have only
their bellies full with petty greed. They are the ones responsible
for Nola, Suessula, and Calatia. We'll have to part from them.
That will be very difficult; we shall have to find wily means and
ways and walk the crooked roads to rid ourselves of them. Before,
I didn't know all this so clearly, but since you came and babbled
nonsense—since then I do know. Have you any more to say?'

'I have,' said Nicos. 'In fact, the essential point is yet to come.
The City Council warns you that Praetor Caius Varinius has
been sent out by the Roman Senate with two full-strength
Legions, to clean up in Campania. In a few days' time his warlike
army will arrive and destroy you.'

The scolding, querulous voice of the old man subsided, he
waited eagerly for the effect of his announcement. He saw the
man with the fur-skin raise his head; his face, beloved of the old
man, which had relaxed in conversation, closed up again, grew
hard and rigid. '. . . He's got something after all,' thought old
Nicos, and for the first time regarded his mission as uncomfortable
and the man in front of him as an enemy. '. . . He is the warlord
and I negotiate with him in the name of the city,' thought Nicos
and made his arid body stiffen.

'Say that again, and more in detail,' said Spartacus.

The torches cast deep shadows over his face, which looked as
though carved inanimately; his eyes held no friendliness. The old
man had to blink his eyes and try to look past him to left and to
right. 'I'm old,' Nicos thought, 'what do I know of him? They

are hard and angry folk.' He wanted to get it all over and done with.

'Two full-strength Legions under Praetor Varinius,' he repeated, 'twelve thousand men. His Legati are Cosinius and Caius Furius. His army is composed of veterans from Lucullus's campaign, and fresh recruits. They are taking their time, but they'll be here before a week has gone, or even sooner. Don't you believe me?'

'If only he would start talking again,' thought Nicos. 'I have never known him like this. He's got something after all.'

Spartacus answered at last, but his eyes did not waver from Nicos's face:

'If it is the truth, then why should you tell me? If an army is on its way to finish us, why then do you warn us? Explain it.'

'I can explain it,' said the old man eagerly and confidentially. 'I told you, the Council has its reasons. The Council of Capua is not interested in being again saved by the soldiers sent by the Senate of Rome. Whenever the Legions of Rome have saved Capua, Capua has had to foot the bill. It was like that with Hannibal and in the Confederate Wars. It's no pleasure, thus speaks the Council of Capua, to be rescued by Rome.'

He was silent and relieved, for he had spoken the truth, and he saw that the man in the fur-skin believed him. Spartacus deliberated for some time:

'Your Councillors are clever men,' he said at last. 'They ask Rome for soldiers to fight us and at the same time they warn us against Rome; they do know the crooked roads well. We will have to learn from you people.'

Nicos said nothing and waited. The man with the fur-skin was more than ever a stranger to him.

'It's getting late,' said Spartacus. 'Do you want to stay the night with us, or do you want to go back?'

'I want to go back,' said the old man.

Already in the doorway and between the quiet bull-necks with their torches, he heard once more the voice of the man in the fur-skin calling him. He knew that maybe he heard it for the last time.

'Come with us, Nicos,' said the voice. 'You're weary, my father, and there are woods in Lucania'.

Nicos hesitated for an instant, stood, a small, brittle old man, between the bull-necked servants. He did not turn. 'No,' he said. He started forward, the servants with him, their torches held high above his head.

Once more the voice came after him, Nicos could hear the smile it held:

'Is it the way of evil, my father?'

He did not turn and did not answer, walked into the darkness, old and puny under the raised torches of the servants.

'Farewell, Father,' came the voice from the temple for the last time. But he was out of earshot.

Again the meeting had brought no result.

Again they had sat around the long stone table, hour after hour, had talked and silently hated each other. Crixus had glumly looked at them and drowsed; Castus the little fellow had played with his necklace, in a piercing voice he had called Varinius's legions a fairy-tale, had demanded attack on Rome. The spokesman of Fannius's servants had got on everybody's nerves with his bull-necked righteousness. The bullet-headed sage had uttered nebulous quotations, and no one knew what he meant. Oenomaus had said nothing and looked at the man with the fur-skin. The blue vein on his forehead swelled with mute excitement, and his shy delicacy had got equally on their nerves. They talked; each one rehashed his already hackneyed pronouncements, knowing that the others were not listening. The stale solemnity of the council weighed heavily on them; they knew one another very well indeed—and knew more than they wished to say or hear at a council. When, in non-committal colloquy, they called a spade a spade, they understood each other; but although, assembled here, they were but the sum of colloquies materialised, the debate was by no means the sum of their conversations, only their ceremoniously vapid surface. They knew this, and knew also of the silent contempt of the man with the fur-skin, whose eyes trekked after their rotating words, eyes which had lost all kindliness. They knew he had detached himself and in his detachment had outgrown them, but he did not speak the relieving word and did not strike the relieving blow; he let them drag on in harness, with ten thousand more hanging in harness, or were they twenty thousand now, stuck fast in mud and stubbles and drenched tents. And those who were to lead them all tugged each in an opposite direction, knowing of their own hatred's impotence, and yet imprisoned by it, and could not advance one single step.

And over there stood the walls of Capua, petrified derision. And on the wall stood the slaves of Capua and aimed their weapons at them—for their hopes lay burnt and smothered and buried in Nola, Suessula, Calatia. All this they knew well and stared in impotent fury at Castus and the Hyaenas. But Castus played smilingly with his necklace; there were many in the camp who listened only to him, there were more than a thousand of them, they lived apart and dressed in rags, stank of blood-lust and lechery.

The gladiators sat around the long stone table, talked, argued and got drunk. Later they rose and went away, tramped back through the wet stubblefields, and again they had decided nothing.

When they had gone, Spartacus detained the man with the bullet-head.

'Sit down and listen,' he said, surly.

The Essene wagged his head and looked at him. 'For that which will now be you'll need other advisers,' he said and raised his shoulders as though chilled.

Spartacus paid no attention to him and continued:

'Rome is sending Varinius and twelve thousand soldiers. We must go to Lucania, the land of mountains and herdsmen, so that we may live in peace and according to our ideas. But there are some among us who won't obey orders. They have spoilt the Sun State for us, and they don't want to go to Lucania either. They want to go and meet Varinius who will destroy them—if we let them go alone.'

The Essene shrugged his shoulders and drew his head in like a tortoise. The sun shone straight at Spartacus's face; he screwed up his eyes, which made him look still more harsh and surly.

'If we let them go alone . . .' Spartacus repeated. 'It all depends on us. They are fools. If we let them, they'll run straight into their own destruction: Varinius will butcher them like lambs. And we will be rid of them. Then they cannot hamper us any longer, and will not prevent our building the Sun State. And now you say nothing.'

The Essene was silent. He did not even wag his head. He sat quite still.

'Now you say nothing,' said Spartacus. 'But in the old days, in the clouds on the mountains, you had a lot to say. Lots of nice, rounded words came from your lips. But the road you showed me did not lead to the Sun State but to Nola, Suessula and Calatia. You have nothing to say, but I must keep to the road now. There were too many among us who would not obey orders; now we must send them to Varinius so that he may butcher them like sheep, sacrifices for your Sun State. For we must destroy them else they destroy us. It is true, they are the chaff and we the wheat, but the same stalk bore us and it goes against the grain of nature, this thing we must do now.'

The Essene sat quite still. Small and shrivelled, he sat opposite Spartacus and marvelled, as old Nicos had marvelled, at how strange to him this man had become, and thought, just as old Nicos had thought: 'They are gladiators, hard, angry men. What do I know of them?' Then he resumed shaking his head, and after a while he said:

'God created the world in five days, and he was in too much of a hurry. Many things went wrong in all his hurry, and when he arrived at the making of man on the sixth day, he was irritable and tired perhaps, and burdened man with curses. But the worst curse of all is that he must tread the evil road for the sake of the good and right, that he must make detours and walk crookedly so that he may reach the straight goal. And I tell you: for that which is to be now you need other advisers.'

Spartacus did not look up when the Essene went through the door; he sat straddling by the table and drank great gurgling draughts from the wine jug. The Essene turned round once more, looked into the other's broad, bony face, and it was as though he were seeing this man for the first time that night.

Spartacus went on drinking until night fell. When night had fallen, Crixus came, and they talked. They did not talk much for they were troubled by each knowing the other's thoughts. That which was now to be, had matured inside them as the sap underneath the bark rises slowly from the roots, and when at last their words came out they fell like over-ripe fruit. So now it had been said and decided; and it had grown quite dark. They ate their meal and when they lay on the rugs, satisfied, with the table rising up between them, both thought of the night on Vesuvius, the night after the victory, spent in the tent of Praetor Clodius Glaber. That night, too, Crixus had reached over the table-top, groped for a chunk of meat, placed it in his mouth, smacked, wiped the grease off his fingers on the mat. Both knew they thought the same, and they were silent. Spartacus lay on his back, arms crossed behind his neck; Crixus smacked his lips, took a gulp from the jug, dug bits of food from between his teeth with the tip of his tongue. They did not look at each other.

Later Castus, the little fellow, came into the sanctuary and announced that the camp was stirred by a rumour which said the gladiators had quarrelled, and that the horde was going to split up. Castus remained in the doorway, screwed up his eyes to get used to the gloom, and smiled uneasily. He received no answer at all; so he went on standing where he was and played with his thin necklace.

Crixus took a gulp, spat it out. 'Why do you come here and tell tales?' he said to the little fellow.

Castus smiled:

'I thought you might be interested.'

'We're not interested,' said Crixus. He turned to Spartacus and asked: 'Are we interested?'

'No,' said Spartacus. 'It has been decided that part of us depart tomorrow to meet Varinius,' he said to the little fellow; it was meant to sound quite casual.

'Really,' said the little fellow. 'Part of us?'

'Yes,' said Spartacus. 'Those who wish it.'

They were silent, all three. Castus was still in the doorway, came no closer.

'And the others?' he asked.

'We will go to Lucania. To the mountains and herdsmen,' said Spartacus.

Again there was a pause, a longer one this time. From somewhere came the bellow of a mule, it took some time to calm down. After that all was quiet.

At last the little fellow asked the darkness in the direction of Crixus:

'Are you going to Lucania too?'

Crixus did not reply. Spartacus said:

'No, he's going with you.'

The little fellow smiled with relief and began to fondle his necklace again. 'To Rome, eh?' he said. 'Mirmillo, we're going to Rome.'

Crixus gulped more wine from the jug.

'To Rome,' he said. 'Or somewhere else,' he said.

Castus could not see him, but he knew that the fish-eyes of Crixus gazed at him muddily out of the heavy seal's-head.

The little fellow felt a slight shudder; he thought of the next night, when he would again have to share his mattress with Crixus.

6

THE ADVENTURES
OF FULVIUS THE LAWYER

During the night the pettifogger and author Fulvius had succeeded in scrambling over the city wall and so escaping from the stupid patriots of the town Capua. It had been quite an acrobatic feat, and the little lawyer with his bald, bumpy head and short-sighted eyes could not think how he had managed it. He plumped into the sodden clayey soil outside the wall, and there he sat for a while. Before him stretched the set stubble-fields, the broad, empty strip of No Man's Land, and somewhere beyond must be the camp of the besiegers. Nothing could be seen of it, and all one heard was the steady hiss and rustle of the rain: quite possibly the bandits, their camp, and the great Spartacus, Leader of the Oppressed, Liberator of the Wretched, did not exist at all. There he sat in the squelchy clay, the wet soaking through his clothes, and he felt the clammy cold of the wall against his back. The wall was very high; when he twisted his face to look up at it, it lowered slantingly down at him. On the wall-top a sentry marched up and down, a Parthian slave, his torso bare, a spear in his hand. Fulvius came to the conclusion that he could not go on sitting there like that for ever; only now he became aware of how miserably wet he was behind. After he had taken a few steps the hoarse, throaty cry of the Parthian stopped him. Fulvius stood and looked up. He saw the silhouette of the sentry craning forward, its knee bent slightly, the spear held ready to throw.

'Where are you going?' shouted the Parthian in his hoarse, throaty voice.

'Just over there,' the lawyer shouted back with the greatest

unmilitary unconcern he could muster. But at the same time he
knew well that his answer could not satisfy the warlike silhouette,
and he began to run out into the rain, and as soon as he ran he
got frightened. The Parthian above him yelled shrilly, and his
spear came whizzing past and splashed into the slush not far
from its running target.

'Well, you won't get that back,' thought the lawyer in all his
panting terror, 'what a pointless profession.'

They were probably shooting arrows after him now, but after
twenty paces rain and darkness had swallowed him up. He
stumbled down a little declivity beyond which olive trees strained
their twisted branches. He stopped, breathless, and clung to a tree.

'For whose sake is that foreigner throwing darts at me?' he
thought. 'For whose sake, pray, is he being heroic?'

He resolved to delve more into this question—when he wrote
his great chronicle of the Slave Campaign. Heroism was obviously the outcome of man's physical ineptitude in attempting to
assert Idea against the alien forces and menaces of Nature. But
that a slave should place his heroism at the disposal of his master
without either threat or ideal did still seem strange.

He tried to get his bearings and squelched on through rain and
mud. It was a wretchedly dark night with no moon or stars—one
could scarcely see more than twenty paces ahead into the sheet of
rain. He would use his wanderings in this boundless yet clinging
darkness as the starting point of his chronicle.

Suddenly a voice hailed him out of the rain. He stopped and
peered short-sightedly. That must be already a sentry of the
Slave Army—but at this moment it seemed quite incredible that
there should be such a thing. The rain poured down and the
voice called out a second time. He must answer, otherwise he
might yet be erroneously killed by those he wished to join. They
probably had a password—the foolish city of Capua resounded
with passwords.

'Spartacus,' shouted the lawyer hoarsely into the rushing patter
of the rain. It seemed the most likely word. Then he was seized
by a fit of coughing.

The sentry came closer, he materialised fitfully out of the
gloom, a dripping hood over his head.

'What are you yelling "Spartacus" for?' asked the sentry in a
broad Lucanian accent, and showed his teeth in surprise.

The lawyer was still coughing—he must have caught cold—and said:

'I am the lawyer and author Fulvius of Capua. Where is your army?'

'Where?' the sentry asked, still more astounded. 'Why, here—everywhere. What do you want?'

It was only then the lawyer noticed the blurred outlines of some tents not thirty paces from him. Apparently they had been there all along, and they looked utterly deserted. True, what was it he wanted with those deserted tents?

'I am an author,' he said and started coughing again. 'I want to go to Spartacus so that I can write a chronicle of your campaign.'

'Write our chronicle?' The brigand-sentry had large protruding horsy teeth which shone yellow through the dark; he looked much more peaceable than the spear-throwing Parthian on the wall. 'Whatever for?'

'Such things are written down so that later on people may know what happened.'

'But does that interest them?' asked the guard. He appeared to feel quite comfortable in the rain and gloom, and inclined to carry on a lengthy conversation.

'Everybody is interested in what happened before he was born,' said the lawyer.

'That's true,' said Hermios the shepherd, 'sometimes I wonder about such things myself. But how can you find out?'

'It is written down in books,' said the lawyer.

'Do you write books?'

'I am going to write the history of your campaign,' said the lawyer and coughed.

'But that isn't interesting,' said the sentry. 'You just go on from town to town and from one scrap to another.'

'A hundred years from now,' recited the lawyer, for he had long prepared himself for a conversation of this sort, 'what am I saying, a thousand years hence, the world will still talk of Spartacus who freed the slaves of Rome.' He had another fit of coughing; rain oozed from his clothes.

'Just fancy, what things you do think of,' said the sentry admiringly. 'But maybe you're wet and would like some hot wine?'

'Ah yes,' the lawyer said and blinked longingly in the direction of the deserted tents. 'That would be nice.'

'Come along then.' And the sentry strode off through the rain. The lawyer hurried after him. 'And who'll stand guard now?' he asked as they approached the canvas town.

'Someone else, maybe,' the shepherd answered him. 'But, you know, when it rains like this nobody is likely to come anyway.'

The news of the army's splitting in two had caused great uproar in the camp. Not that it had come entirely unexpectedly; things had obviously been coming to a head; had they not squabbled and cursed and repeated every day that 'things couldn't go on like this'? But now, when things really would not go on, when the breach was complete and beyond repeal, the camp was confused with wonder and incredulous astonishment.

The servants of Fannius had borne the message, had publicly announced the Decision with their loud, resounding voices and unmoved mien from every corner of the camp. The Slave Army, thus they cried out with memorised words, was to split up into two parties according to the opposed opinions in the camp and the decision of the gladiators' council. One party would march to the north and Rome in accordance with their own desire and the intention of engaging in battle with the approaching Legions. Those would be led by the gladiators Crixus and Castus from the institute of Lentulus Batuatus of Capua. Whosoever honestly and thoroughly agreed with this troop should join them.

But all those who thought differently and were resolved to follow Spartacus, would leave for Lucania, led by him to the land of mountains and herdsmen. For it was Spartacus's will and opinion that further strife and plunder and robbery should be avoided. Instead, the great summons should go round among all the serfs and mean shepherds of southern Italy, in the cities and fields and in the mountains, so that they might unite in the great confederation of justice and goodwill, promised from the beginning of time, from the days of Saturn, and whose name was to be 'the Sun State'. But Spartacus, they proclaimed, demanded of all those who would follow him on the southward march unconditional obedience and submission to his authority.

This then Fannius's servants had announced in the first hour after sunset, and at once people flocked together with much noise and indecision. But in all confusion and variance of conviction, the grave and secret intention of Spartacus began to be carried out: chaff and wheat were about to separate.

When the lawyer and author Fulvius and his guide, Hermios the shepherd, rain-soaked to the skin, walked into the camp, they met arguing clusters everywhere. None paid any attention to them.

'Is it always so with you people here?' asked Fulvius.

'No,' said the shepherd, 'it's because of the separation.' He sighed dejectedly. 'We're in a bad way, brother, we are. We're unreasonable like sheep and lambs: some run hither, others thither, you can't keep them together.'

'What is the reason for the quarrel?' asked the lawyer.

'I couldn't tell you, brother,' sighed the shepherd. 'It's always been like this, even inside Vesuvius when we had nothing to eat and brawled all the time. There are wicked men among us who side with Castus and the Hyaenas. But now maybe we'll get rid of them, and the Romans will mow them down. Then we'll have peace.'

During his last words Zozimos the rhetorician had caught up with them between the tents; he was still wearing his tattered, grimy toga and flapped his sleeves excitedly:

'What are you saying!' he yelled at Hermios and tugged at his arm, trying to keep up with him. 'We'll have peace, you say, while they send our brethren, ignorant of danger as they are, to certain death: crafty and unscrupulous, factious policy . . . And who is this?' he asked, interrupting himself to stare mistrustfully at the shivering lawyer.

'He's caught cold and must get some hot wine,' explained Hermios. 'He's a deserter from Capua. He writes books,' he added in a mysterious whisper.

'The philosopher Zozimos salutes you, colleague,' said the rhetorician, jovial and acidulous. He made a sweeping gesture and the wet toga slapped his belt.

But Fulvius could not return the introduction as he was seized by coughing again. The pompous man inspired in him a mixture of repugnance and pity. In spite of all his grand antics the man looked wasted and sad, like one who has taken many beatings in his time.

'Come on in,' said Hermios to his protégé. 'Here lives a friend of mine, an old man. You must crawl in under the canvas, take care you don't soil your knees.'

Old Vibius sat leaning against the canvas wall, immobile in the light of an oil wick; one could not make out whether he was sleeping or meditating. It was pleasantly musty and dusky inside, the rain rapped on the canvas roof—a well-meaning rain, this, which did not make them wet.

'Here's a guess for you,' said Hermios in a loud voice, for the old man had lately grown hard of hearing. 'He comes from Capua.'

'I salute you,' said the old man. Zozimos flustered about in a corner.

'You too, Zozimos,' said the old man.

The lawyer bowed to the lord of the tent, and they all sat down on the ground sheet.

'He'd like some hot wine,' said the shepherd. 'He's caught a cold.'

Old Vibius fetched a rag-swathed jug and handed it to the lawyer who took a deep draught, coughed, took another. The rich Falernian, brewed with cinnamon and cloves, raised a motley fog inside him. He was happy in this tent, he had arrived.

For a while they said nothing and passed the jug round. Then the old man asked:

'What are people in Capua saying?'

'People in Capua,' said the lawyer and rubbed the bumps on his head, 'are very foolish, my father. They act contrary to their own interests, praise their tormentors and persecute their deliverers with hate and pointed Parthian spears. And, strangely enough, their stupidity is an honest one. They lust after humiliation, and they honestly and worthily despise the new, the foreign and the elevating. Can you tell me why this is so? I used to know the answer, but it has slipped my mind.'

He drank from the jug and tossed his head back as he always did on the track of an idea; he was astonished that the beam over his head was missing. He stroked his pate, but no new bump had sprung up. It disturbed him—he did not know what it was, but he missed something and it disturbed him. He drank another mouthful. Even his sorrow for the foolishness of mankind was now transfigured by musty dusk, like the air inside the tent.

'That question is as old as the world itself,' said Old Vibius.

'The explanation is lack of reason,' said Zozimos the rhetorician, 'as well as the lacking ability to be inspired by the higher things of life.'

'Empty words,' said the old man. 'No man lives wholly without inspiration, else his sap would dry up and his soul wither away.'

'Quite true,' said the lawyer. 'You just go to Capua and have a look at the flag-waving and spear-shaking, and see whether you won't find it difficult not to catch the smallpox of inspired enthusiasm.'

'That's what I said,' replied Zozimos. 'They're always inspired by the wrong thing.'

'But maybe to them it's the right thing,' said Hermios and bared his yellow teeth in embarrassment, startled by his own audacity.

'No,' said the old man. 'It's a wicked inspiredness that makes the calf fraternise with the butcher and the slave with his master.' He broke off and took several small, shaky gulps from the jug. The others were silent too. The rain beat a tattoo on the tent-roof; a well-meaning rain which stayed outside and left them dry; and a multitude of unassorted thoughts drummed in the lawyer's brain, abloom with red Falernian brewed with cloves and cinnamon. Hermios had dropped asleep, he slept sitting and nodding as shepherds will. Old Vibius, too, had closed his eyes. He sat, dried-out like a swaddled corpse from Egypt, and meditated; only the tattered rhetorician was still fluttering with his toga-ends and, by way of tying up loose ends of talk, he repeated Old Vibius's last words:

'Yes, that is bad,' he said, 'when calf and butcher fraternise. But it is worse when the calves send each other to the slaughter. And that's what this Spartacus of ours is doing right now.'

At the mention of the name the shepherd's eyes opened. 'Are you slandering him again, Zozimos?' he spluttered, drunk with sleep and wine.

'This man Spartacus has grown very clever lately,' persisted the rhetorician, 'too clever for my liking. He who yearns for the Sun State and the Realm of Goodwill should not use political wiles and sinister factious tricks.'

The lawyer was abruptly sobered, he remembered the chronicle of the campaign he was set on writing.

'The law of detours,' he said. 'No one can act outside it. Every one with a goal in front is forced on to its baleful track.'

'Detours, you say? He sends them the shortest road to Death without their knowing it,' insisted Zozimos. 'True, Castus and their men committed outrages, but was it their fault? No one is guilty if fate makes him a sinner by sowing the greed of long privation in his innards. They are still our brethren. Are you asleep, Vibius?'

But it appeared that the old man was wide awake and had probably merely been meditating. 'I hear your words and disapprove of them,' he said and drank the jug's last drops. 'He who aims to plant a garden must start out by weeding.'

'All right,' said Zozimos who seemed honestly grieved because of the split-up. 'But you can't treat men like cabbages. I'd like to see whether your wisdom would persist if they sent your son to the slaughter because his stomach growled too loudly.'

'But every one is to choose as he likes,' said the shepherd. 'That's what Fannius's servants announced to all and sundry.'

'All right,' said Zozimos. 'But did they disclose the strength of Varinius's army, towards whom they are to march? Two full-strength Legions, twelve thousand soldiers, they kept silence about that, didn't they? Those poor scatterbrains know of rumours only and they don't bother their heads and think they'll finish off Varinius as easily as they did Clodius Glaber. Yet they are only three thousand men, those greedy and unreasonable ones who will migrate north, badly armed and undisciplined. They'll all be killed, and this Spartacus cunningly lets them run to their deaths in order to be rid of them: "everyone as he likes", indeed.'

'But their leaders,' asked the lawyer, 'those Crixus and Castus or whoever they are, surely they know all about it?'

'Castus is a little fellow, he's only cheeky and knows nothing of warfare, no more than do the rest. But with Crixus it's a different matter,' said Zozimos in the confidentially lowered tones of camp gossip. 'Nobody can make him out. He is sure to know the strength of the Roman army just as well as Spartacus himself, sure to know what the whole thing means—and yet he does not know it. He isn't a one to calculate. He doesn't know himself what it is he wants. Or perhaps that which will be is all right

with him. He hates Spartacus and yet he loves him like a brother.
It is said that the day they escaped from Lentulus in Capua, they
had been destined to duel in the arena. Thus one would have
killed the other, and they knew it all the time, do you understand? And they know it still. It is difficult to explain. They're
sure to have got used to it in those days that one would have to
kill the other in order to live on. And perhaps neither has yet got
used to it that they are both alive. When Crixus goes off now and
parts from Spartacus, perhaps that which will be suits him.
Perhaps both feel that it must be that way, and perhaps they do
not even know why. But that is difficult to explain.'

'The things you do think of,' said the shepherd, puzzled.

Fulvius, too, looked in surprise at the pompous rhetorician.
Had he underestimated the man with the fanciful toga? Again he
was struck with the whipped expression in his lean face, that trait
which excited his pity. How hard a task to read people, thought
the lawyer. He himself had once seen better days: and despite his
earnest endeavours to do so he had never been able to imagine
the mental make-up of a man who had never seen better days.

'. . . And it is still a dastardly thing to do,' said Zozimos, again
in his swaggering, quarrelsome tones. 'Your Spartacus is acting
in a most dastardly manner. You talk of detours which lead to the
goal? Dirty detours, they are. Dangerous detours, I say to you,
for you never know where all those detours will land you in the
end. Many a man has strutted the road of tyranny, at the outset
solely with the purpose of serving his lofty ideals, and in the end
the road alone made him carry on. Just remember the dictatorship of the People's Friend Marius, and what became of it. Just
think . . .'

'What are you drivelling there, of dictatorship and tyranny?'
Fulvius interrupted the speaker who waved his arms excitedly.

'I am speaking of the laws of detours,' shrieked Zozimos
sneeringly, his voice breaking. 'Such detours, you know, have the
most disagreeable laws of their own. Did I mention dictatorship
and tyranny? You people started it with the Detours, and they
led us on to Dictatorship and Tyranny.'

'Ho-ho,' laughed the shepherd and showed his teeth, 'do you
think Spartacus will become a tyrant?'

'I am indeed talking of Spartacus, O you leader of sheep and
lambs.'

'You're like a bleating sheep yourself,' replied the shepherd with a friendly grin and decided to go on sleeping. But this time he curled up on the ground and pulled his knees up to his belly.

Fulvius was tired of dispute; he had gathered enough material to start his chronicle of the Slave Campaign. From afar he had imagined revolution more straightforward and less interlaced—but he should have known that everything looked different close to. All these confused and involved and so far impenetrable matters had to be thought about.

He said good night to the others and stretched out on the ground along the tent wall, his head next to the coarse boots of the shepherd. They smelled strongly but not repellently. The rain drummed evenly and lullingly against the canvas. Had it really all happened this very night, had he run through the rain with the spear thrown by the martial silhouette splashing into the mud beside him? Behold, then, and see how some hours in life widen and fill up to the brim, whereas others, hollow, puny beads strung up on the necklace of Time, are insubstantial and dissolve into the past.

THE CHRONICLE
OF FULVIUS THE LAWYER

T HE chronicle of the lawyer Fulvius from Capua was to have a
strange fate. It was never completed, just as the story it told was
never completed. But those rolls of parchment on which it was
recorded were preserved for a time, evoking a feeling of strange
respect based on hatred, perplexity and horror. They were passed
on with many intentional mutilations and supplements, and were
forgotten and brought to light again whenever history herself
seemed to make an effort to complete what she had begun at that
time.

Thus it happened that the lawyer Fulvius was in a way to be
proved right in what he had said that night to the shepherd, soaking wet and with chattering teeth: that people are interested in
what happened in the world before they were born. Incidentally,
he only half believed in his own words, as man only half believes
that anything real can happen in the world before his birth or
after his death, which amount to the same. Those who were to
read his book in after days were to him of as dim and not very
concrete reality as he to them; only exhaustive abstract reflection
could convince them of each other's existence. Although, as a
further reflection might show, no more than sixty-seven genera-
tions form that chain which links narrator and listeners in the
void of time; no more than sixty-seven times have the fathers had
to make way for their sons and fade before them, to contribute
their share to the great pallid reality of the Past.

Yet Fulvius from the start felt urged to correct a little here and
there the story he recorded. By no means did he intend to

embellish and trim history with his partly intended and partly
involuntary corrections; he was no aesthete—had he been an
aesthete he would never have jumped off the wall of Capua. In
fact, it was for him a question of arranging history like a lucid
manuscript, as it were, and smoothing out the confused crinkles
and creases crushed into its pages by chance and hazard. In this
respect he took his work very seriously, and strictly watched over
details with the jealousy of craftsmanship; although he faced the
point of writing as such with the same scepticism as he confronted the rhetorician Zozimos's outpourings. For all this toga-
flapping invocation of the centuries seemed to him but wan
consolation for the one reality of history: that of you yourself
enduring it.

The strange fate of his rolled-up parchment book, written with
much meditative sighing and pate-stroking, seemed indeed to
confirm this sober conception of his. For, as has been said already, they were dragged again and again from the paleness of
the Past, deliberately supplemented and newly read, whenever
an attempt was made at long last to conclude in reality the in-
complete story itself. They were no beginnings, these parchment
scrolls of the Capuan lawyer Fulvius; their content had long lain
etched in the common people's age-old longing for lost justice;
and they were passed on from hand to hand, like rods in a wrathful relay race which began in primeval gloom, when the luxuriant
god of agriculture and towns murdered the god of deserts and
herdsmen.

FROM THE CHRONICLE OF FULVIUS THE LAWYER OF CAPUA

1.... And when the city of Capua resisted and declined to open
her gates to Spartacus, discord arose in the camp of the rebels.
Spartacus, convinced that inexperienced audacity would be no
match for the strategy of a trained army, intended to avoid
approaching C. Varinius and his forces by withdrawing from the
open fields of Campania and retreating to Lucania, whose mountains would offer cover and shelter and whose herdsmen's fraternal
disposition towards them promised the slaves at once security and
the realisation of their proud plans. The Gauls, on the other
hand, and all those whose objectives were murder, looting, and
the gain of baser advantages, set forth with their commanders
Castus and Crixus and marched to meet the Romans. To many

the latter course may appear more manly and upright than the prudent attitude of Spartacus, but prey to this error will fall only he who is uninformed of the fact that a mean disposition couples with courage as frequently as with cowardice. Now, these apostates, numbering on three thousand, left the communal camp in the course of an extremely rainy night, in the first hour after sunset. Those remaining faithful to Spartacus stood before their tents and observed the disorderly crowd deserting the camp with much noise and manifold bold jests. Many shouts of derision and abuse were also directed at those standing before their tents, but the latter suffered it in silence, although no previous agreement to this effect had been made. Folk with eyes to see realised that these villains were approaching evil fate; for their armament was deficient and by no means equal to a combat with Roman mercenaries, in other words, warriors of a professional nature. The attire of these people consisted of malodorous rags and un-tanned wolves'-hides, as though they wished to proclaim by appearances alone their diversity from the other insurgents; for so flagrant a disregard of body could testify to nothing but a meritless disposition.

However, their departure was conducted with an air most confident, and when they had assembled at the extreme borders of the camp, they set out on their march with blasts of loud and strident music, as produced by their short flutes, which resembled the sort of whistles used by the Etrurian shepherds. They also had a timbal whose noisome and, as some thought, baleful drumming was still audible when eyes could no longer accompany the train in the vast area of mire which surrounds the river Volturnus at that time of year.

When after a while distance smothered even this powerful kettle-drum, those remaining behind fell victims to great dejection.

2. It had been the intention of Spartacus to decamp as well, with his trusty comrades, whose number is estimated as approximately eighteen thousand, and go to Lucania, immediately after the departure of the former mob, whose fate in all probability he foresaw. But his departure was delayed for several days, as preparations for the ordered migration of so great a multitude required sensible plans and suitable measures. Also, the insurgents were consumed with the desire to learn of their erstwhile comrades' fate, before they themselves turned south.

The news came to them on the morning of the third day. At this time, then, two wretched fugitives reached the camp from different directions, neither knowing of the other, but their message was the same. Soon intelligence spread to the effect that Castus and his fellows had been attacked and defeated by the Romans, not far to the north of the Volturnus. Two thousand of them fell there and then, but Castus was assassinated by his own men during their communal flight through the swamps. For the Roman Legionaries did in no way regard the fight as proper battle, rather they had chased their scattered, desperate adversaries singly into the swamps, after the manner of beast-baiting in the arena, firing them with the cries of jocular encouragement customary at the circus games. This, then, had roused the fugitives to such fury as to induce them to slay their own commanders whom they felt to be responsible for their misfortune, after which they hurled themselves with bared talons at their mailed pursuers, whose conviction of dealing not with warlike adversaries but with savage beasts, was thus strengthened. Close on five hundred of the survivors, so the escaped men concluded their tale, had been captured and nailed to the trees of the Appian Way; an evil death at this time of year, as the falling rains would tease the thirsting and delay his decease.

The news of the horrible end meted out to the deserters who had departed but three days ago with the sounds of shrill flutes, sped rapidly through the camp which up till then had held many a hesitating, dubious man. Even those who had reproached the man Spartacus for being either unable or unwilling to prevent their former comrades' perdition, now held their tongues. All and sundry obeyed his commands, and they withdrew to the Apennines.

3. It had been the intention of Spartacus to discard warfare and to instigate a great fraternisation of all shepherds, field-labourers and serfs of the south, as well as setting up a confederation of cities in accordance with the ideals of justice and goodwill. This lofty plan of his was, at least partly, realised at the city of Thurium, but only after he had vanquished first the minor leaders of the Roman army and later Varinius himself. For the Romans could not but realise that a community of a nature as planned by Spartacus would menace, even without warlike intentions, by virtue of its mere existence, the stability of their own Republic, erected on a fundament of usury and injustice as it was; just as health and disease cannot inhabit the same body at once, and either sickness or health will finally reign supreme. For disease cherishes a great longing for health, and health is the righteousness of body. Therefore disease will never be content with the

possession of the one organ already overcome, but will in fact send its noxious juices into all remaining organs.

Therefore the Praetor Varinius delayed not for one moment the pursuit of the rebels and entangled the latter in months of campaigning. Thus Spartacus was driven to make many a detour not helpful to his aims.

4. Now, in the course of this campaign a wealth of incidents occurred as produced by chance and circumstance. It is well-known that chance invariably abounds wherever man's scheming reason has left interstices; and the fact that every war is based on force rather than scheming reason explains why chance is so predominant in this particular sphere. Therefore it would be idle to record all the minute incidents involved in this lengthy campaign; the very fact that it ended with the complete victory of the slaves should offer sufficient proof of the planning ingenuity of Spartacus.

An excellent example of this congenital gift was exhibited by him when, soon after the commencement of the campaign, the insurgents had fallen into an extremely difficult position and appeared already to be lost. Varinius had succeeded in entrapping them in a barren district between the mountains and the strait bay of Tarentum. Lucania has a number of such waste stretches of land, where mountains consist of bare rock, and the soil of nothing but white chalk. Therefore the Donotrians or Greeks, who formerly populated the said country, bestowed on it the name of 'Lucania', which, in their tongue, means: the white country.

Now, as the insurgents were surrounded at all sides and had consumed their provisions, their fate seemed sealed, and again pusillanimity and depression held sway over them. Many recalled the days of misery they had spent in the crater of Mount Vesuvius, and marvelled at fate's well-known inclination to repeat conditions and reconstruct the same collection of circumstances, as though it had forgotten the first time to lead events to a conclusion, and desired to make up for this neglect in the above manner. But again Spartacus found an appropriate way out: he made it possible for all his men to slink out of the camp at the time of the second night-watch. One trumpeter was left behind to give the usual intermittent signal-blasts, and they had tied corpses to stakes driven in the ground at moderate intervals around the camp, which gave an appearance of sentries standing guard. Mighty bonfires burned all over the camp and illuminated the dead sentries, and from time to time the trumpet signalled to the deserted tents. In such manner the enemy was completely deceived, and Spartacus, aided by dark night, led his horde through a narrow pass in which they would have perished had they been discovered.

5. However, to ascribe to *one* man's ingenuity the great and memorable success of this untrained horde over the Legions of Rome would be idle, for the insurrection owed its success in equal measure to the fact that the peasants and herdsmen of South Italy were in agreement with the Slaves, whose plight the former regarded as their own.

For, the same lawlessness and unjust order which had aided rebellion in Campania, also flourished in Bruttium and Lucania. The Roman gentry shared the possession of mountains and valley between them and owned each several thousand slaves who were obliged to guard their enormous herds. These slaves were marked with brands, and allowed to roam free over fields and mountains. Here these unfortunate creatures sought to make up for the bad food and clothing they received by plundering, and unfortunately their masters' parsimony not only permitted, but encouraged them to lessen in this way the expenditure on their keep. These branded slaves, then, fell upon the peasant cabins at night with ever-waxing temerity, ate, drank and did as they pleased, so that in all these particular districts in Italy there was practically no security whatsoever. These men were strong and powerfully built, accustomed to spend their days and nights in the open air, no matter how rough the weather. Knotty, wedge-shaped sticks or hobnailed poles served them as weapons. Their attire consisted of wolf's-skins or boar's-hides, which is why they looked so much like Barbarian warriors. In addition they were ever accompanied by huge and extremely fierce sheepdogs.

These semi-savage shepherds had long spread all over the mountains; no one dared to charge them with their crimes, as the majority of their masters were Roman Knights who themselves administered justice. This shows the state the southern districts of Italy were in. And when Spartacus and his Slave Legion appeared there and sent out heralds and emissaries who called on the common people to join the Lucanian Brotherhood, the entire country rose up against the Romans.

6. The contents of these heralds' and emissaries' proclamations were about as follows:

First they denounced the effeminacy and tyranny of those who grew fat on the labour of so many unfortunate wretches while treating the same with so rigorous a severity. 'What could be easier,' they cried, 'than to suppress these effeminates whose strength has been sapped by wanton luxury, people who at their banquets boast gold and silver plate, which should be used in divine service alone? What can they do against us and without us, if you will make use of your physical superiority, for who else but we, trusty comrades, is entitled to rule, as we surpass them in strength and in number? Nature has bestowed, not wealth on one man and poverty on the other, but strength and talents; the abhorred difference between master and slave was not instituted by Her, no more than She wanted the strong to serve the weak, the Few to rule the Many. Let us obey her law then, it is the only just law, the law valid for all times and all lands. Let your name be celebrated for ever by all mankind, by restoring their natural claim to the wretched who all groan under the same yoke that weighs you down. Well, then, brothers, do not hesitate; courage wanes with lengthy consideration. The righteously resolved have a world to win!'

7. The Praetor Varinius already mourned the loss of his two legati Furius and Cosinius. His forces also were seriously weakened by these losses, and the commander-in-chief was deprived of the soldiers' confidence, as they held him responsible for their plight. A part of the army suffered from the customary autumn sickness, and the remainder showed themselves as refractory as they were cowardly.

Now Spartacus believed himself ready to hold his own against the Romans in open battle. So far they had conducted but raids and scattered skirmish; but this time the rebels marched to meet Varinius in regular order and, for the greater part, well-equipped. In fact, all the arms they had so far either taken in booty, purchased or forged, had been sufficient only for part of the horde. The rest were armed with sickles, pitchforks, rakes, flails, axes and other agricultural implements, or, where even these were lacking, with sharpened stakes, long poles, wedges and other wooden tools which, after having been hardened in fire, had been pointed and sharpened to suit requirement, and were as serviceable as iron weapons. Hatred for their erstwhile tormentors made the rebels ingenious: many brought with them their own fetters in order to forge arrowheads and swords from them.

The Romans also were now of more elated spirits. The Roman Senate had granted Varinius reinforcements. These fresh troops, who thought as meanly of Spartacus and his forces as did the capital, talked of the former only in the most disparaging manner called them lowly rabble who ought to be shackled again, and thought nothing could be easier than to disperse this gang of brigands. Their bragging had at least the effect of shaming the old troops' cowardice and inspiring them with fresh courage. Their impetuosity, however, decreased as they gradually made their adversaries' acquaintance. The Praetor himself was circumspect rather than bold and did not lead them into battle before they had accustomed themselves to the sight of their terrible foe.

8. Shortly before engaging in battle, Spartacus's forces had also received great exhortation, for that Gallic gladiator Crixus, believed to have fallen in the swamps in the company of the other deserters, had unexpectedly found his way back to the camp. This almost miraculous escape of the powerful leader who enjoyed a respect among the insurgents second only to that enjoyed by Spartacus, excited them greatly, especially because the surly man denied reply to any questions about his fate, so that many were induced to regard this as a real miracle and omen.
The battle took place in the extreme south of the Italian peninsula, in the neighbourhood of the town Thurii or Thurium, by the banks of the river Sybaris.

9. Before engaging in battle, Spartacus, in order to act the part of a true war-lord, addressed his comrades and admonished them to behave like genuine warriors: now, so he said, the actual war was about to commence, whose finish would be decided in this their first battle; they would either be vanquished or forced to withstand the powers that be with continuous victories, as there was no other possible alternative between this and an ignominious death. Loud acclamations answered him.
Now, hardly did the Roman cohorts behold their opponents approaching from the opposite bank, when a strange change came over their own ranks. At first they were startled, and marched more slowly when the gladiators raised their terrible war-cries; they grew ever more doubtful and quiet, so that they started the battle without that boastful demeanour with which they had demanded it.
At the same instant when the Roman front line came to blows with the enemy, Crixus who, unknown to the Romans, had crossed the river upstream some time ago and hidden in the deep bed of a creek, at the head of his Gauls, fell with great suddenness upon the Roman second line. The Romans fled in so general a

confusion as to leave behind their commander-in-chief. He and his horse crashed to the ground, and the Praetor was very nearly taken prisoner by the gladiators. His white steed, his purple gown, his fasces, in other words, all the insignia of his office, fell into the victor's hands, and the latter brought them back triumphantly to their leader.

From now on Spartacus himself was seen to be clothed and invested with the insignia of a Roman Imperator; and the inhabitants of the provinces regarded them with reverence as he came parading them, with the fasces borne in front of him.

10. Here it might be requisite to say a few words on origin and character of this unusual man whom fate thus seemed to offer the key to the future. Spartacus came from a tribe of nomadic herdsmen and had been born at a small village in Thrace from which he derived his name. Originally without education, a particular gift enabled him to absorb and transform into actions the ideas and doctrines with which his singular fate brought him in contact. Rays of light from opposite directions mingle in a piece of glass of convex cut and leave the same in the shape of one single, very hot beam; in a like manner the aims and thoughts of men concentrated in Spartacus: this gift also enabled him to master ever heavier tasks set to him by fate, as the power of his personality grew in proportion with the increasing size and weight of the tasks.

11. Spartacus's development, then, soon made him rise above the level of his companions, and made him realise that the latter acted like blind men or ignorant beasts who must be watched and forcibly guided upon the right road. The various incidents in the siege of Capua, and the experience gained in the lengthy campaign against Varinius, which loaded the responsibility for the lives of so many on to his shoulders, had robbed him of his initial affability and induced him to take many a measure which made him appear hard and haughty in the eyes of his men.

But he who guides the blind may not shirk a reputation of haughtiness. He must harden himself against their sufferings, be deaf to their cries. For he must defend their interests against their own want of reason, which attitude will often force him to inflict measures which may appear as arbitrary as they are difficult to understand. He will have to make detours whose point is lost on others; for he alone can see, while they are blind.

12. Thus ended the first campaign; and now the Romans had a

chance to see whether they had judged wisely when they first regarded this rebellion as a momentary disturbance instigated by a handful of bandits.

All Southern Italy was now in the possession of the brotherhood of insurgents, and all was now prepared for their realising their plans and erecting a commonwealth of justice and goodwill, which they intended to name 'The Sun State'.

BOOK THREE

THE SUN STATE

I

HEGIO, A CITIZEN
OF THURIUM THE CITY

HEGIO, a citizen of Thurium, awoke before sunrise in the consciousness that this was the break of a festive day; the house was to be decorated with sprigs and garlands to celebrate the entry of the Prince of Thrace, the new Hannibal. He resolved to go to the vineyards early to fetch vines and mistletoe. He glanced at his sleeping wife, slipped into his sandals, ascended to the flat roof of his house.

As yet it was still dark and chilly, but the sea, which formed a steep vault over his horizon, was already beginning to change colour. Hegio loved this hour dearly, loved its brilliance and its scents. The breath of the sea under the sunny blast of noon differed from its tang at night. At night it smelled of a crystalline coolness, like salt and stars; the morning gave it the fragrance of seaweed, and noon the stench of fish and steaming decay. He sniffed the sea air and looked across at the mountains—first to the north where, if he was not mistaken, traces of snow whitened the peaks of the Lucanian Apennines, though it might have been the morning mist. Then he turned south, to the distant, violet bulk of Sila—he was a shareholder of the Pitch and Resin Production Company there. In fallow magnificence the mountains encircled the valley of the Crathis, but the east was guarded by the dome of sea whose extreme brim began at last to smoulder, and broke into flame under the touch of the still invisible disk.

One cock crowed, then a second; finally all the cocks of Thurium competed eagerly in their officious, alarmist cheers to the rising sun. Hegio decided that only Roman fowls could crow so discordantly and vaingloriously; in his Attic homeland even the cocks' voices held more harmony.

> 'Harsh to the ear of the Greek sounds the
> crow of the cocks of Latinum,'

he improvised.

He did not like the Romans. He did not despise them, but their coarse conceit and pressing self-assurance made him smile. Efficiency oozed out of their every pore. Despite this he, Hegio, a man who traced his ancestors back to the Trojan warriors, had married a Roman. She lay downstairs on the ample marriage bed, moist with the sweat of a satisfied matron in her slumber. Her satisfaction was not derived from the festive day which would bring Spartacus, Thracian Prince, second Hannibal—but from the fact that he, Hegio, descendant of Trojan heroes, had done his conjugal duty last night after a long interval.

The sea, now fully ablaze, sent its smell into his nostrils; he seemed at once boyish and senile in his eagerness. He liked the mild moon-scents better than the blaze of sun, and the cool charm of Greek youths gave him more delight than did the dutiful pleasures of procreation with his matron.

What was the use? The entire Attic family tree was not worth five vines, nor a single share of the Pitch and Resin Production Company. At the foot of the pale mountain lay the ruins of legendary Sybaris, the fairy-city, built by his ancestors in ancient times. Greek colonists of refined customs, with silver coins, harps, and a knowledge of geometry, they had owned the whole strip of South Italian coast, and that at a time when the Latins, clad in bearskins, were busy climbing trees.

The cocks crowed a second time, and someone came puffing up the stairs. It was the matron.

'What are you doing on the roof so early in the morning?' she asked with that kindly sternness which is so suitable in the treatment of the very young and very old.

'I am looking, my dear, merely looking.' He did not mind being taken for a child or an aged man; the creased face on his lean body crumpled into boyishly sly wrinkles.

'What's there to look at?' the matron said disapprovingly. She yawned and stood by his side at the edge of the roof, her hand on his shoulder. That shoulder was boyish and bony; recollecting the events of the night she shivered pleasantly under the frost of dawn.

They gazed down at the town. She was still asleep, a large village of stone rather than a town, a white village of many pillars, lovely and very sad in her morning stillness. Her lanes twisted between the walls like dried-up creeks. The houses were flat-roofed and huddled confidently against the hillside. But on top of the hill the village grew into a proper town with wide, square-cut avenues, in her centre the market place and fountain. After Sybaris had been destroyed, Hippodamus, famed architect, had designed this heart of the city according to carefully drawn and coloured plans. Chalk-white houses stood between blue mountains and blue sea. Thus Thurium had been created, new city of the Sybarites, now very old as well. All the original families were very old; they had many ancestors and few children. They spoke a purer Greek than the Greeks themselves, now extinct everywhere except in Alexandria; they were descended from Trojan knights, or at least from that man Smyndirides whose bed was spoilt for him by a crumpled rose leaf beneath his sheet.

Now and then they married the daughters of the Roman colonists who had been forced on them by the Senate as a punishment for their siding with Hannibal and against Rome during the last Punic war. Those colonists had their own quarter north-east of the town, they multiplied rapidly, worked hard and well, and were heartily hated; it was said that they blew their noses on their elbows. They had had the presumption to re-name the town: 'Copia' was the name of the Roman quarter, the whole of Thurium was now supposed to bear that new name; all official documents called her thus. Naturally the old families persisted in calling their town by her proper name, Attica remained Attica, Thurium stayed Thurium. And naturally they were going to side with Spartacus, that new Hannibal, no matter whether he was Carthagian or Thracian; the main thing was that he knocked a few teeth out of those capable elbow-snufflers. The entire town looked forward to his entry with the joy of children or the aged.

The city awoke by degrees; the first few shepherds, unwashed early-birds, drove their sleep-warmed goats through the narrow alleys. The scattered goats' bells tingled absentmindedly, the shepherds whistled shrilly on their short flutes. The sea waved its morning fumes across the roof: seaweed and sands. Far away, on the fields by the hills, grazed herds of white buffalo; they mingled with the morning mist by the river, and the steers, white as chalky Lucania herself, stared with stiffly raised heads at the Apennines.

'Come and have breakfast,' said the matron.

Hegio smiled: 'I'm going to the river to fetch sprigs and leaves for the Entry.'

'Surely not before breakfast,' said the matron.

'I shall take the boys with me,' said Hegio, 'afterwards they can help us decorating.'

'The boys will stay here,' said the matron.

She was a colonist's daughter. The colonists were against the Thracian Prince. They went about with gloomy frowns on their hostile patriotic countenances. Perhaps thev were afraid.

'Then I'll have to go on my own,' said Hegio.

'In your nightdress?' asked the matron.

'I'll put something on. You'll see how many sprigs I shall bring home.'

He climbed down the stairs, the matron followed with slight snorts of irritation. Downstairs Publibor, the only slave of the household, brought the dog his breakfast.

'You're going with me to the river,' said Hegio to his slave. 'We're going to get sprigs and leaves. You're coming too,' he said to the dog, a calf-sized brute who pulled at his chain, yapping and howling.

They were off: Hegio came first, the slave a few paces behind; the dog frolicked in front, let them pass ahead, only to overtake them again at a furious rate. At the outskirts of the town where garden walls were no longer of stone but of sun-dried clay and dung, they encountered Tyndarus the greengrocer, who was pushing a cart laden with fresh lettuces and herbs to the city.

'Where to, so early?' asked the greengrocer.

'I, my slave and my dog are going to get leaves and sprigs for the entry of the Thracian Prince,' said Hegio.

'Between you and me,' said Tyndarus and propped his cart against a wall, 'I hear he hasn't much claim to any title. People say he used to be a gladiator and bandit, if not worse.'

'Nonsense,' said Hegio. 'There's always tittle-tattling about

those in power. At any rate, he struck Rome a whacking blow.
A second Hannibal, that's what he is, and anyhow, it is a pleasant
change.'

'Quite,' said the greengrocer who liked to keep in with everybody. 'But they do say he's going to give all slaves equal civic
rights, that he's going to rob people of their money and houses,
and that he'll turn everything topsy-turvy.'

'Nonsense,' said Hegio and turned to his young slave. 'Would
you like to leave service and lead a new life?'

'I would,' said Publibor.

'There, you see,' said the greengrocer and harnessed himself to
his cart again. 'It is a dangerous affair, I told you so.'

Hegio was enjoying himself. 'What cheek!' he said. 'Only
because the matron is a trifle strict and moody? I don't have an
easy time of it, either. Don't I treat you well?'

'You do.'

The boy looked at him seriously. He seemed to take everything
seriously. He had a serious face. Hegio had never noticed before
that he had a face at all. This made him thoughtful.

'Didn't I even permit you to join a cremation society?'

'You did.'

'He is in the same society as I,' said the greengrocer. 'We had a
general meeting the day before yesterday.'

'There you are,' said Hegio, surprised. 'Just like a free man.'

'It is my only privilege,' said Publibor.

'Your only one?' said Hegio, more surprised. 'Well yes, perhaps so, according to the law. But it is something. And I shall
leave you your freedom in my will. Do I live too long for your
liking?'

'You do, master.'

Hegio grinned, the greengrocer sighed:

'What did I tell you? I said this was dangerous. I should have
him whipped.'

'Is freedom of such importance to you, then?' said Hegio. 'If
you ask me, it's only an illusion. Didn't you admit just now that
you're having a good time with me?'

'I did.'

'You've saved money.'

'I have.'

'That's the worst of it,' said the greengrocer. 'In the old days that would have been impossible. Private property creates an appetite for more. I should take his savings away and have him flogged.'

'That might be an idea,' said Hegio, taking his departure. 'In the meantime we will go and get sprigs and leaves for the entry of the Prince of Thrace.'

When they had gathered enough vines and leafy branches they sat down near one of the grazing herds by the river Crathis. The dog was tired too, he lay on his belly, his front legs spaced out gracefully like those of the Sphinx of Thebes.

'Look here,' said Hegio to his slave. 'Here we sit, two people by a river, not far from stately mountains. Are you really waiting for my death?'

The youth looked at him and said:

'Are you really my lord, and am I really your property?'

'I'm afraid so,' said Hegio. 'It's a fact, from whatever angle you look at it. Even now, while we're alone together, sitting by a river with stately mountains before our eyes, even now you feel each of your words to be cheek and presumption, and I believe mine to be full of gracious condescension. Tell the truth: Isn't it so?'

'It is,' said the youth after a pause.

'Let us proceed then,' said Hegio. 'Anything that exists is real, you can't get round it. Here I sit in the sun and roast my back, you sit in the shade and freeze. True, it is an unjust division, but it happens to be so, and the gods must have had some idea at the back of their minds when they made it so. Had they thought of the reverse, the reverse it would have been. Reality is rather a forceful argument, don't you think?'

'I do,' said the slave. 'But if I gave you just a little push I should be sitting in the sun and you would be in the river, O master.'

'Why don't you do it, then?' asked Hegio smilingly. 'Do try. Or do you fear the whip?'

For the first time the boy averted his eyes. He said nothing.

'Well?' asked Hegio. 'Why don't you? Here we sit, two people by a river, and you are the stronger. If you kill me and run to the Thracian, you need not even fear punishment. Why don't you do it?'

The lad was silent and pulled out handfuls of grass, his eyes cast down.

'Right here the great Pythagoras taught that the rulers should receive divine adoration and the servants the treatment of cattle. Do you agree with that?'

'I do not,' said Publibor.

'In that case, why don't you throw me in the river, especially as nothing can happen to you if you do? Why don't you make use of your strength? Why does your soul feel shamed now, and why is mine filled with exalted emotion and condescension? Or is it not so?'

'It is,' said the slave. After a while he added:

'It is only habit.'

'Do you think so? Do you think the Thracian will import new habits? If he did, he would be greater than Hannibal. There is nothing greater than to change the habits of thought.'

'Yes,' said the slave.

'Where did you get all these thoughts, anyway?' asked Hegio. 'You've always been hard-working and dumb, I never noticed that you had a face, that you could smile. Maybe laugh—yes. But smile—tell me, do you know how that is done?'

The slave was silent. Hegio regarded him attentively, smiling the smile of children or aged ones.

'Are you wishing for my death now?' he asked. 'He who waits cannot smile. Look at those pebbles at the bottom of the river: the water is quite transparent, you can even see blades of grass down there. When the water brushes over the pebbles and grass, it gives the faintest humming sound. Can you see and hear such things?'

'I cannot, master. I never had time to lie in the grass.'

'Blind and deaf and gloomy you go through this world of ours, and you wait for my death, though I have eyes to see and know all of the many scents of the sea. That is the cause of your shame and the source of my smiling condescension. A man in misfortune is never lovable.'

The slave tore out bushels of grass. After a while he said:

'You said yourself I was the stronger.'

'Yes, but since when have you known that? It is not as obvious a thought as it seems to be. The matron has beaten you frequently, not very hard, it is true, but she did beat you, and it has never occurred to you that you were stronger than she.'

'It did not,' said the slave. And after a pause: 'That was habit.'

'And now? Has the Thracian suddenly informed you of your strength? People say his agents and emissaries are everywhere, inciting the serfs. Is that true?'

'It is.'

'And you believe in his teachings?'

'I do.'

'And do all of your kind believe in him?'

'Many.'

'Why not all of them?'

'The old habits are too strong.'

'What does he look like, that Slave-Hannibal of yours?'

'He wears the skin of a beast and rides a white horse, and a guard of strong men carries the fasces before him.'

'Just like the Roman Imperators, eh?'

'No, for his ensigns are not silver eagles, but broken chains.'

'An original idea,' said Hegio. 'I do believe both of us can safely expect some pleasant diversion. Don't you think so?'

'I do, master,' said the slave, gazing at him earnestly.

For a while they were silent, lay back on the grass and looked at the mountains that had shed their morning veils and enclosed the horizon with their naked, powerful blue. The sun had broken away from the sea, rose higher, warmed the air and sucked in the scent of morn in the fields. In the olive and lemon orchards people were bent on their work today as on all other days.

Before they started on their way home, Hegio said:

'It is strange to think that the Thracian will arrive this very day, that he will probably change everything, yet neither you nor I can really believe in it. It is the same as with war: everybody discusses it, some are for it, some against, but no one honestly believes that it will eventually materialise; and when it is really upon them, they are astounded that they were right. There is no surprise greater than that of the prophet whose prophecies come true. For there is a great laziness of habit in the thoughts of man, and a smiling voice deeply buried inside him, which whispers that Tomorrow will be just like Today and Yesterday. And, against his better judgment, he believes it. And that is really a mercy, for otherwise he could not live with the knowledge of his certain death.

'And now come on, let us go and decorate the house with these sprigs and leaves, so that we may greet the Prince of Thrace as is his due.'

2

THE ENTRY

THE sun rose higher, and the city was full of joyous activity; the citizens of Thurium adorned their houses with vines and leafy garlands. The houses were flat-roofed, and white like the chalky land Lucania herself. The descendants of Trojan warriors looked forward to this pleasant change in humdrum life, the Thracian Prince with the fur-skin. They shoved and jostled each other in the streets which were narrow and winding like the pebbly beds of dried-up creeks. The Roman colonists stood apart and scowled patriotically. Perhaps they were afraid.

Nor was the Council of Thurium entirely happy. True, this strange Imperator had struck Rome a whacking blow and they were pleased with him for that. They were less pleased with him in all other respects. He called himself 'Liberator of Slaves, Leader of the Oppressed'. You could, of course, interpret it symbolically, especially with reference to an alliance with the Greek cities of the south, groaning under Roman yoke; had not Thurium and the other South Italian cities once sided with Hannibal? But Hannibal had been a great general and a prince in his native country, whereas the less said the better about the antecedents of this man Spartacus. For, once you started saying things, you would have to admit that he was a Prince only by the grace of Thurium's Senate for reasons of urban self-respect: the descendants of Trojan warriors would hardly form an alliance with a vagabond gladiator. And form an alliance they must, else it would be the end of Thurium; to be quite honest, the Council of Thurium had been overjoyed and amazed when the gladiator did as much as enter negotiations. These negotiations had taken a rather strange course, as will be seen; but finally a treaty had been signed whose main points were as follows:

Outside the city of Thurium, in the plain which stretched between the rivers Sybaris and Crathis, protected by mountains on one side and by sea on the other, the Slave Army will erect its permanent camp and build a city with the name of 'Sun City'. The Corporation of Thurium will cede to the Thracian Prince all fields and pastureland in the said area; likewise the Corporation shall undertake the maintenance of the Slave Army until the latter is provided with food by the produce of its own soil. Spartacus's soldiers, on the other hand, after the Army's ceremonial entry into Thurium—which is to be of merely symbolical import—will molest the city no further. Spartacus, furthermore, shall undertake to cease to incite the slaves of Thurium as soon as the alliance is settled.

The delegates of Spartacus had met this last demand with fierce opposition, but in the end they granted it.

'They must be coming any minute now,' said the greengrocer Tyndarus to Hegio, his neighbour in the queue.

They had been waiting for over an hour, wedged in the convivial crowd which hemmed the wide avenue that led to the agora, waiting for the Entry of the Thracian Prince. Over their heads garlands and leafy branches hung down the white housefronts; over the houses a chubby blazing sun stood in the skies; and across the roofs the sea blew its midday breath, reeking of fish and decay. The citizens of Thurium were waiting and gossiping and pressing together and sweating a great deal.

But when the sun stood vertically above them, the great moment came at last.

'They're coming!' cried Hegio's little boy, 'they're coming!'

They were really coming, a slow cloud of dust at the other end of the avenue. The queuing citizens giggled, groaned, pushed one another, surged forward. Blustering officials pushed them back, straightened the queue. They were coming.

'How many are they?' asked Tyndarus the greengrocer and craned his neck.

'A hundred thousand,' screamed the little boy who was very

well-informed, 'a hundred thousand robbers, and they'll turn everything upside-down.'

'As many as that can't possibly pass here,' said Tyndarus. 'They would clog up the whole city.'

'Only their show-troops will take part in the Entry,' said his left-hand neighbour. 'The rest will have to stay outside. That's how it has been settled.'

'Settled, indeed,' sighed Tyndarus. 'And you think they'll abide by it?'

The cloud of dust was coming closer. The citizens of Thurium in their queues craned their necks. Most of them were dressed in white; the young women wore thin, airy garments. The self-important officials scurried back and forth.

By and by they could distinguish the foremost ranks of the Slave Army, two rows of ten strong-boned, bull-necked men, their heavy boots spurring the dust. They did not glance to right or left, Thurium did not interest them; they carried the fasces and, in the place of the axes, broken iron chains.

A few of the citizens in their queues cheered tentatively but the majority did not follow suit. The citizens were painfully surprised, the grave and dingy procession disappointed them.

And now, right behind the stamping men, they beheld the white horse, and on it the Thracian Prince in his fur-skin. By his side rode a fat man with a doleful face and dangling moustaches. He rode his horse as though it were a mule. The purple velum was borne in front of them.

The citizens knew what was expected of them: they yelled, waved their hands and flapped their sleeves. The Imperator acknowledged their cheers, raised his arm in salute; his horse began to amble; but he did not smile and his eyes were not friendly. Still, the citizens liked him quite well; they were not exactly bowled over, but they quite liked him. The fat man with the moustaches they liked far less. He did not even acknowledge their cheering, looked straight ahead with unfocused eyes. The queue on his side receded a little as he passed. His face impressed itself on their memories far deeper than the Imperator's; years later they would still remember it.

They would speak of Spartacus as 'the Prince' or 'the Imperator' or the second Hannibal; but his picture was blurred and dim in their minds' eye. Many of them were to doubt later on that he had really ridden past them on his white steed, with the velum in front.

The march towards the market place quickened as though the strangers wanted to get the Entry over and done with. Boisterous mass-feeling had been nipped in the bud.

Behind the leaders came more infantry, raking the dust and glancing woodenly out of dirty faces. What strange soldiers they were, these new allies who had given the Romans so sound a beating. What strange ensigns they carried ahead, how solemn and how sinister: crude wooden crosses. The bearers staggered under them and had to crush the shafts to their chests in order not to fall under their weight. And solemn and sinister the broken fetters and iron chains recurred. The leader of a troop of particularly ruffianly characters, a pock-marked lout, carried a giant muraena-eel with a human head made of rags in its jaws. Hegio's little boy stretched on tiptoe and asked in his shrill little voice:

'What's that, Father? Are there fish who eat people?'

Hegio smiled as the very young or the very old smile, but the greengrocer clapped his hand over the child's mouth:

'Hush, my boy, hush, hush,' he said. 'You mustn't ask questions, otherwise the soldiers will be cross.'

For the queue had gradually grown very quiet. The citizens had given up banter and acclamation, the smiles had been wiped off their faces. Frightened, the boy stopped talking. Only the thunder of the marching Army was heard in the avenue, their feet made the dust whirl up and envelop them in a vaporous cloud.

Cavalry came riding past now, men on small Lucanian horses; but Hegio's little boy, whom toy-soldiers had instructed as to the proper looks of classified professional warriors, was by no means the only one to wonder, for even the peace-loving citizens in their queues were amazed, nay, horrified, by the unmilitary appearance of their new allies. Not only did almost the entire heavy cavalry lack armour for man and beast—at most one or the other was protected by a clanging bit of tin tied with hempen cord to arm or leg; not only were most of their lances wooden, their shields of reed and hide; not only did most of them flourish scythes, pitchforks and axes instead of swords; no: not even *uniforms* did they have, nor glittering helmets! Some were bareheaded and waved slings, others wore black felt hats, bleached and so worn that the brims fell like fringes into their bearded faces; their shirts and linen blouses were equally slashed; but half of them wore nothing from the girdle up, rode past with tanned and shaggy chests, shamelessly naked between matted beard and belt.

A moan passed over the queue, and many men of Thurium averted their heads in shame; but the women had glinting eyes and sighed. A matron fainted and had to be carried away.

And the new allies went past; again infantry came marching and tramped the dust, glanced woodenly out of dirty faces. Those who passed now were organised according to nationalities: coarse Gauls and Germans with moustaches; tall Thracians with luminous eyes and peculiarly springy walk; Barbarians from Numidia and Asia whose skin was dark and dry; black men with earrings and thick lips moistly open over bared teeth.

'What a mess!' the greengrocer whispered to Hegio.

'A pleasant change, I think,' smiled Hegio and bent down to the little boy: 'Don't you like it? Isn't it rather gay and colourful?'

'Yes, it is,' nodded the boy. 'Just like a circus.'

'Hush,' said the greengrocer, 'that's the very thing you mustn't say.'

A new cloud of dust approached, and oxcarts came, loaded with the sick and wounded. They lay with their backs on filthy blankets; some gazed quietly up at the sky, others writhed in pain, others again stuck out their tongues and grimaced. Their faces were speckled with flies which crawled into their eye-sockets and stuck fast to their rugs. Hegio's little boy began to cry.

'What do they show us all that for?' asked the greengrocer. 'Are these part of their show-troops?'

'No,' smiled Hegio. 'Still it is an original Entry.'

Three more carts went by, in better condition than the rest, and drawn by oxen. On each of the carts lay one corpse covered with swarms of flies, the ensign of the broken chain at his head. They sent out fetid smells.

And that was the end of the procession.

The queues had thinned out a little, but most of the citizens had not dared to go away. Fear kept them at their places. Even now, when the entertainment was finished, they remained in the streets, abashed.

3

THE NEW LAW

THE citizens of Thurium calmed down; no soldier of the slave army approached their walls. Outside, on the plain between the rivers Crathis and Sybaris, they were building their camp, the Sun City.

It was nearly spring at that time. Aromatic fumes rose up from the soil, the stormy March breezes blew from the sea. Slaves with axes scrambled up the mountains so furry with trees, and, returning with timber trunks lugged by white buffaloes, they sawed planks and beams for the first granaries and dining halls of their new town. The Celts dug firm, tough clay from the banks of the river Crathis, moulded bricks and dried them in the sun; for the Celts all wanted to live in brick houses. The Thracians sewed tents of blackened goat-skins, plaited pliant twigs into hoops for the frames of their roofs, and laid the floor with soft carpets so that talk might be quiet and sedate when they had guests. The Lucanians and Samnites mixed peat with dung and rubble, and formed their tiny conical houses from the paste; they sprinkled the floor with chaff and straw, and their houses smelled wholesomely of stable. The black men with the earrings twined rushes into an ingenious mesh, and tied the braid to pegs; their huts looked fragile and toy-like, but they stood fast and dry in storm and rain.

The sun was shining, the earth steaming, crops spouting from the clods. The town grew rapidly as though the sun had coaxed her from the soil, fertile with rottenness, bursting with long restrained live juices. There were seventy thousand of them, marked with the brand, cast out by fortune and scattered over the earth; now they were building their own town. They lugged tree-trunks, carried stone blocks, hammered, glued, sawed. It was going to be a very marvellous town, property of the destitute, home of the homeless, refuge of the wretched. Each one built his house, and the house was his.

The city grew. A stretch of land had been allotted to every tribe, Celts, Thracians, Syrians, Africans; each might build his house as he liked. But the ground-plan was uniform, designed according to the strict Roman rules of camp construction, with straight walls and straight, parallel streets. Outer rampart and moat formed a severe square in the plain between Crathis and Sybaris, at the foot of the valiant, nicked, blue mountains. Austere and defiant, the Slave Town lay embedded in the plain, her four gates guarded by forbidding sentries, silent and bull-necked; before each gate the ensign of the town, the broken chain, looked far into the country. On a hill in the centre of the town stood the great tent with the purple velum, the Imperator's tent, from which issued the new laws to rule the town. The hill was encircled by the dens of his captains, the gladiators; the community buildings formed a second, wider ring around it: tool-sheds and sword-smithies, granaries, corrals, communal dining halls. For, each might build his house as he liked in the allotments, but corn and cattle, arms, tools, and the yield of all labour were common property. And the new laws decreed by the Imperator on the very founding of the city, recorded by Fulvius the Lawyer of Capua, read as follows:

1. No longer shall man distress and oppress his neighbour with covetousness and greed in his struggle for the necessities of life; for the Communal Brotherhood undertakes to care for all.

2. Nor shall anyone serve the other from now on, nor the strong subject the weak, nor he who won a sack of meal enslave him who took no booty; for all shall serve the Communal Brotherhood.

3. Therefore no man shall hoard victuals to last for more than one half day, nor amass in his house any other goods or merchandise; for all will be fed with the acquirements of all in the great dining halls, as behoves brethren.

4. Likewise, the requirements of all as regards material for building or weapons, and the well-being of life and limb, will be met, in return for labour done by each one according to his abilities, to further common welfare, be it by the building of houses or the forging of swords, cultivating the soil and tending the flocks. And each one shall do the work he is suited to in strength and ability, and there shall be no differentiation in the sharing out of all worldly goods, but all will share and share alike.

5. Therefore the possibility shall be abolished of one gaining advantages by imposing on the other in buying and selling, or of his gaining possession of property beyond his share in the shape of notes of hand or coin. Therefore the Lucanian Brotherhood will abolish the use of gold and silver coins, and those of lesser metals; and whosoever is discovered in the possession of such shall incur the penalty of ejection and death.

Such were the laws decreed by Spartacus to rule life in the growing Sun City. Very novel laws they were—and yet as old as the hills. When they had first started to build the camp and dug in the earth, they had found the ruins of mythical Sybaris— those weather-eaten walls, clay pottery and broken vases had seen the age of Saturn whose memory is longingly cherished by the people, the age that was ruled by justice and goodwill. They had found inscriptions dealing with the hero Lykurgos and the Spartan state of communal store houses and dining-halls—these new laws of Spartacus, was it not as though corroded stone, chiselled by long-dead hands which were guided by long-expired souls, decreed them here and now? It was the soul and spirit of a country which had borne the ancestors of Thurium's citizens. And the citizens of Thurium, watching the growth of the new town and shaking their heads, crowding and prying before her gates as no outsider was ever admitted—the citizens of Thurium likewise remembered the stories of a long-gone era, and they were strangely affected by them: stories of a good King Agis, a Panchee island, memories of old Plato's unworldly reveries of a republic of wisdom, which one read at school, faintly bored, touched and smiling, as one deigns to read the classics, as present day condescends to submerged past. Sublime and dusty were these traditional legends, but they most certainly had no relation to reality and the present times, thought the citizens of Thurium. And that a nondescript Thracian Prince, if a Prince he was and not, as was rumoured, a circus-gladiator, that such a man should suddenly appear from nowhere, defeat the Romans and build a city in which all these unworldly dreams became real as orders of the day—that was indeed an extravagant spectacle.

But the city grew.

Sternly and squarely walled, she grew, and her straight streets grew, her store houses and dining halls. New, just and inexorable were her laws. On a hill in the centre of the town, guarded by a double line of sentinels, stood the Imperator's tent from which issued the laws. In an out-of-the-way spot, in the corner of the North Gate wall, stood the crosses for those who broke the laws.

Several died there every day in the interest of common welfare, with fractured limbs and black tongues; and in their last tremors they cursed the tent with the purple velum and the Sun State.

4

THE NET

THE negotiations which preceded the settlement of the alliance between the Imperator on the one, and Thurium on the other hand, were of a slightly weird nature, and the gentlemen of the Town Council had experienced several surprises.

The delegates alone, sent by the Imperator into the sumptuous audience chamber of the Corporation of Thurium, had been very peculiar people: a shrivelled lawyer with a bumpy bald head and a tall, shy youth with lowered eyes and frequent blushes, on whose high forehead a blue vein swelled the thin skin: both of insignificant appearance, impossible dress and complete ignorance of diplomatic ceremony. The two Chief Councillors of Thurium were painfully surprised and not quite sure how to behave. When one of them, an old man with slightly protruding eyes, prefaced the parley with the usual embroidery and spoke of 'your lord, the glorious conqueror of Rome and Princely Imperator', the bald-headed little man interrupted him:

'Do you mean Spartacus? We thought you knew who he is.'

The dignified old gentleman got completely muddled, and his colleague, a thick-set business man and owner of one of the largest pitch refineries in Sila, had to help him out. He said:

'We were informed that your leader rides a white horse, exhibits the insignia of Praetor Varinius and has the fasces and axes carried before him. Those are the insignia of an Imperator. Anyhow, the formalities are irrelevant.'

'Just as a point of order,' replied the lawyer of Capua, 'let me say that it is not a question of fasces or axes but of symbolical ensigns. But, as you say, such formalities are irrelevant,' he concluded with a touch of sarcasm.

'What sort of ensigns?' asked the old gentleman, who was inquisitive and liked accuracy.

'As we heard, they have merely symbolical significance,' said the business man glibly. The old man shook his head but did not pursue the matter. What could that mean: 'symbolical ensigns'? There was a snag somewhere. The whole alliance had a snag somewhere.

Both sides insisted no longer and turned to the actual matter in hand. The suggestions made by the lawyer Fulvius on behalf of his Imperator, occasionally stroking his pate, and interrupted by frequent coughs, were about as follows:

The city of Thurium shall form an alliance with Spartucus's Army. The city of Thurium shall thus cease to be under the sovereignty of the Roman Republic. The payment of poll-tax, tithe and municipal rates to the Roman exchequer will be stopped. All cornfields, pastureland and other fertile soil near and around the city shall, so long as they have hitherto been Roman territory, become the property of the municipality.

'What about the resin and pitch refineries?' asked the business man.

'Those which are State property will become that of the city. In the case of those rented by private individuals not domiciled in the city, the lease will be cancelled.'

'Excellent,' said the burly Senator. 'So far everything is reasonable and deserves approval.'

'But is your Prince entitled to cancel contracts?' asked the old Councillor. But nobody paid any attention to him, and the lawyer Fulvius went on:

'Further, we suggest this: the city of Thurium shall be declared a free-port. Roman customs duty and other tolls on imported and exported goods are suspended, which measure will affect trade with overseas ports as well as other Roman ports.'

'What does it mean?' asked the old man. 'Is that symbolical too? I am ignorant of the laws of trade, and I always thought that an alliance is mainly concerned with martial affairs.'

'It means,' explained the business man enthusiastically, 'it means that Thurium will steal a march on the ports of Brundisium, Tarentum, Metapontum, etcetera etcetera, and become the most important port of the south. It means wealth and blessings for this city and—who knows—the end, perhaps, of Roman world commerce- and fleet-monopolies.'

'The sea is full of pirates,' said the old man, 'the sea is not safe.'

'As to the pirates,' said the lawyer Fulvius calmly, 'we will form an alliance with them.'

'With the pirates?' asked the old man, horrified. 'Why, they are murdererers and bandits and quite definitely not decent people.'

There was an uncomfortable silence. The business man was also stunned this time, his expression was flustered and inane; and as Oenomaus did not contribute anything except a timidly polite smile, they had to wait for the lawyer to finish coughing in order to hear an explanation of an alliance with pirates.

'Why not?' he said. 'Piracy is as much a consequence of the Roman naval trade monopoly, as robbery on land is a consequence of the land monopolies and great land-owning combines. Only, as you know, the pirates of Cilicia are far better organised than the miserable bandits used to be before the coming of Spartacus. They have a well-ordered, military sort of floating state, with admirals and strict laws. King Mithridates formed an alliance with them, and so did the Roman emigrants under Sertorius. Rome calls it piracy, but in reality it is the holy war of the oppressed of the seas. So we too will make an alliance with the pirates and include them in the Lucanian Brotherhood.'

'Wouldn't you like to make an ally of Mithridates too?' asked the business man sarcastically.

'We probably will,' replied the lawyer. 'Negotiations are pending.'

'And with the emigrants in Spain too?'

'With them too,' replied the lawyer and looked steadily at him out of his short-sighted eyes.

The aged Councillor shook his head and made no more efforts to understand. The business man silently surveyed these delegates who dressed impossibly and did not know the first thing about diplomatic rites. He was not sure whether he was attending an act of world history or a burlesque farce. He imagined what Crassus or Pompeius or any other great Roman statesman would think if they were invisible witnesses of this conversation. They would probably smile, highly amused at these ambassadors of an obscure gladiator negotiating the fate of the world with a Greek dodderer and a petty industrialist. Of course, it all was sheer amateurism and childishness; take alone the fact of these people as much as entering upon negotiations, instead of marching into the city and taking what they wanted. For who could prevent them, after they had beaten Varinius? Thurium had neither proper walls nor a garrison worth speaking of, and this man Spartacus knew it as well as they did. Only the dignified old man had no idea of it at all and took this farce of a parley seriously. However, if these people would negotiate, one might as well try to get the better of them. That was the only sane point he could see in the whole crazy business.

'Are those your lord's, the Thracian Prince's, ideas?' he asked in the end.

'These ideas have been in the air for a long time,' said the lawyer. 'All that was needed was for somebody to take them up.'

'All right,' said the business man. 'That's your affair and rather beyond the authority of this conference. Permit me to return to the actual issue. What I mean is this: what sort of duties would we incur in an alliance as proposed by you, or, to be more direct: what do you want of us?'

'That's easily said,' said the lawyer amiably. 'We want you to grant us voluntarily all that which we could easily take by force.'

The Councillor nearly swooned. 'That sounds very general,' he stuttered. 'You just can't consider things in such a one-sided way.'

But Fulvius disregarded his protests with dry incivility and came out with their demands: The Corporation is to cede the area between the rivers Crathis and Sybaris to the Slave Army as a site for a new town; the Corporation, furthermore, is to undertake supplying the Army with building material and food until the Army is able to live on the produce of its land.

'How many are you?' asked the business man in a matter-of-fact way.

'Seventy thousand so far,' said Fulvius, 'but we'll soon be a hundred thousand, or more.'

'Out of the question,' said the Councillor decidedly. 'We have fifty thousand inhabitants, we can't possibly maintain twice as many more.'

'We have quite substantial herds,' said Fulvius, 'so that about a third of our consumption of meat and milk is covered. Apart from that, the free-port of Thurium will import food; also metals and other material necessary for armament.'

'And who'll pay?' asked the business man.

'We will,' said Fulvius, and the business man lost his composure for the second time in the course of this conversation. He regained it only when the lawyer added:

'To be sure, we will fix the prices—in agreement with the Corporation, of course.'

'We can't possibly tell every shopkeeper what price to take for a cucumber or a pickled herring when one of your soldiers asks for them.'

'As a matter of fact that would be quite superfluous,' said Fulvius, 'for we will buy everything in bulk for the needs of the entire town, as ours will be a co-operative society. And, by the way, we shall abolish money.'

After a fairly long pause during which the busines man visibly swallowed the wealth of remarks at the tip of his tongue and breathed audibly, he said at last:

'What you want to do inside your camp is your affair.'

'Quite,' said Fulvius. 'Besides, we had better speak of a town instead of a camp, because we shall start building. It will be called the Sun City.'

'How lyrical,' said the business man; and again there was a pause.

He was thinking: let these fools do what they liked—as far as Thurium's fate was concerned, he had been prepared for worse. The site for the camp had for the greater part been Roman State property; Spartacus took it from the Romans and presented it to the Corporation, who in turn presented it to Spartacus. It could have been done more simply and without legal footnotes, as it were, but if these people were so keen on symbols he would not grudge them the pleasure. Whether they would abide by the treaty or not was quite a different question. But Thurium was in their power, and a treaty, however questionable, was better than no treaty at all. As a whole the business man was very pleased indeed, and he turned to his aged colleague:

'These seem to me rather heavy demands, but one might consider them. What do you think?'

The old man looked at him with slightly protruding eyes and said:

'I understand only an infinitesimal part of all this. Will you, ambassador of the Thracian Prince, permit me to ask one question? I have heard that you wish to take all our money, houses, wives, daughters and servants away from us and turn everything generally upside-down. Is that true?'

'I'm sure that is all idle talk,' said the business man quickly. 'These things may have been said, but should not be taken quite so literally.' He shot a smiling glance at the two delegates, it expressed understanding and wheedled for corroboration.

Oenomaus blushed under this glance and lowered his eyes. He did not want an understanding with this man, and longed to be miles away. He thought of the crater inside Vesuvius and how simple things had been then.

The old man seemed not to have heard his colleague's remarks. He looked first at Oenomaus, then at the lawyer, looked them straight in the face and waited for his question to be answered.

Fulvius had been expecting a question of this kind and had prepared a precise and matter-of-fact answer. But to his painful surprise he became aware of having forgotten it. He felt the glance of the old man who sat facing him, hunched in an attitude of listening. He had wrinkled pouches below the slightly protruding, but clear, eyes. Strangely enough the lawyer and author Fulvius suddenly thought of his father—a thing he had not done in years. His discomfort grew, unexpectedly he had a guilty conscience, which annoyed him. Finally he said:

'We want law and order—but new and just laws and order.' He coughed.

'Words,' said the old man. 'Nothing but words, ambassador of the Thracian Prince, you do avoid the real issue. You speak of customs duties, import, export and symbols; but I asked you whether you want to take my house from me or not.'

The business man cleared his throat: 'This isn't the point.' Again he sent Oenomaus an imploring glance. But Oenomaus kept his eyes lowered.

'Rubbish,' said the old man with angry obstinacy. 'It is the only point. If one man has a house and another man wants to take it away from him, the two of them cannot form an alliance because it would be sheer hypocrisy.'

Fulvius was silent. The old man reminded him strangely of his father whom he had long forgotten. The same feeling that forced young Oenomaus's lids down made him forget his arguments, made them look like meaningless quibble. Clear and straight was only the road of force—and the sublime stupidity reflected in the old man's eyes. For—and this was the discovery which so disconcerted the chronicler Fulvius and paralysed his eloquence—there was a stupidity so sublime and venerable as to abash the clever. There was an injustice so ingrained and self-assured as to make the just doubt himself. There was a dignity of property which behaved with such natural grace as to make the dispossessed's desire for the same fortune appear unnatural.

The lawyer Fulvius made a decision and straightened with a jerk. Immediately and instinctively he felt his skull: he missed the wooden beam over his desk in the attic which made him pay with a bump on his head for every bold thought. He missed this beam now; it was difficult to get used to this new mode of life.

'You have a right to this question,' he said to the old man and paused.

He could almost hear the business man's sigh of relief; he felt young Oenomaus's searching glance; he saw the childlike trust in the old man's eyes. He coughed and went on:

'The aims pursued by our movement and' (here he coughed again) 'the Thracian Prince would, to be sure, lead to a complete change of system and conditions in this country. But the achievement of this aim is still very distant. At the moment we need security for the new city we will build, the security of alliances. Our allies will have nothing to fear from us.'

'No disorder?' asked the old man. 'That means you will not take our houses away and send no more emissaries into our city who incite our slaves to rebellion?'

Again the lawyer bounded up; again he missed banging against the beam. This time, in fact, the lack fairly troubled him. Had his brain functioned better when the beam was a constant threat? Had too much freedom from such brutal, tangible warnings a corrupting effect on one's ideas? The horde would never understand why they should renounce winning over the slaves of their neighbouring city. And yet one must consent to it in order to have peace at last for the great experiment, for the building of the Sun City. Fulvius was silent and recalled the conversation of the first night he had spent in Spartacus's camp: the *law of detours*, there it was again, hampering every new step with new demands, muddy and impenetrable.

The lawyer Fulvius would have liked to break off negotiations. That which he had always refused to believe, almost seemed true now: that only the direct road was the clean one. But had the road of Nola, Suessula, Calatia been any cleaner? Was it cleaner to put a spear through the dignified old Councillor's bowels instead of . . . ? Well yes, instead of making rotten compromises, agreeing to conditions which the horde would never understand.

'We won't take your houses away and we won't send any emissaries,' he said curtly. 'Are you reassured now?'

'I accept your word,' said the old man in his clear, slightly tremulous voice.

Refreshments were brought in; the treaty was drawn up with some haste and signed immediately. Both parties were in quite a hurry now and refrained from discussing details. The document embroidered Spartacus's name with all the reverential appellations to which a foreign Prince was entitled; the delegates had raised no more objections.

Such had been the negotiations which preceded the founding of the city, and other negotiations had followed it. It was to be a Sun City and life within her walls was to run on independently of what happened outside; her citizens free and untouched by the world's laws and orders. But from her very foundation on, this city was tied to existing order by a thousand threads, invisibly and yet inescapably caught in the net.

It had been nearly spring at that time. And since then the city had grown rapidly out of bare earth; she had been planned for seventy thousand, and already a hundred thousand lived within her walls. Granaries grew up, sword smithies, communal dining halls; and also crosses grew in a corner by the North Gate, on which died those whose lives were forfeited in the interests of common welfare, those who had not been able to submit to the stern laws of freedom.

5

THE NEW-COMER

A NEW-COMER among many new-comers had come to the
town, a youth named Publibor. He had run away from
Hegio his master, and now he was here. Not that he had led too
bad a life with his master. Even the matron had beaten him only
seldom, when her mood was particularly black, and there were
many who had a worse time of it. But he had heard the message of
the Sun State—in the days before the alliance had forbidden
Spartacus's emissaries to solicit the slaves of Thurium. And the
message had sown the seed of longing into his heart, and it had
budded and blossomed forth, until he had to go to the camp
city.

Now he was here, one youth, one among a hundred thousand,
and was little noticed. With a longing in his heart he had come,
in his mind the picture of the new life, as painted by the agents
and emissaries—in the days before they had to refrain from
courting the slaves of Thurium. He walked through the clean
new streets of the camp city, astonished and intimidated; nobody
bothered about him. People here were very active and busy,
building, hammering, construction work was going on everywhere; and there was no one whom he could tell of his burning
joy: he had arrived in the Sun State.

He had not had an easy time at the gate. Guards stood there,
stiff and forbidding, with the disdainful air of all men in uniform
about them. Halloh there, whither was the lad going, they had
asked scornfully.

Smiling and trustingly he had replied that he had come to live with them under the new laws of the Lucanian Brotherhood, that he had been a slave until today and had run away from his master in Thurium.

But his disclosures did not effect a change for the friendlier in the uniformed men; they remained discouraging and adverse. Had they not understood his words? Yes, they did seem to have understood them. Callously they told him he might not enter and would have to go back to his master; no slave from Thurium might be admitted into the city, thus it had been settled in the treaty with the Council of Thurium; therefore: off with him.

But he would not go off. He screamed that they had not understood him, that it was all a terrible misunderstanding, for he was a slave and wanted to live in the Slave Town ruled by justice and goodwill. But when the soldiers, laughing at first and soon getting tired of his screams, tried to drive him away with cuffs and blows, he clung to the gate post, quite beside himself, and screamed they could not do that to him, he wanted to go to Spartacus who most certainly would accept him into his state; and tears poured from his eyes. For he was a shy and meek young man who had never before in his life made such a fuss, and he was very much ashamed of his own screams. But more and more people had come to the gate to see what was up, and in the end the guard had to lead him inside, growlingly, and bring him to his captain.

All's well now, thought the youth Publibor, wiped the tears off his face and became shy and sedate once more. They did not have far to go; the captain's shack was only a few paces from the inner rampart. It was a wooden shack covered with tarred cloth on which the sun burned down. Around the shack stood and sat many people, tightly packed in all this heat, they looked down at the heel and tired, as after a long march; children were among them too, and nursing mothers; they were guarded by soldiers. The sentry who had brought Publibor spoke to one of the soldiers and went back to his place; Publibor was told to wait with the rest. He sat down in the dust, well satisfied that he had after all succeeded in entering the city.

Time passed, the sun was very hot, the people sitting in the dust around Publibor chatted anxiously and dejectedly ate what they had brought along; some mothers suckled their crying babies. There were several hundred of them waiting here in front of the shack, guarded by soldiers; from time to time a group was called inside. Hurriedly and with great excitement, they stumbled into the wooden building; the others gazed after them. You never saw anyone come out again, they were led off in another direction.

'Are they all new-comers?' Publibor asked the man who sat next to him. The man had a peaked, bird-like face with a long, pointed nose to which huddled closely his darting eyes; a tramp in all probability. He chewed a slice of bread with onions and paid no attention to the question. In his stead a woman turned her thin, yellow face to Publibor and asked:

'Are you one of those from the mines?'

As she talked she rocked her knee on which lay an ugly infant with the end of her baggy breast in his mouth.

'No,' said Publibor, 'I'm from Thurium.'

He would have liked to tell her more, but the woman had turned back again and rocked her child. She probably had not listened to his answer at all.

The tramp had stopped eating and said:

'If you're from Thurium they'll send you back. They don't want to have any trouble with the Magistrate. Spartacus is quite the gentleman these days.'

'They'll keep me all right,' said Publibor. 'Spartacus does not send anybody back who wants to join him.'

'Spartacus has his head full with more important things than you,' said the tramp and rolled his shifty eyes in all directions. 'Yesterday the ambassadors of Mithridates were with him, today he's palavering with the agents of Sertorius. Great bees he's got in his bonnet. That one will be sent back too,' he concluded in a whisper, and jerked his thumb at the yellow-skinned woman.

'Don't jabber so much. Everyone's turn will come,' said one of the soldiers good-naturedly, and wiped the sweat from under his helmet.

A new group was being shepherded into the shack.

The woman turned to Publibor.

'They're sure to keep the ones from the mines,' she said. She talked with a strange, absent haste and turned back at once without waiting for an answer. She rocked the baby, took the breast from him and crammed the other one in his mouth. The child seemed asleep, flies crawled over his face.

'I'll say they'll keep the ones from the mines,' said the tramp. He pointed at a troop of broad-shouldered men with shiny, naked torsos, who sat quietly in a corner. 'They're men all right—I'll say they can use them. But my likes aren't good enough for their Sun State. And what should they do with old hags? She's got nipples like a withered goat's udder, she hasn't had any milk for years.'

Publibor felt the same anxiety as outside the gate.

'Do so many people come, then?' he asked.

The tramp embraced the whole country, fields, mountains, seas, with a gesture. 'Three from four are sent back,' he said.

'I thought,' said Publibor, 'that all the poor and humble can find a place in the Sun State.'

The tramp grazed him with a look and pulled a face.

'Trying to be funny, aren't you,' he said, and began to chew his slice of bread again.

But all went well in the end; towards evening Publibor had been called in together with some of the others, the soldiers had forgotten to report that Publibor came from Thurium, and as he was young and vigorous, he was allowed to stay, and was received into the Lucanian Brotherhood. Tomorrow his military training was to begin, and he had also been put into a carpenter's brigade which built pens, but today he was free and allowed to go through the streets and look at the new city, the Sun State.

All the people here were his brothers, but they were also very busy, no one had any time for him. He was too timid to start a conversation, but he would have liked to, if only someone had encouraged him. Nobody encouraged him. He stopped in front of a forge, and watched two sooty lads of about his own age work the bellows; a third, older one held the red-hot metal on the anvil, a fourth swung the heavy hammer over his head and brought it down. It clanged in one's ears, red sparks flew up. Publibor looked on; these were his brothers. Eagerly he scanned their faces: should not the happiness be reflected in them, the happiness of being free and living according to the New Law? All of them looked darkly at the metal, and did not talk; the one who held the tongs spat and swore angrily at the material. Did they not feel this precious change in their lives, had they already forgotten what it had been like before? Publibor called out with a timid salute. Only one of them turned his head indifferently, and spat black saliva; Publibor went on.

The dwelling huts and tents were almost empty. It was working time. The store houses stood lined up in a geometrically severe row, pointed pyramids, white and grey in the glaring sun. The sheds, workshops and dining halls were built of wood, white buffaloes had lugged the thick planks down from the mountains; the buildings smelled of forests still, and resin oozed from the joints. Publibor turned into a wide, gently ascending street; up on the hill he saw huge leather tents and in the middle the largest, a purple velum hanging slackly from a high mast in front of it. Publibor stood still when he saw it. A hot wave washed over his heart and he felt his eyes fill with tears. But up on the hill stood haughtily the bull-necked guards, gruff, and with discouraging faces; so he turned back again.

Again he walked through the streets, walked between mud houses and workshops, peered into faces, searched them for a reflection of joyful excitement. He came to the African quarter of black giants with thick lips, woolly heads, round, friendly, stolid eyes. They grinned at him but he did not understand the deep sounds that came huskily and yet melodiously from their throats. How many varieties of man there were! Were these also his brothers? Did they, too, think of the Sun State? They had different gods, different bodies, different stuff inside their skulls. He accosted one of them who carried a stripped tree on his shoulder, so heavy that three Publibors could scarcely have lifted it. The giant stopped; with a mixture of friendliness and fear he looked down at Publibor, who faced him in the empty street under the dazzling sun.

'Heavy,' said Publibor. 'Heavy, heavy.'

The giant pointed gravely at the mountains. He probably thought that the lad had asked him where such trees grew.

'Heavy, heavy,' repeated Publibor, already a trifle embarrassed, and made a heaving gesture.

Frightened, the giant shook his head: he would not let him have the tree. He uttered animal noises, cried plaintively, it almost seemed as though he were going to weep. Is he frightened that I'll take that beam from him, is he afraid of me? thought Publibor, very puzzled. Has he been treated so badly in the past that he is afraid of me? He had an idea. 'Spartacus,' he

cried, smiled, and pointed with his finger in the direction
of the tent with the velum. 'Surely he'll understand that,'
said Publibor to himself. But the black man suddenly struck
him on the chest and began to run. Running, he looked
round once more, his eyes rolling madly and fearfully. After
that he disappeared.

The joyous wave which had carried him high ever since his
flight from Hegio's house was gradually ebbing away. He was
wearied from all that aimless strolling through streets, but he
could not rid himself of an unreal, dreamlike feeling. It had not
been easy to tear through the network of everyday and habit;
only an hour before he escaped, it had seemed to him that he
would never have sufficient courage to do it. But afterwards,
during those horrible minutes outside the gate, a feeling that he
was dreaming had never left him, so that the nasty quarrel and
his own shrill screams had only touched him as from afar. And
now the tide of his festive joy was receding, but perplexity
stayed, together with the expectation of something strange and
singular that must happen to him. He went on walking through
the streets, sedate and already tired, when the voice of a young
woman called out to him.

She was sitting on the threshold of a long wooden house, and
with thin, quick fingers stripped a corn cob of its grains. Inside,
in a large, fusty hall, other women were at work, equally speedily
and busily; it was one of the great communal kitchens which
prepared the meals for the dining halls.

Publibor had not understood the woman's words, but her
voice still echoed in his ear. It was a voice of husky, yet tinkling
timbre, like the touch and texture of some precious, supple
material whose surface is slightly roughened. He stood still,
blushed, and said apologetically:

'I'm a new-comer.'

'I can see that,' said the girl with a swift smile, without looking
up from the maize. As she sat bent down he could not see her
eyes, only her lashes, the oval of her face and the loose knot of
hair. She spoke Greek.

'How can you see that?' he asked.

She did not answer, merely smiled; the maize ran in swift
beads through her fingers into the bowl. She threw the stripped

cob into a pail, took a fresh one out; she seemed to have forgotten about him. At last Publibor thought up a new question:

'Have you been in the Brotherhood long?'

'What?'

'Have you been long in the Brotherhood, I said.'

She laughed ringingly and threw her head back, for one second he could see her eyes:

'Since Nola I've been in the—Brotherhood.'

He could see no joke and gravely asked the question which obviously had to come next:

'Are you happy?'

This time she only smiled and said: 'Hand me another corn cob. Not that one—the big one.' After that she was serious again and continued stripping the grains off very rapidly.

Publibor knew that he was making a fool of himself and should have walked on. Instead he asked:

'I suppose you ran away from your master in Nola?'

'They killed him,' she said without interrupting her work.

'Were you glad when they came and killed him?'

'Glad? What for?'

'Because you are free now,' said Publibor. 'Before, your master could do with you as he pleased.'

It seemed as though she were about to laugh again, but she only gave him an amused look. 'That he could,' she said, smiling.

'He could have you whipped,' said Publibor.

'Whipped? What for?'

'He could, if he wanted to,' said Publibor obstinately.

'Well, is that so terrible?'

He pondered, did no longer know himself what it was he wanted. Then he asked:

'Isn't it marvellous to be free?'

'What's the difference?' she asked indifferently. 'Don't I have to go on working? Free is he who needn't work.'

'Before, you worked for your master, now we work for ourselves. Is there no difference in that?'

She had got herself a fresh corn cob. 'Oh yes,' she said, obviously bored.

Standing opposite her in the street for a while longer, he found nothing more to say. Finally he murmured a farewell and slowly went away. She did not look up, nor did she return his salute. Very rapidly the beads of maize flowed through her slender fingers into the bowl.

He grew more and more tired; in the end he got hungry as well. He should have asked the girl the way to the carpenters' dining hall; now he dared not ask anybody. He had come to the Celtic quarter with its little thatched houses of raw clay bricks; they did not look very clean. He thought of the white verandas and roof gardens of Thurium, of the black shadows on the pillars; all that seemed years back. His old master, Hegio, was probably returning from his morning walk now, playing with the dog and answering with childlike banter the matron's nagging on the subject of his, Publibor's, disappearance. Here, in the outer ring, the streets were almost empty, everybody was either working or eating, the few he did meet were sweating fat men in coarse smocks, with tufty whiskers and peevish eyes—Barbarians from Gaul. He came to a wide, open square already bordering on the outer wall, not far from the North Gate. The square was completely empty, he started to cross it to ask the guard by the North Gate the way to the dining hall, when suddenly his heart almost stopped.

In the left-hand corner of the square, close to the moat, he saw three wooden posts with unplaned crossbeams, from which men were suspended. Their heads had fallen forward on to their chests, whose ribs stood out sharply. Their limbs were unnaturally contorted; their wrists tied to the crossbeams with ropes, they hung like birds held up by their wings. Publibor had never seen a crucified man before; every one had laughed at him because he never went to executions. Now he had to lean against the wall, he felt sick, and vomited. When he looked again, one of the twisted forms was slowly lifting his head and looked at him, Publibor, with those eyes of his. His tongue, dark and shapeless, came out of his mouth, and wiped slowly, slowly along his teeth, to the right first, and then to the left, while his eyes did not leave Publibor. Publibor's fingers scraped the wall behind him, his throat was constricted, he did not know whether he coughed or sobbed. Then the skin of the hanged man's face began to crinkle slowly, wrinkles formed around mouth and eyes, no doubt the man was trying to grin. He swallowed a few times, you could see the spasms travel down his throat, after that he shut his eyes, the head sunk slowly down again, tried to rest on the shoulder, until finally the chin slid back on the chest. At the same time a hand touched Publibor's arm, it was the guard who had been standing in the shade of the wall.

'What are you doing here?' asked the sentry. But Publibor was incapable of answering. He merely stared at the sentry, his Roman uniform and the helmet above his flushed neck.

'I suppose you're new here,' said the sentry. 'Go along then, you've no business here.'

'Why,' groaned Publibor and tilted his shivering chin at the three posts, 'why did they do that to those over there?'

The sentry shrugged and did not answer. He also looked over at the crucified men, but after a while he averted his head and mopped the sweat off his face.

'It's for the sake of discipline, and to warn others,' he said. 'If you give them something to drink it takes even longer. Go on then, off with you.'

Again Publibor strayed through the streets of the town, he did not know for how long, hours, it seemed to him. The eyes of the twisted man on the cross did not leave him, again and again he saw the tongue slip slowly along the teeth, to the right first and then to the left. But when his tired feet almost refused to carry him and his stomach burned with hunger, the picture gradually paled. 'It's for the sake of discipline, and to warn others,' the sentry had said. If he said so, that's what it was then, surely the sentry was the one to know, and if Spartacus had people crucified, he probably had his reasons. By and by he calmed down and even gathered sufficient courage to ask the way to the dining hall.

The dining hall was a long wooden building, only just finished. The fresh planks oozed resin from the joints like all the fresh planks in the town. When Publibor sat down on the bench along the extremely long, unplaned table, in an extremely long line of men, and his elbows touched those of his two neighbours, he felt that everything was well and good again, and that the festive joy which had surged through him when he set foot in the city was warming him once more. The meal consisted of a strong maize and onion soup; every six men had one pot between them, bent their heads over it and ate it all together with their wooden ladles.

The hall was big enough to hold nearly a hundred such pot-partnerships at one and the same time. The men at the long tables ate their soup and did not talk much; the sweat of their day's work dried but slowly, they were tired; yet the hall was filled with an even hum of voices. The five men who shared Publibor's pot with him and whose spoons constantly crossed and accidentally hit his, had not talked up to now. Publibor, who already loved these five as his brothers, did not dare address them, afraid to say the wrong thing, as he seemed to have done the wrong thing all day long. But he noticed that the man opposite him was dressed in a gown vastly different from the smocks of the others: he wore a worn cloth which might have been a toga once, wound several times around his body; the fluttering sleeves were in constant danger of dipping into the soup dish. The man had a gaunt bird's face distantly resembling that of the tramp; but a secret pain had been engraved into the skin around his eyes, which formed a queer contrast to his exaggerated, flurried gestures. He was the first to address the new-comer:

'How tastes the bread of freedom?' he asked and beat with his spoon against the rim of the dish.

'Fine,' said Publibor readily. Previously he had always imag-ined speech in the Brotherhood just like this, but now he was slightly repelled by the pompous tone.

'I can see it in your eyes,' said Zozimos. 'Soon you will be full up.'

'I am already,' said Publibor, smiling, and leaned back on his bench.

'As yet only your body is full up,' said Zozimos, 'but your soul is still puffed with high emotions and great expectations. You just wait until that goes.'

He was the only one still eating; kept on dipping his spoon in the soup with a sort of tormented greed while he talked. The others listened indolently.

'The soul forgets sooner than does the body,' he said and waved his spoon instructively. 'Just have a look around you, and see how they all sit by their pots, in stupid and vain satisfaction about their day's work; what do they care for their hungry brothers in all Italy? Alas, their thirst was quenched when they had but sipped a drop from the cup of freedom; they have long forgotten what they dreamed of when their palates withered on Mount Vesuvius. And Spartacus calls himself "Imperator" and has dealings with the mighty of this world and forms alliances with them. Wait, only wait, new-comer, until your eyes are opened, for so far they are still glued together with the sticky liquid of emotion.'

Publibor did not know what to say, he was a new-comer, sure enough. But he was very much surprised that the others around the table were keeping silent and did not take any interest in the conversation. The man who sat next to Publibor, a red-haired giant with the eternally homesick eyes of the Thracian mountaineer, rose clumsily from his bench, nodded, friendly and awkward, and stamped out. The hall emptied gradually. But Zozimos went on talking:

'Nearly two months it is since we have been sitting here, building our little homes, as though all of mankind's probems had been solved. Where is the rising of our Italian brethren? They tell each other fairy tales about Spartacus before they go to sleep at night and are proud of the fact that there is a Slave City in Italy. And when the master kicks their behinds, they yell: you wait till Spartacus comes and gets you! And that consoles them, and that is all which happens. Alas, our cause makes no progress, humanity is dull-brained and deaf. But we build little homes and eat our soup and forget about the misery of the others.'

Zozimos had underlined his words with sweeping gestures; now he let his arms fall back with grief. As nobody answered him, he sighed and scraped the dregs of the soup out of the pot. His gluttony seemed uncommonly funny to young Publibor; yet he had the impression that genuine sorrow inspired the rhetorician's speech.

The hall was empty now; in one corner only a few men sat throwing dice from a leather cup. Publibor was tired and sleepy, it had all been too much for one day; and when the rhetorician started off again with another tirade on the Sun State, he did not bother to listen—just as the girl with the maize had not bothered to listen to him. His eyes, which the rhetorician said were stuck together with the moisture of emotion, closed on their own accord; he fell asleep in sitting.

6

WORLD POLITICS

THE slaves of Italy had not heeded the call.

In the northern parts, in Etruria and Umbria, a number of
big landowners were murdered; their corpses were found in the
mornings with the ensign, the broken chain, beside them. But
no more than that happened. In a few towns, in Capua and Metapontum, occasional riots clogged up the markets. They were
suppressed; and that was all that happened. The great uprising
the Essene had prattled of on Mount Vesuvius; the insurrection
of the Italian slaves predicted by the lawyer Fulvius in the steambaths, had not come to pass. True, people from far away were still
flocking to join the Slave City; seventy thousand had built her,
a hundred thousand were already living within her walls—but
the town, the Sun City, remained the only one of her kind. Stern
and solitary, she stood in the plain between Crathis and Sybaris,
at the foot of the mountains. The people within her walls lived
according to her own laws, as though she lay not within the
Roman Empire but on a foreign planet.

His parchment scrolls squeezed under his arm, the chronicler
Fulvius strolled through the streets of the town, stroked his
bumpy pate and racked his brains as to where the fault lay. The
Roman Empire was finished, he had said it in his speeches, had
repeated it over and over again. The peasantry had been bled
empty, free workers had been supplanted by slave labour, those
who once earned their living had to go abegging or become
bandits. Rome was full of working hands, no hands were wanted.
Rome was flooded with cheap wheat—it rotted in the granaries,

and for the poor there was no bread. Not ten years went by without revolution and civil war; a new world and a new order were knocking at all doors, any child could see that nowadays. Where, then, lay the fault, mused the lawyer Fulvius, and missed the wooden beam over his desk. Why, then, did the Sun State remain alone, without the world responding, as though its walls stood on a foreign planet?

The last one to try saving this putrid order had been Sulla. He saw the abyss towards which the State was driving, heard the cries of the wretched and famished down below, and knew that a new era was about to dawn. And so he presumed to turn back the wheel of history: the legendary order of far-back times, the age of patriarchs, was to be resurrected, an age that knew not world commerce nor the Rights of Man; whose vision was narrow and devoutly limited; an age of evil, bloodthirsty gods ruling the mind of mankind. Only those who could prove that the blood in their veins was that of the superior She-Wolf-Race were to be the Lords and Masters in this State; every one else was as nothing before him. But when he went forth seeking to re-erect the heroic past, his conjuring call into space and time was answered by the thousand tongues of informers, blackmailers, adventurers and spies. Like merry sharks they splashed about in the sea of spilt blood and grew fat on the victims' corpses, clung to the cliffs of favouritism. And the country's best men went into exile.

Truly, this dictator walked the earth as in a trance, claimed to converse with gods in his sleep, called himself 'Sulla the Fortunate', and surrounded his own life with a guard of ten thousand bloodlusty men; the hell-hounds of his phantom realm.

But then the lice got hold of great Sulla, and the lice ate him up, which they call phthiriasis.

His rule had been but a nightmare interlude, the last attempt to delay the end of the doomed State by magic spells. True, the constitution bequeathed by him was still extant, the banished democrats were still in exile—but it was a question of mere years, perhaps of months only, until the reins would slip from the listless, senile hands of the Roman aristocracy.

But who should be the heir? Who possessed both firm grasp and exalted conviction, to bring about the new era? The slaves of Italy were deaf, they had not answered the call. There were twice as many slaves as free citizens in Italy, yet the Sun City remained alone. Her only allies were in Thurium; the lords of the Corporation had grasped the position more rapidly than those for whose sake the whole thing had been started. Where was the fault? Ought one to look for other allies?

The lawyer Fulvius remembered the treatise he had begun to write when the slaves of Capua thronged to man the walls instead of joining Spartacus; 'On the Causes which Induce Man to Act Contrary to His Own Interests', had been the heading of the treatise. Would he ever finish it? A sudden anxiety contracted the lawyer Fulvius's throat; a presentiment, perhaps, although he did not believe in presentiments. What was in store for him? One rainy night he had scrambled over the walls to join the revolution, now he was a chronicler, and adviser to the Imperator of the Sun State—but the revolution had not come about. What was in store for all of them? Perhaps this entire city which had sprouted from the soil with such impetuous rapidity, perhaps she too was but an interlude, destined to equally rapid extinction? An interlude, like the haunting nightmare of Sulla's dictatorship, but in opposite direction; there was no reason why history should not dream different, pleasanter dreams once in a while—and wake again, to go its own way.

But what sort of way? All these sufferings, all these turbid detours which it was said one had to take for the sake of the goal —were they perhaps not means to an end at all, were they the law of history itself; and the goal only human fancy—without any reality to back it up?

The lawyer Fulvius stood still in the middle of the street, so terrified suddenly that his parchment rolls dropped in the dust. What had got into his thoughts? Extremely turbid thoughts were these, pernicious, almost suicidal. If one's mind went thus astray while he was a political adviser, he did verily deserve to be strung up on one of the posts by the North Gate, in order to get rid of the ill, and in the interest of common welfare.

It is not good, thought the lawyer Fulvius, it is not good for people with responsibilities to think too much. And if they do, it would be far better for them to have a wooden beam hanging over their heads, which gives them beneficial bumps as a warning not to let their ideas get lost in blue eternity.

The lawyer Fulvius sighed and collected his parchment scrolls.

Oh yes, one had to look for new allies all right, that was the important thing right now. One must negotiate with all sorts of people, make all sorts of detours, regardless of where they might lead. The lawyer Fulvius squeezed the scrolls firmly under his arm, and continued his uphill way to the tent with the purple velum.

The tent with the purple velum was beginning to be a factor in world politics.

The camp saw the Imperator but rarely. His guards with their lustrous helmets and stern eyes broadcast his orders. The hammering of humming activity came distantly low into the tent, like the faraway breath of the mountains.

From a mast in front of the tent hung the purple velum, and flapped tremulously in the air when the sirocco drove it ahead; it slapped, heavy and saturated, against the mast when it rained. The sentries let no one pass without orders; they had harsh, intimidating faces.

And yet manifold visitors of strangely varied character were continually entering and leaving the tent. There were the Councillors of Thurium, who came to discuss the question of provisions, metal and building material. There were delegates who came to lodge complaints, sent chiefly by the ever-dissatisfied Gauls: quarrels had to be tried, judgment pronounced. There were the gladiators and minor leaders, who came to the daily conferences, brief now and almost mere formality—for the time of endless arguments was past, and the Imperator's frugal words decided and closed the meetings.

There were gentlemen of stately appearance and of a slightly flashy elegance who came and went regularly, escorted by a guard of honour which the Council of Thurium had provided: the ambassadors of the Pirate State. Their magnificent flagships rocked in the harbour, reverently gaped at by Thurium's citizens. Their fleet supplied the Slave Army with metals and weapons, and corn and merchandise for the rising trade of the new free-port of Thurium. The pirates were stately, proud gentlemen, though for the greater part slightly damaged; the admiral had a black patch over his left eye, his aide-de-camp limped a little, and all the gentlemen of the suite had lost minor parts of their bodies through the perils of naval life: a bit of ear, a few fingers or toes;

what else there might be missing was hidden by their sumptuous
finery. On Roman soil the gallows awaited them according to the
established law; now the Council of Thurium greeted them with
guards of honour.

There were travellers from Spain. They came clothed like
merchants, quiet and with small retinue: ambassadors of the
emigrants' army.

And in great splendour and pomp, announced by heralds,
acclaimed by the people, with Barbarian, glittering dress, with
idol-like, unmoved faces, came the diplomatic ambassadors of
Great King Mithridates.

All of these came and disappeared into the tent with the
purple velum, sat and parleyed with the new Imperator, the
ruler of South Italy, who was of obscure origin and had beaten
the Legions of the Roman Senate, who commanded an Army of
a hundred thousand; and who sat opposite them in a dusky corner
of his tent, and spoke tight and few words in a hoarse, Thracian
tone of voice, his face in a twilight of shadow.

In the evenings came the lawyer Fulvius. For many hours he
sat facing the Imperator in his tent at night, when the bluster of
the camp died down and the black mountains seemed to move
closer together around the city. Interrupted by much coughing,
dry and monotonous, he spoke of Roman politics in which he had
for so long a time taken an active part, in the radical wing of the
Democratic Party, until dictatorship forced him to go to earth in
Capua as an author, rhetorician and pettifogger. He talked of
the enemies of the Roman Empire, the Pontian King Mithridates,
the Armenian King Tigranes, the Pirate State, the Emigrants'
Army in Spain; of the network of treaties which connected these
powers from Asia to the Atlantic coast, from the Pyrenees to
Sicily. He talked also of the unrest, and of the lacking ability of
the Roman statesmen. Verily, the end of the lords of Rome was
near, power trembled in their senile hands, the only question was
who would be the first to wrest it from them. The Imperator
listened motionless.

'Take the refugees in Spain,' said Fulvius, 'most of them were
members of the old Democratic Party. Some of its members died
in the civil war, others on the scaffold; the rest fled abroad.

'There were several thousand of them, the intellectual élite of

Rome. At first they fared badly in exile, journeyed from one country to the next, not one wanted them. On old barges, which the pirates had given them from pity, they collected in the southern part of the Mediterranean, and put into all the Sicilian and North African ports for shelter and protection—but every one rejected them.

'Thus they went as far as Numidia, whose desert coast and sandy dunes became their winter refuge. It turned out, however, that the King of Numidia, who had seemed friendly and put them off with all sorts of promises, had only done so in order to make them feel safe, and extradite them to the dictator; for dictator Sulla's power reached far and his thirst for vengeance was unquenchable; and his agents and spies had pressed Hiempsal— that was the Numidian King's name—with so many threats and promises, that in the end he consented to this faithless breach of hospitality. The refugees escaped extradition by the skin of their teeth and found a new hide-out on a small island off the coast of Tunis. Thus they led wretchedly adventurous lives, pitied by all and condemned by all, for pity and contempt are twin brothers.

'Until the day when the greatest of all revolutionaries, the former governor of Spain deposed by Sulla—until Sertorius became their leader did they live thus; and from that day on the miserable band of emigrants became Rome's most potent foe.

'The people of Spain rose up against the new governors sent by the dictator, and received the refugees into their country. And now Sertorius recruited the Spaniards to his army, which became a very imposing one, and although he had no money to pay them with, had nothing but his fiery eloquence and the force of his arguments, thousands of the noblest Spaniards swore undying fealty to Sertorius and his fellows, and acknowledged him their legitimate governor. All those banished from Rome were enrolled as officers; King Mithridates and the Pirate State, who at first had not wanted anything to do with them, became their allies. And so the emigrants' war began, first against Sulla, and later against the heirs to his rule, a war that has lasted for eight years to this day.'

The lawyer paused, but Spartacus kept silent; one could not guess his thoughts. In three days' time the ambassadors of Sertorius were to arrive; messengers had announced their visit. Fulvius foresaw that the negotiations about an alliance would be distinctly difficult. He recalled the first parleys with the Council of Thurium, and felt a dry discomfort at the thought of the impending one. He longed to know the Imperator's opinion. But the Imperator kept silent.

Fulvius cleared his throat, he longed to be in his own tent, or better still, at the desk in his attic, writing his chronicle there; so that events would be helpfully purified by filtering through distance, before they came to him. He waited to see whether the Imperator would not say something after all, then he went on:

'Great is Sertorius's power. He has formed an Emigrants' Senate in Spain, which decrees laws and claims to be the constitutional government of Rome. His treaty with Mithridates cedes the King four Asiatic states under Roman protectorate, against which Mithridates places three thousand Gold Talents and forty men of war at his disposal. They say that this fleet, manned with the ablest of the refugees, and commanded by Marius the Younger, will shortly land on the Italian coast.

'It is probable that the delegates from Spain will ask us questions before they conclude an alliance. They will be tricky questions.'

At last the Imperator said out of his corner:

'Tell me the questions they will ask.'

'They are easy to predict,' replied Fulvius. 'They will ask us exactly what the Thurium-people asked us. Is it true that you want to rob the citizen of his house, the master of his servant? Is it true that you want to turn everything upside-down? Is it true that you want to give land not only to the farmer, but also to the slave? And the worst of it is, they will ask only partly from egotism and worry for their petty welfare; and partly they will ask in all honesty of conviction and great blindness. And if we answered them in all honesty of conviction, they would not understand us.'

'And what shall we answer?' said Spartacus.

The lawyer did not reply at once. Discomfort blocked his throat. Finally he said:

'We have conquered Varinius—Rome will send fresh Legions. Sertorius has an army many times superior to ours in number, arms and trained mercenaries; yet he has been trying for eight years to finish off the Legions of Rome. The State is weak and almost dead, but the Legions are as strong as ever. The enemies of Rome can be victorious only if united, their struggle is our struggle.'

'Is their victory our victory?'

'No. But every alliance has a false bottom.'

'And what will the horde have to say to such an alliance?'

'They won't understand it,' said Fulvius. 'But we are acting in their name and interest.'

Spartacus was silent.

The oil lamp flickered, about to go out, and the lawyer rose fumblingly to replace the wick with a new one.

'Leave it alone,' said Spartacus sharply, from his corner.

'I can't talk into the dark,' said the lawyer.

'You don't need a light for talking,' said Spartacus. 'The old man who used to talk a lot to me before you came along, could arrange his words best when it was dark.'

'There are matters better talked about in the dark, and matters better talked about in the light,' said the lawyer Fulvius.

'What's the difference?'

'The former appeal to Sentiment which has its roots in darkness, the latter to Reason which needs every sense on the alert to assert itself.'

They were both silent. Fulvius was exhausted and caught his eyelids drooping. He had a strange feeling of himself not speaking his own mind at all, but merely wording that which the other wished to hear. Who was the leader here and who was being led? This impenetrable son of the mountains began to make him feel uneasy, the way he was still sitting, motionless in his corner, elbows propped on his knees, like a wood-cutter, his face expressionless. Was he crafty or a simpleton, knowing or but carried along? Or were these differentiations that did not exist in the field of action? He emitted great power which forced every one about him to offer up their innermost knowledge; his eyes fastened on one and sucked dry the deepest wells of one's being; but it did not seem as though he cared very much. Did these lengthy conversations help him to make up his mind—or did he only want them to confirm long-established decisions?

During the long silence the tent-walls began to sway, touched by a wind that had set out from the sea. The purple velum outside beat against its mast with slapping blows and went silent again; but the sea breeze stayed and returned at intervals, swept clear the darkness between the stars, and shook the fusty air out of the tent. A cock strained his voice in crowing, others joined in irregular chorus; morn was approaching.

Fulvius started up. The man opposite had risen, stretched himself, suddenly filled the tent. Blinking, the lawyer looked up at him, looked at that broad and hard face whose planes were already tinged with the yellow light of day. Controlling himself and his heavy tongue, Fulvius asked:

'Will you enter the alliance . . . ?'

. . . and was startled by the full and ringing voice of the Imperator above him, who had already flung back the tent flap and called from outside, alien and distant: he, Fulvius, might have it announced that the Slaves would unite with the enemies of Rome, the Pirates and the Emigrants and Great King Mithridates; unite in joint struggle against the lords of the earth, the Roman Senate.

And he saw the Imperator descend the hill and disappear between the two rows of guards who, reeling up from heavy sleep, saluted him with up-raised arms; across his broad back stretched shaggily the dappled fur.

7

THE LONGING

IN spring, when March blew reckless breezes and the crops sprouted from the clods, they had built their city; now it was summer, and the heat had set in.

The soil was cracked, its saps dried up. The sea was like lead, reflecting the heaven's blast in unbearable glitter. The mould pulverised into dust, the dust covered everything once moist and green with a floury powder. The brooks shrank, slowed, died the Dry Death.

The cattle grew slothful, the white buffaloes lay in the shade with heaving flanks. Men and women, too, grew slothful; first their bodies, then their minds.

There were a hundred thousand of them.

When the rains set in they had dreamt of a firm city, of a firm city to hibernate in, a town with walls which was their own.

Now they had their town, she had firm walls and belonged to them.

Why should the strong serve the weak, they had asked, why should the Many serve the Few? Now they were strong and numerous and served themselves.

We guard their cattle, they had complained, and drag the bloody calf out of the cow, but not into our herds. We build them houses but may not live in them. We are to fight battles, but for the interests of others. Now they were doing all that for themselves.

For lost justice they had longed, for the age of Saturn, an age

201

that knew, not masters and slaves, but equal rights and good-will. Now they were free and had their new law.

They lived, a hundred thousand strong, in the new town which stood in the present, visible from afar between seas and mountains. No longer a mirage of the future, no past grown questionable with distance, here and now were the mountains, the town, fulfilment. . . .

Was it fulfilment?

That sloth which had come over them in the hot, sizzling air, was it the sloth of satiety and contentment? Had they no goal, no longing, no desires left?

Life in the town took its course. The shepherds drove the cattle to the meadows, farm-hands, weeders, mowers went about their work, the women cooked, the children played in the dust, the law-breakers died on the stakes by the North Gate, the gods toused about the hot streets. It was as though everything had been like this for years. In the evenings people told each other stories about the wicked time of slavery, it lay far behind them, and now only half of it was true.

A kind of drowsiness hung over the city, possibly produced by the heat. And a musty, unhealthy expectation was inside the people, of which they themselves knew nothing.

When the Slave Town had seen five months pass, food grew scarce, the granaries stood empty, and the meals inside the dining halls became scantier. General feeling sank rapidly.

Young Publibor noticed it every time he entered the dining hall. As before, six of them dipped into the soup in the joint bowl, but it was only half-full; the wooden ladles travelled considerably faster and clanged together more often. The greatest dexterity was exhibited by the rhetorician Zozimos; his ladle travelled the road between pot and mouth twice as often as the others' in the same space of time; his sleeves fluttered, and in addition he talked almost incessantly. His most frequent topic was the posts by the North Gate which had lately increased in number.

'Discipline and warning, indeed,' scoffed Zozimos. 'Did we fight and endure the most unusual hardships in order to exchange the old yoke for a new one? In the old days your belly growled with wrath, now it growls with discipline. Life in the Sun Town has become jaded and narrow; enthusiasm and fraternity of yore

—what has become of them? The old chasm between leaders and
common people has opened again, the Imperator meets only
with Councillors and diplomats—to whose entertainment, I
might add, the scarcity of provisions does not seem to apply; but
no matter. Of course, we have learnt that it is all done to further
higher interests and our own welfare—things that we unfortunately don't know anything about. So we must needs be herded
like sheep who would not find the way to the pasture on their
own; well and good, let us suppose that it is so. But the meadow
is barren, and the sheep start bleating as one might have expected.
And now listen well, my lad, listen to what else happens, for this
is the important point. Suddenly, you see, the shepherd begins
to talk to the sheep as though they were reasoning creatures, and
talks to them of patience and discipline and lofty reasons, and
declares that those who will not understand and go on bleating,
must be slaughtered to serve a higher cause.

'That's what the philosophers call a paradoxon. Can you
reply to this, my lad?'

No, Publibor could not. He had been listening in a spirit of
contradictory confusion; repelled by the agitated sleeve-flapping
of the other, he felt at the same time that the man, despite all his
antics, was honest in his grief. Ah yes, it was difficult to get one's
bearings in this town, whose life was so very different from what
one had imagined it to be like! He remembered the day of his
arrival, his horror at the sight of the wooden crosses by the
North Gate; and, as though in apology for a sinful thought, he
muttered hastily:

'Still, the Imperator surely means well, whatever he does.'

But these seemed to be the very words the other had been
waiting for. He even put his spoon down and, gesticulating
frantically, fairly pounced on poor Publibor:

'He means well, you say? Of course he means well, that's the
worst of it. There is no more dangerous tyrant than he who is
convinced he is the selfless guardian of the people. For the damage
done by the congenitally wicked tyrant is confined to the field of
his personal interests and his personal cruelty; but the well-
meaning tyrant who has a lofty reason for everything, can do un-
limited damage. Just think of the God Jehovah, my lad: ever
since the unfortunate Hebrews chose to adhere to Him, they've
had one calamity after the other, from lofty reasons every time,

because He means so well. Give me our old bloodthirsty gods
every time: you throw them a sacrifice now and then, and they
leave you in peace.'

To this naturally Publibor could not say anything either. But
that was unnecessary anyhow, for Zozimos talked on irrepressibly.
Publibor noticed that the other men at the table who never used
to listen to the rhetorician and had always got up as soon as they
had finished their meal, were now staying on and listening
attentively.

'But,' Zozimos went on, 'we aren't talking of gods but of
human beings. And I tell you, it is dangerous to combine so
much power in the fist, and so many lofty reasons in the head, of
one single person. In the beginning the head will always order
the fist to strike from lofty reasons; later on the fist strikes of its
own accord and the head supplies the lofty reasons afterwards;
and the person does not even notice the difference. That's human
nature, my lad. Many a man has started out as a friend of the
people and ended up as a tyrant; but history gives not a single
example of a man starting out as a tyrant and ending up as a
friend of the people. Therefore I tell you again: there is nothing
so dangerous as a dictator who means well.'

Everyone was silent, and Zozimos tried to scrape the last
drops of soup from the dish. But the red-haired giant with the
eternally homesick eyes of the Thracian shepherds who sat next
to Publibor, sighed suddenly and said:

'You talk a lot of muck, you do. We should all go home, to
the mountains, where we came from.'

'Did you hear that!' cried Zozimos. 'Every day you can hear
such talk. They think of the past instead of the future. All of a
sudden they all want to go home.'

The giant nodded in agreement. 'Everybody says so. What do
we gain, fighting the Romans all the time? If you kill one, along
comes another. We should go back, to the mountains, now that
no one can stop us . . .'

Outraged, Zozimos flung both arms up in the air. His sleeves
aflutter, he got ready for a great speech of protest. But this time
Publibor anticipated him. Blushing with shock at his own
temerity, he said to the giant:

'Wouldn't you be sorry to go away from the town and never
to live in this way again?'

But the giant avoided answering; perhaps he did not know how. 'In the mountains we were free, too,' was all he said, 'before the naked-skull came and chased us. And there was plenty of sun too in the mountains. We should go back now. That's where Spartacus should lead us.'

'But he certainly won't,' cried Zozimos, 'he has other bees in his bonnet.'

'Well, well,' said the man and rose clumsily. 'How do you know what's inside Spartacus's head? We'll have to wait, that's all, and then he'll lead us all back home.'

He sighed once more and, like the rest, left the hall without bidding them good-bye.

Every day Publibor heard similar talk in the dining hall. More and more people began to talk of going home. At night the Thracians and Celts sang the songs of their native lands, emerging from years-old oblivion. Many had never known those legendary countries, had been born in captivity as their fathers and grandfathers before them; others had only dimmed memories left. But all of them talked of those countries now; homesickness and longing haunted men and women as once fever had haunted them in the swamp-island by the Clanius. And there was no medicine against this infection.

A blurred, expectant, unhealthy longing infested men and women. From the tent with the purple velum issued the announcement that the cause of dearth was a passing stoppage in the food-supply. Patience, and all will soon be well. Also, the allied fleet is on its way, the emigrants' fleet, commanded by Young Marius.

But that did not fill the pots, and the guards with the lustrous helmets who broadcast the Imperator's message to the town, were confronted more and more by unreceptive faces and ears. Many said enough words and decrees had by now come out of the tent with the purple velum; you had not fought and shed your blood and conquered the Romans in order to bend once more under the yoke of labour and drink once more your own sweat. Particularly glib and loud were those who had neither fought nor shed their blood, but had come quite recently, begging to be let in; among them a tramp with a bird's head and eyes which lay close together and shifted incessantly in their orbits.

But they found a following among many people who would no longer listen to the words from the tent with the purple velum; and the meals in the dining halls became ever smaller. Not that they were starving, but very nearly so. Many, in fact most of the hundred thousand, had in their past lives known hunger more intimately and regarded it as the natural companion of their existence. But past experience evaporates quickly from the memory of man, and the more tormenting the experience, the quicker it devours every trace of itself. And so, when the forgotten and yet so familiar burning arose once more in the innards of the people, they erupted in angry words against the tent with the purple velum, against the false advisers and haughty blindness of Spartacus, who parleyed with ambassadors and diplomats instead of taking for himself and his fellows that for which their stomachs growled. Was not their neighbour the fair city of Thurium with her full store houses? Were there not plenty of bountiful cities in Lucania? What could prevent them from taking what was their, the victors', due? What kind of crazy law was this which enjoined them to ever waxing privation and barred the logical way out of their pressing want? Had they not had a fine time at the beginning of the rising, when one celebrated merry entries into Nola, Suessula and Calatia?

A blurred, unhealthy longing was in men and women, and as they lived together, a hundred thousand, densely packed, the longing found a hundred thousand echoes.

At night the Thracians and Celts sang their traditional songs, believed to have been forgotten. And in those days one name was in every one's mouth, a name believed to have been equally forgotten: the name of Crixus.

Ever since his return Crixus had retired from public affairs.

In the days of the siege of Capua the renegades had elected him to be their leader. He had done nothing towards promoting the split-up and done nothing towards preventing it; without his doing they had elected him. The renegades had been slaughtered by the Romans, but he had been miraculously spared and came back to the camp; was taciturn as he had always been; fought, gloomy and savage, as he had always fought. When they had finished campaigning and began building their city between mountains and seas, Crixus had again stepped aside and left leadership to Spartacus. He said nothing when they entered the alliance with Thurium, said nothing when Spartacus decreed the new laws, said nothing when Sertorius and the Asiatic King began negotiations. Sullenly he moved his heavy bulk about the camp, his sad fish-eyes watched them hammer and build; at night he got drunk and lay with maidens and boys. But even then he remained gloomy and taciturn; nobody had ever seen him smile with the joy of the flesh.

He was little loved, yet secretly the Gauls and Germans still regarded him as their rightful leader; for he spoke their language and wore a moustache like them, and like them a silver necklace round his thick neck.

The Gauls and Germans numbered about thirty thousand; they constituted a third of the town's inhabitants. But all the others who also harboured in their hearts the unhealthy longing and the memories of the time of Nola, Suessula and Calatia, raised their eyes to the taciturn man. He decreed no laws and issued no commands, did not negotiate with foreign ambassadors, yet he seemed to many mightier than the Imperator himself. They felt drawn to him in a different, turbid way to which they could give no name, they saw in him the dismal embodiment of their fate.

He did nothing towards accelerating developments, and nothing towards staying them. But at mealtimes there was less and less, and the memories of the fine days of Nola, Suessula and Calatia lived on in many minds. The discontented, victims of restlessness and turbid longing, knew: the gloomy one was the man for them.

8

THE LITTLE RED VEINS

Directly responsible for the emptiness in the store houses and the scantiness of the meals was the Concil of Thurium who of late seemed more and more inclined to make trouble.

Ever since the gentlemen of the Council had realised to their amazement that this extraordinary Prince or brigand-chief, whichever you liked, kept strictly to the letter of the agreement and watched sternly over his men's respect for the immunity of the citizens, ever since then their confidence had returned; and a feeling of security clears one's head and makes room in it for all sorts of thoughts and considerations.

Above all, it was to be noted that no other districts of Italy showed any signs of the rebellion's spreading. In vain the emissaries of the Brotherhood travelled across the whole country, from the Gulf of Tarentum to Gallia Cisalpina, from the Adriatic to the Tyrrhenic seas. The slaves did not rise up, the emissaries met with approbation but no readiness to act. Perhaps overgreat misery had macerated their courage of action, perhaps the reaction of the hundred years' civil war became apparent only now, with the symptoms of paralysing weariness; perhaps they were all living in a period of abortive revolutions. Whatever it was, the Thracian could go on waiting for his Italian revolution until he was black in the face.

But what about the powerful allies of the brigand-chief? A variety of reports and rumours had reached Thurium during the last few days. It was said that discord was dividing the refugees in Spain, they were always at each other's throats as it was, the

Anti-Senate itself was split up into opposed factions; people were talking of a serious defeat suffered by the Emigrants' Army at the hands of Pompeius. Nor did fate seem to be smiling on Mithridates; his father-in-law, Great King Tigranes, had let him down—he who staked his hopes on these gentry might yet live to experience all sorts of disappointments. It certainly looked as though the Romans had recaptured their luck of battle which traditionally set in whenever everything seemed lost.

The gods knew with what mixed feelings the gentlemen of the Council of Thurium received these reports; but one had to look at things realistically.

There was still the emigrants' fleet in the charge of Young Marius. It was supposed to consist of no less than fifty galleys and frigates, manned with ten thousand picked warriors, the cream of the Roman refugees, commanded by the son of the gallant champion of liberty, Marius the Younger in person. If they did land on Italian soil, revolution had indeed a very good chance. In that case the most reputable citizens of democratic leanings would join in, as well as all those entrenched cities which now faced the gladiator with barred gates and spear-bristling walls.

So far, so good. The load of anxiety lifted off their chests, the Councillors of Thurium considered without prejudice the world situation, weighed arguments and counter-arguments in their heads and came to the conclusion that the position of both parties was so far about equal.

But that was changed on the day on which one of the pirate captains—who were quite at home in the free-port now, came and went like homing pigeons and had dinner with the very best people, customary rite among distinguished business acquaintances—when one of these portly captains, without the habitual guard of honour, accompanied by only one aide-de-camp, entered in some haste the offices of the Council of Thurium.

Athenodoros was the captain's name. He came straight from a long voyage; his gilt galley, laden with iron and copper for the Slave Town, rocked on the blue waves of the bay of Thurium, cheered and gaped at by the people. The captain was at once received by the gentlemen of the Council; they expressed their regret at not having been allowed time to provide the guard of honour. The captain waved it aside; he had brought more important news with him, never mind escort and formality.

A great battle had been fought in the waters of Asia Minor; fire signals had transmitted the news from isle to isle, the mounted messengers of the Roman trading companies had borne it across the Greek mainland, the pirate ships' flags had waved it on through the Adriatic. Captain Athenodoros was the first to set foot on Italian soil. The emigrants' fleet was annihilated.

Nobody knew any details as yet. All that was known was that the Roman general Lucullus with part of his fleet had taken by surprise and sunk fifteen hostile galleys between the Trojan coast and the island of Tenedos. The main force of the emigrants' fleet had been stationed by the small island of Neae near Lemnos. It appeared that, in criminal levity, the refugees had cast anchor by the beach and scattered all over the island in order to enjoy its daughters. Evidently they had not even sent scouts cruising, remarked the pirate captain scornfully. Thus Lucullus surprised them. He seized the badly guarded men of war and hounded the scattered crew together like hares. Young Marius himself, and with him the cream of the emigrants, died fighting on the island. The rest were herded and trapped in one spot and imprisoned on their own ships. That was the end of the emigrants' fleet. King Mithridates, who had been financing them, had thus also lost his navy.

Well, if that was not news, what was? It had to be weighed and thought over with reinvigorated brains. The scales, trembling in balance up to now with the forces and tensions in the world, tipped noticeably. Poor old gladiator-Prince and bandit, you devout keeper of agreements, we weighed you, you were too light. Go on minding peace and order in that town of yours; go on waiting for your mighty allies, they won't come; events are turning over a new leaf now . . . Does the worthy captain intend to let the Thracian Imperator have this priceless information?

He did not see any occasion to do so, said the worthy and portly captain. Sooner or later the Imperators would hear of it anyway. On the other hand, as regards the impending fluctuations in the price of corn, the sole possession of such news was, as the gentlemen themselves had said so aptly, priceless indeed.

'Indeed, yes,' confirmed the gentlemen of the Thurium Town Council, and very soon an agreement on the price was reached.

The captain further notified them that he would in future supply the Sicilian corn for the Slave Town only against immediate payment. Until now the pirates had allowed the Council credit for Spartacus.

Several hours later the Council of Thurium met for a confidential conference. On the agenda were: Change of policy with a view to the altered situation, and the deliberation of certain measures concerning the sustenance of the Sun City; which were soon to have a distressing effect on her dining halls.

Present at this historical session were the First and Second Councillors—a dignified old gentleman with slightly protruding eyes, and a sturdy business man; also Hegio, retired philosopher, the greengrocer Tyndarus and several other members of the Council.

Most of those present approved of the proposed measures. Some, though, voiced the objection whether these might not endanger the safety of Thurium—in case the bandits, affected by the measures in question, decided to break the treaty after all and indulge their baser instincts. The greengrocer Tyndarus in particular mentioned the well-known bowstring which must not be over-stretched, the fierce lion one must not tease, and more such figurative turns of speech, inspired partly by fear and partly by the endeavour to impress his colleagues with his education. In the course of all this they happened, for the first time, on the name of the town *Metapontum*.

The dignified old gentleman was the one to pronounce it. 'Why should we be the ones to suffer all the time?' he cried, his voice trembling with virtuous indignation. 'Why we and we alone, why not Metapontum for once?' His protruding eyes rested on every one in turn; they had all grown quiet. Their re-invigorated brains had quickly grasped meaning and range of this exclamation. Metapontum, the second largest city on the coast by the Gulf of Tarentum, was also a Greek settlement; sixty Roman miles and a century-old commercial feud separated the two cities.

'Why we and we alone?' repeated the old man, and his venerable head shook slightly. 'After all, we did enter into an alliance with the Thracian Prince. If the Prince yearns for booty or martial feats he might seek them with those who failed to do so.'

The Councillors were silent. They had not thought that the dignified old gentleman had so much practical sense in him; even the greengrocer Tyndarus suppressed a picturesque simile which had just occurred to him. Only Hegio whistled thinly with both boyish and senile bad manners; he thought of great Pythagoras having taught in Metapontum, which thus became the cradle of the so-called Italian trend in philosophy; and thought further that, if the dignified old man should be proved right, Metapontum would be levelled to the ground. He thought also of his escaped slave Publibor who had confessed in his shyly sedate way that he was waiting for his, Hegio's, death. By all the gods and philosophers, Hegio could hardly blame him at this moment; yet he kept silent and whistled thinly. For the third thing to come into his thoughts after Pythagoras and young Publibor had been his shares in the pitch refineries at Sila, and simultaneously his wife, the Roman matron, of whom he was afraid because he could fulfil his connubial duties but rarely.

Such a labyrinthine maze of ideas was conjured up by the word 'Metapontum', when it emerged for the first time from the toothless gums of an aged man.

From this day on the food supply to the Slave Town began to flow even more scantily; stoppages, irregularities occurred. Also, a large percentage of the victuals supplied were rotten and inedible. The store houses had to be opened, soon they were emptied of provisions.

Called to account, the gentlemen of the Thurium Corporation used subterfuges. Whenever they possibly could, they sent the dignified old Councillor to the front. With his trembling voice full of guileless equitability he gave the reasons: reasons of a technical or financial nature about which he knew nothing at all. It was all very moving. He deplored the unreliability of the pirates; things had been different when he was young—that's what happened when you did business with such lawless folk.

On hearing this, young Oenomaus instinctively lowered his eyes, and the pettifogger Fulvius cleared his throat uncertainly. He thought of his own saying that every alliance has a false bottom: perhaps that was why he felt so completely left in the air now. When he looked into those protruding eyes, traversed by a net of little red veins, he felt reduced to insignificance. He stroked his bumpy lawyer's skull, dearly missed the wooden beam above the desk in his Capuan attic, and asked a deliberately dry question about a wagon-load of rotten turnips. What did a white-whiskered patrician know of rotten turnips? But he let it pass in great dignity and indulgence, he showed no irritation, the suspicion of angry pink on his aged cheeks was hardly noticeable. He actually consented to discuss the turnips, he knew nothing about them and offered completely senseless explanations: his efforts were all the more touching. After half an hour of it Fulvius, frayed, usually gave it up. The little red veins were so forceful an argument that he could not stand up to it. Oenomaus had for a long time been but a silent nonentity with lowered eyes.

Thus several weeks went by and yet no conclusion had been arrived at. After each conference the people in the Slave Town hoped the error would be rectified, the puzzle solved—and knew they were deceiving themselves. The captains demanded coercive measures and reprisals against Thurium: Fulvius wavered, Spartacus resisted. For some time now they had been receiving provisions on credit, the booty-treasure had molten into the sword smithies; iron and copper were most important, were still paid for in cash, were still punctually delivered.

When the dearth got worse and worse—not starvation yet, but a state of affairs sadly like it—the captains got together and demanded that steps be taken against Thurium. They did not say what sort of steps. For the first time since Capua Crixus made an appearance at this meeting; he said nothing, but the fact that he was there made a deep impression on everyone present and affected the general feeling in the city. Spartacus would not comply, he demanded time. Was not Marius's fleet on its way? Was it not expected to land on the Italian coast any day now? One must not spoil everything because of petty greed and impatient guts. Remember Nola, Suessula, Calatia! We poured blood all over the land Campania, and everybody turned against us, even our brothers. Remember how we camped before Capua, in bog and rain, and had soiled the name of the Sun State—and darkness and horror clouded our road. . . .

Vehement and forceful, the man with the fur-skin spoke to them, countered their petty reasons with great reasons, their short-sighted demand for straight roads with the laws of detours; his voice was the voice of the days in the swamps by the Clanius and inside the crater of Vesuvius; he had been right in all their times of trial. He demanded time, argued well and vehemently.

The captains grumbled and subsided. Fulvius wavered. Crixus said nothing.

But the town was haunted in those days by a name whispered from mouth to ear, which set up a goal for the unhealthy longing and greed: Metapontum.

9

DESTRUCTION OF
THE TOWN METAPONTUM

FROM THE CHRONICLE OF FULVIUS THE LAWYER

31. Inasmuch as the serfs of Italy had failed to rebel, and the allies of Spartacus, ill favoured by luck of battle, had made no appearance on the Italian scene, the Slaves in their City were left alone to defy a hostile world. The Age of Justice on which they had set their hopes and whose advent had seemingly been predicted by all manner of signs, had not descended upon Italy. Rather, everything remained as it had been heretofore, and all over the inhabited world traditional law and order persevered. In such circumstances the Sun City, built by Spartacus and ruled by the Slave Law, could not but give the impression of not being a concrete reality of the present, but the product of another age, an outlandish continent even, or a foreign planet.
But man is not allowed to shape his existence independently of the system, conditions and laws of his time.

33. And so it happened with the Slaves in their City.
Fate and a wicked order had condemned these people to the predicament of slavery, and had sown hunger and greed into their entrails, so that they became like wolves. And like a pack of wolves released from their cages, they had hurled themselves upon Nola, Suessula and Calatia, until their greed yielded to satiety. Meanwhile they had shed the shaggy hide and turned tame. They had built their City, had dreamed of leading a life of Justice and Goodwill within her walls. But the period in which these unfortunate men lived would have none of it. It reached across their walls and reminded them that beyond not the laws of the Sun

State reigned supreme, but the law of the stronger, which left slaves no choice besides servitude or the use of brute force. Those who had desired to live like humans, were compelled to become wolves once again.

Now they awoke from their dream and saw that they had again grown claws. Roars issued from their throats, and they set out again to tear their tormentors limb from limb. Their goal was the town Metapontum, which they destroyed.

But, by relapsing into ferocity and wolf's countenance of yore they had destroyed the fundaments on which their own City rested, and no one was able to stay her decline and fall after this.

A few men had come out with the idea, and quickly the name of Metapontum had impressed itself on many minds. A most marvellous city was Metapontum, her store houses were bursting with fruit and bacon, her temples were bursting with bars of solid silver and gold.

When they rose from the empty dishes in the dining halls, one would nudge the other stealthily, it was like a secret password: 'What will we eat in Metapontum?' 'Fieldfare with bacon, that's what we'll eat in Metapontum.' 'What will we drink in Metapontum?' 'Wine from Carmel, wine from Vesuvius, that's what we'll drink in Metapontum.' 'What will the girls be like in Metapontum?' 'Like opened oranges—that's what they will be like.' 'How far is it to Metapontum?' 'Sixty miles from here, one night and one day.'

A few men had come out with the idea: those who frequently went to Thurium on business, to supervise the unloading of cargo, and to talk with the gentlemen of the Town Council.

Every day they came back and had more to say about the bounty of Metapontum. And these men no longer had as famished a look about them as had the rest. They were living on the good things of Metapontum in advance.

The conference of the captains, during which Spartacus had demanded time, Fulvius wavered, and Crixus said nothing, had taken place at noon. Now it is eventide; the night will be a dark one, the moon will not rise.

The moon has gone on a trip, she will take her time before she comes back.

Already it is quite dark, you cannot even see the mountain's outlines, but you can hear the sea. A secretive, whispering activity rustles through the camp, footsteps patter through the lightless streets; after that the silence is more choking than before. The sentries' footfalls die away—and at once the hiss and whisper and tapping of hurried sandals come back from every nook. The Celtic quarter in particular, populated by Gauls and Germans, is filled with the stifled noises. The uninitiated listen warily in their tents and keep quiet.

But among those in the know, a secret password goes from mouth to ear: 'How far is it to Metapontum?' 'Sixty miles, one dark night and one short day.' And a whispered rumour is passed on: Crixus is with us.

The night is very dark, you cannot even see the mountain's outlines. The sirocco charges darkness with heat, men and women groan in their sleep, afflicted with nightmares. In the tent with the purple velum the Imperator sits in his corner behind the oil lamp, opposite him the lawyer Fulvius, reading in a husky voice the Council of Thurium's report on the causes of the irregularities in the transport of turnips.

But at this hour the three thousand conspirators had already left the camp and were trotting at full speed along the highway which followed the edge of the twinkling sea to the town Metapontum.

The town of Metapontum also traced her foundation to the Trojan wars; the faded records in the Magistrate's archives stated that Nestor, leader of the Pylians, had built her when his warriors had conquered this land of wine and beef, and brought unto the Italian Barbarians Asiatic splendour, arts and sciences. A wonderful coin collection was kept under lock and key in the Magistrate's library, behind coloured Phoenician glass; they were unlike the clumsy, thick pieces of Roman silver, stamped on one side only, which could be easily forged in lesser metals if the State had a mind to do so—no, they were flat, thin silver discs, voluptuously smooth, with neat and dainty inscriptions in whose elucidation the philologists could prove their sagacity. The town had lived through eight centuries, survived dozens of invasions, always smilingly submissive to the victor, taming him with her graceful compliance. She had opened her gates to Hannibal as well as Pythagoras, hunted out by the Crotoniates; had bowed to numerous masters and numerous deities, even if most zealously to Anadyomene; her cellars hoarded opulent sweet wine, and the white cows turned on the spits over her hearths. None of her prophets, augurs and erudite astronomers had predicted her ghastly end.

It happened after sunset, after a day that had been like all other days. The gates had not been closed yet, farmers were still bent on their work in the fields. Already they unharnessed the buffaloes from the ploughs, led the thirsty beasts to their water troughs, shouldered their tools on their peaceable way home, when a cloud of dust blotted out the southern highway. Curious, they looked and wondered what it could be that rolled toward their walls, howling and with clattering hoofs. But already the cattle roared plaintively, and broke loose and galloped across the fields. The dismayed farmers sped after their cattle, and the riders on foaming horses sped after the farmers; iron bit hotly into their skulls before they knew what was happening. Thus the massacre began outside their walls and rolled on into the town through every gate at once, and drowned her with a deluge of fire and blood which lasted the whole night through. But the night was dark because the moon had taken a trip, and hour followed hour without the outcry of the murdered city weakening or pausing; for the cries of fury, death and lust were mingling in a horrible chorus which strangled the thundering of the surf. When the cocks crowed for the second time, the whole city was burning away, from the harbour to the Latin Gate; and when the sun raised his head at last from the waves, he looked pale and weary and screened his face with the veil which rose black and flaky from the pillars of flame. All the cities the slaves had sacked in the course of their campaign had suffered and been maimed through the wrath of the oppressed; but the town Metapontum suffered only for one night, for in the morning the town Metapontum was no more.

Trojan warriors had founded her, for eight centuries she had given herself smilingly to every conqueror, the spits over her hearths had never stopped turning. Now she had been erased from the surface of the inhabited earth. Charred walls left for weather to gnaw, cindery flesh dispersed by the winds, dully iridescent lumps of silver coins and coloured Phoenician glass: such harvest saw the morn.

I O

THE LOFTY REASONS

WHEN, towards morning, they broke the news to the Imperator in his tent, he understood at once that this meant the end of the Sun City.

Two of the guards had been sent as messengers, and they were very frightened of his anger. They wore gleaming helmets above their flushed necks; at an inn by the Appian Way they had joined the horde, had served it faithfully ever since. Brave and awkward, sparing with their words, they reported: part of the Brotherhood, three thousand maybe, disappeared from the town last night. They took horses. There is reason to suppose that they set out to pillage the town of Metapontum.

Briefly and simply they talked, as though reporting as on all other days; straight, bull-necked, they stood before him, clutched their torches and were frightened.

But the Imperator did not get angry. He sat quite still and said nothing at all. The servants of Fannius were surprised. For quite some time he sat in his habitual, motionless way; the torches' light coaxed sparks from his fur-skin. Afterwards he asked for details in his usual, harsh Thracian tones. The servants stood straight and amazed. By and by they noticed the animal sadness in the Imperator's eyes. They stood before him and clutched their torches. Outside it was already growing light. Then he gave them their orders.

The orders sounded clipped and determined as always. The servants exchanged looks: he really was a proper Imperator. The conspirators numbered three thousand; six thousand of his most reliable men, all Thracians and Lucanians, he sent after them. They were to bring back the runaways, by force if necessary. They had about twelve hours' start; the pursuers would find them in Metapontum, enfeebled with looting and debauchery. In two days' time at the latest pursuers and pursued would be back.

In the meantime he sent a message to Thurium. The message said that, unless the stoppages in food supply ceased immediately, the Imperator would hold the gentlemen of the Council personally responsible and would make an example of them. The gentlemen were perturbed. He was a brigand-chief after all, they should never have had any dealings with him. They promised to do their best.

After that everybody waited for the return of those at Metapontum. A tensive suspense hung over the Celtic quarter. Life in the town stopped pulsating; nobody worked, they were waiting. Everyone knew that a turning point was at hand. The dining halls witnessed the first brawls.

They came back the next evening, pursuers and pursued; but of the nine thousand only six thousand were left. The Celts and Germans had offered resistance, the pursuers had had to surround them among the ruins of Metapontum, there had been gruesome fighting. Every third man on both sides had been killed. At last the insurgents had surrendered, were disarmed and brought back. Crixus was not among them. The prisoners, their hands bound, tied together in groups with long ropes, were led through the East Gate by the Thracians and Lucanians.

Immediately after their arrival, the Slave City split up into two parties. Both mourned their dead, accused the opponents of fratricide. Both were prolific with arguments and had some of the right on their side. That night was rent by rioting and uproar.

That night the Imperator delivered a speech to the assembled captains. He declared that, if they wanted to save the Sun City, they must not shrink from any measures. In his everyday voice he ordered twenty-four of the ringleaders to be crucified without delay. That, he said, was what he had had them brought back for. If one wanted to prevent the Army's dissolving into looting gangs, one had no other choice.

For the first time since Capua the captains raised objections.

They wrangled for some time, the town sent muddled noise and outcry into the tent, street fighting was going on; the Celts had begun to pilfer the store houses. After letting the captains wrangle for a while, Spartacus repeated that they had no choice if they wanted to prevent the Army's disbanding, and that they could not afford to lose any time; then he asked them very quietly who among them intended to oppose his orders. Five Celtic captains, gladiators of the Old Horde all of them, declared that they would. Before they had time to draw arms they were overpowered by the guards who had been waiting outside the tent. The rest of the captains realised that they had walked into a trap, and kept silent. When the Imperator, always with the same quiet voice, told them that these five would share the ringleaders' fate, they dared not object, with the exception of timid Oenomaus who had been silent up to then. When the guards seized him, the Imperator for the first time looked away.

These six were led off, bound hand and foot. They cursed and kicked and struggled, one of them wept with rage and shame; Oenomaus hung his head, the blue vein swelling on his bruised forehead. All six were gladiators, comrades of the Imperator, from the school of Lentulus Batuatus in Capua.

That was the end of the conference, and the captains went back to their stations. Crixus had made no appearance.

There were not enough crosses by the North Gate, new ones had to be hurriedly constructed. When the two Thracian platoons hauled the thirty condemned men, among them young Oenomaus, to the square, there was more fighting and several casualties. Then the crowd was forced back, and the bull-necks bent about tying the condemned men to the crosses.

The thirty crosses lay side by side on the ground. They dragged one culprit after the other to his cross, threw him down, pressed his back to the shaft, forced his arms apart and tied his wrists to the cross beam. After that they untied his feet, pulled at them so that the bodies might hang in position afterwards, and bound his ankles to the shaft. They let him lie and threw the next one down. The rest looked on and waited their turn. Those of the condemned still on their feet were fairly quiet now; only when they lay, already thrown, and the tying work started, did they swear, toss their heads from side to side, groan and spit into the bull-necks' faces above them. Fannius's servants wiped their faces and turned to the next.

At last all thirty lay tied to their crosses, side by side. Their behaviour varied. Some went on cursing, others sang loudly, kept silent or yelled jokes at each other; a fat man lay still, tears streaming down his face, his tied-up arm twitched again and again as he wanted to wipe them off. Young Oenomaus turned his head from left to right and kept his eyes shut. Then the crosses were raised; the captain called upon a whole platoon to do it, so that it might be done in one go and not take up too much time. A trio of soldiers took hold of each one cross from behind, groaned and called out to each other in encouragement. The crosses rose slowly, stood upright at last and were speedily implanted in the earth. The delinquents' arms strained and contorted, their joints cracked, their bodies reared up, convulsed. One of the hastily constructed crosses broke in the middle, the man on it dropped to the ground and with him the whole procedure had to start anew. It was the fat, weeping man. When they untied him, he rubbed his face with both hands. After that they tied him up again.

The town was silent as though suddenly frozen. People went home, torches were extinguished, in dead silence the town lay on the plain below the stars.

But after a time the thirty crucified men began to cry out. First they screamed apart and confusedly in their agony, then they screamed all at once at regular intervals. Their screams resounded through the whole muted town; broke into the darkened houses, shrilled through the empty dining halls, forced, at regular intervals, their way into the tent with the purple velum.

In it lay Spartacus, alone, in the dark, arms crossed behind his neck, little beads of sweat on his forehead. Nobody could see him now, he might shut his eyes when the scream came inside. Now he might even talk aloud and argue with himself as they do in the mountains; now he need not be an Imperator. He who guides the blind may not fear his own pride; he must make them suffer for their own good. For he alone can see while they are blind. There must be but *one* will, the will of the knowing. For he alone can see the goal, the end of bad detours, the progress in apparent retrocession. He must force them upon the road so that they may not be scattered about the earth; ruthless to their sufferings, deaf to their cries. He must defend their interests against their own want of reason, with all and any means, however cruel and incomprehensible they might appear.

Again the drawn-out screams of the crucified penetrated the gloom in the tent. The thirty hanging men were still screaming in chorus, only the pauses had become longer. At first they had screamed out with coherent words, roared for mercy, yelled for their brothers' aid. Now they only screamed disconnected sounds, but still in chorus.

Spartacus went on lying on his rug in the dark, alone, prickling with sweat; nobody could see him, his lips working. After a while he called for the servants, and they brought the huge drinking horn from Mount Vesuvius. Then they left him alone and refused all visitors, even the gentlemen of the Council of Thurium who had actually come at night to confer about turnips, and even Fulvius the lawyer.

'What's the Imperator doing?' asked the lawyer.

'He wants to get drunk,' replied the servants of Fannius, very grave and solemn.

But in his tent lay the man with the fur-skin, the drinking horn in front of him and the tent flap fastened, so that it might be quite dark around him while he got drunk. He had not been drunk for a long time, ever since the night after the victory on Vesuvius; but he knew it was good to get drunk. Drunkenness lifted the weight off you and the stern thoughts in your head began to smile.

He lay on his back, the drinking horn in front of him and his hands linked behind his neck, and he waited.

But drunkenness did not come to him. Only foggy images came, rose from a deep shaft inside him and looked into his closed eyes.

Who cast the die, decided a man's life before he was born? He gave noses unto all of them, stuck eyeballs into them, guts and sex, without much difference. But he set them apart in their mothers' wombs already, some were never to smile, nor be smiled at, the others were dragged into the light of day, and for them shone the sun. And they had set out, sinister multitude, had torn asunder the cellar walls and broken the iron chains, to bask their

skin in the sun. Now, so they thought and blinked, now everything will be all right, mouldiness will evaporate from our bodies,
we will not exude it any more. But a light world without walls
was not for them to enjoy, they were far too unaccustomed to
the strident light. They kicked and struggled like blind men,
whatever they grasped they broke to bits. One had to watch
over them as over wild beasts, one had to guide them.

First he had guided them upon the straight, wild road, and
they had sown fire, reaped hatred and ashes. It had been the
wrong road. He had led them along smooth highways, winding
and roundabout, hard to follow with the eye; and the goal had
sunk from their sight. And again they kicked and struggled like
blind men, the stench of ignominy never left them, their wolf's
claws grew again.

A great anger and wretchedness came over him. He gripped
the drinking horn, lay back and closed his eyes in great weariness.
Then he saw Crixus lying at the other side of the table, his head
propped up on the bare arm, reaching out for a hunk of meat.
'The corpses must be burned,' said Spartacus, 'they're stinking.'
Crixus smacked and wiped his dripping fingers on the mattress.
'Eat or be eaten,' he said dolefully, 'or do you know of something
better?' He leaned forward and gazed into Crixus's dull fish-eyes;
and he saw the great sadness lie like a lake behind the pupils, and
the longing for Alexandria.

But Crixus had vanished and in his place sat the aged Essene
and wagged his head. 'Do you know of something better?'
Spartacus asked him.

'Perhaps,' said the old one, 'for it is written that the power of
the Four Beasts had ended and One climbed up a mountain, the
Son of man.'

But his words were drowned in distant cries: the thirty men on
their crosses by the North Gate; and in the sage's stead sat the
coughing lawyer and stroked his bald head. Spartacus did not
like him much, but he leaned forward and put his hand on the
other's shoulder. 'You heard what Crixus said,' he told him, 'I
don't like it, do you know of something better?'

'Things are never black or white,' said the lawyer, 'and there
are only detours.'

Again the Thirty on their crosses roared through the night,
one of them was the youth Oenomaus. Moisture trickled down

Spartacus's forehead. 'Hear it, then, hear where your detours lead us,' he groaned.

'You never see that until you have arrived—and it takes a long time,' said the lawyer, but his voice sounded uncertain.

'But we can't wait that long,' shouted Spartacus, and became so angry that he woke.

Before him stood the two bull-necks; but they held no torches because it had grown quite light outside.

I I

THE TURNING POINT

WHEN it was daylight, more and more people crowded by the North Gate. Two platoons of Thracians and Lucanians formed a spear-bristling semi-circle around the open side of the square.

The thirty crucified men were still screaming. In steadily lengthening intervals they had been screaming the whole night long. When one of them fainted with pain and exhaustion, he was torn back into consciousness by the cries of the rest, and he cried with them. Screaming detained their slowly dwindling life.

A number of Germans and Celts had stood in the open square all night, hour after hour, in silence. When it dawned, they were joined by more and more; they were all still silent; a further platoon had to line up. When the sun rose, the entire square was filled with a dense crowd. They were no longer silent. They yelled at the crosses, called for Crixus; at regular intervals the crucified screamed in answer. Two more platoons had to line up.

The sun disentangled himself from the morning mists, the crucified hung in the brilliant light. When they were silent, their heads hung down like those of dead birds; when the scream wrenched out of them, they threw their heads up so that they beat against the wood, and showed the whites of their eyes. The crowd grew silent when they screamed; but when the scream had died the crowd raised its voice again, louder, more menacing every time. The soldiers began to feel uneasy. Their captain, a Thracian gladiator, sent a message to the tent with the purple velum; things could not go on like this much longer, he declined responsibility, for his men as well. The captain was a friend of the youth Oenomaus, the only one of the thirty who raised his head no more.

Before the messenger had returned, one man in the crowd pressed forward, using his elbows until he had reached the front row. It was Zozimos the rhetorician, clad, as always, in his grimy toga. He talked feverishly, fluttered excited sleeves and took one step forward from the row.

Hermios the shepherd, who stood with ready lance in the guarding semi-circle, was the first to see him. Disconsolate, he bared his yellow horse's teeth, smiled helplessly.

'You must go back, Zozimos,' he said.

Zozimos stopped, and the crowd behind him was suddenly silent. His gaunt bird's face was more sunken than usual, he was shockingly pale, his face as grey as the linen of his garment. He stood and stared at the shepherd as though he did not know him.

'You must go back, dear Zozimos,' the shepherd reiterated, nearly weeping with distress. 'We must keep an empty space between us and you.'

But Zozimos took one step farther and began to shriek: 'Brethren, brethren,' he shrieked at the crucified, 'can you hear me?'

They flung their heads up and screamed.

'Can you hear them, brethren, do you hear them?' shrieked Zozimos and waved his sleeves like banners. 'Do you hang well, brethren? Does freedom cut nicely into your limbs? Do its splinters tear your flesh? It's the Sun State, that stuff which flows red from your mouths. They've skewered you like worms, so that every one may see the time of Justice and Goodwill is come.'

A few in the crowd laughed, the rest were silent. A hoarse voice cried: 'Get Crixus, he'll put a stop to it all.' Other voices joined in, the whole square roared. Hermios, near to tears, brandished his lance desperately as Zozimos came closer. He tried to catch his clothes with the point of his lance in order to force him back gently. But Zozimos in all actuality tore the rags from his bare chest:

'Drive it home, tyrant's menial,' he shrieked.

His eyes agape, Hermios receded a step. His neighbours to left and right quickly crossed their spears in order to bar Zozimos's way. It grew very quiet, and Zozimos suddenly realised that he stood alone in the empty space between soldiers and people. His knees gave, he reeled. Several men leapt forward because they thought he had been killed, and supported him with their arms. As the guards did nothing to prevent them, the rest surged forward too, and in a trice the empty space had been obliterated by the crowd which pressed around the soldiers. The soldiers lowered their lances, averse to stabbing into the crowd; they were tired, wearied with heat and hunger, the screams of the crucified, the whole senseless situation.

Uncertainly the captain tried to command attack. Nobody paid any attention; if anything he was glad of it. Unmolested, he made his way through the crowd and went quickly to the tent with the purple velum where the captains were meeting.

The entire, very large square by the North Gate was now flooded with a constantly growing crowd. The four platoons were welded into it, not one of the soldiers liked the idea of further scuffle. Everybody was talking at once, aimless and not very loud; but the steady hum of these thousands penetrated even into the Imperator's tent. The crucified men screamed again, with hope this time; only young Oenomaus no longer raised his head. Women came running across the square, they carried pitchers full of water, held them up to the delinquents, put them to their black lips. Several men fetched knives and axes, cut the ropes, took the men down from their crosses and carried them off; with the exception of young Oenomaus they were all still alive. After that the men hacked the crosses to pieces. Hermios and a few other soldiers wondered loudly what Spartacus would say. They were pushed aside, indifferently, without hostility. Again a voice called for Crixus. This time everybody joined in. Crixus should come, they cried, put a stop to it all, lead them back home. The whole teeming square called for Crixus; the voices held no wrath, only great weariness and a longing to be led somewhere, anywhere, as long as it was home.

Zozimos had reappeared. He had climbed up one of the demolished crosses and let his sleeves fly in the wind.

'Brethren,' he yelled across the sea of heads, 'do you think you've done enough? Can't you see how you've been betrayed? Woe, for a new tyrant has emerged from the bleeding womb of revolution; woe unto us who assisted at his birth! From the broken chains we ourselves forged new chains; the burnt crosses sprouted up again. A new world we were going to erect, and what happened? Spartacus negotiates alliances with the lords, and the more compromises he yields unto them, the more blood and gore he spills among his own ranks. In boundless pride he believes it's for our own good to see the reward for blood and sacrifices further and further removed from our just greed, that he makes us walk the crooked roads until the goal is lost from our sight, for our own good. Woe unto us unfortunate beings who are of the seed of Tantalus! What kind of a freedom is this, which does not free us from the yoke of labour? What kind of justice is it that we are to go on swallowing but our own spittle, drinking our own sweat, always gazing into the future instead of embracing Today? What kind of fraternity is this: one man commands and the rest obey? Verily, his truculent pride knows no bounds because he can justify every deed before his own conscience with the thought that it was done for the good of us all. Kill him, kill him, brethren, for a well-meaning tyrant is worse than a man-eating beast. . . .'

His voice squeaked and broke, his sleeves fluttered above the splintered cross, but this time his words met with no approbation. The crowd was silent, suddenly a voice called out for Crixus again, others took it up. Crixus shall come, put a stop to it all, lead them back home. The square was crammed with mainly Celts and Germans, several thousands of them; their voices held no wrath, only great weariness, only the longing to get away from this unnatural City, this insane campaign, this infernal Italy, to hear no more speeches, no more incomprehensible laws and tirades—just to go away, go home. Crixus was one of them, he wore a silver necklace; they had confidence in him. He will lead them home, and on their way they will live merrily as in Metapontum.

Crixus was the man for them. He talked little. He decreed no laws. He was the man to lead them.

Spartacus had the entire Celtic quarter surrounded. A hundred thousand lived in the town, about thirty thousand were Celts and Germans. He could rely on the Thracians and Lucanians, the Daci, the black men, and the Getae. He stationed armed troops on every street that led to the Celtic quarter, and on the outside of the North Gate as well. It was the third hour after sunrise when he went to the large square, where the crowd around the demolished crosses was becoming more and more clamorous and shouted for Crixus. Crixus went with him, dismal and silent as always. Behind them walked only the small troop of Fannius's servants.

Mutely the crowd made way for them, and Spartacus climbed up on a ledge in the wall, raised his hand, indicating that he wished to speak. The humming dulled, but it did not become completely still.

He looked at the crowd. People were strewn loosely all over the extremely large square; his glance merged them all into one single thousand-limbed breathing clot. He sensed the self-contained, aloof hostility, the malign stupidity of the buzzing human mass. His eyes singled out heads, dived exploringly into their glances, confronted nothing but dullness, animal bluntness, and callously hostile defensiveness. Bitter saliva filled his mouth, disgust and retching contempt.

He began to speak; his voice, too, had altered, it cut through the air and fell on the mass like a lash. First he spoke about the rumours of the approach of a new Roman army whose vanguard was said to have entered Apulia this very day, while they were busy mangling each other. He spoke about this century of failed revolutions, every rising of the tormented masses having died of their own disunity. He spoke—and the bitter saliva in his mouth thickened with nausea—of the lords' and Masters' grinning triumph, enjoying as in the arena the sight of the self-destroying enemies. He told them that they would have to pay for their releasing the crucified ringleaders and mutineers a thousand, a million times, if they did not change their minds. He spoke of the twenty thousand crucified in the Sicilian rising, the ten thousand corpses of the counter revolution under Sulla, the carnage of the Roman slaves following on Cinna's abortive rebellion. He asked them—and the sunny square darkened before his eyes—whether they had still not learnt their lesson from so many horrible defeats, whether the fate of bleating sheep seemed to them more desirable than that of the disciplined soldiers of revolution. He asked them whether they wished to confirm by their behaviour the jeering assertion of the enemy that mankind was not mature enough for a better system, did not even want justice, preferred things to remain as they were.

After the first few words he had felt that he could not move the

inert multitude beneath him, that his cry did not penetrate the
crust of their wicked sloth. Scathing like whip lashes were his
words, but it was like the impotent effort of one who whips the
sea with rods and believes to move it thus. Again his eyes singled
out heads in the crowd; their glances held the same dull in-
difference as before, some grinned at him with the murderous
superiority of the stupid; one of them cried they wanted decent
food instead of these eternal recitals. Another cried this was
neither revolution nor freedom, which did not abolish the yoke
of labour; for, as everyone knew well, free was only he who need
not work. And when, at the same time, the call for Crixus went
up again, everybody joined in: *he*, Crixus, should put a stop to it
all and lead them home. And when one voice rose pealingly above
the rest: in Gaul, in Germania alone was real freedom, the entire
square roared with enthusiasm for the first time.

Spartacus looked at Crixus beside him. Doleful and silent as
ever, the gloomy man returned his glance. And it was as in the
days of Clodius Glaber's tent, and again later when they parted
before Capua: again both knew that their thoughts were the
same. It would have been better if that duel had taken place
before they left the school of Lentulus. One of them would have
died, probably he, Spartacus. And Crixus would have been the
sole leader of the horde, would have drowned all Italy in blood
and hit out at everything and destroyed everything. And perhaps
his would have been the right way.

Louder and louder the crowd clamoured for Crixus. The
rest of the City was devoted to him, Spartacus. The leader of
Fannius's servants stepped forward. He waited for orders. The
crowd in the square was unarmed, the Celtic quarter was sur-
rounded; the weapons were in the arsenal-shed by the South
Gate. Silent, devoted, a blush on his stiff neck, the spokesman of
Fannius's servants stood behind Spartacus, awaiting the
Imperator's orders.

But Spartacus was silent.

He hesitated only for the fraction of a second, although he
realised with acrid clarity that now and here, at this moment,
the future was being determined. If he gave the orders awaited
by the silent bull-neck behind him—if he did, a fresh and very
bloody massacre would rack the camp itself, and he, Spartacus,
would most probably prevail—a much hated, much feared victor

and absolute leader of the revolution. That would be the very bloody and very unjust detour which alone could lead to salvation. The other, kind, friendly, humane road inevitably led to rupture and hence to perdition.

All this he realised very clearly, it passed his mind's eye like a chain of pictures, and yet had it no longer any power over his actions. For this roundabout wisdom was native to a sphere different from that of live feelings. And the screams of the crucified were more strident in his mind's ear than the husky voice of the lawyer. Wisdom and knowledge alone did no longer carry enough weight to make him give the order. Where was the great, angry pride of a few minutes ago? Empty and hollow, he faced the thousand-headed, bawling mass. For their own good he would have to have them slain; thus decreed the law of detours. But within him another law, fed from a different source, demanded his silence, demanded that he signalled Crixus to climb up beside him. As from great distance he heard the cry which rose brayingly from the thousand-headed, thousand-limbed monster. As from great distance he beheld Crixus, gloomy, doleful as ever, standing beside him on the ledge. With quiet clarity he knew that the irrevocable had happened, that the Army's division had been accomplished, the fate of the revolution sealed. For, wondrous though the gift of knowledge is, it has little moving power over the happening.

From great distance he saw the gloomy one raise his arm, and heard the crowd grow silent. Was all this really happening now and here? Deep down in the past he had once already lived through it, that which took place now was long familiar and could not be escaped. How simply and straightforwardly the man of gloom spoke to the crowd! 'The Imperator wishes that your will be done.' Rejoicing, enthusiasm. Was not everything clear and simple on the straight road? They wished it, their will be done. Were they acting against their own interest, burying the revolution in great joy? They were, but what good was knowledge. Impotent, it faced the happening; withered and sour was the taste of wisdom when the black saps of enthusiasm flowed through the veins of the thousand-headed monster.

No, one could neither guide it from outside nor from above, not with the pride of the lonely seer, nor with the cunning of detours, nor with the cruel kindness of the prophet. The century of abortive revolutions had been completed; others will come, receive the word and pass it on in a great wrathful relay-race through the ages; and from the bloody birth-pangs of revolution again and again a new tyrant will be born—until at last the groaning human clod would itself begin to think with its thousand heads; until knowledge was no longer foisted on it from outside, but was born in laboured torment out of its own body, thus gaining from within power over the happening.

12

THE END OF THE SUN CITY

THE meeting of the captains was quickly over. They were very tired; tired particularly of words. Everybody was glad that the separation seemed to go off quietly. While discussing the details of decamping from the Sun City, everybody tried to affect a plain, friendly manner, as though worrying about a very minor point, such as the building of a new barrack by the South Gate, or the changing of the guards. They avoided raising their voices or exchanging looks, as far as possible. Spartacus's talk was plain and simple too, just as in the old days. The people had announced its will, he declared, and so the leadership had been relieved of responsibility. The Celts and Germans, he said, thirty thousand of them, had chosen Crixus for their leader. Crixus, he said, would lead them across the Alps and the river Padus, to Gaul. He, Spartacus himself, with the Thracians and Lucanians and the others who had remained faithful to him, intended to stay in the camp for a few days longer, until reliable information from the allies reached him. He reserved the right, he said, to act according to the nature of this information later on.

The departure of the Celts and Germans went off smoothly and without incident. The departing men were in the most congenial mood imaginable, they proposed cheers to Crixus and to Spartacus, too. The two leaders embraced in farewell by the North Gate. In the embrace Spartacus said in a low voice:

'Wouldn't it have been better after all if one of us had killed the other, Mirmillo?'

Crixus looked at him petulantly. He answered:

'It wouldn't have made any difference.'

After that they departed, whisked the dust and vanished on the northern highway, thirty thousand men, five thousand women and children; it took many hours. Those who stayed behind were quiet and gazed after the last cloud of dust, and great depression took hold of them. Afterwards they went about their work. A third of the town lay deserted. The remaining two-thirds would only exist for a few days longer.

The period stipulated by Spartacus elapsed quicker than one should have thought. The day after the Celts' departure, the gentlemen of the Council of Thurium at last decided to make a clean breast of everything.

In Rome Lucius Gellius and Gneius Lentullus, both members of the reactionary Aristocrats' Party, had been elected Consuls for this year, the 683rd since the foundation of the city. They were determined to put a stop to the South Italian slave-trouble. The senate had immediately furnished them with extraordinary authority. The latest, highly favourable reports from the Spanish and Asiatic fronts were useful: the newly levied soldiers as well as the newly recruited mercenaries could all be used in the Slave Campaign. Two well-trained armies, totalling twelve full-strength Legions, had already left Rome. The two Consuls took over the command in person, a thing that had but rarely happened in the annals of the Republic, in times of greatest emergency.

This news, together with that of the destruction of the emigrants' fleet, had considerably steeled the spines of the gentlemen of Thurium, and they hesitated no longer to let the Thracian Prince know most courteously that the Council, to its regret, was unable further to guarantee supplying the Slave Army with bread and corn. The world situation, they said, had changed completely during the last few months, Rome had recaptured her traditional though undeserved luck of battle; Thurium was unfortunately forced to take into account the altered circumstances, her own store houses being empty down to the last sack.

This was incidentally true, and it was also a consequence of the changed political situation: for their wheat came from Sicily. Up to now the Roman governor of Sicily, a shrewd gentleman by the name of Verres, had been gambling on revolution in Rome, which he believed not far off, and supplied the pirates with wheat on credit, knowing full well that they would lend it to the opposition city of Thurium, who in turn would lend it to the brigand-chief Spartacus. The Lord Verres, immortalised by the lawyer Cicero as an arch scoundrel, cut-throat and paragon of wickedness, on whom thus depended the welfare of the Sun City, had now suddenly turned pro-Senate. In consequence the granaries of Thurium stood as empty as those of the Sun City, and the dignified aged Councillor with the protruding eyes, whom they had once more sent to the front, was able to confirm this truthfully. He added that he personally knew nothing about the rules of the wheat trade. After that he inquired for young Oenomaus whose presence he missed, and whom he described as a well-bred young man; whereupon he looked at Fulvius out of red-veined eyes. After Fulvius had got over a fit of coughing, and muttered evasively, the aged Councillor begged him to convey his best regards to the Thracian Prince, beckoned his attendance and departed with faintly shaky steps.

On the next day the long overdue messenger of the Spanish emigrants' army arrived at last.

In the first place the messenger brought a letter from the emigrants' leader, Sertorius, in which he accepted the conditions for an alliance against Rome; and secondly he brought the news that Sertorius had been murdered the night after the composing of the letter. From the beginning strife and discord had rent the refugees' camp, they had split up into factions, faithful images of political division in Rome; they had neither forgotten nor learnt anything. Some time ago a rather doubtful customer had appeared among them, a man called Perpenna. He criticised Sertorius's ponderous way of conducting the war, none of the General's measures satisfied his fiery revolutionary zeal. Finally he voiced open distrust: the leader spent his days feasting, he said, dissipating money and time alike. Oddly enough, Perpenna himself was provided with ample monetary means of unknown origin, which he squandered generously for the gaining of supporters. When finally Sertorius told him straight to his face that he was a paid provocateur of the Roman Senate, Perpenna and his friends decided to act: at headquarters in Osca they arranged for a banquet in honour of the General, and when the guests were incensed with wine, they started a prearranged brawl. Disgusted,

Sertorius lay back on his sofa and closed his eyes: he was never to open them again. More than a hundred daggers lacerated his body, while Mark Antony, his neighbour at table, held the victim's arms and legs. So now the collapse of the emigrants' army and Pompeius's victory were a mere matter of months or weeks.

The democratic opposition of Rome had been defeated because of the incapacity of its leaders; the refugees had destroyed themselves with inner discord. The opponents' weakness, not its own strength, had once again—and how often before!—saved the doddering regime which had lived beyond its time. And how many times more in the course of centuries to come will the pitiable spectacle be repeated?

Fulvius, chronicler and lawyer, was the one to ask this last question. He put it more to himself than to Spartacus, who sat opposite him in the tent with the purple velum and who, strangely enough, did not seem in the least affected by this devastating news. He even smiled his old good-natured smile again, as in the early days of the horde—even though this hilarity might well be fed from far removed sources, like those remarkably clear brooks which spring forth from the granite pressure and sweat of the mountains. Their conversation was conducted in daylight this time, the sun glared down outside. Fulvius himself felt very distressed, his dry cough vexed him, as well as the bad rheumatism he had caught in the rainy night before Capua. How many times more, he repeated sadly, will this pitiable spectacle be revived again by the centuries to come?

But the man in the fur-skin sat opposite him, legs astride, like the wood-cutters of the mountains, and smiled. What was there to smile at, when everything was finished and the ghosts of the past celebrated their return into the soul of the broken and desperate?

'And what do you intend to do now?' he asked the Imperator, in a dry and hostile tone.

But the Imperator smiled, friendly, absent-minded, relieved.

'We'll all go home,' he said, in that slightly bewildered tone with which one repeats what has long been known and decided.

All of a sudden verve and busy activity came back to the people in the Slave City. It was as though after long and deadly calm, when the first gust of wind leaps into the ship's sail, the masts creak in their joints and the keel ploughs merrily through the foam once more. Joyous and excited, they had hauled the timber from the mountains, had built sheds and barracks, erected their city—rejoicing now, they attacked the buildings with axes and saws, tore laboriously constructed walls asunder, razed the town to the ground. The straight, measured streets became covered with ruins and debris, all objects of use had been taken from the workshops and loaded on carts, granaries were emptied, the tent poles torn from the resisting earth. For some days the Celtic quarter had lain waste; now it was no longer an oppressive memory, but an example to be emulated. And the same hammering and bluster, the same joyous activity held sway when they demolished, as when they had built the city.

Spartacus walked about the camp, looked at the destruction, laughed, encouraged his Thracians in their joyous task, went to work himself when the big dining halls were pulled down. Again they loved him dearly. He was their laughing comrade, companion of old, the One with the fur-skin. The harsh glint in his eyes had been put out, at night he drank gallantly from the drinking horn and slept again with his woman, the dark, slender one whom he had been neglecting all this time. A heavy weight had been taken off him; he need no longer guide the blind, need make no more murky detours. Even the memory of young Oenomaus, victim of his own timid righteousness, had faded; he was filled with a mild and merry void.

Everybody looked forward to the march home. In the mountains reigned the true Sun State. In the mountains there is room for all, for the Lucanians too, and for the black men, every one who wants to join them will be welcome. Pale and anaemic this town had been, with her straitlaced streets, her straight, stern laws. The allies had never come, the Italian brothers had not answered the call, the age of Saturn had not dawned. This age was either too young or too old, the crops decayed or not yet ripe—who wants to know and who wants to ballast his mind.

And they were very glad indeed. A festive mood, as when they had first come, was in the camp on the eve of the departure. The workshops, the granaries, the dining halls, burned in towering, blazing flames: torches of farewell in the plain.

On the eve of departure the man with the bullet-head sat in a corner of his tent, reading a page of rolled-up parchment which he held on his knee, in the light of an oil wick. His lips moved zealously, he murmured some passages in a wrathful chant, performed ardent little bows with his torso, other passages he accompanied with head-wagging and protestingly upturned palms; his whole body was reading. Thus Hermios the shepherd found him when he came to pay the old man a little visit.

'What on earth are you doing?' asked Hermios the shepherd, astonished.

'I'm quarrelling with God,' said the old man.

'But is that allowed?'

'It depends,' said the old man. 'My God demands that we quarrel with him. He needs it, otherwise he feels uneasy about both himself and mankind. Therefore he teases them with all sorts of pranks in order to provoke them.'

'What kind of pranks?' asked Hermios inquisitively. He had actually come to let the old man console him, for he was terribly sad about the departure from the Sun City. But now he had forgotten about his sorrow and was longing to hear with what sort of pranks the quarrelsome God of the man with the bullet-head provoked the mortals.

'It is written,' began the old man, 'that many men once came wandering from the East and came to a valley between two rivers and settled there and desired to build a city.'

'Where was that valley?' asked Hermios the shepherd who had sat down on the ground and listened piously.

'Fairly far away,' said the old man, 'between high mountains and the sea; but you need not be in any way surprised, because there are valleys everywhere, between mountains and seas. But the people said unto each other: lo, let us build a city the like of which has never before existed, so that we may not be scattered over the earth in all our misery. And they felled trees and made buffaloes lug them down into the valley, and they had bricks for stone and slime had they for mortar; and thus their city grew up. But these people were not content, and they said unto each other: lo, let us build a tower the like of which has never before existed, so that all of us may be able to behold it and we may not be scattered all over the earth.'

'A tower?' asked Hermios, disappointed. 'I don't know anything about a tower.'

'That need not surprise you either,' said the old man, 'for the
mortals build many sorts of towers, some are made of brick and
some are not. But above sits God and sees the towers shoot up into
his own cloud realm, which he wishes to withhold from man,
just like a certain tree in a certain garden. But the humans build
their tower in order to be great before all other living creatures,
and in honour of their creator, and also to annoy him. And God
looks on as they build, and is both flattered and angry, and
ponders what sort of prank he might tease them with. And so he
hears that they all speak the same language and understand one
another, as is only natural among creatures with the same aim
and in the same plight. And God thinks: hey, where would it
lead? Far too well do these mortals understand one another, far
too high do they build this tower of theirs; and if this is only the
beginning—what would the end be like? Perhaps they will even
reach their goal in the end and remain at peace, which would
grossly violate the rules of my game with the humans. Lo, let us
rush down upon them and tease them with a prank and let us
confuse their language, so that there is left but stammer and
angry stutter and cries, and not one understands the other,
although they are beings with one common aim and one common
plight. And thus he did do, and they did no longer understand
one another and left their tower and scattered all over the earth.'

Hermios grinned sadly and showed his yellow teeth. 'That is
an awful tale,' he said.

'They are all awful tales,' said the man with the bullet-head
and nodded vacantly. 'Tales, all of them merely begun and
never finished. There is one about an apple which was only half-
eaten; there is one about a ladder on which one man almost
conquered, but his hip-bone was dislocated so that he limped all
his life; there is the one about the tower only half-completed, and
rain and gale wearing it down again.'

Hermios was silent and sad. After a while he asked:

'Is that why you were quarrelling with the God when I came?'

'You've guessed it,' said the old man, 'with whom else should
I be quarrelling on account of the beautiful tower? With the rain
perhaps, or with the night, or the sirocco who whips a purple
velum to and fro upon its flag-pole?'

.   .   .   .   .

The camp was in a festive mood as when they had first arrived. Workshops, granaries, and dining halls burned in towering, blazing flames: farewell torches. The Council of Thurium, too, was doing things handsomely: twenty barrels of old Falernian came rolling as their farewell gift. So then several hundred from the camp set out in the middle of the night to pay a thanksgiving visit to the magnanimous city. Without great secrecy, they looted, extorted and raped with moderation. The citizens of Thurium could be glad to have got off so lightly. Spartacus pretended to know, see, hear nothing.

The next morning they departed.

There were still forty thousand of them. Thirty thousand had gone with Crixus; the remainder had scattered over the earth.

Behind them glowed the embers of the Sun City.

13

THE DESIRE TO REMAIN

On the morning after the departure of the Slave Army, Hegio, a citizen of Thurium, again stood on the flat roof of his house. The glowing rim of the sun-disk had only just risen from the sea, the waters were still sending over the fresh, crystalline scents of seaweed and stars; yet this would be a hot day, a day like any other.

The cocks had begun with their hoarse cries, the large village of many white columns was already waking from its serene morning stillness. The first shepherds herded their goats through the winding little alleys between the stone walls, playing their shrill flutes. Far away, the white herds of buffalo were grazing in the fields at the foot of the mountains; their heads stiffly raised, they sniffed up the smell of burning which drifted over from the deserted Slave City. Hegio's flat roof overlooked the entire squarely walled area, its dead, straight streets, the smouldering remains of workshops and dining halls in what had been the City of the Hundred Thousand. Soon the walls will begin to crumble, the dry, hot dust will cover them by and by; the children of Thurium's citizens will stalk around the bewitched spot with pounding hearts, will impudently climb over the walls, and play at robbers and soldiers in the empty streets. And more dust will settle on the ruins, rain will spray down and combine with it into clay, and future men with ploughs and buffaloes will furrow the ground, as they now till the soil entombing Sybaris. And some day, perhaps, learned men and historians will remember the legends of the strange Sun State, whose fundaments rested on even more ancient legends, they will tunnel down into the realm of the past and find a broken chain, ensign of the Slave Army, or the earthen platter of Publibor my servant.

Hegio smiled his smile of an aged man or a child. He sighed and gazed down once more at the dead town. Hunger and a guilty conscience worried him, for he had not done his conjugal duty since the night before the entry of the Thracian Prince. At last he made up his mind to descend the iron stairs, to wake the matron and demand his breakfast. Suddenly his gaze fell on a youth, motionless and quite forlorn in the as yet pale shadow of the opposite wall, who looked up at him; and it was Publibor his slave. Hegio felt pleased rather than surprised, though apprehensive at the thought of what the matron would say when she heard of the young rebel's return; she was a Roman, she took things damned seriously and had no sense of humour. He had better talk it over with her alone, at breakfast.

With the sly air of a conspirator he signalled the lad to wait for him outside. The lad did not answer, nodded timidly, and remained motionless in the shadow of the wall.

He was still there when Hegio came out half an hour later and cheerfully asked him to accompany his master on his customary morning walk to the river Crathis. He took the dog off the chain, the beast romped and yapped around the youth who seemed equally glad to see it and gravely stroked its head. Hegio watched the two of them with amused, resigned, and slightly disgusted eyes.

'Well,' he asked the slave. 'Do you still wish for my death?'

The boy returned his gaze earnestly, pondered, and slowly shook his head.

'I see,' said Hegio. 'You haven't learnt a thing. It would at least have been effective if you had said yes.'

He actually seemed to be annoyed at Publibor's no longer wishing for his death. In silence they left the town, Hegio in front, the slave a pace behind him, the dog gambolling backwards and forwards.

'By the way,' said Hegio after a while and turned his head without slackening his pace, 'the matron, of course, insists on your being chastised before she forgives you. I suppose the procedure will be symbolical rather than painful. You realise she is within her rights.'

Publibor did not answer, he kept his glance on the cobbles, a faint blush suffused his cheeks; he had not slowed down either. In silence they continued on their way.

When they had arrived by the river Crathis and lay down in the grass, Hegio began again:

'I probably did you an injustice just now. I too might have acted in a more effective manner by simply declaring you freed, when you came back disappointed, with your hopes betrayed. That would indeed have been a beautiful solution—a philosophical gesture with a pious moral. Ah well, one always expects the other person to act in an effective manner.'

They were silent, and watched the goats graze near the walls of the deserted town, and listened to the distant tinkling of their bells. Mighty and gently nicked, the mountains framed the horizon.

'As for your returning, I can see quite well why you did it,' said Hegio. 'I too have within me those two opposed energies: the desire to depart and the desire to remain. You might also call them the desire to destroy and the desire to preserve. There are only those two whether you search without or within you; and their strife is eternal. For each victory gained by one over the other is but a sham-conquest which cannot last; just as the change from life into death has its vicious circle and is only seemingly final. He who departs remains chained to his memories, and he who stays abandons himself to painful longings. And throughout the ages men and women have crouched on ruins, lamenting.'

'They said,' replied the slave, without taking his eyes off the wall around the deserted City, 'they said: the time is not ripe, it is either too young or too old.'

'There is truth in that also,' said Hegio and smiled his stirring smile which was at once young and old. 'To your misfortune you people happened into a world that can neither live nor die. For a long time every thing this world brings forth has been senseless and barren; but the forces of perseverance are tenacious. You just go and ask the matron, and see what little flattering ideas she has on my strength and power. She too thinks me too old to be productive and too young to die; and so, my poor Publibor, you will have to put up with me for some time yet—even though my death seems no longer to be quite so desirable to you. . . .'

Hegio's hand, which had rested as though comforting on the boy's shoulder, began to glide down his body; his smiling, resigned, and slightly disgusted gaze did not leave the boy's. Astonished and apathetic, Publibor gave himself up to it.

'You see,' murmured Hegio after a while, 'this is also a solution, and a way to enjoy one another. You can regard it as a symbol if you wish. For, considering what the two of us are and represent, I cannot think of anything better for us to do.'

The sun stood higher in the skies, and the olive trees no longer afforded any shade. The dog lay in the grass, with trembling sides; its tongue hung from between its teeth, it turned its head and watched them with a glassy stare.

BOOK FOUR

DECLINE

Interlude

THE DOLPHINS

THE clerk Quintus Apronius enters the covered walk of the Steambaths in the best of moods.

In a few months' time he will have been a civil servant for exactly twenty years, and the Market Judge, his superior, has promised to accept him as his official protégé. Apronius, whose hands have become a trifle unsteady of late, will no longer have to take minutes; he will stroll through the streets, a member of the suite of the Market Judge, dignified, his robe held high; he will supervise the doings of his erstwhile colleagues and sternly watch that all is as it should be; and he will be invited to the family parties at the house of the patron and protector. Apart from that, there is reason to hope and to believe that the 'Friends of Diana and Antinous' will elect their Secretary of many years' standing to the position of this year's President.

The usual bustle enlivens the arch-roofed shelter of the baths; only the bald-headed lawyer Fulvius, seditious agitator, has not been seen here for some time now. People say he has gone and joined the robbers, and that he excels in murder, the looting of temples and the raping of virgins. Apronius has always been struck with an expression of lasciviousness and cruelty about this lawyer Fulvius's face; well, it won't be long now before a just fate overtakes him and his accomplices. For it is said that the bandits have left their crazy town down south, and that their end is close at hand.

Cheerfully Apronius enters the Hall of the Dolphins, where he at once espies two acquaintances, impresario Rufus and games-director Lentulus, engrossed in thoughtful digestive colloquy; as he takes his habitual seat they salute him, a little monosyllabic and reserved. But Apronius is in too good a mood to be discomfited by this, his physical functions are perfectly shipshape again, and soon, ah, very soon he will no longer need to sound anybody about free tickets; on the contrary, they will consider it an honour to spend the hours of siesta in the company of The Honorary President of a reputed club, and an intimate protégé of the Market Judge. Cheerily he starts conversation with a few general reflections on expiation and dire requital, soon to be the lot of the brazen rebels, and is justly surprised when his remarks fetch only moderate response. The impresario in his fashionable bathrobe—Apronius decided some months ago to acquire an exact replica—shrugs his shoulders and pulls a wry face:

'What are you so happy about?' Rufus asks the clerk. 'Do you think you'll be any better off when those people have been done to death? You just wait and see; afterwards the fat will be more than ever in the fire. The Exchequer is empty as never before, the price of wheat is constantly rising to nobody knows what heights, and everything in Rome is at sixes and sevens; only a short time ago the People's Tribune Licinius Macer delivered a speech in which he frankly invited the populace to refuse military service to the State. If the Senate still manages to put down the rebellion, it will be solely due to the fact that those people were so obliging as to quarrel among themselves just at the decisive moment; a phenomenon apparently in character with all revolutions, which thus furnish their own safeguarding antidote. But that's no reason why you should have any illusions about the future.'

The clerk Apronius wonders what has come over the impresario and his charming wit, why he is so venomous all of a sudden? But he won't let anything impair his genial mood; he decides that evidently Rufus is thwarted in his digestive efforts. So he remarks conciliatorily, the fact that the two Consuls are personally conducting the campaign should surely prove that there are still Men in Rome, which certainly ought to reassure everyone.

But impresario Rufus contributes but a pitying smile, and the games-director stares gloomily in front of him; the two of them had, until a short time ago, counted on the victory of Spartacus's allies, the emigrants in Spain, and backed a corresponding slump in wheat; the triumph of the worthy scribe with his digestive philosophy is getting on their nerves more than ever.

'Men? In Rome?' says Rufus, and in order to vex the gaunt clerk he adds pugnaciously that maybe Spartacus is a Man; but as for the lords of Rome, they rule over their inherited empire in the manner of the proverbial rider who when asked whither he was so stormily bound, replied: 'Don't ask me, ask the horse.' For, ever since the popular army was replaced by mercenary forces, the real power is not wielded by the State, but by its generals. A new military dictatorship, perhaps even restoration of the monarchy, is on its way; this living corpse of a Republic will breathe its last with voluptuous relief when a mailed fist does actually grip its throat . . . And then what?

'Look around you, do, my esteemed friend,' cries the bulky impresario, prophetic on his Dolphins' throne. 'Do open your eyes and have a look round. The bases of economics and the chances for individual prosperity are shrinking and dwindling from day to day; not even children are produced in this country nowadays. The Suburra is full of child-charmers, women of the people stab the foetus in their womb, kill it with knitting needles, and the midwives' fees for abortion are twice as high as those assisting at births. The race of the she-wolf is dying out, my friend; jackals may replace it later on . . .'

Bitter grief has rather raised Rufus's voice; several people on nearby marble seats are looking. Quintus Apronius rises and takes a somewhat hasty departure. He does not want his good temper spoilt, and it is scarcely advisable in times like these to be seen too frequently in the company of people with openly seditious sentiments.

On his way home through the Oscian quarter he once more calls to mind the impresario's words. Had he not fairly advertised his sympathies with the foes of the Republic, had he not more or less proclaimed the runaway gladiator and revolutionist the only Man in all Rome? Apronius ponders whether it would not be his duty as a patriot and future club-president to mention the matter to the Market Judge. It is high time that a stop is put to the machinations of folk with obscure antecedents, who incite honest citizens against Authority without ever once providing them with a free ticket; it is time that law and order are restored.

I

THE BATTLE
BY THE GARGANUS

AT THAT time Marcus Cato was twenty-three years old. As a boy he had shot up too quickly, and now his lanky body seemed unable to fill out into manly proportions. He was never to be seen without a book or manuscript under his arm, and his lips worked constantly, even when he was alone. He had volunteered to join the campaign of Consul Gellius; the soldiers laughed at him a good deal and feared the dry monotony of the lectures he used to force on them. They knew that, like King Romulus, he wore no undergarment, that he slept with neither women nor men, that he sought to imitate the puritan life led by his great-great-grandfather, Old Cato. They mocked him, but in their heart of hearts they were discomfited by the fanatical youth. A wit had once named him 'Cato the Younger' in a moment of mock pathos, and the name had stuck.

Cato's elder brother, Captain Caepio, was also taking part in the campaign. He was the Consul's right-hand man. Caepio, a man of handsome, manly appearance, spoilt by the Roman ladies, was very depressed over his failure of a brother. Cato should long ago have been an officer, should occupy a place in the army as befitted the scion of an ancient aristocratic family; but the lad insisted on serving his time like any private, declined promotion to his brother's Legion, and contemptuously avoided the worldly Caepio.

'He's making a fool of himself,' said Caepio despairingly to Consul Gellius. The Consul smiled; he thought the young Puritan not undeserving of interest.

'Your brother is quite a remarkable young man,' he said. 'He will probably found another Stoic sect, or commit a political assassination, or some other effusive absurdity, which, according to the circumstances, will either be regarded as a schoolboy prank or as a heroic accomplishment.'

'Perhaps he'll grow out of it yet,' said Caepio.

'Not he, take my word for it,' said the Consul. 'I know the type. He'll remain an adolescent all his life. The Younger Gracchus was cut after the same pattern. There seem to be periods of human evolution during which the making of history is reserved to this type of the Forever-Adolescent. It is not the type's fault, but History's. And I fear, my friend, that once more we live in one of those half-baked, immature times.'

Consul Lucius Gellius Publicola had a weakness for philosophical reflections. He liked to quote his friend, the author Varro, who maintained that nothing comes anywhere near a genuine old philosophers' wrangle, on the principle that a Stoic bout far surpasses any feat of the arena. Some years ago Gellius, then governor of Greece, had enacted a farce that had rocked all Rome, Gellius himself more than anyone. He had summoned the representatives of the conflicting philosophical schools in Athens, locked them up in a hall, and demanded that they should at last come to a unanimous definition of Truth; he himself would be the chairman, and would not let anyone leave before that unity had been achieved. The undertaking took a disastrous course, the governor's armed bodyguard had to take a strong hand in the proceedings, till finally Gellius was forced to have the doors unlocked before Truth had been discovered, in order to avoid further bloodshed. Nevertheless, Gellius had scored a pedagogical triumph, for the philosophers of Athens showed a unity unparalleled in their known history by addressing a joint petition to the Roman Senate, demanding the resignation of the Governor. Atticus, then staying in Athens, sent a faithful account of the incident to Cicero, and Gellius won a popularity which proved a vital asset in his election for Consul.

In Northern Apulia, beside the river Garganus, the Roman vanguard encountered the army of Crixus and his thirty thousand Celts and Germans. The hostile armies occupied two hills that faced each other on the northern bank of the river.

The two Roman Consuls with their armies had separated, partly from strategical considerations, partly because they were not over-fond of each other, and each wanted to claim the victory his own. Gellius had advanced to meet the enemy in Apulia, his colleague Gneius Lentullus was to guard northern Italy against a possible onslaught by the Slave Army. This could scarcely be called a very logical arrangement, but the Senate had for a long time been afraid to interfere with its generals, and this time the Consuls themselves were acting as generals, which more or less amounted to a form of interior siege.

The first night by the river Garganus passed peacefully. The Romans fortified their castra, the Celts barricaded their hill with the classic wagon fortress. A Roman scout had observed the process from a vantage point and reported to Captain Caepio, who in turn informed the Consul.

'They're no army, they're a whole, travelling people,' Captain Caepio told the Consul, bewildered. 'Women, children, horses, ox-carts, cattle, asses. They're using those carts and all the lumber they have with them, to build a barricade all around the hill; and they're reinforcing this wall of rubbish with all kinds of things, even sacks of grain and living cattle.'

'Appalling,' said the Consul. 'These people give war such a private, personal odour. Win or lose—in either case we will be humiliated.'

'One might try,' said Caepio, 'to set their barricade on fire. It encircles the entire camp. The ground inside is only dry grass. At least half their people would be roasted alive.'

'Does the idea appeal to you much?' asked Gellius. 'For God's sake don't answer me, "War is War", or something like that.'

Caepio shrugged.

'This whole war does not appeal to me any more than to you. But I shouldn't think that things are any more refined in the war against Mithridates. He has the wells poisoned.'

'But he does at least poison you in style,' said the Consul. He knew how much his unsoldierly witticisms infuriated Captain Caepio, but he really could not bring himself to order the enemy camp set on fire. The mere thought of the stench of burning flesh almost made him sick.

Decision was made easy for him, though, for the guard by the tent door announced Captain Roscius of the Third. Captain

Roscius entered immediately, stood to grim attention, saluted with grave emphasis. This Captain Roscius, a veteran of Sulla's time, invariably treated the Consul with this emphatic military formality; it was a kind of protest against Gellius's easy-going worldliness. Gellius guessed by the smirk that twitched his mighty whiskers, that the Captain bore unpleasant news.

A deputy of the enemy side had been brought before him, reported Captain Roscius, and had suggested on behalf of his general to fix the day and hour of battle: an ancient Celtic-German custom. Besides this—and here the Captain could hardly restrain his hilarity—besides, the enemy war-lord, that is, the circus-gladiator Crixus, proposed a duel between himself and the Roman war-lord Lucius Gellius Publicola: another Celtic-German custom. He, the Captain, was now awaiting instructions as to how the suggestions should be dealt with.

Young Caepio flushed with shame and anger. Captain Roscius grinned. The Consul smiled. For one fleeting second he felt tempted to accept the challenge, if only to frustrate Captain Roscius and, by means of such a duel, to inflame beyond endurance the wound caused by this humiliating war against slaves and gladiators. Or would that humiliation thus dissolve itself? What a poser for his philosopher friends of Athens. But at once his calm and reason reasserted themselves: of course it was utterly impossible to treat history as an arena.

He beamed amiably into Captain Roscius's blinking veteran eyes, ordered the messenger to be hung without unnecessary cruelty, nodded in dismissal. Roscius saluted smartly and thundered out of the tent. Gellius turned back to Captain Caepio and gave the order to attack the enemy position from five points at once, shortly before sunrise. Caepio dared not return to the subject of firebrands:

Crixus was inspecting his camp. He dragged his gross body in its cuirass from one group to the next, gloomy and mute. Yet he inspired confidence. Wherever he appeared he was cheered with friendly, juicy curses. He never replied; kicked at a bit of weak structure in the barricade, waited until it had been repaired, passed on.

His plan was a simple one: he intended to leave the attack to the Romans. Let them crack their naked skulls against his en-

campment; when they were wearied after a second or third fruitless attack, the besieged would burst from the hidden gaps in
their wall, from six points at once, and crush their enemy. And,
as soon as that crushing had been attended to, they would
continue on their homeward, northward march.

Their homeward, northward march. Was that a goal? Crixus
asked no questions. To the north was the river Padus, behind it
Gallia Cisalpina, Liguria, the country of Lepontia. Then
mountains. They were high, were those mountains; avalanches
roared down from them, warm summer snow covered them, gods
and demons raced in the gales around them. The summits were
regions of silence. But beyond all this, beyond heaven's threshold,
began the lands of memory. Was it really memory, or was it
merely the longing for dreamed-of tradition? Crixus asked no
questions. Barefooted processions of priestesses and druids in
long white shrouds marched quietly along the highways of Gaul
and Britain. In his silvered chariot, surrounded by glittering
attendance—hunters with leashed hounds, wandering bands of
bards—the Year's King rode through his domain, squandered
gold as he passed. Adorned with silver necklaces and fearful
moustaches, the knights feasted at long tables; in between two
courses they would fight with shields and swords, in deadly
earnest, for the loin, fattest morsel of pork, prize of the bravest.
And, no more wine in the thirsty knight's cup, no more coin in
his purse, he would offer his life for five barrels of wine, would
treat his friends, and lie down on the shield with heavy head to
await placidly his own slaughter by the hand of his creditor.

This homeland beyond the river Padus, beyond the snow-
covered heavenly threshold, did it really still exist? Crixus asked
no questions. They were northward bound, for the foggy realm of
their past. They were going home. Vesuvius, and that Sun State
of vapid laws, their whole misshapen, miscarried future—all this
they would leave far behind. In front of them lay the past, called
homeland, the primeval mist which had borne them. Was there
any doubt as to their choice? They asked no questions. They
followed that north which called them back to their origin, to
complete the dimmed rotation.

Towards morning, shortly before the Romans' first attack,
Crixus dreamed once more of Alexandria. Standing, with his
back against a badly built section of barricade, he had fallen

asleep. He dreamed of a woman who sang as he shared her bed. Never had he known a wench who sang thus. He listened to find out whether she sang madly or softly, and sensed that he had dreamed that dream before, on Vesuvius, in the tent of Praetor Clodius Glaber. Soon after, he woke, and his dismal eyes held no memory of the dream. He kicked the faulty section, watched until it had been mended, and went forth on his circuit, ironclad, gloomy and mute.

The Romans attacked soon after sunrise. It was no pleasant task to storm up a hill against a fortress; to run up against showers of arrows and javelins, and against the baneful silence that lurked behind those barricades. The attack was handled most correctly; both of the two storming Legions lost half their men, waited for the bugle calling the retreat, and ran back downhill in splendid order.

Caepio and Consul Gellius watched the battle from a nearby hill. Caepio paled as he saw his Legions flood down the hill; he thought of the firebrands, and gnawed his lip. The Consul's arm swept in a crescent that embraced the entire battle ground and all its running, falling, dead and wounded men.

'Personified absurdity,' he said. 'It is almost incredible that grown-up men can behave like this.'

Caepio grew still paler, he was white with fury:

'Your philosophy, sir, has so far cost us three thousand Roman lives.'

The Consul's eyebrows arched in surprise, but his retort was drowned by the bugle giving the signal for the second attack, driving a further flood of breathing flesh uphill into the rain of javelins and arrows. Before he could think up an answer, that rain had already swamped down the foremost ranks; they covered the slope in strangely twisted positions, their arms and legs like the dislocated limbs of broken puppets.

'Did I hear you say "philosophy"?' yelled the Consul, trying to rise over the din.

Caepio had arrived at the exact limit of his self-control. His choked-back fury so racked his nerves, sinews and muscles that his toes strained, cramped, in their straps, his calves in their armour.

'Are you feeling sick?' yelled the Consul.

'Permit me to lead the attack myself, sir,' the Captain yelled back, but in the middle of his sentence the bugle broke off, so that his unwontedly raised voice sounded ridiculous in the sudden silence.

The second attack had been repulsed. Again Caepio's men ran down the hill in fairly good order. Some even stooped in their run to lift a wounded friend but, seeing themselves left behind, they ran on again before having loaded such heavy burden on their shoulders. The wounded tried to cling to their comrades' legs, causing many to fall head over heels. The wind had turned, and so no sound, no cry could be heard on the other hill; the unpleasant action reeled on dumbly in the transparent air.

'It is indeed very repellent,' said the Consul, who had also grown pale. 'But, of course, that is a purely aesthetic point of view. One tends to forget completely that all those people would certainly have died in any case within the next twenty years, probably in much crueller ways and without such emotional alleviation of the procedure. The only difference is that war concentrates those individual death-processes in one confined space, and in one defined hour. It lends their death a sort of collective meaning, and, in its nauseating accumulation, shows up its complete senselessness at the same time. But do not be deceived: any private death-process is quite senseless and disgusting. It is not the absurdity of War, but the absurdity of Death as such, which is revealed by such drastic multiplication.'

'Sir,' said Caepio, incapable of controlling himself any longer, 'if you had taken my advice, all these people would still be alive.'

'And to make up for it, the others would be dead—what is the difference?' said the Consul, and regretted it immediately. Decidedly he had gone too far, that phrase could drag him before the State Court, and cost him his head. The Captain stared at him in unbelieving horror, turned on his heel and went without any further word.

Gellius shrugged his shoulders. Serve him right if he engaged in follies like war, martial dignity, and Consulship, he said to himself. He should have stayed with his philosophers. But they were even greater fools and their folly even less dignified. The Consul frowned, trying to think something out: what does a sensible man do when he happens into a world totally upside-down? He found no solution. Curious, he looked across at the field of battle.

Making good use of the short pause in the fighting, a swarm of blackbirds had alighted on the hill. Well-directed promptitude, thought the Consul, when a bugle sounded the attack once more; the swarm of black dots fluttered up into the air, yielding the field to the attackers. With what precision, what ingenuity, functions the senseless, thought the Consul; if one of those birds joined in the march now or one of the soldiers flew up into the air—how astounded they would all be. Yet it would be no crazier than their normal, present behaviour.

Caepio won't get there in time, he thought, and felt pleased. Corpses of friends and acquaintances are particularly nauseating; it gives one's relation with them such a theatrical tinge. Death provokes tactless personalities which one would never permit oneself ordinarily. A well-bred person should never die. And where are my dear attendants? They leave me standing here and fight their battle without a general.

At least one can look on in peace, thought the Consul. After all, such a battle is Experience.

The third attack began like the preceding ones. The Consul was already hardened, he expected the punctual fall of the spear-and arrow-rain; thought it quite natural when the attackers had at last climbed a third of the hill, and it fell, according to programme; thought it natural that the foremost ranks flung their arms up, fidgeted quaintly and lay down in an oddly theatrical manner. Only the continued silence of the spectacle disturbed him. He decided to follow a single man's fate, his glance fastened on a youth of fine bearing who struggled up the hillside; Gellius tried to predict his movements when he was hit. But nothing hit him, the Consul was disappointed and lost him in the crowd. The youth's name was Octavius; he ducked under a spear that nearly grazed his temple, and was to sire an emperor of Rome later on.

This time the hand-to-hand fighting by the barricades took on an extremely stubborn aspect. The terrible lumber, contrary to all rules of war, with which the Celts had built their wall, proved an intricate obstacle. The attackers, trying to climb over it, stuck fast with their legs in the shafts and wheels of latticed wagons; from every gap spears, axes, hammers, stabbed, cut, hit, into the living flesh, crushed the fingers of one, ripped a leg off another, cut off a third's head. Although the Consul could not hear it, the attackers yelled at the top of their voices, some to encourage themselves for they could scarcely see, some in pain and rage; but those behind the barricade worked quietly and efficiently: their spears, axes, hammers, stabbed, cut, hit, hacked the Roman flesh; they panted like butchers at work on the sow.

'That'll turn out badly,' the Consul had just time to think, when the bugle call sliced the air. The attackers promptly left the walls; the Consul found it difficult to overcome the impression that all this was nothing but a prearranged, childish and cruel play. But that which followed now had the effect of an unpredicted improvisation.

For, hardly had the attackers retreated from the wall when, instead of the usual rain of stones and arrows, which should have accompanied their flight, the senders of that rain themselves burst from the apparently air-tight barricades. The effect was so dumbfounding as to make the Consul, absorbed in the spectacle as he was, cry out with the joy he felt when a play took an unexpectedly witty turn. Like an echo, the roar of the Celts came from the other hill, so powerful that it abolished the distance and tore the Consul rudely from his reverie. 'That'll turn out very badly indeed,' he thought; and the slaughter of his soldiers began. They had evidently lost their heads; gone was the principle of honourable warfare, gone were the weapons they threw away as they stumbled over living and dead alike; they fell to their knees with shields raised over their heads, they cut peculiar downward capers, tumbled in clinched somersaults. Their pursuers were over, under, among them, were everywhere at once; their spears, axes, hammers, stabbed, cut, hit: they gasped with satisfaction. The Consul was sick.

The panic swept over the reserves at the foot of the hill when they saw the mad chase racing towards them. First they merely gaped at the nearing avalanche; then a few nervy ones took to their heels, and the rest joined the flight, glad that the decision had been made for them. No one listened to the officers.

After having finished vomiting, the Consul on his lonely hill began to wave his arms about excitedly. No one looked up at him and he himself did not know the meaning of his signals. Soon he stopped waving and searched for Caepio. But he remained invisible. He is probably cross with me, thought the Consul; and sat down in the grass.

.   .   .   .   .

But at a point in direct line with the course of the fleeing stood another observer on another deserted hill. He stood raised on his toes in order to see better, his haggard body swayed awkwardly in trying to keep its balance, and his lips moved all the while. When the first fugitives reached this end of the valley, young Cato rushed from his hill, waving his arms in the air; he shouted excitedly, and made awkward attempts at blocking their flight with his sword. It was such an unusual sight as to make several soldiers actually stop; others followed their example. Anyway, they had left the enemy far behind, after having run more than a mile; it was time to regain their breath. Cato, in the midst of a small group, talked on and on; he preached one of his dreaded sermons on the duties of soldierdom and the virtues of their ancestors. More and more fugitives pressed into the group in order to hear what was up, and, once halted, they remained. When they got bored they sat down on the ground. Cato talked and talked; he had now reached the dangers of gluttonous debauchery, quoted his great-great-grandfather as well as Cicero and Homer. The end of the valley formed a natural close, the group around Cato intercepted the onslaught of further soldiers, the flight was arrested. While the enemy looted the Roman camp, the greater part of the Roman army had collected around Cato. He was still talking; the boredom he secreted had conquered the general panic.

When the Consul and Caepio came running from different directions, the Centurions were already rallying and reassembling their men. They had suffered enormous losses, their camp was in the hands of the enemy; but the majority of the army was saved.

The Consul addressed the assembled soldiers, called young Cato from the ranks, praised his model conduct, promised special reward and promotion. Cato replied with unbearably irritating modesty that he declined promotion, for neither he nor any other man had today done anything to deserve such remuneration. The soldiers grinned. The Consul smiled and declared Cato a worthy successor to his famous ancestor. This moment made Caepio forgive the Consul all his sins; he resolved to box little brother's ears, but saw at once that it would not do. His aversion for little brother had already become so strong as to border on respect.

.   .   .   .   .

Crixus realised that to drop the pursuit had been a serious error. It was now apparent that the power he had over his men waned when his commands were no longer identical with their wishes. As soon as they had taken the Roman castra, and seen the ample provisions in wine and food, they lost all interest in their enemies: let them run, the naked-skulls, meanwhile they would have a really good time. When Crixus tried to reason with them, they laughed at him: 'Are you trying to be Spartacus or something?' So he said no more, went into the tent of Consul Gellius, had wine and meat brought to him, stretched out on the Consul's rug, and got himself drunk, lonely and silent.

Sentries had been posted, but he felt convinced that they too were drunk. One should really inspect them, shatter their dreams with one's heavy step, frighten them with one's dismal face, punish them, talk, act—like Spartacus. One should curse their vices—one's own; should condemn their greed—one's own; deny their drunkenness—one's own drunkenness. One should obey the law of detours. Crixus realised the decisive error of not inspecting the guard.

He smacked his lips. He was full up. He was sick of it all, bloody sick. He groped for a bit of meat on the table above his head, ate, wiped his fingers on Consul Gellius's rug. He groped for the jug, washed down the last gulp, picked his teeth with the tip of his tongue, shut his eyes.

Silence filled the tent, dusky, hot silence. His flesh stirred under the darkness. He remembered a young Celtic priestess. At times she had showed the whites of her eyes when she moaned for death in his embrace. He remembered Castus who had bitten the air, turning female without possessing woman's alien eeriness, akin even in oblivion, a brother under the skin, familiar in his lust. But he was sick of all that now, sick of women, sick of men. Once the one in the fur-skin had spoken of a girl who sang as he lay with her. He should have had this girl. Anything else was not worth while.

To sleep with a woman who sang—why had it been denied to him? That and that alone had been the point of all his deeds, from the days of Capua, down to the Present. Why did the goal mock at him, throw him stray crumbs, only to keep back the Real Thing, which bounced, singing and smiling, into the masters' laps? Chasing it was useless; you never caught up with it. Too many clung to your legs, driven by the very same hunger, the same starved longing of the flesh. Right at the beginning he should have gone off by himself; now it was too late for Alexandria.

It certainly was a grave error not to inspect the guards. Spartacus would have done it. Had you asked him what for and why, you would have started him off on his Sun State again. Pale Sun, too many thirst for his rays, too few of them fall on the single man. Chilly Sun, found only after strangest detours; it takes time before he warms, it takes too long, longer than life itself; and the death of life means death to all desires. Only swelled-headed fools care a straw for the Will-be.

Darkness, silence and heat filled the tent. Just before he fell asleep, Crixus thought once more of inspecting the guards—perhaps he fell asleep with the intention. But no one lets sleep take him unawares unless he wills it so. His sleep was so deep that nothing woke him when the Romans raided the camp in the middle of the night. The heavy, sad seal's head lay on his naked biceps, the closed eyelids parted the darkness of the tent from the darkness of sleep which was curiously reflected in his fish-like eyes. He snored, curled up like a sleeping dog, with his short, stocky limbs on the mattress of Consul Gellius. Thus he lay when the first Roman soldier to break into the Consul's tent found him. But such a powerful spell of darkness issued from the sleeping Gladiator, that the soldier backed at first, and stood undecided for a brief while before he severed the heavy seal's head from its body with a blow of his sword, so that the wicked charm might be broken.

During the night and the following morning twenty thousand slaves fell. Five thousand died on the cross, five thousand found their way back to Spartacus. Their wives and children were confiscated and publicly auctioned or sent to work in the mines. The death of Crixus was officially confirmed, but his carcass had disappeared from the tent; and in the dry, official report of Consul Lucius Gellius Publicola one could read the following paragraph:

'Night, who brought forth this man, swallowed back his flesh; so, being unable to honour this dead enemy, I honour the powers of darkness he embodied.'

2

DOWNHILL JOURNEY

FROM THE CHRONICLE OF FULVIUS THE LAWYER

44. As men and women habour a natural fear of dying, they are
fond of talking about this process in a manner which fails to
comply with actuality. They use expressions comparing dying to
falling asleep, which is as incorrect an assumption as the one
which is equally often voiced: the statement that the newborn
babe, just ejected by the bleeding womb, is awakened to living in
a gentle manner. In truth, however, the newborn being does at
once burst out with vehement sounds and gestures which seem to
express melancholy or even despair; and vice versa the aged
person before death is overcome with glad assurance and a delus-
ive feeling of strength. This may be the reason for so many
people's belief that Life and Death, before they, relieving one the
other, succeed to the rule over man, must first of all each pay a
last tribute to the other.

45. It might be advisable to keep the above in mind, for the
behaviour of the Slaves who had remained with Spartacus was
different from what one might have expected when they departed
from the City which they had built with so many high hopes.
It could not but be clear to every one that they were rushing towards their own destruction, and yet the miscarriage of their
proud plans did not produce in them distress but, rather, glad
confidence. Spartacus himself, who knew better than anyone else
what great ideals the departing were burning behind them, was
merrier in those days than anyone had ever seen him before,
and behaved like a man delivered from a heavy load. And the
others appeared to feel the same.

But this seemingly unreasonable merriment had its legitimate reasons: for, it is difficult for man to carry the burden of Future and to accept the detours which it forces upon him. Now, the Slaves had decided to return to their native lands, and he who languishes for Yesterday has an easier road before him than he who travels towards Tomorrow, just as it is invariably easier, merrier and more natural to walk downhill than to struggle pantingly over rock, rubble and glacier frost.

46. Thus the migration of the Slave Army to the north had in fact great likeness to a happy chase down and away from fatiguing heights. In the downward fall all those currents of strength which left the body at the time of ascent, return back into their channels. Down below his death awaits man but does not fail to pay life the last tribute due, by inspiring the falling with treacherous hopes.

This hope became, for the remainder of the Slave Army, the Thracian homeland, which was also to become the homeland of those others willing to join them. Straight through Italy they wished to wander north, stray nowhere, fell to the ground everything that barred their way. And these treacherous hopes of theirs took on ever bolder colouring. All the Slaves on their way, in Samnium, Umbria, Etruria would, so they hoped, join in the march to the north and leave Italy with them. A great migration of the people was to take place, taking all toilers and with them all productive power out of the country and leaving only their tormentors behind—who would then have to look after themselves for once. Like a wine-bag whose contents have run dry, the Roman State would remain, alone and empty; thus the Slaves said unto each other.

47. Though knowing full well—particularly since the news of the end of Crixus's army had reached him—how fallacious were these hopes and how the road would lead only downhill henceforth, Spartacus had never offered more resplendent proof of his strategical gifts than now. With swift marches by day he and the rest of his trusty comrades had traversed the midlands of Italy and irresistibly continued their way to the north. At the frontiers of Etruria Consul Lentulus made as if to bar their way by occupying with his army the mountains on both sides of the Arno. Meanwhile his colleague Gellius, who had vanquished Crixus, came to his aid from the south in order to bar Spartacus's retreat. As between pincers the slaves stood between the two Roman armies—but once more it became apparent that the pincers were

made of wood and the object in between of red-hot iron. On two consecutive days Spartacus completely annihilated the armies of both Consuls. The Consuls themselves escaped death by a hair's breadth, as did a number of distinguished personages who had been in their camp, such as young Marcus Cato and his brother Caepio. The lot of them were recalled to Rome by the infuriated Senate, and the Consuls removed from office.

But the Slaves continued, if a trifle reluctantly, their northward march.

48. They reached the river Padus at the northern frontier of Italy just when the rains were setting in. The river had considerably increased in width through the rains; also, not a single skiff could be procured which might have served for ferrying them, as the natives, seized with fear, had escaped to the other bank, taking with them all the boats they possessed. The other bank was only dimly visible, and the northern plain beyond it was obscured by grey screens of mist.

Now, when they were so near their goal, Spartacus and his fellows would assuredly have been able to overcome this final natural obstacle, after having triumphed over so many others by virtue of their courage and skill. However, with growing proximity the goal did not appear to them to be of such tempting colours as distance had led them to believe. They were still hesitating by the river, when messengers arriving from Thrace brought to them a report which slew all their hopes with one blow. In the Thracian mountains a great battle had been fought; Sadalas, King of the Odrysi, had prostrated himself under the Roman yoke; in Uscudum and Tomoi, Kalatis and Odessos, sat Roman governors. Even in their native land no Sun was left for them.

49. Thus the Slaves had in vain traversed the whole of Italy, from the extreme southern to the extreme northern end; the gate through which they had hoped to pass into freedom had slid closed before their very eyes like a trap. There was nothing left for them to do but to retrace their steps and turn to the south once more, without any other aim this time than that of keeping body and soul together and avoiding capture by their tormentors. As the beast of prey in its cage walks incessantly to and fro, so Spartacus and his forces wandered through Italy now, back again, from north to south.

50. They had no hopes left and no lofty plans. They looted the

cities which they passed on their restless wanderings and strayed through the land like a pack of hungry wolves. But the awe they inspired was greater than ever, for their number had again increased to fifty thousand, and their victory over the two Consuls had been followed by fresh ones over the Praetor Arrius and other generals as arrogant as they were incompetent.

51. This fear grew even greater when Spartacus, who presumably sensed despite his victories that the days of the revolt were numbered, undertook a venture felt by the Romans to be the greatest humiliation ever suffered by their State. Before he left the river Padus, for the south, he honoured his comrade Crixus with a funeral celebration of a splendour equal to those customarily given for the Roman Imperators. On this occasion he forced three hundred captive Romans to duel like gladiators and kill one another in front of the pyre on which a waxen image of Crixus was being fed to the flames. This remarkable spectacle was to be a memorial of the vengeance the Slaves had wreaked on their tormentors, as well as a memorial of their friendship for their former leader.

The three hundred sacrifices of this sepulchral celebration were all free Roman citizens; some were young aristocrats of patrician families. The fact that the latter were forced to such derisive transposition and compelled to slaughter each other for the entertainment of the assembled Slaves—that was an ignominy the possibility of which had never as much as entered the thoughts of a Roman, let alone come to his ears.

52. Of all the defeats meted out to them by the despised circus-gladiator, none had cut the hearts of the Roman lords so deeply and painfully as this occurrence.

Confusion and fright in the capital grew to such an extent that on the day on which new war-lords were to be elected, nobody applied for this honour; nor could a candidate for the Municipal Praetorate be found. For, no one wished to occupy these offices in a war where victory would bring no glory, defeat the worst shame. Confusion was increased by the fact that the Senate had been forced to buy enormous quantities of wheat and distribute them gratuitously to soothe the grumbling people; this, and the expenditure on the maintenance of so many campaigns abroad, had exhausted the State treasury. Even if an able general could have been obtained, he would have found little or no money in the treasuries to pay his soldiers.

All these ordeals afflicted the people with the most terrible fear, and in Rome the belief held sway that the fierce gladiator-chieftain with whose name mothers threatened their disobedient children, was already the master of their gates.

53. Thus fate played the strangest game with the Slaves. When, wearied by long wandering, they were already about to give themselves up as lost, fate for the last time introduced treacherous hope into their hearts. Without protection and defence, Rome seemed to lie at their feet, exposed, waiting like submissive prey for her own destruction. Like the flame which flickers up a last time before dying, hope flared up once more in the hearts of the exhausted Slave Horde; already they thought themselves the lords of Rome and masters of the world's destiny.

54. The man who in those days saved Rome and destroyed any hopes for a new order in the world: that man was no general and had never distinguished himself with martial feats.
He was the banker Marcus Crassus, who was hard of hearing, stocky and fat in appearance. Like all deaf or half-deaf men, he was of gauche and distrustful demeanour, and, because of his monstrous wealth, he was dreaded by all and loved by few.

55. Marcus Crassus had reached his forty-third year without ever having achieved any special glory. Now at last be believed the moment come to achieve great honours and boost himself as the saviour of Rome, by means of relatively little strenuous efforts. For in his calculating way he realised that, in spite of Spartacus's great strategical talents, the latter's victories were based less on the strength of his army than on the weakness and block-headed-ness of the Roman generals with whom he had been dealing hitherto.
So, when the fright had reached its zenith in Rome, Marcus Crassus with his attendants betook himself to the Campus Martius and declared before the assembled people that he was prepared to take on the Praetorate and to equip a fresh army out of his own pocket, trusting that the State would, at a later date, refund the expenses he would thus incur. This statement naturally caused great jubilation, and soon Crassus was in charge of eight full-strength Legions whom he intended to use for the crushing of the Slave Rising in the immediate present, and for his own ambitious ends at a later time.

56. When his vanguard, after the first skirmish with the Slaves, ran away as was their habit, Crassus's first action in his capacity

of commander-in-chief consisted of the order that every tenth man of the guilty regiments was to be flogged to death in full view of his comrades. The Legions saw that a hand different from those of Varinius or Clodius Glaber was pulling the reins, and began at last to behave themselves. Their excellent equipment and the superiority of their weapons, in the purchase of which Crassus had exercised no niggardliness, soon caused the routing of Spartacus in Apulia.

57. This was the first defeat suffered by the Slaves under the command of Spartacus, and it had the effect of depressing them greatly, though their valour was by no means broken. Spartacus himself did not desire to fight in open combat against so superior an adversary, and withdrew farther south.

Thus the Slaves traversed the land Lucania for the second time on this sorry march, the same land they had entered with such audacious hopes the previous year. They passed the ruins of their own former City and beheld the remains of granaries and dining halls covered with dust and rubbish—a sight which cut them to the quick. For, the more the Sun City receded into the past, the more brilliant and colourful did their memory paint the life they had formerly led within her walls.

58. But not even here did the Legions of Crassus leave the Slaves in peace, and so Spartacus and his Army were forced to seek refuge in the extreme southern cusp of the peninsula. They flooded the rugged land of Bruttium, on the border of which Crassus surprisingly suspended the pursuit.

This remarkable man who did not exercise his military authority in the traditional manner, but rather handled it in the prudently calculating way in which wheat agents and property speculators set about their work, had another plan. Presumably he realised that the Slaves would each defend his life to the very end; also the land Bruttium was mountainous and clothed in the densest woods of all Italy; and these circumstances would have tended to assist the Slaves in the form of warfare peculiar to them, while at the same time annulling the Romans' superiority in the way of arms.

59. Therefore Crassus arrested the march of his army and designed a plan whose execution would have been thought ridiculous or even impossible by any professional soldier.

While the Slaves were bent on their customary raids at the southern coast, the banker had his Legions dig a trench right across the entire peninsula, between the Sylacian and the Hyppomic Gulfs. This trench was fifteen feet deep and as wide, so that it completely cut off the southern tip of Italy from the rest of the country. As the neck of land at the said point has a width of only three and twenty Roman miles from sea to sea, the eight Legions spread out by Crassus along the entire stretch of land, who all worked simultaneously, were able to complete this work within a few days. Now Crassus had ramparts and turrets built along the trench, and decided patiently to wait his chance behind these entrenchments until the Slaves should have exhausted their provisions in this rough region, and would thus be forced either to surrender to their tormentors or perish miserably.

It is said that Crassus told his Legions that, in order to exterminate these dangerous curs, he had turned all Bruttium into a rat-trap; henceforth they would be unable to bite.

60. Hardships and privation of this lengthy campaign, as well as the usual autumnal epidemics, had reduced Spartacus's forces to less than half their previous number. Twenty thousand creatures turned savage, the last survivors of the greatest revolution that had ever shaken the Roman Empire, wandered restlessly through the mountains and forests of Bruttium, south of the huge earthwork which cut them off from the rest of humanity.

3

THE TOMBSTONES

OVER mountains and through forests, they wandered across the land of Bruttium. The past lay behind them, their future was no more. Spartacus rode at their head, alone now.

They came to the necropolis of Rhegium. The man with the fur-skin gazed out into the rain-drenched country, at the scanty palms and many tombstones. His gaze was arrested by an inscription:

SCOFFING AT ILLUSION I LIE HERE IN ETERNAL SLUMBER

His mind stored the phrase. Next to it stood another stone:

TITUS LOLLIUS LAY DOWN HERE BY THE ROAD SO THAT
THE PASSING WANDERER MAY SAY: GREETINGS, LOLLIUS

'Greetings, Lollius,' said the man with the fur-skin and smiled the good-natured smile of the old days. How different men remained even in death: one still jeered at life which could not concern him any longer; the other whined after it like a puppy frightened of loneliness.

Long strings of rain fell on the tombstone of the sociable Lollius, and shivered into tiny water beads; others ran in fat drops down the inscription.

The man with the fur-skin felt the silent train of the horde behind him, the silent train of those who were left. He thought of Hermios, the shepherd with the horsy teeth, killed in Apulia by a spear from the army of the banker Crassus. He looked at the rain-bathed tombstones and tried to make up an epitaph for Hermios:

> THIS IS THE LAST RESTING PLACE OF HERMIOS, A LUCANIAN SHEPHERD; HE LONGED TO EAT FIELDFARE WITH BACON JUST ONCE BUT WAS PREVENTED. YOU WHO PASS HERE, REMEMBER THAT NO ONE SHOULD EAT FIELDFARE WITH BACON AS LONG AS ONE MAN LIVES ON THIS EARTH WHO MAY NOT TASTE OF THEM

The rain did not cease; the horde's pace dragged more and more. The man with the fur-skin at their head felt lonely; in bygone days fat Crixus used to be at his side, riding his horse as though it were a mule. Now Hades had swallowed up the sulky man; the one with the fur-skin composed an epitaph for him:

> HERE LIES CRIXUS, A CELTIC GLADIATOR, WHO WOULD HAVE LIKED TO SHARE THE BED OF A MAID WHO SANG. YOU WHO READ THIS, REMEMBER THAT MAIDS SHALL NOT SING AS LONG AS THERE IS BUT ONE MAN ON THIS EARTH WHO MAY NOT HEAR THEIR SONG

The rain went on falling; the man with the fur-skin thought of Zozimos the rhetorician who had caught the fever by the river Padus; now he no longer flapped the wings of his toga.

> ZOZIMOS, AN ORATOR, WHO CHERISHED NOBLE SPEECH AND DEMANDED JUST GOVERNMENT, REMAINED BY THE ROADSIDE HERE. PASSING WANDERER, REMEMBER THAT THERE CAN BE NO NOBLE SPEECH AND NO JUST GOVERN- MENT AS LONG AS THERE ARE PEOPLE EXCLUDED FROM JUSTICE

The rain got worse, the mountains were curtained with the drooping clouds. Beyond lay the fertile plains of Lucania, the succulent land of Campania, the rich and wonderful cities—all cut off by the trench the banker Crassus had dug across the whole country, from coast to coast. They must perish here like rats in a trap.

The man with the fur-skin could feel the long procession of misery behind his back, the ragged, savage men, the women with their wet hair and slack breasts, the barrows full of sick people trailing swarms of lazy flies. Rain drizzled down his face; he made up an epitaph for all of them:

> THEY WERE OF THE SEED OF TANTALUS AND DEBARRED
> FROM THE ENJOYMENT OF THE GOOD THINGS OF THE
> WORLD. PASSING WANDERER, HALT AND QUAKE WITH
> SHAME AS YOU THINK OF THEM

There was one last chance for them: that of crossing to the isle of Sicily with the aid of the pirate fleet.

The slaves of Sicily were even worse off than those of the Italian mainland; the great risings kindled by the Syrian Eunus and the Thracian Athenion less than a generation ago had not yet been extinguished from their memories. For three years during the first rising, and four years during the second, the slaves had ruled over almost the whole of Sicily; perhaps the horde might succeed in rekindling the fire.

But they had no boats, and between them and the island was the dreaded channel, guarded on one side by the cliff of Scylla, on the other by the vortex of Charybdis. Their deliverance depended on the pirate fleet.

In his temporary camp at the coast of Rhegium, Spartacus met the admiral of the pirate fleet stationed in the Ionic sea. He received him in his leather tent. The tattered purple velum hung from its mast outside: the last two of Fannius's servants had nursed it through all their journeys across Italy and carried it on.

The pirate state was then at the height of its power. The pirates commanded nearly a thousand naval units, for the greater part small, open racing barges teamed into squadrons; each squadron was protected by a number of heavy two- and three-storeyed galleys; at its head sailed the flagship, painted in gold and purple. They formed a self-contained military state with strict discipline and a judiciously thought-out system for the sharing out of booty; their home was the sea and its isles, from Asia Minor to the Pillar of Hercules which stood guard over the thoroughfare between Africa and the southern patch of Spain. The heart of their dominion was the isle of Crete; the Cicilian woods yielded the timber for their ships, and their wharves stood in the town Side in Pamphylia, which was also the entrepôt for prisoners of war. Their women, children and treasures were kept at fortresses scattered over a number of islands, which communicated by means of bonfire signals and mail barges. They entered into political alliances with Asiatic kings, insurgent Greek cities, and factions of the Roman opposition. The largest Roman ports, including Ostia and Brundisium, paid them an annual tribute; only a short time ago their Ionic squadron had occupied the port of Syracuse. Of such might was the power on whose behalf the Admiral Demetrius took up negotiations with the Slaves, after one year's pause.

Admiral Demetrius had so far never met the Thracian Prince in person, but he knew all about the negotiations at Thurium and disapproved of them. His stately barge rocked out in the bay; he disembarked, clad in gala uniform, and searched for the guard of honour. There was none. Two unkempt, bull-necked ruffians with helmets of rusty tin escorted the Admiral through the cluster of dripping tents that reeked of misery and disease, and led him to their leader.

The Admiral disliked this leader at first sight: he was a tall, coarsely-built man with a slight stoop and awkward poise, dressed in nothing but a shaggy fur-skin. He received Demetrius in his tent, alone, had wine brought in, as well as bread and salt, said little, looked sickly and rather sad. The Admiral had expected an invitation to dinner; rigid in all his portliness, somewhat damaged by the perils of navigation, he sat on the rug, his one sound eye swept disapprovingly through the badly furnished tent, while the other eye, made of polished coloured stone, stared straight in front. Was this supposed to be the famous brigand-chief, aspirant ally of the filibuster state? He had not even a silver wash basin, no jester or household poet nor any agreeable female attendance. Truly, this man was just about fit to be a Roman People's Tribune, a preacher of social revolution; it was a sure bet that he had never even heard of the fashionable poet Phineas of Athens.

Admiral Demetrius fidgeted uncomfortably on the hard mattress; possibly it was full of vermin, trust the friend of the people and sinister democrat for that. Out of politeness he essayed a conversation on the weather and Thracian deities.

But that landlubber cut him short with unsurpassable rudeness, asked dryly on what conditions he would be prepared to convey the Slave Army to Sicily.

Thereupon the Admiral indulged in a voluble lecture on the world situation which, he said, had considerably changed since the days of Thurium; with the remaining three fingers of his right hand he pointed down at the ground, at Hades: that's where the fleet of the arrogant Spanish emigrants had got to; and Mithridates too would soon share their fate, after the defeat inflicted on him by the glutton Lucullus near the town Kabeira; which just went to show that a sense for palatal delights and the virtue of hospitality did by no means diminish the military greatness of a man.

After this catty thrust which seemed, however, to have made no impression on the fur-clad rebel and plebeian, the Admiral took a deep gulp to fortify himself, baring a missing row of teeth dedicated to the God of War, and declared that the one and only power in the world capable of gallantly standing up to Rome was the buccaneer state, for Rome had no fleet worthy of the name. He, Admiral Demetrius, therefore regretted not to be interested in an alliance with the Thracian Prince and to be in a position of regarding the transport of his Army only in the light of a business enterprise. The cost, he said, was five Sestertii per passenger, in other words: one and a quarter Denarii or twelve and a half Asses.

The man with the fur-skin did not reply. He made an effort to multiply by twenty thousand the sum named by the portly visitor. The Admiral was watching him.

'In other words,' said Demetrius, 'a total of one hundred thousand Sestertii or twenty-five thousand Denarii; if you wish to have it translated into Greek currency: four Talents. As usual, half of this sum should be paid down in advance; the squadron is at present anchored off Syracuse, and so you should be able to embark within the next five days. The sick must of course be left behind; danger of infection and all that, you know.'

The man with the fur-skin knew that he had no choice and that the other knew it as well as he did. He haggled stubbornly without ever taking his leaden, ailing glance off the visitor, who was beginning to feel ill at ease. In the end they agreed on sixty thousand Sestertii; that was the last of the slaves' booty-treasure.

The two bodyguards dragged rough sacks filled with half the amount into the tent, counted it in the presence of the Admiral, and transported it to his barge. After which the Admiral expressed his regret at being unable to stay any longer, as a banquet awaited him on board; he rose in all his stateliness, ceremoniously saluted his lord and brother the Thracian Prince, and, escorted by the guards with their rusty helmets, made his way to the magnificent barge and went aboard.

The slaves waited for five days; young hope in their hearts, they peered across the rain-screened sea; but the pirate fleet did not come.

Impatient as they were, they tried to make rafts out of tree trunks. The stormy waves lifted them up, spun them around like whirligigs; they were dashed to pieces against the rock Scylla, sucked into Charybdis's voracious abyss. They could do nothing but wait.

A second week passed, a third—the pirate ships did not come.

When four weeks had passed they heard that Admiral Demetrius and his squadron had long left the port of Syracuse and sailed forth to the coast of Asia Minor.

When a further three weeks had passed and the remainder of the horde, decimated by starvation and illness, began to scatter about the mountains, Spartacus decided to end it all. He requested the hostile generalissimo Marcus Licinius Crassus for an interview.

4

THE INTERVIEW

MARCUS CRASSUS was forty-three years of age and owned a fortune of one hundred and fifty million Sestertii. He was fat, hard of hearing, and suffered from asthma.

Although an offspring of the ancient family of the Licinii, which should and would have paved his way in the political hierarchy, he had for years trod a lone path. Whereas his contemporaries and rivals quarrelled for leading commissions in Spain and Asia Minor, aiming to seize power one day, Crassus had turned almost exclusively to affairs of finance. He laid the foundations of his fortune in the years of terror under Sulla by informing on members of the opposition and appropriating their fortunes after they had been executed. One day it was proved that he had forged a name in the proscription lists; in consequence there was a slight drop in the temperature of his and the dictator's personal relations, and Crassus turned to land speculation.

He bought up depreciated or fire-damaged houses and sites first one by one, and later by whole streets and quarters, until quite a considerable part of the capital had become his property. Next, he bought up the best masons, carpenters and building-slaves on the market, in so systematic a manner, that after a few years he held an architectural monopoly for Rome and some of the provincial cities. He owned silver-mines in Greece and quarries in Italy, which supplied his own concern with building materials; so that henceforth small-fry with building ambitions had to order their future houses through Crassus, from site to finished roof, including architects and labour. As he did not feel up to conducting so complicated an enterprise on his own, he advanced capital to a number of his freedmen and clients, and went into partnership with them.

But after a time it became evident that the fluctuations in the building-contracting business caused frequent unemployment to part of the building-slaves, while their maintenance required considerable sums. In order to remedy this, Crassus's enterprise grew a new branch which gave the finishing touch of perfection to the Whole: he founded the first Roman fire brigade.

Since most of the houses in Rome were built of wood, fires occurred quite often, in fact, every day. Crassus's fire brigade consisted of his unoccupied building-slaves who were equipped with carts and fire-bells. The carts carried axes and water-buckets; but it was said that Crassus's fire brigade made more diligent use of the axes than of the buckets. In addition, the fire wardens were commissioned to begin fighting the flames only after the unfortunate owner of the burning house had agreed to the fee for the salvage work; and as a rule these negotiations ended with the owner being obliged to sell both house and property to Crassus, before they had burnt down completely.

Years ago Crassus had coined the saying that only a man capable of supporting an army of his own on the interest of his capital had the right to call himself wealthy. All Rome thought him avaricious and miserly; Crassus did nothing to disabuse them. He knew exactly what it was he strove for; he had made a discovery.

He owed this discovery to an experience which was to decide his entire future: an encounter with his rival Pompeius which had taken place several years ago.

Ever since his childhood, Crassus had been overshadowed by Pompeius, had measured all his deeds, thoughts, dreams by his; and in every respect Pompeius had outdone him.

During the civil war Crassus, nearly thirty years old, a man without either past or future, had wandered about Spain with a hired band of mercenaries, waiting for an opportunity to take a hand in politics. The opportunity made no appearance; but meanwhile Pompeius, his junior by eight years, had acquitted himself with distinction under Sulla, and already called himself 'Imperator'.

In the last years of the civil war Crassus as well as Pompeius was in charge of a Legion. Both fought with some success: Crassus was accused of having embezzled the booty from the town Todi, Pompeius was charged with the theft of birds'-snares and books from Asculum. Finally the revolution was routed and Sulla became dictator. Crassus was paid off with a seat in the Senate, but Pompeius was publicly embraced by a bare-headed Sulla and addressed as 'Magnus', 'the Great'.

Crassus was at that time thirty-two, Pompeius twenty-four. Crassus had already grown slightly deaf and asthmatic, Pompeius vied with his soldiers in sporting-feats and contests. Crassus was married to an honourable matron, Pompeius was having his third divorce and became Sulla's son-in-law. Senator Crassus, half-deaf, embittered and despondent, was considering whether to retire from public affairs, seclude himself on his country estate and write his memoirs, when events took the decisive turn which led to the said discovery: Pompeius borrowed money from him.

It was a matter of a largish sum which Pompeius needed at any price in order to bribe a few jurors, for once more he was involved in some shady affair or other. He mumbled and carried on, bashful like a schoolboy before Crassus. Crassus let him hanker in suspense for a while, then he lent him the money—without interest and without security. When Pompeius left the house, his athlete's face fiery red with mortification, tripping and nearly falling over the doorstep, Crassus locked himself in his study and burst into tears. He was thirty-three years old, and this was the first happy day of his life.

The scales fell from his eyes. He and all of his kind knew all about the use of money, but no one had so far drawn the obvious conclusion. Crassus did so now. The conclusion was: money is not the means to profit and pleasure, but the means to power.

It was a simple enough discovery; all that mattered now was to amplify it into a system. Crassus's system was as simple as it was revolutionary: he amassed his capital, the largest in all Rome, and lent it out—but without interest and security. The usurers' capital brought them percentage-profits; Crassus's yielded power.

While Pompeius bedecked himself with new glories in the Spanish war, Crassus lent money out rate-free to the influential men of every party, irrespective of their political ends. Half the

Senate was in his debt; all the party leaders were dependent on him. The most reckless of zealots bewared of getting in his way; people spoke of him as a bull with hay on his horns.

Crassus knew as well as his competitors that the Republic was putrid to the core, and that only a new dictatorship could save the State. A dictatorship which ruthlessly finished with the old constitution and the old methods, and progressed along utterly new paths in the spirit of the time: perhaps that of fighting the moribund Senate by making use of the army and the rebellious section of the people; perhaps that of establishing a monarchy. A monarchy that leaned not on the conservative aristocracy but on the People's tribunes and the masses.

He knew that most of the leading politicians had the same ideas and aimed at the same goal; but Lucullus was too frivolous, Sertorius dead, Caesar too young; the only serious competitor was still the rival of old, Pompeius.

Crassus was bored with the campaign; he considered warfare inferior activity. He did not think much of palatal delights, excepting candied dates and sweetmeats for which he had special recipes; his banquets were all that was expected of a patrician, but he himself had plain fare. Women likewise did not tempt him; all the love affairs in his life had been unsatisfactory. The only thing apart from his candied dates which gave him honest pleasure was lengthy mealtime conversations, preferably with youthful fanatics and theorists whom he made fun of in his own way, without their noticing it. For, although the half-deaf banker almost never laughed, he had a sense of humour of his own.

One of the participants in his campaign was Young Cato, who again had volunteered as a common soldier; against his wish Crassus had forced the rank of a Tribune on him. The ascetic youth had not changed; he still went about with manuscripts in his arms, and lectured on the Stoa and on the forefathers' virtues, which drove everybody except Crassus to distraction. The fat generalissimo would patiently let him talk on, put a hand to his deaf ear, and nod now and then with deadly solemnity.

After dinner on the day before that fixed for the meeting with Spartacus, to which Crassus looked forward with a certain amount of expectation, Young Cato expounded his views on the slave question. He quoted his Stoic teachers, Antipater of Tyre and

Antiochus of Askalon, and gesticulated vigorously with his lanky arms, while his lips let forth a lively pin-point spray which Crassus discreetly tried to elude.

'Real liberty,' explained Cato, 'is contained in virtue alone, which is also the loftiest wisdom; real slavery results from vice. Passion gainsays reason; and since Nature is administered by immortal Reason, instincts and baser desires are unnatural. The hordes who have forced us into this campaign are goaded by the basest of appetites; therefore they are clearly acting against Reason and Nature. But also among ourselves an evil state of affairs has gained ground. Our forefathers knew how to live simply and in accord with Nature; but we are surrounded by effeminacy, vice and debauchery. If Rome continues on this disastrous road, she will soon come to certain perdition.'

Crassus had been listening patiently; he nodded his head and placed a handful of sweetmeats in his mouth.

'You're right, the Republic is doomed,' he said and wheezed asthmatically. 'She is smothered in vice and intemperance. And do you know what is the root of all that debauchery?'

'It is the estrangement of mankind from the Natural virtues,' said the youth, but, eagerly about to resume, he was cut short by a gesture of Crassus's plump hand.

'Pardon me,' he said. 'The root of all moral depravity is the depreciating ground-rent, and the decline of export.'

'I know nothing about that,' said Cato, 'but in the times of my grandfather . . .'

'Pardon me,' said Crassus. 'Do you think Lucullus would build his crazy fish-ponds if it were more profitable to grow wheat? Do you think our nobility would waste its capital on circus-games in the most lunatic manner, if they could invest it profitably in agriculture, as was the case in your venerable grandfather's time? But since then the ground-rent has fallen, and it is no longer lucrative to grow wheat in Italy. That is the reason for the decline of our peasantry, for the flooding of our towns with the agrarian proletariat; that is why Roman capital is no longer productive, does no longer create work for the people, which is reduced to either beggary or robbery.'

'The reason for that is the moral degeneracy of the people,' cried Young Cato. 'They fight shy of work, prefer to live on the corn-dole for the unemployed, to run to their street-clubs and listen to the demagogues. What we need is discipline, the law and order of our fathers.'

'Pardon me,' said Crassus. 'Discipline and law and order are all very nice, but they are no remedies for the agricultural crisis, that is, the falling ground-rent. And do you know what the falling ground-rent results from?'

'No,' said Cato defiantly, and the red chastity-pimples on his face grew even redder. 'I have never bothered my head about that.'

'More's the pity,' said Crassus and chewed his candy. 'A grave neglect, for a young philosopher and future politician. I'll explain the connection to you, and you will find it more useful than your Antipater of Tyre with all his Stoicism. If you look at the Roman State Balance Sheet, you will see that on the world market we are represented by only two articles of export: (a) wine, (b) oil. On the other hand, we import goods from all over the world, from corn to labour power—slaves—and all the luxuries with which are markets are overrun. How, do you think, does Rome pay for this colossal import-surplus?'

'With money, I suppose, that is to say with silver,' said Cato.

'Wrong,' said Crassus, and spat out the date-stones. 'There aren't any silver-mines in Italy. The sublime trick of the Roman State is its receiving goods from its colonies without paying for them. That means, for example, that everything our deplorable Asiatic subjects export to Rome is merely credited to the account of taxes to be rendered. In other words, we get everything for nothing—and, strangely enough, that is just what we're dying of. For is it no longer worth the Roman burgess's while to produce things: farmers can't compete with the cheap imported wheat, artisans can't complete with the cheap slave labour. That is why half the free population is unemployed these days, and why there are twice as many slaves as burgesses in Italy. Rome has literally become a parasite State—the "Vampire of the World", as one of our excitable young poets describes it. As work has lost the capacity of tempting anyone in Italy, our productive powers don't develop either; the Gallic Barbarians' agricultural equipment is technically far superior to ours, and in most of our provinces industry has reached a far higher stage of development than here; all we ever invent are war- and gambling-machines. If any sort of stoppage occurs in the supply of overseas wheat, we have a famine on our hands—just as it happened two years ago—as well as revolution. With the wheat-supply at its normal rate we choke in corn, and a good harvest becomes the farmer's curse; he has to sell his field and go to the capital, to receive by charity the wheat he may no longer produce by his labour. Isn't that an insane state of affairs?'

Crassus leaned back and took a handful of dates. With caustically screwed-up eyes he looked at the lean youth who squirmed on his seat. Cato's face was getting redder and redder.

'I have never put my mind to those things,' he said stubbornly. 'But do you think they are all that important? Is not rather everything a matter of moral pulchritude and the spirit in the State? In olden times . . .'

But Crassus was inexorable. 'Pardon me,' he said. 'If you look at all that bunkum still more closely, you must come to the conclusion that the State itself no longer knows what it is living on. For the State, that is the Roman official-caste, is far too block-headed even to discriminate between a real mortgage and a debenture; and besides, tradition and class-arrogance prevent them from understanding the laws of economics. The consequence is that the tax-contractors, the lords of the public stock companies, the masters of the shipping trade, the slave-dealers, and the mining-licensees, have in point of fact the whole State in their hands, have power of decision over war and peace, prosperity and ruin of the nation. You read our great historian Polybios, who wrote a hundred years ago that these sort of people do not only control our legal apparatus, but also the elections—either by simply bribing the voters or through the honest votes of the small shareholders, who often constitute the majority of the small boroughs.

'Can you doubt that the competition between the Roman and Phoenician wheat trades was the direct cause of the Punic wars? And that the war against Jugurtha was drawn out over six years because the African knew his onions and candidly bribed the important knights and Senators? Just look up the Senatorial minutes of the time. Look up the records of the Permanent Blackmail Commission. And you talk of morals and the forefathers' virtues. . . .'

Cato did not know what to reply; he was horrified at the cynicism of his commander-in-chief. He begged to take his departure, and departed, with a crimson face. Crassus gazed after him and spat out date-stones; the conversation had pleased him.

It had not been easy for Spartacus to start out on this excursion, but it had not been as hard as many of his fellows thought.

He knew that this was the end. His horde was beginning to scatter about the woods. One month longer, and the Romans could hunt them down one by one. The best of them had fallen, the rest were going to the dogs. The men in the camp had grown hollow-eyed, despair covered their livid faces as with cobwebs. Every day the women came running through the streets of the camp, in their arms infants with big heads and spidery limbs, and screamed they should surrender, so that everything might become as it once had been. They ran through the camp, with babies at their loose breasts and with wild, tangled hair, and screamed wildly that they did not want to die.

The men did not want to die either. They stood by the beach, watched the waves rolling close, filled their lungs with the cool fragrance of the seaweed and thought it was good to be alive, and felt that the worst sort of life was still better than the best of deaths.

Despair and the wish to live deprived men and women of their reason. They talked of throwing their weapons away and going over to the Romans, and they believed they would be forgiven. They came to Spartacus and looked at him with the childish, trusting glances of their sunken eyes, like wounded animals, and believed that he would save them. But he knew that everything was finished; and when three weeks had passed after the pirates' breach of trust, he decided to go to Crassus. It was not easy for him; he thought of Zozimos the rhetorician: he would probably have flapped excited sleeves, harangued of Pride and Honour, shrieked of shame and iniquity. But Zozimos was dead, and the others wanted to live. And when at night they listened to the waves and smelled the sea breeze, words like honour and shame were nothing but maudlin stutter lost in the thunder-drone of the surf.

The rains were as good as past and spring was already drawing near, when Spartacus started on his way to Crassus. His attendants might only escort him to the rampart, Crassus had stipulated. The trench he was to cross alone.

On the other side the Roman Guards were waiting for him. As soon as he set eyes on them, the man with the fur-skin was aware of setting foot into another world, and the first impression moved him deeply. It moved him to look at the brisk, well-fed soldiers, their shining, contented eyes, the polished metal of their armour, the flawless leather of their straps. The Guards escorted him and did not speak. They looked haughtily straight ahead; the freshly starched linen of their kilts crunched with every step they took, an odour of pomatum and ointments floated round them. Spartacus in his shaggy fur-skin walked between them; he was taller than they, but his back was hunched and his chin hairy; at first he took pains to keep his head up, but he left off soon, and let it droop.

They walked for some time. The Guards escorted him and said nothing and looked straight ahead.

They passed many soldiers, singly and in cohorts. With curiosity they looked at the approaching Guards with the tall, shaggy man in their midst, but made no move to line their way. They all looked clean, sprightly and contented. As the small troop strode past them, the soldiers kept silent, at most they nudged one another. Their clear eyes held no hostility, only quizzical bewilderment.

It was a long way. As they approached the camp, they passed three chatting officers. All three veered round to watch them coming. One of the officers wore smart riding habit, he was nearly as tall as Spartacus and had stern, regular features. The Guards who escorted Spartacus saluted. The officer did not return salute; he looked at the fur-clad man. He raised his eyebrows; his cool glance slowly travelled down the fur-skin to the torn footwear; in rhythm with the Guards' footsteps he slapped his thigh with the riding crop.

It was a long way. At last they could see the first tents.

When they turned into the main street of the camp, a battalion in marching order came towards them. The mailed legs of the column beat down on the road so precisely and simultaneously, that every time only one short sharp clap was heard. When the captain of the regiment saw the group with the man in the fur-skin coming to meet him, he turned into a side street. The column wheeled with sharp thunder-claps; Spartacus could see only their armour-plated backs; not one of the soldiers turned his head.

Finally the Guards stopped in front of the generalissimo's tent. A sentry took the man with the fur-skin in his charge; the Guards turned and marched off. They had not exchanged one word with the sentry. Nor did the sentry say anything to the man in the fur-skin. Dumb, he led him over soft carpets into the wide, spacious tent, turned on his heel and fastened the tent flap from outside.

Inside the tent, the carpet on the floor was so thick as to stun the sounds of Spartacus's footsteps. When he entered, Crassus sat at his desk in the centre of the tent, writing. He did not rise and did not look up. He had flung back the sleeves of his purple-edged toga; his short, bare arms, covered with gooseflesh, were propped on the table. Spartacus noticed immediately that the expression in the Roman generalissimo's face reminded him of Crixus. True, his gross face was clean-shaven, and so was his skull. But the heavy, dismal, unmoved glance below the padded lids was perplexingly like that of dead Crixus.

The generalissimo clapped his hands, a dumb cuirassier aide-de-camp appeared, saluted, received the document and departed, after having brushed the man in the fur-skin with a rapid glance. Spartacus had sat down on the sofa opposite the desk, and waited.

At last the generalissimo raised his eyes to him. 'A wounded beast,' thought Crassus. 'You wish to negotiate the conditions of surrender,' he said. He propped his stumpy bare arms on the desk. 'There are no conditions.'

His petulant glance did not waver from the sitting man. If you put him in decent uniform, thought Crassus, and took the animal sadness out of his eyes, he would cut a better figure than Pompeius. He waited for an answer, put a hand to his ear. 'Did you say anything?' he asked.

Spartacus marvelled at the beautifully clear, almost dainty Latin which came from the lips of the fat generalissimo. On his desk stood a small, cubic inkwell of cut glass; it had a hole in each side without the ink running out. The carpets on floor and walls obliterated every sound from outside. The complete quiet in the tent was different from the nightly silence of the mountains that he knew; it was a soft, cushiony silence, like the sofa on which he was sitting. He had difficulty in calling to mind that the words spoken here would decide the fate of twenty thousand human beings, and of the Italian revolt.

'I am slightly deaf in my right ear,' said the generalissimo in the same clear, glossy accents. 'Please speak distinctly if you have anything to say.'

Spartacus kept silent and contemplated the desk. The clouds of Mount Vesuvius, the prophetic babble of the aged masseur, the hoarse lectures of the little lawyer—all of that had no reality inside this tent, in the face of the cut, polished inkwell; it was blotted out by the stuffed silence. When you looked at the generalissimo's plump hand curving round his deaf ear, everything said or thought down there beyond the earthwork seemed absurdly unreal and indigent.

'You know how things are with us,' said Spartacus. 'It can't be in anybody's interest to have twenty thousand people go to ruin.'

Crassus shrugged imperceptibly; he was still thinking of what Pompeius would look and act like in the place of this creature. Probably even more pitiably. This Barbarian at least did not pretend; he probably talked just as measuredly, in the same harsh, guttural Thracian tones, when issuing martial commands from his horse. Crassus could easily imagine him at a triumphal entry, striding through underneath the arch, acclaimed by the frenzied, queueing people, with an unmoved face. Really, everything depended on the period in which such a man was born, thought Crassus, whether time threw him on the rubbish heap or allowed him to make history. Born one century earlier or later, this wounded animal would have turned the world inside-out, more thoroughly than Alexander and Hannibal. 'In other words, you surrender unconditionally,' said Crassus.

He leaned forward slightly and waited.

'That would depend on what would happen to my people,' said Spartacus.

'The Senate of Rome will decide that,' said Crassus.

After a brief pause Spartacus said:

'I'm not talking of the leaders, but of the men and the women.'

'Pardon me,' said Crassus. 'We were talking of unconditional surrender. Everything else will be decided by the Senate.'

Spartacus was silent. He looked at the glass inkwell; he still could not bring himself to believe in the reality of what they were saying. He could not understand why the ink did not run out although the glass cube had holes for dipping in on every one of its six sides. Then he saw that within the cubic glass case a small bowl was suspended from two hoop-links: whatever way you placed the cube, the little bowl would always swing horizontally on its hoops. He felt pleased to have seen through this bit of mechanism; for an instant a smile hovered on his face.

At that moment two orderlies entered, with wine, cups, candied dates and sweetmeats on a tray, put it down on a three-legged, lo‧v table and vanished soundlessly.

Crassus had followed Spartacus's glance, he took up the inkwell and tilted it, unsmiling.

'Have you never seen anything like that?' he asked.

'No, I haven't,' said Spartacus. Crassus handed him the glass cube, he took it in his hand, tilted it too and put it back on the table.

'Our conditions,' said Spartacus, 'are: the serfs can go back to where they used to be in service without fear of punishment, and the rest are enrolled in your army.'

Crassus shrugged his shoulders. 'You are pleased to jest,' he said. 'You don't seem to have much of an idea of Roman martial law. Besides, the decision lies with the Senate. All that is in my power to do would be to recommend the utmost leniency.'

Spartacus shook his head.

'In that case I must go back,' he said. 'Our conditions would be that we disband and everything becomes as it used to be; but before we could do that, you would have to withdraw your army, so that there is no possibility of a trap.'

Crassus shrugged, took a small draught of wine and shoved a handful of sweetmeats in his mouth. He had foreseen that this parley would have no result, and had agreed to the meeting mainly from curiosity. He could, of course, have the man detained and strung up here and now, but as his victory was certain anyway, there seemed no point in marring it and laying oneself open to the Opposition Tribunes' reproaches. His short, bare arm pointed to the second cup. 'Are you afraid it is poisoned?' he asked, unsmiling.

Spartacus shook his head; he was thirsty and drained the cup in one go. It was filled with rich, sweet, oily wine such as he had never drunk before. The silence that filled the tent became still more perceptible.

'The conditions would apply only to the men and women,' he said after a while. 'Our chiefs and leaders need no conditions.'

'I understand,' said Crassus and chewed his dates. 'It is a touching idea of yours: the leaders sacrifice themselves to save their people and presumably expect that the Senate erects tombstones to them, with moving inscriptions. You have a curious conception of the times we live in.'

Spartacus drained his second cup and wondered at this fat war-lord talking to him without annoyance in his beautiful Latin, chewing sweetmeats all the while. Decidedly the little lawyer of Capua had described him far too spitefully.

Crassus sat watching the man in the fur-skin, just as he was accustomed to watch Cato during their mealtime discourses. He felt stimulated. 'In fact, what do you know of this our time?' he went on. 'You are the dilettanti of revolution. You want to abolish slavery and have not even considered that if you did so, you would have to close down all the quarries and mines, would have to forgo the benefits of road-making, bridge-construction, aqueducts; that you would cripple the shipping business and traffic, and generally reduce the world to a state of barbarism. For the word "liberty" means to every present-day man and woman solely this: not to have to work. If your intentions were serious, you should have invented a new religion which should have raised labour to the station of a creed and cult, and declared sweat to be ambrosia. You should have brazenly claimed that only digging and road-mending, the sawing of planks and the rowing of galleys, manifest the destiny and nobility of mankind, whereas serene idleness and leisurely contemplation are contemptible and bestial. Contrary to every experience ever made, you should have assured the world that poverty holds blessing and distinction, while wealth is but a curse. You should have dethroned the lazy and licentious gods of Olympus, and invented new gods corresponding to your aims and interests. All this you neglected to do. Your Sun City perished because you failed to invent a new god and priests to serve him.'

Spartacus shook his head.

'All priests and prophets are swindlers,' he said. 'We didn't need any, and thousands of people came to join us. And they weren't only slaves, you know, we had farmers, too, who had been hounded off their fields by the big landowners. The farmers and small tenants don't need a new religion, what they need is land.'

'Pardon me,' said Crassus, 'again you only visualise part of the connection between cause and effect. Why, in your opinion, does the Italian peasantry suffer itself to be bought up by the oligarchy and to be chased off the soil? Surely not because the farmers are innocent lambs, as you keep on telling us, but because the import of overseas wheat lowers the price of corn to such an extent that only the big landowners can keep their heads above water. Following all this to its logical conclusion, you should demand that Rome resigns her colonies, that world commerce is stopped, the earth contracted to its old size, and all progress cancelled. All your amateurish attempts at reform, beginning with those of the Gracchi, were actually ultra-reactionary. As long as no one comes along and invents a new god who declares the Barbarian peoples to be on equal footing with us and forces them to produce at the same price as we, as long as that has not been attended to, the real champions of progress are and remain, in spite of everything, those two thousand Roman aristocrats and idlers who let the rest of the world work for them and yet enforce progress, without knowing how they are doing it. Until one day the in- flated belly of our State will burst asunder, and the devil get us all.'

Crassus wheezed contentedly and held his hand up to his ear to catch possible objections. But Spartacus was at a loss for a reply, and he doubted whether the pious masseur or the little pettifogger would have fared any better. Suddenly he realised that his conditions had been declined, that there was no escape for his people, and impotent hatred rose up inside him. Why in hell's name had he let himself in for this entire discourse in which he played such a poor part, instead of rejoining the horde at once, after the negotiations had failed?

Hate and grief welled up in his throat and effaced all his embarrassment. 'If you know it all so well,' he said hoarsely and so loudly as to make the generalissimo arch his eyebrows, 'if you know so much about it all and yourself say that the devil will carry off that State of yours—how then can you ask for our unconditional surrender and make the injustice even worse?'

He was going to say more, but Crassus cut him short with a gesture of his burly arm.

'Pardon me,' said Crassus. 'Have you ever stopped to consider that a human being lives only for approximately fifteen thousand days? Quite a lot more than that will pass before Rome goes to the dogs. Since I do not have the honour of knowing my great-grand-children, I see no occasion to humour them in my actions.'

He sipped his wine and looked gloomily at Spartacus. Spartacus's wrath had vanished as quickly as it had come; he thought the generalissimo looked particularly like Crixus at this moment. 'Eat, or be eaten,' Crixus had said; and if you came to think of it, the Roman with his cultured pronunciation really said the same. Only a fool cares a straw for the Will-be.

He drank his third cupful; it tasted even more aromatic and strange than the first two.

Crassus sat watching him. If he succeeded after all in inducing these people to surrender, his Consulship was assured, even before Pompeius returned from Spain. True, he had reckoned with the failure of the parley from the beginning, but there was one last possibility which he had not lost sight of.

'. . . Fifteen thousand days,' Crassus repeated and leaned heavily on his propped-up arms. 'I have approximately five thousand left, which posterity could never refund to me. As things are, the amount left to you is about ten or twenty. From whatever angle you look at it, there is a considerable difference; and posterity won't pay *you* back the subtracted remainder either. I, on the other hand, might be in a position to do so. In the case of surrender the Senate decides the fate of your people, but for yourself there might be different possibilities. Such as, for instance, a passport with an arch-Roman name and a ship to Alexandria.' He stopped and looked gloomily at Spartacus.

Spartacus was not surprised; ever since he had entered this queerly silent tent, he had felt that this would come, or rather, that something he had once before experienced would repeat itself. Where was it he had experienced it? Long ago, at the inn by the Appian Way. 'If you and me went off now,' Crixus had said, 'no skipper would ask for our passports.' That had been ages ago, in the days when all of this was just beginning; and now when the end was approaching, Crixus, through the mouth of this naked-skulled generalissimo, spoke to him a last time. And Crixus had always been right in the end.

They were probably right, the two fat ones with the dismal eyes. Eat or be eaten—who ever knew of anything better? Ten thousand days—where was the deity who would refund it to you? And the horde, those men and women on the other side of the trench—they could not escape their fate, must perish, with him or without. Whom would he serve by returning beyond the trench?

He had never been to Alexandria. But he knew that was where the light, wide avenues were, and women, and the ten times thousand days . . . 'What shall we eat in Alexandria? Fieldfare with bacon, that's what we'll eat in Alexandria. What shall we drink in Alexandria? Wine from Vesuvius, wine from Carmel, that's what we'll drink in Alexandria. What will the girls be like in Alexandria? Like opened oranges—that's what they will be like . . .' He had never been to Alexandria. But he knew all the same that at night a wind rustled through the leaves in the avenues, and he knew of the homesickness that lives in unknown women. No, it did not look as though he would ever come to Alexandria, now.

Crassus sat behind his desk, looked at him, chewed his dates and waited. Spartacus shook his head. Crassus spat out the date-stones, rose and clapped his hands. Spartacus rose too. The tent flap was flung back; outside stood the Guards who had escorted him across the trench.

'I did rather expect this turn of proceedings,' said Crassus. 'Nevertheless I should be interested to know what sort of reasons induced you to refuse my proposal, which would, after all, have been of considerable advantage to you, without altering the fate of your companions in any way.'

Spartacus stood in the middle of the tent; now as they were both standing, he was almost a whole head taller than the generalissimo. He smiled, vaguely and faintly embarrassed; how could you explain it to the fat man in his toga? Then he remembered the aged Essene:

'One must keep on the road to the end,' said Spartacus in that tone of voice in which one explains to children something they refuse to understand. 'One must keep on walking to the end, else the chain is broken. That is what it must be like, and one may not ask for the reason why.'

But as he saw that the fat man still did not understand him, he took up the wine cup from the little low table. 'One must not leave any dregs,' he said and smilingly drank the last drops out of the cup. 'So that one may hand it in a clean state to the Next One who will come.'

After that he joined the armour-plated Guards; without a word, as they had come, they walked back to the trench.

5

THE BATTLE
BY THE SILARUS

A WEEK after his conference with the Slave Leader, Crassus
made the decisive error of his life, never to be rectified.
When he received word that Spartacus and the remainder of
his Army had broken out of Bruttium and were now this side of
the trench, he lost his head and sent a message to the Senate,
demanding that Pompeius be recalled from Spain to his succour.

This break had occurred during a cold night, thick with falling
snow. The remainder of the Slave Army, gathered by Spartacus
for one last desperate attempt, had taken by surprise the Third
Cohort under Cato, immediately by the west coast near the Gulf
of Euphemia, and forced its way through to the north. In order
to have quick passage for the ox-carts with the sick, wounded and
the children, they filled and bridged the trench with tree-
trunks, brushwood, snow, horse-carrion, and the prisoners from
the Third Cohort, after having strangled them. After that the
Twenty Thousand wandered across; covered by darkness and
wrapped in snow; driven by hunger, they wandered into the last
combat against an overwhelmingly superior enemy; they
wandered to meet death, and knew it.

One day later Crassus knew as well that the break had been but
an act of despair, and that the adversary was no longer a menace
to him. But now it was too late. For years, coolly and prudently,
he had built step by step the ladder for his ascent, had lent out
his money without interest, chewed sweetmeats and waited for
his opportunity, when Power would fall in his lap, a ripe fruit.
One hour had ruined it all. His panic-stricken cry for aid to the

Senate had cast him for all times in the role of Pompeius's inferior.

In later times, Crassus himself could not understand how it had happened that cold winter morn that he had so inexplicably lost his head. Eight days before, the man with the fur-skin had been sitting on the sofa opposite his desk, awkward and embarrassed, and had played with his inkwell; one month later he was destroyed by Crassus's army. What mocking power had, in between those two dates, frightened him so terribly with the mere shadow of the self-same man, and driven him to political suicide?

In the eighteen years or six thousand five hundred days Crassus had still to live, not a single one passed without his brooding over this question. It still bothered him in the hour when, in front of the town Sinnata in the Mesopotamian desert, the dagger of a Parthian groom inflicted on him an inglorious and pointless end. The bloody head of the man who had realised that money has more might than the sword, who had crushed the greatest rebellion in Italy, and had dreamed of becoming Emperor of Rome, was carried by actors across the stage of a Princely court in Asia Minor. The Prince's name was Orodes, and in honour of his son's wedding feast *The Bacchae* by Euripides was being enacted, when a messenger from the battlefield brought the freshly severed head of Crassus. So the actor in the part of Agave exchanged the puppet-head of Pentheus for the genuine head of the banker Marcus Crassus, and sang his song, under the frenzied enthusiasm of the audience:

'Lo, from the trunk new-shorn—Hither a Mountain Thorn—
Bear we! O Asia-born—Bacchanals, bless this chase!'

When Crassus sent his cry for help to the Senate, Pompeius and his army had successfully terminated the Spanish war, and were already on their way home. Crassus wanted to put an end to it all, at least before Pompeius reached Italy. The Slaves, too, after three years' wanderings without hope or goal, yearned for the end; it came to them in the battle by the river Silarus, which only a few survived.

On the eve of the battle by the river Silarus an old man arrived at the camp. His name was Nicos; he was a former servant of the games-director Lentulus Batuatus, and had walked the long way from Capua to Apulia on foot. His appearance caused great amazement among the fighters of the original horde who knew him of old; he was at once brought to Spartacus's tent. And there he sat now, old, arid and infirm, and talked to him on the eve of the last battle.

The man with the fur-skin received him kindly and without overgreat surprise; the springs of wonder and surprise had run dry inside him, and whatever happened in these last days seemed to him familiar of old, and long expected.

'Have you at last come home to us?' he greeted old Nicos. 'We waited a long time for you; you always said we would take a bad end, and now you're just in time to see it happen.'

Old Nicos nodded gravely. His eyes were dimmed by cataract, he could no longer see clearly. Yet he saw how much the man with the fur-skin had changed since their last meeting in Capua; he felt that all haughtiness had left him, felt the peaceful repose that went out from the former gladiator, and the sad yet transparent look in his eyes.

'It took me a long time,' said old Nicos, 'and I had to become a very old man and nearly blind, before I realised that one may not run away from one's inner fate. For forty years I served, and when I got freed pride dazzled me, and I prattled silly stuff and nonsense in the Diana Temple on Mount Tifata. But now I know that I had to come to you, now that you've reached your journeys' end.'

Spartacus smiled: 'So you no longer believe it to be the evil road, my father?'

'I still do,' said Nicos. 'Yours was the way of evil, the way of disruption, and yet I had to come to you, to share your end. I know more about it than you do, for I was born in bondage, and that is why I belong with you. But you used to live in the mountains of your homeland, though not long enough to recognise the limits of freedom. You believe yourself free and yet you are caught in a net of manifold threads. There are day, and night, and your neighbour, and the alienness of woman, and the wicked blinking of the stars: borders, which shut you in; threads, from whose mesh you can't escape. There is no feeling you can wholly draw, and no thought you may fully think out. There is only one thing you can entirely fill: service.'

Spartacus shook his head: 'Why then do you come to us?'

'Your way was not mine, but your end is my end,' said the old man. 'Peace be with all of us. Freedom is beset by walls, run up against them with your head—the wall will remain, but your head will receive bumps. There is nothing on earth that achieves perfection, and all action is wicked; even the action you think good throws a shadow which is wicked. Blessed are the serving and oppressed who fall at the hand of the wicked and evil, for they will find peace. That is why I came to you.'

Spartacus smiled: 'You are welcome, my father, even though your old head harbours curious thoughts. There are only few alive of those you used to know; we welcome you.'

With increasing darkness they could see the Roman torches on the adjoining hill. Both camps were making the last preparations for the battle. Crassus held a short review; on his white horse he rode along the spreading line of his infantry, his glance glided dolefully up and down the shining armour which stretched like a steel wall along the hill; he did not address his soldiers, and they noticed that he chewed sweetmeats all through the parade.

Spartacus also assembled his ragged, barefooted men at the highest point of his hill. Up there, in full view of the Romans, he had a cross erected with a Roman prisoner nailed to it. It was the last display of his decrepit Army, parade of the wretched and desperate; they thronged the hill all around the cross on which the Roman squirmed and bled, and they could not grasp the meaning of that miserable spectacle. And the man with the fur-skin told them they should deeply imprint this picture on their minds, for this was the end in store for every one who surrendered or whom the Romans got alive. They understood what he meant then, and he knew that they understood him.

He had his horse brought, the white steed of Praetor Varinius, led it to the cross, affectionately stroked its nostrils, and cut its throat. 'Dead men need no horses,' he said to the mute horde, 'and living men can get themselves new ones.'

Afterwards he had the last provisions in food and wine distributed and went into his tent.

Night progressed, the last of the great horde ate, drank and loved the last of the women. On the adjoining hill bright dots scintillated through the night like glow-worms: the torches of the enemy. Sometimes the wind would carry over shreds of the tunes sung by the Romans on their hill; hardy, gay songs, patriotic songs, drunk with wine and the nearness of victory.

One could hear them in the tent of the little lawyer Fulvius, who sat there in the light of an oil-wick and wrote his chronicle, now never to be completed. He could hear the intoxicated Roman songsters, and he recalled the last days in the foolish city of Capua, when the patriots had marched through the streets with waving flags and rattling spears. He remembered the treatise he had at that time begun to write, which would never be completed now, either. The little bald-headed lawyer's heart ached sorely; through the open tent flap he could see the baneful red dots move in the distance, and pitiful fear overcame him; he did not want to be alone this last night. He rolled up his parchment, caressed it nimbly, and went through the pitch-dark camp-alleys to the tent of the Essene.

He found him quarrelling strenuously with old Nicos from Capua. The two old men sat side by side on the rug, sipping wine out of a jug, hot wine brewed with cloves and cinnamon, and quarrelled about the course of the world, while the Romans up on their hill rattled their spears and sang bloodthirsty songs. The tepid wind that made the canvas shiver mildly from time to time, waved the sounds across.

'Can you hear the song of evil?' said old Nicos, and his aged lips drew small, gurgling sips of the hot wine. 'There you can see now what forcible action leads to. They've all caught the small-pox of enthusiasm.'

The Essene vigorously shook his head in protest. 'No man can live without enthusiasm,' he said, 'for otherwise he would wither away like a tree without roots. But there are two kinds of enthusiasm: a merry one, derived from Life, and a gloomy one which stealthily draws its saps from Death. To be sure, the second kind is far more frequent. For, from the beginning the gods deprived man of serene merriment and taught him to obey prohibitions and renounce his desires. And the fatal gift of renunciation, which makes him different from all other creatures, has become so much the second nature of men, that they use it like a weapon which they direct against one another, as a means of the Few oppressing the Many, as a means of oppression in every respect. The necessity of renunciation has been instilled into their blood from the beginning of time, so that they can only regard as truly noble that enthusiasm in which they may abnegate themselves and their very own interests. But does not really all negation fall into the domain of Death, by acting against and opposing Life? This might be the explanation of how it came about that humanity has always been more susceptible to the enthusiasm of the black Death-saps, to foolish and hostile-to-life mass mentality, rather than to the other kind.'

The lawyer had sat down on the mat and poured himself some wine. His fear of the red torches abated slightly; immediately on entering the tent he had begun to feel well and warm.

Old Nicos visibly disliked the Essene's talk. His speech had already grown a trifle indistinct. 'Blessed are the meek who serve and do not resist,' he said. 'You spoke of an evil enthusiasm as though there were another sort. What kind of another sort might that be? All passion is evil.'

'The other sort,' said the lawyer, and stroked his bumpy pate, 'is that enthusiasm which does not aim at renunciation but at the heightened enjoyment of life. True, through the habit of observing prohibitions, which likens virtue to self-negation and lauds Death as the loftiest sacrifice—true, in this intoxication of the black juices any other sort of enthusiasm appears low and vulgar. Does not the foolish order of things force us to seek the satisfaction of all our desires in the lowest and most vulgar ways? The shopkeeper must use false weights in order to live. The slave must scheme and rob his master in order to live; the farmer must be hard and mean, for else he cannot live. Is, therefore, not everything that serves Life and one's own interests, low and vulgar? Is it not so, that only the opposites, renunciation, sacrifice and death, are exalted and deemed worthy of enthusiasm? The petty misery of their existence has made men and women unreceptive for the serene, merry-making enthusiasm, and spurs them on towards the drunkenness of the black saps. That is what induces mankind to act contrary to the interests of others when isolated, and to act contrary to their own interests when associated in groups or crowds.'

Behold, he had again arrived at the heading of his treatise. Perhaps, if they had left him time, he might have completed it after all—but now it was too late.

The lawyer coughed gently and rubbed his bald pate. O that
he might sit at his desk, with the good old wooden beam over his
head! Those fools over there sang and rattled their spears into the
night, and got themselves ready to act against their own interests
and kill him, the chronicler Fulvius. Why on earth should a
chronicler dive into adventures, climb over walls and commit
himself to mortal perils, instead of staying with his desk and
beam?

The lawyer Fulvius hastily emptied his cup. 'To be sure,' he
went on, 'the serene sort of enthusiasm, affirmative of Life, must
also be prepared for sacrifices and often assign itself to Death.
But the difference lies in what way you die, whether you place
Death itself at Life's disposal, or whether you push Life into
thraldom to Death. True, it is easier to live for Death, like the
soldiers who rattle their spears, than to die for Life and serene
merriment, as the law of detours will sometimes demand.'

Old Nicos nodded in his corner, asleep; but the Essene was still
awake and circumspectly wagged his head.

'Well, well,' he said, 'this may be our last night, the Sun City
was burnt to the ground, humanity is the prey of the black saps,
and God is dissatisfied with Himself. He started it all, and
behold, everything went all wrong from the start. For, hardly
had He populated heaven, earth and waters, when all and sundry
began to eat up each other. Naturally He was annoyed by this;
but in order to save His face He announced that it was His law
which decreed that all living creatures should eat up each other,
and in fact the big should always be eating up the small. Anyone,
of course, can order things in such a way, there's nothing to it—
the other way round, *that* would be something.'

'But that's impossible, isn't it,' said old Nicos, who had started
up from the light slumber of the aged.

'What is He a God for, then?' asked the Essene and wagged
his head disapprovingly. 'Anybody could work it in that way,
you don't need to be a God to do it. Things didn't go so well
with the animals, but they only went properly wrong when He
came to the humans; right in the first few days He started to
wrangle with them. I might add that He was really very much in
the wrong in that affair about the tree. If He didn't want man
and woman to have a certain apple, why did He dangle it right
above their noses? It just isn't done.'

'So that they might learn to renounce,' said old Nicos, 'and get used to the existence of forbidden fruit.'

'That's just it. Can you understand why He invents a world full of forbidden things if He could just as easily invent one without any? Can you understand that? I can't.'

'Yes I can,' said old Nicos. 'Man must renounce, serve and suffer. Blessed are the meek who die at the hands of the wicked and evil.'

'But that was not provided for in the programme of creation,' said the Essene and crinkled his faun's nose. 'And if it *was* provided for—in that case it just was a bad programme, and it would have been much better if He had kept His hands off it.' He wagged disapprovingly; then he went down on his knees and performed his morning prayer.

The signal blasts of the Romans sounded closer and clearer. It was still dark outside, but day was not far off.

The night progressed, and Spartacus lay on his rug. He had not wanted to be alone this last night either, beside him breathed the woman, dark and slender, little more than a child. He had neglected her for a long time; she had never entered the tent with the purple velum in the Sun City. She had frequently been seen with Crixus, more often on her own. Far from the City, quite alone, she had roamed the woods for days, sleeping underneath tree trunks, or below the white rocks of the chalky land of Lucania. A shepherd from the Brotherhood, searching for a stray ram, had surprised her once; she was lying on a projecting ledge of rock, talked aloud although no one else was there, and showed the whites of her eyes. The shepherd hailed her. She was much scared, and looked at him as though he were the weirdest apparition. But then she said that he would find the animal he was looking for at a certain spot behind that distant hill, near a hamlet in a valley not visible from here; and that was where he did find it. Similar incidents occurred quite often, and helped to strengthen her reputation as a seer of the hidden and obscure, and a herald of things as yet concealed by the future.

For she had gained this reputation earlier on, being a former priestess of Bacchos of Thrace, initiate of the Orphic cult; had she not announced to Spartacus the terrible power in store for him, when he was a mere common circus-gladiator? He had been

lying on the floor, asleep, but the woman watched a serpent
sneaking towards him and coiling round his head without
harming him in any way; and thus she had known of all
that was to be.

Spartacus had been neglecting her for a long time; and people
said he shunned her to avoid meeting and touching the dark and
allusive powers she bore within her. It was said he wanted to
have nothing to do with these powers of twilight and obscurity,
ever since he went about with ambassadors and Asiatic diplomats
and had for his chief counsellor a bald-headed lawyer. But when
the Sun City crumpled in ruins, he took her with him again;
and now as the night progressed, she breathed beside him on the
rug, slim, girlish and frail, and alien still in the embrace.

Before, he had shunned her for the sake of her eery powers;
but now he wanted her because of them. For he too had seen the
red torches move about and heard the Romans sing through the
night, drunken with the certainty of their victory; and he too
knew that this night was his last, and he would have liked to hear
about what happened afterwards, when the sun rose no more and
breath was still. He had long forgotten the illboding gods of
Thrace, and he had been ashamed to ask the aged Essene; and
also it seemed to him that a woman's embrace might bring you
closer to the answer than the company of all the priests and magi
of this world.

So now she lay beside him again, her breath still laboured and
heavy; and had withheld the answer and was a stranger more
than ever. He lay still, and longed to know the answer to his
question. He had searched for it in the touch of her body, and
now he looked for it within her eyes, until she began to feel uncomfortable and averted her head. So he let her go, disappointed,
and knew that here there was no answer neither.

He rose and stepped outside the tent. He walked through the
dark camp, inspected the sentries, heard the hoarse cry of the
cocks and the hoarse signal blast of the Romans, and returned
to his tent, tired and chilled. The woman had gone, but her odour
lingered still about the tent, and the warmth of her body was still
on the rug. He lay down in the hollow she had made on the rug
and closed his eyes; and knew that he would never find the
answer to his quest, now, and fell asleep.

He did not find it on the next day either, in the battle by the river Silarus, during which his Army was destroyed and he himself killed.

The battle started shortly before sunrise. The Slaves were the attackers. Their African drums, wooden boxes covered with hide, droned like subterranean thunder in the morning twilight. The district was hilly and barren. The Lucanian sling-shooters on their lean, half-starved nags rode in front; they were received by a rain of arrows; the superior flexibility and range of the Roman bows made their slings appear like toys. The Lucanian lines spread out, scattered, performed acrobatic tricks as they wielded their slings, flitting like swarms of gnats in front of the Celtic infantry which advanced with raucous cries. Light increased rapidly. The Roman lines did not budge; but the cavalry at their flanks began to move.

Spartacus knew that he had not enough cavalry to prevent the Romans closing in on his flanks. He had no choice but to concentrate attack on the enemy centre, to break the triple line of Roman infantry before they encircled his Army completely. The Celts in their clattering tin armour, with wooden spears, axes and sickles, advanced, roaring; the African drums thundered. The Roman front line gave way; the heavy javelins of the second line broke through the Celts' tin armour and hurled them back. The third Roman line, the steel wall of the veterans, did not go into action until hours later, after the Slaves had carried on wave after wave of attack, and wave after wave had been shattered against them.

When the sun stood almost vertically in the sky, half of the Slave Army had been annihilated; the rest fought, barefooted, against the mailed men, with wood against iron, flesh against steel. It was a massacre rather than a battle; and the victims, driven by despair and fascinated by death, voluntarily rushed into their executioners' arms. When the sun had passed his zenith, the Romans had accomplished the surrounding of the Slaves, and their mailed cohorts advanced concentrically in counter-attack, marching over hills and corpses.

The battle had begun shortly before sunrise: shortly before sunset it was over. The Slave Army was non-existent; fifteen thousand corpses in malodorous rags, unworthy of plunder and disgusting to the victors, lay strewn about the hilly area by the river Silarus.

The Slave Leader, the gladiator Spartacus, fell some time around noon, a few moments before the sun stood vertically. At the head of his Thracians, he had led the attack against Crassus's Fifth Cohort; very tall and conspicuous in his shaggy fur-skin, he hewed his way through the Roman lines with his gladiator's-sword. The last two of Fannius's servants in their rusty helmets kept close behind him, even when he put more and more distance between himself and the others. On a small hillock not a hundred paces from him, the man with the fur-skin had caught a glimpse of a Roman officer in smart riding habit, with stern, regular features, the riding crop in his hand; and he was his object. He had already cut down two Roman Centurions who barred his way; the turmoil around him had decreased in density, the two bull-necks were no longer behind him either; only about thirty paces separated him from the officer, who had also recognised him and watched his approach with slightly raised eyebrows.

The ring around Spartacus closed in again; only twenty paces were between him and the officer, when the spear pierced his hip and a short, hard, terrible blow fell between his eyes. Once more, in falling, he beheld the officer, who had not moved at all, gazing over at him and slowly slapping his thigh with the riding crop; but he felt nothing towards him any longer, felt only the clayey earth on his cheeks, and shut his eyes.

Far away, in deaf distance, behind misty veils, the clamouring went on, men stabbed one another and crashed to the ground. Stampeding feet with hard, angular shoes pushed into his body like battering rams, every part of him hurt and seemed brittle; but even pain came from far away, toned down and overshadowed by clouds.

'Is that all?' he thought, and rolled on his belly, pressing his teeth into the clay which yielded and scratched palate and lips with a pungent, bitter taste. 'Is that all?' he had just time to think, and with a short, sharp snapping of his jaws he bit into the clay. Thus they found the leader of the Italian revolution towards evening, covered by his shaggy fur-skin, which was stiff with blood; his mouth full of earth, his fingers burrowed, claw-like, in clay and stubbles.

6

THE CROSSES

THE Italian insurrection was over. Fifteen thousand corpses lay strewn about the hilly land by the river Silarus; four thousand women, and the old and infirm who had not taken part in the battle and failed to kill themselves in time, were taken alive by the Romans. Rome breathed with relief, the weight off her chest; and a manhunt chased through the whole land, unequalled in the annals of Italy.

The herdsmen of the Lucanian highlands, the farmers and petty tenants of Apulia, were quarry and prey for Crassus's Legions. Whosoever owned less than one acre or two cows was suspect of revolutionary sympathies, was killed or kidnapped; a quarter of the Italian slave population was extirpated. The rebels had squirted blood over the country, the conquerors turned it into a slaughterhouse. In small troops they marched through villages, singing patriotic songs, erected the crosses in the market place, raped the women, hamstrung the cattle; at night the huts and slave barracks blazed in flames, torches of victory. The drunkenness of the black juices had taken hold of Italy, she extolled the generalissimo who had helped legitimate right to conquer the might of Darkness—general Pompeius.

Pompeius and his army had returned from Spain just in time to encounter a small band of fugitives by the Apennines. He destroyed them and allowed his Legions to participate in the manhunt of their native country, in order to reward them for the hardships they had undergone in Spain; whereupon he reported to the Senate that, although Crassus had defeated the Slaves, he, Pompeius, had stamped out the very roots of revolution.

Pompeius got his triumphal entry; he arrived in Rome on a chariot drawn by four white palfreys. He displayed the laurels in his right, the ebony mace in his left hand; his inane face was rouged, the people roared, and the only thing that jarred his smugness was the fact that the State-slave behind him who held the golden crown of Jove above his head reiterated a bit too often the due, traditional phrase: 'Remember that you are a mortal.'

All Crassus got was an ovation, the entry on foot, followed by a few soldiers; the only special favour granted him was the permission to wear a laurel wreath instead of the ordinary myrtle wreath. And yet the banker Crassus's march home was a spectacle which sent a tremor through the world, and the like of which it had never seen before. Pompeius's parade began on the Campus Martius and ended, two miles farther, before the Capitol; Crassus had caused two rows of wooden crosses to hem the two hundred miles of Appian Way of his homeward march. Six thousand captive slaves, their hands and feet pierced by nails, hung, at regular intervals of fifty metres, on both sides of the highway, in inunterrupted sequence from Capua to Rome.

Crassus's progress was slow; he rested often. He had sent on his engineer troops to construct the posts before he arrived; he himself carried the prisoners with him, bundled in groups and tied together with long ropes. Before his army stretched the road, endless and hemmed with empty crosses; behind his army, every cross bore a hanging man. Crassus took his time. He approached the capital at a leisurely rate, interrupting his march three times a day. During the rest-periods lots were drawn to decide the succession of prisoners to be crucified from here to their next station. The army marched fifteen miles per day, and left behind five hundred crucified per day as their living mile-stones.

His progress caused sensation in the capital. The entire aristocratic youth, and whoever could afford it by hook or by crook, rode to meet Crassus's army in order to see for themselves; a ceaseless stream of tourists, in showy state carriages or hired coaches, on horseback or borne in sedan chairs, drifted south along the Appian Way. Crassus would receive the more eminent among them in his tent during the rest periods, chew candied dates, look sulkily at his visitors and ask them whether they had enjoyed Pompeius's triumphal entry as much. And only then did the ingenuity of Crassus's idea dawn on the visitors, an ingenuity greater than that which had produced his building trust and his fire brigade: Rome had denied Crassus a triumphal entry; now Crassus forced Rome to meet him in homage on the very road.

It was getting on towards spring. The sun diffused some heat already, but not enough as yet to grant the mercy of a quick death to the people on the crosses left behind Crassus's army. Only a few of them succeeded in bribing a soldier of the rearguard to come back at night and kill them. For Crassus had forbidden any initiative in that direction; although he had no particular inclination to cruelty, he liked an idea to be carried out meticulously, without anything to mar the purity of its effect. But, as he was by no means devoid of humane considerations, he had chosen the method of nailing which tended to hasten death, rather than the customary stringing up.

The army's march from Capua to Rome took twelve days; and on every one of them it left behind five hundred crucified at regular, tape-measured intervals. The feebler delinquents lived for a few hours only, the more tenacious for several days. If a man was lucky a nail pierced an artery, and he quickly bled to death, but usually only the bones of hands and feet were splintered, and if he fainted in the process, he came to again when they raised the cross, to curse the lords of creation. Many tore at their nails, some to break loose, some to bleed more rapidly; but they realised that torment puts a limit to even the strongest of wills. Many attempted to shatter their skulls against the posts; but they had to realise that of all living creatures it is yourself that is most difficult to kill.

It was getting on towards spring. Day relieved night and night relieved day; and still they lived on, imprisoned by their torment and pain; and gangrene made their flesh rot away, and their tongues swelled, and the beasts and birds of earth and air came close to them, growling, spitting, and flapping their wings. Day relieved night and night relieved day, and the earth would not open up and the sun would not cease travelling the skies. And that which was happening to them was inflicted beyond measure and guilt; and it was not happening as in mirage of fever, but in that reality from which one cannot wake; and they did not suffer in remembrance nor in anticipation, but suffered it in the present, here and now.

.   .   .   .   .

Chance had spared the chronicler Fulvius and the man with
the bullet-head until the army had reached the river Liris. They
were the last two of the Old Horde; Hermios the shepherd had
been felled by a spear in Apulia, the two Vibiuses, father and son,
had died together in the battle by the Silarus; Spartacus's dark,
slender woman had drowned herself during the battle when no
one as yet knew of his death. Only the two of them were left, and
old Nicos besides, almost blind now, led by the rope which bound
them all, stammering incoherently.

They sat down for the last time, by the river Liris. They were
sitting on the bank, in line with the others whom the lot had
selected for this day; their hands were bound by the rope and
armoured men guarded them. The river Liris was greatly swollen.
It carried shrubs and rotting vegetables, cat- and pig-carrion,
circling incessantly on its slimy whirls. At times the bodies of
slain men drifted past; they had travelled a long way and did not
look much like humans, now.

Upstream, by the camp of the vanguard behind the river's
next bend, tapped the sounds of mallets. The posts for the next
station were not ready yet; the one hundred and fifty men chosen
by the lot had to wait. They were sitting along the bank in one
long row, tied together by the rope, and waited to be fetched;
they did not look much like humans either. They gazed into the
yellow waters of the river Liris. Some swayed back and forth and
moaned, some were singing, some lay with their faces on the
ground, some had bared their body to coax a last bliss out of it
and weaken its vitality.

Old Nicos stammered disconnected phrases. He was the only
one in their row whose fate was still postponed, but as he was
almost blind the soldiers had left him with the other two who
had been guiding him all along. 'Blessed are those who renounce
and die at the hands of the evil and wicked,' stammered old
Nicos.

But the Essene beside him smiled and wagged his head:

'Blessed are those who take the sword in their hand to end the
power of the Beasts; those who build towers of stone to gain the
clouds, who climb the ladder to fight with the angel; for they are
the true Sons of man.'

The mallets upstream were less insistent now, their work was
nearly finished. Next to the chronicler Fulvius sat a Calabrian

peasant, a sorry little figure of a man with a tangled beard and gentle, slightly protruding eyes. He nibbled a stalk of lettuce, picked up somewhere or other, bore the name of Nicolaos, and hurriedly told Fulvius a muddled story about his cow Juno who had been about to calve when the soldiers came and pounced upon his wife and set the new barn roof on fire. He interrupted his tale to offer the lawyer some leaves of his lettuce, and asked him whether he thought that the soldiers would give them something to eat beforehand.

The lawyer Fulvius cleared his throat. 'It will be better not to have anything in one's bowels,' he said huskily.

He thought of his unfinished treatise and his parchment scrolls, wrested from him by a young officer when they took him prisoner. He felt almost indifferent to death, but he was very frightened indeed of that which would precede it, and he would have liked to know what had become of his parchment scrolls.

The mallets stopped completely; the mail-clad men came and led off the first ten in the row. Soon after, those who remained behind could hear hammering blows again, at regular intervals in ever receding distance, but they sounded duller now than before and were accompanied by oddly inhuman yells. The hundred and forty roped men sat quietly side by side and listened.

'Blessed are those who die at the hand of evil,' babbled old Nicos. 'The man-built towers crash to the ground, and the angel punished the bold one who climbed the ladder by dislocating his hip. Blessed are those who serve and offer no resistance.'

Nobody answered him; after a while the mail-clad men came back and led off the next ten. The lawyer Fulvius, the Essene and the little peasant with his protruding eyes sat near the end of the line now, among the ten whose turn it would be next. The Essene wagged his head:

'He who receives the Word has a bad time of it,' he said. 'He must carry it on and serve it in many ways, be they good or evil, until he may pass it on.'

The little Calabrian peasant told hurriedly on about Juno his cow, afraid that he might not have time to finish the story. He stopped in the middle of it. 'Aren't you afraid?' he asked the lawyer and went on nibbling his lettuce.

'Every man is afraid of dying,' said the chronicler Fulvius, 'only, every one in a different way. And yet, once the time is come, he forgets about it. For at first he only feels the pain, that means, he thinks of himself only and not of dying; and later, when death is already upon him, he forgets about himself. Nobody can feel both things at once, dying and one's own self.'

The bearded little peasant nodded violently; he did not understand a single one of Fulvius's words, but he wanted to believe in them because he imagined them to be comforting. But the chronicler Fulvius's thoughts were divided between what they were going to do to him, and his lost parchment scrolls. The century of abortive revolutions was completed, the Party of Justice had lost out, its strength was spent and exhausted. Now nothing could impede the greed for power, nothing barred the way to despotism, no barrier to protect the People was left. He whose grasp is the most brutal can now rise to untold heights: dictator, emperor, god. Who will be the first to reach the winning post? Pompeius the soldier, Caesar the Tribune, Cethegus the schemer, Crassus the banker, Cato the puritan? Fulvius knows them all from the days of his earlier career, he knows well what the people's heroes look like, when they bargain for office and position, drag one another before the Blackmail Commission, when they borrow money for games to win popularity, when they address the Senate, white, formal and starchy, every one his own monument. Up above glares the sun, down below flows the river, his hands are tied, the little peasant at his right chatters feverishly of Juno his cow, the next in the line, a black man, sits shamelessly exposed. And the sun will not stand still and no ladder descends from the skies, and there is no escaping from the Now and Here. But the bullet-headed sage smiles and wags his head:

'It is written: the wind comes and the wind goes, and does not leave a trace. Man comes, and man is gone, and knows nothing of the fate of his fathers and has no knowledge of the future of his seed. The rain falls into the river, and the river drowns in the sea, but the sea becomes no greater. All is vanity.'

The black man's pupils have rolled behind his lids, he has covered up his nakedness; he has thrown himself back on the ground and groans and prays to the dismal gods of his homeland.

'That's no consolation,' said the chronicler Fulvius, hoarse with fear, for he could see the mail-clad soldiers coming towards them.

Epilogue

THE DOLPHINS

I T IS night still.
Still no cock has crowed.

But Quintus Apronius, First Scribe of the Market Court, has long got used to the fact that clerks must be earlier risers than cocks. He groans as his toes fish for the sandals on the filthy floor. Once again the sandals are standing the wrong way round, toes facing the bed; twenty years' service have not taught Pomponia to place them in the correct position.

He shuffles along to the window, looks down into the funnel-like inner court; and there she comes climbing up the fire escape, old, bony and dishevelled. The water she brings up is lukewarm, breakfast awful: the morning's second offence. How many more are to come, and for how long a time?

The Dolphins glide across his mind, once splendid climax of his day; but even this pleasure was spoilt for him when his hopes of becoming the Market Judge's official protégé were wrecked. Every time he enters the marble hall these days, Apronius feels beset by gloating and malicious glances.

He descends the fire escape with slightly shaky knees and snatched-up gown; he knows that, broom in hand, Pomponia watches from the window to see that he does not trail its hem over the rungs. The cramped little alley is pale with feeble dawn; the endless train of milk and vegetable barrows clatters past him with many gee-ups.

Where the perfume and ointment stalls meet the fish market he encounters the morning troop of building-slaves herded to their work. They are manacled again as in Sulla's time; their faces are gloomy and stony, their stare charged with hatred. Apronius flattens against the house-front; trembling, he gathers his cloak about him. At last they have passed and he may go on his way.

The wooden hoarding arrests his gaze; a new announcement has been painted on it a few days ago. At the top shines a painted crimson sun, underneath games-director Lentulus Batuatus is proud to invite the gracious Capuan public to a super-performance of his new gladiators' team. Follows the list of the performing teams; the main feature being a fight between the Gallic gladiator Nestos and the Thracian ring-bearer Orestes. Perfume will be sprayed throughout the auditorium during the intermissions; seats may be booked in advance with the baker Titus and the authorised ticket-agents.

Apronius knows the placard by heart; shaking his head and muttering with scorn he continues on his way—he has long given up dreams of free tickets. Soon he has arrived at his destination, Minerva's Temple Hall, seat of the Municipal Market Court, where a further mortification is lying in wait for Apronius: the sight of his young colleague, who refused for years before he joined the 'Worshippers of Diana and Antinous'; and whom they have nevertheless elected honorary president, solely for the sake of his newfangled coiffure. Bumptious as a cock he moves about the Hall, stacks the documents, orders the beadles about; and when at long last the Market Judge appears in the midst of his attendants, he fusses busily about his chair for him, whereupon the Judge favours him with a patronising nod.

Proceedings proceed, opponents warm to offensive heat, attorneys wave their sleeves, documents keep piling up—Quintus Apronius sits behind his desk and laboriously traces his minutes, with slightly shaky hands. They are no longer of perfect beauty; gone are the days of the artistic flourishes which once were the pride and glory of his heart.

As the sun beams noon at last, the beadle announces the court's adjournment and Apronius stacks his records; pleading important business, he takes a hasty departure from his colleagues. Pressing his pleats to his hips, at a dignified pace, he strides to the Tavern of the Twin-Wolves. Severely he supervises the cleansing of his drinking bowl, mutters scornful remarks about the quality of the food, which are received with hypocritical dismay by the proprietor. After brief hesitation, and with much growling and grumbling, he suffers a second jug of wine to be forced upon him, a habit he has lately grown fond of. A slight blush on his lean cheeks, the clerk rises from his seat, snips the bread-crumbs off his dress, leaves the Tavern of the Twin-Wolves and betakes himself to the Steambaths.

The covered walk swarms with life as usual, groups lounge in gossip, news and compliments are exchanged, public speakers and ambitious poets hold forth beside the columns. The largest audience has assembled around two speakers who quarrel heatedly about the qualities of this year's two Consuls; one of them, a small, rotund man, lauds the magnanimity of Marcus Crassus, while the other, a gouty veteran, praises the outstanding military distinction of Pompeius Magnus. It looks as though they might resort to physical violence at any moment, for each accuses the other of getting paid for his enthusiasm with fifteen pieces of silver from the electioneering gang-leaders by the Temple of Hercules. The little fat one maintains that Pompeius wants to start a new civil war and set himself up as a new dictator; that is why he keeps his army camping at the very gates of the capital. The veteran, on the other hand, points out that Crassus has not dismissed his army either, pretending to protect the Republic from Pompeius, whereas it is blatantly obvious that he craves the dictatorship for himself.

Apronius shrugs; he has learnt his lesson and knows that politics are nothing but the sinister conspiracy of invisible powers with the aim of robbing the little man and making his life a misery. Slowly he crosses the hall, takes the key to his locker from the attendant and puts on his bathrobe with an aching heart.

It is a garment with red and green stripes, once very dashing; Apronius had had it made in exact imitation of impresario Rufus's bathrobe in the days when the future was still radiant with promise. But what privation paid for this prodigal deed, what hours of copywork at night, what restriction in the way of his meals at the Tavern of the Twin-Wolves! And now the material has grown shabby and dilapidated, the little woolly fibres are dropping out as though infected with mange at elbows and knees. Only its screaming colours have remained, red and green; and whenever Apronius struts through the corridors with the hem of his bathrobe gathered up to his peaky knees, all heads turn to gaze after him.

At last he enters the Hall of the Dolphins. Much to his relief Rufus and the games-director are not there. For the impresario has lately acquired a new marvel of a dressing-gown, a checked one this time, light yellow and puce; and whenever the clerk sees it, he is overcome with a wild desire to become a revolutionist and take the road of the late Spartacus.

He sits down on one of the Dolphins' thrones. Next to him are two strangers of provincial appearance whom he has never seen before; they, too, are talking of the former gladiator-chief and Slave Leader. Bewildered, Apronius listens to their conversation; for, although the Thracian has been dead for nearly a year now, the younger one of the two strangers claims that he has been seen only a short time ago on one of the large estates up north, in Umbria, where the field-slaves had slain their lord. The elderly stranger nods gravely. He is from the south, from the Lucanian country, and has been hearing similar tales: a number of hunters and shepherds had met the man on lonely mountain paths, and he spoke to them kindly words and vanished suddenly; they had known him at once by the shaggy fur-skin, which covered his body as in times of old. And these tidings have spread across the whole of Apulia and Bruttium; and the rich in their cities are scaring the children with the threat that Spartacus will come and get them.

The scribe shakes his head with astonishment; after all, he says to the strangers, everybody knows that the brigand-chief was killed in the battle by the river Silarus, and that his carcass was burnt the next morning, together with many others.

The younger one of the two strangers looks at him disapprovingly; his earnest glance slides down along Apronius's bathrobe, a fleeting smile brightens his face.

'What makes you be so certain about his death?' asks the stranger.

'Well, they did find his corpse,' says Apronius. 'They say he looked appalling, his mouth was full of clay; and then he was burnt the next day.'

'How do you know?' the stranger asks, looking at him with his grave eyes. 'There are others who say that he was indeed pierced by many spears, but when they looked for his body it was no longer there. There has been many a man who went to his grave and came out again and walks the earth, with both feet on the ground.'

Shaking his head, the clerk Quintus Apronius rises from his marble seat; even after the bath, on his way home, he cannot stop wondering at the curious talk of the two strangers.

Dusk veils the narrow criss-cross streets of the Oscian quarter, as he climbs up the fire escape to his apartment. He lets the clothes down his weary old body, repleats them carefully and lays them on the wobbly tripod, puts out the light. Rhythmically thudding footsteps resound from the street: the building-slaves are returning from work. He can see their gloomy, joyless faces and the manacles on their wrists; and in their midst, his glance savage and disdainful, is the man in the fur-skin, with the sword in his hand.

With a pounding heart the scribe Quintus Apronius stares into his bedroom's night. In vain he waits for sleep to come to him, afraid of the dreams it will bring. For, alas, he knows they will be sad and very evil dreams.

Postscript to the Danube Edition of
'THE GLADIATORS'

Novels must speak for themselves; the author's comments ought not to intrude between the work and the reader, at least until the reading is over. Hence this postscript instead of a preface.

The Gladiators is the first novel of a trilogy (the other two are *Darkness at Noon* and *Arrival and Departure*) whose leitmotif is the central question of revolutionary ethics and of political ethics in general: the question whether, or to what extent, the end justifies the means. It is a hoary problem, but it obsessed me during a decisive period in my life. I am referring to the seven years which I spent as a member of the Communist Party and the years which followed immediately after.

I joined the Communist Party in 1931, at the age of twenty-six, when on the editorial staff of a Liberal newspaper in Berlin. I joined the Communists partly as an alternative to the threat of Nazism and partly because, like Auden, Brecht, Malraux, Dos Passos and other writers of my generation, I felt attracted by the Soviet utopia. Since I have described the atmosphere of those days in some detail elsewhere,[1] I need not dwell here further on the subject.

When Hitler came to power I was in the Soviet Union writing a book on the First Five Year Plan; from there I went to Paris where I lived until the collapse of France. My progressive dis-illusionment with the Communist Party reached an acute state in 1935—the year of the Kirov murder, the first purges, the first waves of the Terror which was to sweep most of my comrades

1. *The God that Failed* and *The Invisible Writing*.

away. It was during this crisis that I began to write *The Gladiators*—the story of another revolution that had gone wrong. It took four years; a series of interruptions made the writing of the book a kind of hurdle race. The year after I started it, the Spanish Civil War broke out, in the course of which I was captured by Franco's troops and spent four months in prison; after that I had to write a topical book on Spain;[1] in between I ran out of money and had to do hack-work for a living. I finished the book in the summer of 'thirty-eight—a few months after I had left the Communist Party.

After each interruption the return to the first century B.C. brought peace and relief. It was not so much an escape as a form of occupational therapy which helped me to clarify my ideas; for there existed some obvious parallels between the first pre-Christian century and the present. It had been a century of social unrest, of revolutions and mass-upheavals. Their causes had an equally familiar ring: the breakdown of traditional values, the abrupt transformation of the economic system, unemployment, corruption, and a decadent ruling class. Only against this background could it be understood that a band of seventy circus fighters could grow within a few months into an army, and for two years hold half Italy under its sway.

But why, then, did the revolution go to pieces? The reasons were, of course, of great complexity, yet one factor stood out clearly: Spartacus was a victim of the 'law of detours', which compels the leader on the road to Utopia to be 'ruthless for the sake of pity'. Yet he shrinks from taking the last step—the purge by crucifixion of the dissident Celts and the establishment of a ruthless tyranny; and through this refusal he dooms his revolution to defeat. In *Darkness at Noon*, the Bolshevik Commissar Rubashov goes the opposite way and follows the 'law of detours' to the end—only to discover that 'reason alone was a defective compass which led one such a winding, twisted course that the goal finally disappeared in the mist'. Thus the two novels complement each other—both roads end in a tragic *cul-de-sac*.

The reader of a historic novel has a right to ask how much of it is based on fact and how much on fiction. The original source material on the slave revolt consists of a few passages in Livy,

1. *Spanish Testament.*

Plutarch, Appian and Florus; added together they amount to less than four thousand words. The Roman historians obviously felt the whole episode to be so humiliating that the less said about it the better. The one exception seemed to have been Sallust, but of his *Historiae* only fragments survive.

In contrast to these meagre references to the revolt itself, there is an abundance of background material on the social conditions and political intrigues of the time. And while next to nothing is known about the character of the slave leaders and the ideas that guided them, a great amount is known about their opponents: Pompeius, Crassus, Varinius, the Consuls and Senators of 73–71, their friends and contemporaries. This provided on the one hand an added challenge to the imagination, which had to supply not only the characters of Spartacus and his lieutenants, but also the details of their campaign and the organisation of the slave community. On the other hand, the detailed knowledge available about the period provided a pattern or framework from which much could be deduced; so that the filling in of missing details became a problem of intuitive geometry, the reconstruction of a jigsaw puzzle from which half the pieces are missing.

The sources give no indication of the programme or common idea that held the Slave Army together; yet a number of hints indicate that it must have been a kind of 'socialist' programme, which asserted that all men were born equal, and denied that the distinction between free men and slaves was part of the natural order. And there are further hints to the effect that at one time Spartacus tried to found somewhere in Calabria a Utopian community based on common property. Now such ideas were entirely alien to the Roman proletariat before the advent of primitive Christianity. This led to the wild, but fairly plausible, guess that the Spartacists had been inspired by the same source as the Nazarenes a century later: the Messianism of the Hebrew prophets. There must have been, in the motley crowd of runaway slaves, quite a number of Syrian origin; and some of these may have acquainted Spartacus with the prophecies relating to the Son of Man, sent 'to comfort the captives, to open the eyes of the blind, to free the oppressed'. Every spontaneous movement eventually picks up, by a kind of natural selection, the ideology or mystique best fitted to its purpose. I thus assumed, for the purposes of my jigsaw puzzle, that among the numerous cranks, reformers and sectarians whom his horde must have attracted, Spartacus chose as his mentor and guide a member of the Judaic sect of the Essenes—the only sizeable civilised community that practised primitive Communism at that time, and taught that 'what is mine is thine, and what is thine is mine'. What Spartacus, after his inititial victories, needed most was a programme and credo that would hold his mob together. It seemed to me that the philosophy most likely to appeal to the largest number of the dispossessed must have been the same which a century later found a more sublime expression in the Sermon on the Mount—and which Spartacus, the slave Messiah, had failed to implement.

In contrast to these speculations regarding the unknown heroes of the tale, I felt the need to draw the known historical background with a strict, indeed pedantic accuracy. This led me into the study of such intricate subjects as the nature and shape of Roman underwear, and their complicated ways of fastening clothes by buckles, belts and sashes. In the end, not a word of all this found its way into the novel, and clothes are hardly mentioned in the text; but I found it impossible to write a scene if I could not visualise how the characters were dressed, and how their garments were held together. Similarly, the months spent in studying Roman exports, imports, taxation and related matters yielded less than three pages (pp. 280–4, where Crassus explains to the younger Cato the economic policies of Rome in cynically Marxist terms).

Born in Budapest and educated in Vienna, I wrote first in Hungarian, then in German; and from 1940 onward, when I settled in this country, in English. *The Gladiators* belongs to the end of the German period. It was translated by Edith Simon, then a young Art student, who has subsequently become one of the most imaginative practitioners of the art of the historic novel.

London, Spring 1965   A.K.